MW00713416

Renewal

I Found My Heart in
San Francisco
Book Eighteen

Susan X Meagher

Renewal

I Found My Heart In San Francisco: Book Eighteen

THIS TRADE PAPERBACK ORIGINAL IS PUBLISHED BY BRISK PRESS, BRIELLE, NJ 08730.

FIRST PRINTING: MAY 2015

COVER DESIGN: CAROLYN NORMAN

ISBN-13: 978-0-9899895-8-9

By Susan X Meagher

Novels

Arbor Vitae
All That Matters
Cherry Grove
Girl Meets Girl
The Lies That Bind
The Legacy
Doublecrossed
Smooth Sailing
How To Wrangle a Woman
Almost Heaven
The Crush
The Reunion
Inside Out
Out of Whack
Homecoming

Serial Novel

I Found My Heart In San Francisco
Awakenings: Book One
Beginnings: Book Two
Coalescence: Book Three
Disclosures: Book Four
Entwined: Book Five
Fidelity: Book Six
Getaway: Book Seven
Honesty: Book Eight
Intentions: Book Nine
Journeys: Book Ten
Karma: Book Eleven
Lifeline: Book Twelve
Monogamy: Book Thirteen
Nurture: Book Fourteen
Osmosis: Book Fifteen
Paradigm: Book Sixteen
Quandary: Book Seventeen
Renewal: Book Eighteen

Anthologies

Undercover Tales
Outsiders

Chapter One

Two weeks.

Fourteen days.

And in this ridiculously short amount of time she was supposed to have become "comfortable" with her new-found wealth. "Found" being the perfect word for it.

They'd had a lot of fun playing their stock market game over the past year. Part of the fun, a big part of it for Ryan, had been the fact that it was risk-free. After learning that Jamie had, in fact, been playing with real money, and that half of their profits were now in her name, Ryan had spent untold hours stressing over the entire situation.

Jamie was doing her best to understand how difficult it was to get used to having money, but it was beyond her ken. It was like trying to tell an orphan what it was like to have a very large, very loving family; you could easily comprehend the words, yet still have little true understanding or grasp of how it felt. Understanding the concept wasn't the same as living it and knowing it.

Ryan had told no one about the money, nor had Jamie. Not even Catherine. It wasn't that Ryan was ashamed or embarrassed. She merely wanted to get over the shock; but she was stuck. Part of her problem was not having anyone to discuss it with, at least not anyone who knew what it was like not to have money. She was loath to bring it up with her father or brothers; easily imagining the lecture she'd receive from her father. As much as he loved her, it seemed he took Jamie's side in every dispute. And the boys, even Brendan, would have a hard time sympathizing over being given a pile of cash.

It was tough orienting herself through this realm when she didn't speak the language. Sadly, Jamie was equally clueless when it came to being in Ryan's native land. There was a massive gulf between the mindsets of people who'd never had to consider the cost of anything and those who'd carefully planned and saved for even relatively small purchases.

Even though she'd definitely never been wealthy, Ryan was not under the illusion that she'd ever been poor. She knew that was yet another realm, a third place where she would be just as confused as she was in her present situation. Before Jamie, she'd been happily ensconced in the lower section of the middle class. Being thrust into the lower section of the upper class was actually giving her nightmares.

Not for the first time in her life with Jamie, Ryan was in the awkward position of seeking solace for something she considered upsetting, even tumultuous, but which nearly every other person on earth would consider an unadulterated joy.

It wasn't that she wanted sympathy. There was nothing intrinsically bad about having money. When she was young, she and Rory'd had an on-going fantasy where they dreamt about scraping together a dollar to buy a lottery ticket. They were fairly certain they would win, even though at such a tender age Ryan already had a decent understanding of the laws of probability. But her childish mind allowed her to ignore the hard reality and dream of the toys she and Rory would buy once they got their hands on the dough.

In the preceding two weeks she'd spent a lot of time considering her relationship with money, and she had to admit that she had never in her adult life felt she needed more than she had. Being rich had never been a goal, and she was fairly certain it never would have been. Why this was so wasn't crystal clear, but she suspected it had to do with the fact that she didn't like to stick out from her family any more than she already did. Being gifted in math and science had always created a small wedge between her and everyone in the clan. Math was something she could put her arms around, something almost corporeal, but no one in her life understood that. Now she was going to have to have yet another thing that would make her stand out from the people she most wanted to fit in with.

Ryan had flirted with the idea of creating a big scam in which she'd get everyone in the family to contribute a few bucks to the lottery. Then she'd devise a fake ticket that would miraculously win. Given the lads' lack of computer savvy and non-inquisitive natures, she was certain she could pull it off without breaking a sweat. It wouldn't bother her much to lie to her cousins, but she didn't think she could do it to her father. Besides, he knew her so well he'd likely be able to tell that she was hiding something.

Another idea was to send a check for the whole amount to her aunt Moira and tell her to spend most of it on her grandparents and keep the change. Right before Rory left for Ireland the previous week he'd asked if Ryan had any messages for their relatives. He'd never know how close he'd come to carrying a suitcase full of hundred dollar bills. But she knew Moira would have as difficult a time dispersing the money as she would, and it wasn't fair to burden her with that task.

Her old high school principal, Sister Mary Magdalene, would happily accept every dime. Their former friend and parish priest, Father Pender, would not only take it, he wouldn't ask where she'd gotten it. But those options also seemed like taking the easy road, something she rarely did.

Besides, even if she got rid of the money that was solely in her name, she still had Jamie's money to contend with. That was a considerably greater sum. She'd been fairly successful in convincing herself that the Dunlop/Smith fortune wasn't hers, but she knew the day was coming when she couldn't continue that delusion.

So, this "starter" fortune was probably good for her, as much as she hated to acknowledge that. It was an awful lot of money, but it was nothing compared to the money Jamie would one day have. Instead of foisting it onto a third party, she decided to learn how to live with it.

That left her trying to find someone she could talk to who would understand why she was so ambivalent. The person most in her position was Jim Evans, but she was fairly certain he would've been happy to have every dollar Catherine had ever earned or inherited. Granted, he hadn't demanded anything from their divorce, but Ryan was fairly sure that was primarily because his earning potential was already way, way up there.

No, there was only one person who understood her background, her need to fit in with her family, and, even though she wasn't wealthy yet, she could see the Promised Land in the distance. Sara Andrews was the only person she knew who might have some empathy. That was the thing that was so hard to find. She didn't want sympathy; only a fool would think people should feel sorry for her for having too much money. What she wanted was empathy, someone who understood the difficulties that having money could create.

The problem was that she was always hesitant to call Sara. She had it straight in her mind why there was still a charge between them. That part didn't worry her at all. After their disastrous rapprochement the previous fall, Ryan had done a lot of thinking and was now completely confident that things had worked out perfectly. Her infatuation with Sara was something that belonged to her youth. Without question, her love for Jamie was mature, considered, and permanent. She was equally certain that Sara was happy with Ally. But it was impossible to long for someone like she had pined away for Sara and not feel awkward when you were in her presence. There was just too much water under that bridge.

Nonetheless, Ryan had stated on many occasions that she wanted to have an ongoing relationship with both Sara and Ally.

She was the one who had to make the first move with both of them. But how to get time alone to talk on the phone?

They'd been at the O'Flaherty house for ten days now, and it was hard to get any privacy. Both Conor and Kevin had unpredictable schedules, and her father and her aunt showed up every morning to cook breakfast for anyone who wanted it. It also wasn't odd for one of her aunts to drop by for no particular reason. Since no one called before they showed up, and having the door locked was a sign of crass incivility, Ryan felt a bit like she had when she was first coming out. Then she'd craved privacy to read a book she'd picked up or carefully scan the local gay and lesbian paper, but someone could walk in at any minute.

She began to understand a little better why Jamie had seemed so reluctant to live permanently at the O'Flaherty family home. Privacy wasn't something she'd thought she needed, but she was really craving it now.

She knew Jamie wouldn't mind her being gone for a while; in fact, she'd probably welcome it. Things had been vaguely tense between them, with Jamie disappointed in Ryan's reaction to her wealth and Ryan disappointed in Jamie's lack of understanding. They'd both been trying, but they weren't clicking.

Now that they'd graduated, and had hours of unscheduled free time, they'd both fallen into old habits. Jamie'd taken to reading novels, and Ryan puttered around on her computer. They'd have to get more focused, but each of them seemed to be in a rut—with Jamie not seeming to mind her rut in the least.

It was a typical early June day in San Francisco. Cold and foggy, with just enough of a mist to leave tiny water droplets on your clothing. The sun was probably shining brightly in the South Bay, but they were a long way and several microclimates from there.

Ryan put on her running shoes and by the time she got to the landing, Duffy was standing there, waving his tail excitedly. "Yes, you guessed right. We're going for a run." She ran her hand through his curly hair while he licked her wrist and forearm as though she were made out of Kibble.

Running the few stairs from the landing into the living room, Ryan stood in front of the chair where Jamie was sitting. "I'm gonna take Duff out for a run. Cool?"

Jamie stretched, yawned noisily, and looked her up and down. "I'm gonna turn into stone if I don't get up and move around. Will you wait for me to put some shoes on?"

Ryan's smile faded. She hadn't counted on this. "I might make a stop." Popping up onto her toes a couple of times, she added, "I've got some things to work out."

Jamie settled back into her chair and spent another few moments looking carefully at Ryan's face. "That's fine. Are you sure you want to take Duffy? I could take him over to the park if you want to be alone."

"I'd like to take him. But if you want company..."

"No, I'm good." She put her legs up over the arm of the chair and nestled down into the worn seat. "I don't really care if I turn to stone."

Ryan leaned over and kissed her, feeling Jamie's arms encircle her neck and hold her down for a few seconds. Reading the signal, she said, "We should take a shower together when I get back. Would you like that?"

"Sure would," Jamie purred, showing her most seductive smile. "Hurry back."

With a slight frown, Ryan said, "I can't promise that. I'm gonna try to get out of this funk. That might take a while."

Jamie cupped her butt, patting it a couple of times. "Stay out as long as you need. Just come back horny."

Ryan turned, nearly tripping over Duffy who was anxiously waiting right behind her. "Most women wouldn't send their girlfriends off with that instruction."

"Too bad for them. My girlfriend is a woman of supreme integrity."

"And supreme grouchiness."

"Nah. You've been much, much worse." Jamie blew a kiss,

which Ryan acted like she had to jump to field.

"Got it." She kissed her right hand and tossed it back underhanded. "Love you."

"Ditto. Take your time, but call if you're not going to be home for dinner."

"Will do." She followed Duffy to the front door, affixed his collar, and they took off, bounding down the narrow stairs that led to the street. Duffy pranced to his right and then his left, looking for an indication from his master. When Ryan took her cell phone out of the pocket of her nylon vest, he sat down, mildly disappointed, watching her every move.

She speed dialed a number, then waited for an answer for a few rings.

"Hello?"

"Hi, Sara. It's—"

"Siobhán. How are you?"

Ryan both loved and hated that Sara's soprano voice, paired with using her given name, served to give her a powerful sense memory of her mother. It was like a kick in the teeth every time it happened, but she was slightly better prepared this time. She took in a breath and tried to sound casual. "I'm okay."

Concern colored Sara's voice. "Just okay? That's not like you."

"Busted. To be honest, I'm not good. I need to talk to someone, and you're the person I think would best understand what I'm going through. Do you have any free time?"

"I'll always make time for you. When's good?"

"Now." Ryan laughed at herself. "I think I'm supposed to say 'whenever is convenient for you' or something like that, but I've got some stuff I've—"

"Quit wasting time explaining. I'm at the office but I can leave right now and meet you anywhere you want."

"Oh, damn. It's Friday, isn't it. I forgot."

"Boy," Sara said, laughing, "you really *are* taking the summer off."

"I don't want to screw up your day. We can do this later."

"No, it's fine. I've been here since seven, and I'm getting glassy-eyed. Ally's coming over at six, so I'm free until then. Where do you want to meet?"

"That's a good question. I have Duffy with me and we both need some exercise."

"Fine. You two go for a run to the Marina. That'll tire you both out. Come to my apartment and I'll have water for you both. You can have yours in a glass."

Ryan's brain was bombarded with images of being with Sara in Berkeley and having a near-fatal lapse in judgment when they kissed. She also recalled promising never to be alone with her again, or something to that effect, but Jamie might have said that wasn't necessary, or something like that… What had they agreed to?

"Ryan?"

"Oh! Sorry. I was working out logistics."

"Wanna meet somewhere else?"

"I can't think of anywhere…"

"Your house?"

"No, not good."

"My office?"

"No. I've got Duffy." She spent another moment worrying then made a decision. "Your place is fine. Remind me of the address."

"Oh, right. You've never been there. I'm in the only four-story building on the corner of Prado and Scott. Do you know where that is?"

"I know Scott."

"Just head down Scott; you'll cross Prado. I'm a couple of blocks from the Marina. Are you sure this is cool?"

"Very. I'll be there in… I don't know how long."

"I've run there from my parents' place, so I have a guess. See you soon."

"Right." Disappointing Duffy, Ryan ran back up the stairs.

Jamie looked up from her book. "Forget something?"

"Yeah." Shaking with nerves, she rushed to get it out. "I want to talk to Sara, and the only place we can meet is her apartment. Is that okay?"

Jamie got up and stood right in front of her, rubbing Duffy's head with one hand while the other arm went around Ryan. "Of course it's all right. Do what you need to do."

Ryan looked down into eyes so filled with sympathy and trust that she almost choked up. "Thank you." She kissed Jamie gently then started for the door again, thinking that even though her partner was too polite to say it, she bet Jamie now hoped she wasn't *too* horny when she came home.

It wasn't far to the Marina, maybe four miles, but it was up and down some thigh-cramping hills, just the kind of workout that helped Ryan center herself. She was much less edgy when she rang the bell and heard Sara's voice call out through the intercom, "Come on up."

Duffy had been lagging for the last quarter mile, but he gamely shot up the stairs, not having any idea where he was headed. Ryan dropped his leash and by the time she got to the apartment, Duffy was licking Sara's face, his big paws resting on her waist.

Sara looked fantastic, so good that Ryan was surprised she'd come from work. She'd always had great arms, and the sleeveless sweater she wore showed them in all their glory. Her look was that of an advertising exec or a fashion magazine editor rather than a lawyer, and Ryan had to focus to distract herself from staring. She decided to tend to Duffy, whom she'd let misbehave for too long. "You don't have to let him do that. Say the word and I can make him behave."

"I like him." She tilted her face and Duffy attacked her ear, making her squeal, "I don't like him that much!"

"Duff! Down!" The dog's four paws hit the ground, but he whimpered at the loss of his best friend in the whole world—

whom he'd met two or three times.

Ryan approached the door and hesitated, unsure how to greet Sara. They moved together and exchanged tentative kisses on the cheek, with Ryan breaking the slight tension by saying, "You smell like dog."

Sara gave her a playful push into the apartment. "Come on in and have a drink." Duffy dashed into the place, poking his nose into the bedroom, bathroom, and kitchen before he dove for the cereal bowl Sara had filled with water and placed on the floor. "Your dog's a lot like you," Sara said, smiling at Ryan. "No nonsense."

"True." Ryan took the glass Sara handed her and gulped down the cool water, then handed it back. "More, please."

"That's the biggest glass I have, but I was certain it wouldn't be big enough."

After two more refills, Ryan put the glass on the counter. "Can I have a tour?"

"Sure. It won't take long. This is the kitchen."

"Got it. Nice." They went into the living room. "Nice again. Your good taste is showing. It doesn't look like your mom's house at all." She slapped her hand over her mouth. "I didn't mean that like it sounded."

Sara smiled warmly. "I know how you meant it. My mom's stuck in the Eighties—lots of powder blue and rose. I wanted a more modern look."

"It's really nice."

"It's all from the usual design stores people our age shop at. I don't have the time or the inclination to really do my own decorating; I figure the gay guys at the big chains can do that for me."

"You've always had a good eye for color. If it weren't for you, I never would have figured out what colors look best on me."

Sara sat on a sleek brown leather chair that rocked when she leaned over to set her glass down on a small table. Winking, she said, "If not for me, you would've worn sweats and T-shirts every minute you weren't wearing a uniform."

"True. I didn't know girls were supposed to have a style. Actually, I didn't know what a style was. My aunts were always trying to get me to wear things they liked, but you were my role model."

"That's a nice thing for you to say. I'm not sure I had style, I just spent more time looking at fashion magazines than you did."

Ryan was sitting on the edge of the sofa. "Any amount of time would have been more than I spent."

"You look like you're perching more than sitting. What's wrong?"

"Can I stretch for a minute? I know they say it's not helpful, but I always feel better if I stretch after a run."

"Sure." She looked more carefully at Ryan's limp clothing. "I'll get you a dry shirt."

"I'm okay…" Ryan called as Sara left the room.

She was back in a moment, holding up a shirt that advertised a bar in North Carolina. "One of Ally's. She only keeps T-shirts and a toothbrush here."

Ryan took the proffered garment and went into the bathroom. After changing, she did her stretching in the small room, just getting her hamstrings and calves loosened up. "Much better," she said as she went into the kitchen for another refill of water. Duffy was right next to her, and followed her into the living room, but as soon as Ryan sat down, he went over to Sara and flopped down at her feet.

"Duff isn't in great shape right now," Ryan explained. "He hasn't been running regularly and I think I stressed him too much today. I've got to ease up on him."

"Are you in the city now?"

"We have been." Ryan took a drink. "I'm not sure we'll stay. It's not perfect having Conor and Kevin there. It's more like a fraternity house now that Da's gone and women are allowed to stay over."

"Eww." Sara made a face. "That must be weird."

"It is. I don't know why, but I don't like knowing that Conor's in Da's room knocking boots with some stranger. It's really ridiculous of me, but it makes me grouchy." She shrugged and took another drink. "Of course, I've been so grouchy anyway that it's hard to tell what's due to what."

"Tell me about this grouchiness. That's not like you."

"If you don't think I get grouchy, your memory is failing." Ryan smiled fondly at her.

"No, you do, but not for long. You tend to work things out."

"Right. But I've been having trouble with this one. Ready?"

"Hit me."

Once again Ryan perched on the edge of the sofa. "When Jamie was taking a business course, she and I had a stock picking game. We played it for fun, but we were both pretty competitive."

"You? No!" Sara feigned shock.

"Yeah. Hard to believe, but Jamie's almost as competitive as I am. Anyway, two weeks ago she told me that she'd actually bought the stocks I picked. She bought her own portfolio, too, but she bought mine in my name." Even now it was hard to keep the anger from her voice.

"You look like you want to kick something. Why did that make you mad?"

"She didn't have my permission!"

"So? She's got money and she wanted to make the game real. It was probably easier for her to get into it that way."

"Not for me!" Ryan's eyes were blazing. "I never, ever would have thrown money away like that. It's institutional betting. I'd feel more secure playing poker at a casino."

"I'm not sure what's really going on here. This doesn't sound like you. You seem really angry at Jamie for doing something pretty benign. She gave you a gift, right? Am I missing something?"

"I'm rich!" Ryan got to her feet, making Duffy jump up and start barking, at what, he did not know. "Shh," she said, patting him gently. "Sorry I woke you up. Good boy. Go lie down. Go on." He wouldn't move until she sat down and stayed quiet. Then he went back to Sara, but he kept giving Ryan the fish eye for another minute before he put his head down and went back to sleep. Ryan purposely spoke in a calm tone. "Between Jamie and my father and my dog, I don't get to have a private thought."

"Okay," Sara said with finality, "how much money are we talking about? Billions?"

Ryan's head shot up a couple of inches. "No!"

"Then millions."

She could almost feel the wind leave her sails. "No, not millions. Not even a million." She shook her head mournfully. "Listen to me; I even talk like a rich person. As if a few hundred thousand dollars isn't a huge deal."

"You were rich before, weren't you? You and Jamie share money, right?"

"Yeah, in a way. Jamie thinks we share, but I don't. I try to live like I always have."

"How can you do that?"

"It's not easy. I do most of the shopping, and I have to buy those French and Italian cheeses and cold cuts and olives she likes. Nice bottles of wine…" She made a face.

"You don't like that stuff?"

"No, I do, it's delicious, but I wouldn't buy it for myself. I wouldn't order carry-outs like we do, either. I could live on fifty dollars a week."

Sara nodded, like she was starting to get the picture. "So you've had access to money, but you don't spend it like it's yours."

"Right. It's Jamie's and I spend it on her. I haven't bought a pair of shoes all year, mainly because I don't want to spend her money. I'm itching to get back to work so I can have some cash."

"But I thought you were taking a year off."

"We are." Ryan hung her head, feeling totally defeated. "I don't want to, but I promised."

"So you've got too much money and too much time off."

Annoyed, Ryan looked up and snapped, “I know I’m an idiot. This isn’t the first time in my life I’ve complained about something that anyone else would kill for.”

Sara got up and moved across the room, accompanied by a dog who looked like he was rolling his eyes in frustration. She sat on the sofa and put her hand on Ryan’s shoulder. “I don’t think you’re an idiot. I know you. I can only guess how much you hate not being able to work.”

“I do!” Ryan stared at her, eyes wide. “I know it’s nuts, but I want to work.”

“Poor you.” Sara patted her shoulder and Ryan fought the urge to seek solace in a hug. “Your father instilled the work ethic into you from the time you could talk. It must drive you mad to rely on Jamie for money.”

“I don’t rely on her; I just don’t buy the things I want. Eventually Jamie will notice my shoes are falling apart and she’ll buy mc a hundred pairs.” She looked into Sara’s dark brown eyes and asked, “Do you understand at all?”

“I do,” Sara soothed. “I understand. I’d have a very hard time letting Ally support me.”

“Even if she was rich?”

“Yeah, I think so. It’s more about me than her. I like having my autonomy.”

“Exactly!” Ryan felt her first genuine smile of the afternoon blossom. It was small and brief, but it was genuine. “I need to work, to earn my keep. And having Jamie hand me a ton of money is being rewarded for doing nothing. I hate that!”

“Well, it’s not for nothing since you picked the stocks. People *do* earn a living doing that.”

“Yeah, I know, but it was supposed to be a game. She tricked me.”

“Would you have played if you’d known?”

“Hell, no!”

“I rest my case. She wanted to play and she got more of a charge out of it by playing with real money. Once she saw you were doing well she wanted to capture the profit. Rich people get rich by recognizing and taking advantage of opportunity, Ryan. It's in their genes." She grinned playfully.

"Yeah. Her ancestors got rich off immigrants. They were in coal. I wonder how many cases of black lung her money accounts for."

"You're getting a little dark, pal." Sara put a hand on her shoulder and pushed her. "You can't blame her for what her relatives did. Some of my dad's ancestors owned slaves."

"My ancestors *were* slaves," Ryan said, a sly grin forming. "Well, indentured servants."

Sara sat quietly for a few moments, then she said, "Do you want my opinion?"

"Yeah. That's why I came. Hit me."

"I think you're in danger of making this a wedge issue. I can't imagine you want that, but listen to yourself."

"What?" She could feel her hackles rise.

"Siobhán," Sara said, her voice soft and gentle. Just hearing that tone made her relax a little. It was like a narcotic. "*Really* listen to yourself. You make it sound like money's dirty, like it's something that'll harm you."

"I think it is," Ryan said, interrupting. "I honestly do."

"Money's not bad. People might use it badly but money is just a thing. In the right hands, it can fix things and make people more secure, more comfortable. Your view is so dark. Why?"

Ryan got up and walked to the window. Duffy lazily looked up, but seeing she was only a few feet away, he put his head back down. The view was limited, mostly the side of another building, but Ryan was able to see a sliver of water in the distance, and she focused on it. "I haven't seen much good come from this kind of money. So many people use it to oppress others. I don't want to be in the group of people who make their problems go away by waving money at them."

"That's ridiculous," Sara said, making Ryan turn and stare at her. "Bad people with money are dangerous. Good people with money can make the world a better place. I know that's something you want to do. Why not use this as another tool?"

"I didn't earn it," Ryan said, her voice almost breaking.

"Yes, you did. You earned it fair and square, doing the same thing that everybody on Wall Street does. Give it up, Ryan. You're being childish about this and you're going to mess things up if you persist in this attitude. Nobody likes to feel you think you're superior to them. That includes Jamie."

"I don't think I'm superior to Jamie!"

"If I were Jamie, I'd be furious with you. She gave you this fantastic opportunity to have your own money and you act like she gave you a venereal disease."

"She doesn't think that." A flash of doubt crept through her. "At least I don't think she does."

"Here's the truth. With or without money, you're the same person. But we both know not everyone in your family will believe that. Your father will probably have a hard time with it; some of your cousins will make a big deal about it. God knows how Conor will react. So don't tell them. It's no one's business that you have this money. Live like you've always lived, but respect Jamie's lifestyle too."

"I try to," Ryan said quietly. "But it's so, so different from mine."

"It's the same for her. She seems awfully down to earth to me. Has she cut back on her spending to make you happy?"

"Yeah, she has." Ryan's head dropped and she glumly looked at the floor.

"Who's compromised further, her or you?"

"She has." Ryan looked up briefly. "She loves to travel and go out to nice restaurants, while I fight to stay home."

"You've got to stop. I know you, and I know your needs are simple, but hers aren't. Be respectful of that. This isn't all about you; it's about the two of you as a couple."

"You're right, you're right, you're right." Ryan slid down the wall, her Lycra leggings letting her glide along the surface until she was crouched down so far her butt was resting on her heels. "I'm such a jackass."

"You don't like change. You never have. I understand this is hard for you, but you've got to think about what's best for Jamie, too. So take the money and do something positive with it. Just stop whining!" She said it with a smile, but Ryan knew she meant every word.

Nodding her head a few times, Ryan tensed her thighs and slowly pushed upward. "Got it." She extended her fist and Sara bumped it with her own.

"Just for the record, it's been an adjustment for me to make the kind of money I'm making."

"Yeah?"

"I make more than my dad does and that's weird."

Ryan started to stretch her arms over her head, limbering up for the run home. "How do you handle it?"

"Since my parents don't know what I make, it's not a very big deal, but if I stay in this job it'll be obvious. I'm sure I'll blow most of it on vacations and massages and expensive wine, like most of the partners, so they'll catch on."

"I'll go halfsies with you on a yacht." Teasing made the whole thing seem less onerous.

"We'll see. Maybe I'll tag along with Jamie on some of that travel she hasn't been getting."

"And I'll stay here with Ally and work out. We could all be happy."

"Not so fast! I want my big girl with me. And I think you'd go nuts without Jamie after two days."

"Probably one," Ryan admitted. "'Tis desperate." She shook her arms out and rocked up onto her toes a few times. "I'd better get going. Jamie will want to know what I want for dinner. She likes to shop right before she cooks."

"Does she cook every night?"

Ryan smiled contentedly. "Yeah. It's great."

"For *you*," Sara said, giving Ryan a pointed look.

Her smile evaporated. "Right. That's right." Shaking her head again, she said, "Relationships are a full time job."

"So concentrate on your job and do it well. You've got the time and all of the tools. Get busy, O'Flaherty."

"I'll start today." She headed for the bath, putting her wet shirt back on. When she returned to the living room, she placed Ally's shirt on the arm of the sofa. "Thanks for the loan."

When Ryan slapped her leg, Duffy immediately got up and moved to her. He sat down, waiting for her to put his leash on. "Time to go home, buddy." She clipped him in and gave Sara a one-armed hug. It was very brief, the kind of hug she'd give someone she barely knew, but it let her feel in control, something she was determined to do while resuscitating their relationship. "Thanks for your time." She stepped back and added, "I appreciate that you went out of your way to talk to me."

"I always will. I really like that you knew you could call. That's a good sign."

"Really good." Smiling happily, Ryan moved toward the door. As she walked out she said, "We'll be in touch."

Sara lightly placed her hand on Ryan's shoulder. "One more thing."

"Yeah?" They were standing close to each other in the doorway, a little too close for Ryan's comfort. But they'd always kept only a small amount of personal space between them, and to step back would have been rude.

"You have a tendency," Sara began, "just a small tendency…" she put her thumb and forefinger an inch apart, "to ascribe good motives to the less wealthy and bad motives to the rich. You might want to reconsider that position."

Ryan looked into warm brown eyes, searching them carefully. "Do I really do that?"

"Yeah. You have since you were a kid."

Muttering under her breath, Ryan said, "That's not a good trait, considering the family I'm marrying into."

"I'd think not."

"It's tough. I've just had so many nasty interactions with people who think they can buy me or pay off the little people who get in their way."

"I realize that. But think about your da's father. Think about Michael's father. You can be a very bad person and as poor as dirt. Rich people don't have a monopoly on evil. There's plenty to go around."

"Right." Ryan looked at Sara and shrugged. "I've got my work cut out for me."

"Call me anytime you need a reminder."

"Will do."

Sara moved closer and gently kissed Ryan's cheek. The spot grew warm and Ryan could feel a wave of heat rise.

"I'll count on it, Siobhán." Sara pulled away and Ryan grasped Duffy's leash, letting him propel her down the stairs and out of the range of Sara's primal pull.

Chapter Two

The front door of the O'Flaherty house opened and Duffy burst through, scampering up the stairs and into the living room where he bounced against the chair and began to joyously lick Jamie's face. By the time Ryan got there, Jamie was giggling and pushing the frantic dog away. "Stop him!" she begged.

Ryan could have easily done so. Instead, she got down on her knees and joined the game. Looking puzzled, Duffy cast a glance at her then went back to his task. Ryan was a little gentler and expelled a lot less saliva than her dog did. Her technique was to burrow her nose into Jamie's armpits, then against her belly, anywhere she could fit to make her laugh. Deciding that Jamie had had enough, Ryan sat on her haunches then tapped Duffy on his. She had to poke him a few times, but he finally got the message and sat back, staring at Jamie with his huge dark eyes.

"Only one of you is evil." Jamie scratched under both of their chins, drawing smiles. "You both know better, but *you* know better than he does." She patted Ryan's head. "Luckily, I love you both." She leaned over and put both arms around Duffy's neck and tossed him back and forth in a raucous hug. He turned, pulling Jamie off the chair, then the two of them rolled around on the floor for a moment, with Ryan laughing at their antics.

"I don't want to break up the party, but I'm going to go down and shower." She gave Jamie a lecherous gaze. "I could sure use some help."

Jamie released her hold on Duffy and let Ryan pull her to her feet. "I was hoping you'd come home dirtier than normal."

They all went downstairs together, but only two of them were allowed into the bathroom. Jamie spent a moment peeling Ryan's wet running clothes off, then she got into the shower and adjusted the temperature. Ryan joined her, bringing her toothbrush. While Jamie continued to adjust the water, Ryan wet her brush and gave her teeth a thorough cleansing.

"I don't know why brushing my teeth in the shower doesn't appeal to me, but it really doesn't," Jamie commented.

"It's much more efficient to do it this way. You can rinse the foam right off."

Ryan stood in front of the water and Jamie watched the bubbly white rivulet roll down her face. "I know you have a point—you always do—but to me, brushing belongs in front of the sink. I don't think I can change. Besides, I brushed mine after lunch."

Ryan leaned down and kissed her, then she pulled away and said, "You still taste fresh."

"You taste fresher." With the water raining down on them and the minty scent of toothpaste still in the air, Jamie slipped her hands up Ryan's back and pulled her close. Then she tilted her head and kissed her several times, each time putting a little more energy into it. She finally pulled away, her eyes half closed.

"You look so sexy when you're kissing me," Ryan murmured. "You get this cute half smile and look like you're going to do something that you're really looking forward to."

"Truer words…"

Ryan took the bar of soap and lathered her partner up, with several detours to harden her nipples. Jamie returned the attention, spending a little longer than was absolutely necessary to clean Ryan's most private parts. Completing their lovemaking right then and there would probably have been Ryan's preference, but Jamie stopped and began to rinse both of them with the handheld attachment.

"We're stopping?" Ryan asked, sounding just a little

pathetic.

"We're just starting, silly. Don't be in such a rush."

Once they were well rinsed, Jamie grabbed a towel and put it around her shoulders then took another and started to dry Ryan off. When they were both reasonably dry, she opened the bathroom door, finding, as expected, Duffy lying right in front of it. "You tired your poor dog out."

"I know I did. We came home pretty slowly. He's really gotten out of shape just going on walks and occasional runs with Conor. I'll have to take it a little easier on him."

Jamie pulled out the hairdryer and started to work a wide comb through Ryan's hair while she blew it dry. Ryan rarely asked for this kind of pampering, but Jamie knew she loved it. It took quite a few minutes but once she was done, Ryan stood and tossed her hair back and it settled against her shoulders, fluffy and model beautiful. "I love the way you dry my hair. You do a much better job than I do."

"I'd like being a stylist if I only had you as a client. My turn."

"Want me to do it?"

"No thanks. Mine takes a certain amount of technique now that I'm trying to grow it out. I have to account for a couple of cowlicks that'll show up if I don't dry it the right way."

Ryan sat on the edge of the tub and watched Jamie concentrate on getting her hair just right. "It's going to be messed up in about two minutes. A waste of time if you ask me."

"No it's not. If I get it right, I only have to comb it after you've thoroughly messed it up." She turned and gave Ryan a lascivious wink which she knew didn't look very lascivious at all. Ryan always said her wink made her look about six years old.

When they were both completely clean and dry, they went into the bedroom and got under the sheet. It was still chilly in the room, but they would warm up quickly.

When Jamie put her hand on the small of Ryan's back to pull her close, Ryan's leg automatically slid between Jamie's. Their heads were on the same pillow, faces mere inches apart. "Want to tell me about your day?"

"Sure. I'll tell you about it over dinner. Luckily, I made a very good choice in talking to Sara. She was the right person at the right time. And," she said dramatically, "I'm giving myself bonus points for coming back into the house and telling you that's where I was going."

Frowning slightly, Jamie said, "You don't have to get permission from me to see whomever you want."

"This isn't about you; it's about me. Seeing Sara is always charged for me, and when I'm doing something that has an emotional charge, it's best for me to tell you I'm doing it. I don't like to feel like I'm going behind your back."

Jamie disentangled herself and rolled over, lying on her belly. "You can go behind my back now. I need a massage. Sitting in a chair for what…six hours? That wasn't the most intelligent thing I could have done with my day."

Ryan started to work on her stiff muscles. "Did you have a good day?"

Purring with pleasure, Jamie said, "It was an excellent day. I read a book that really pulled me into the royal court in St. Petersburg during the time of Nicholas the Great. It was fantastic."

When Ryan didn't comment, Jamie said, "You don't ever get that feeling from reading, do you."

"Nope. Sounds cool, though."

"We definitely have some differences, but a few things really bring us together." She reached back and guided one of Ryan's hands to her ass. When Ryan started to knead it, she mused that the things that brought them together were much more fun than the things that separated them.

About a half-hour later, Ryan woke at the sensation of Jamie trying to creep out of bed. "Where you going? I'm not done with you."

Sitting on the edge of the bed, Jamie turned and raised an eyebrow. "Really? The fact that you were asleep led me to think you were not only done, you'd moved on to another activity."

"Just a catnap. Two or three minutes was all I needed." She held her hands out. "Come back to me."

Jamie leaned back and gently rubbed Ryan's warm belly. "It's getting late and I've got to get to the store. How many do you think we'll have for dinner?" As she spoke, the front door opened and at least two sets of footsteps climbed the stairs after the front door slammed.

"I can't tell who that is." It sounded as though the footsteps stayed in the living room, then stopped. "That's Kevin and somebody else. If it was Conor, he would've gone into his room."

"Good deducing. I think you're right. I'll go get a head-count."

Ryan dove for her, wrapping both arms around Jamie's waist. "Don't go."

"I have to. I can't have three or four sets of hungry eyes staring balefully at me right at six o'clock."

"Tonight there will only be one set of eyes staring at you, and they're not going to be full of bale." Ryan paused, uncertain about that last word.

"What do you mean?"

"We, you and I, are going out to dinner."

"We are?" Jamie said excitedly.

She said it with so much enthusiasm Ryan felt like a tremendous jerk. Jamie truly got a lot of enjoyment out of going out to dinner, and the only reason they didn't go more often was because Ryan didn't care for it. She realized once again that when they had a difference of opinion, Jamie almost always deferred. That just wasn't right, and Ryan vowed to rededicate herself to changing the dynamic.

"We're not only going out, we're going out to a real restaurant—silverware, cloth napkins, tablecloths." She said this with great élan.

Jamie jumped to her feet "Tablecloths?" She joyously hopped around in a circle.

"And real servers—people who know what's on the menu and how stuff is made."

Putting her hand to her chest, Jamie stumbled around as though she were having a spell. "What's gotten into you?"

"I decided to be thoughtful for a change. We're going to a new place your mom likes. She got us reservations, something I think I would've had a tough time doing."

Jamie knelt on the bed and took Ryan's face into her hands. "I can't tell you how much I appreciate this. The fact that you're not only willing to go, but that you called my mom to find a good place really means a lot to me."

She leaned all the way over and kissed Ryan several times, her heartfelt enthusiasm making Ryan feel like an even bigger idiot. But she fought through it and reminded herself not to wallow in self-rebuke. If she was going to do something nice for Jamie, she had to just do it and get over it. "We're going at seven. Is that too early?"

"Seven is perfect. How dressed up should I get?"

"It's in SoMa. Your mom said it'll be filled with people from the nearby art galleries wearing black. Does that tell you enough?"

"That tells me everything I need to know." Jamie leaned down and gave Ryan one last smooch, then hurriedly put on her discarded clothes. "I'll go tell the boys they're on their own."

"Wanna bet if the house is gonna smell like pizza or burritos when we get home?"

"Nope." Jamie gave her a big smile. "Their favorite burrito place doesn't deliver."

Chapter Three

At seven-thirty, Jamie looked over her wineglass, smiling at Ryan. "You look lovely," she said for the fourth time.

Ryan smirked. "Then why did every guy and a couple of women turn and watch you walk ahead of me?"

"They were just trying to make sure they had enough room to get behind me to grab you."

"Not a chance. They knew who the beauty was, and so do I."

"I still say they were all looking at you."

"Only to figure out why you were completely dry and my suit was covered with droplets of rain. I could just see people trying to figure out if I'd been walking on a different side of the street and got caught in a tiny storm."

Jamie laughed and squeezed Ryan's hand. "Silly girl. You'd be dry if you'd used an umbrella."

Ryan made a sour face. "I hate umbrellas. They're bulky and they drip all over the place. I always leave the little ones somewhere, and the big ones are a pain."

"You could have worn your rain jacket."

With an even more sour look, Ryan said, "I can't wear a neon-bright rain jacket over my nice suit." She ran her hand down a lapel. "That would look way stupid. I should have a real raincoat."

Jamie could feel her eyes grow as wide as saucers. "Are you seriously considering buying non-sports related clothing?"

"Yes, dear, I am." Ryan's smile was sickly. "I want to look like an adult, and adults have raincoats. I can get one on the Internet."

"No you can't. Your arms are too long to find one that'll fit."

Ryan took a sip of her drink, something from the specialty drink menu that contained several types of liquor and some cranberry juice. The choice had surprised Jamie, but she liked that Ryan was trying to find a drink that suited her. "I suppose you have a solution to that?"

"You know I do, so stop playing cat and mouse and tell me what kind of raincoat you want."

Ryan's forehead furrowed for a few minutes, and Jamie could almost see the thoughts running through her head, with color and style and length all zipping along.

"I want one like private detectives in old movies wear."

Blinking slowly, Jamie reminded herself that she and Ryan thought about fashion in different ways. "Okay. What color?"

"I don't know. The movies were in black and white."

Trying not to laugh, Jamie led her along. "You can have any color you want. Khaki is kinda standard, but you can have anything from off-white to black."

"Hmm." Ryan took another sip of her drink, clearly thinking. "Let's go black." She put her drink down and quickly added, "But make sure it's got those flaps up here." She patted the spot right above her breast, "and a belt."

"You want a traditional trench coat."

"Whatever. Just don't make it too warm. I don't want lining or anything."

"Honey," Jamie said, again trying to make sure her voice didn't betray how funny she found this, "you have to have lining. But I'll make sure it's very lightweight. I know you'll want to wear it all year."

"Yeah, I will. I love my winter coat, but I can only wear it when it's really cold outside."

"I understand completely: lightweight, black, and

traditional."

"Make sure it has stuff like buttons and flaps and a belt," Ryan said, looking very serious.

Making sure the smirk she felt didn't show, Jamie nodded solemnly. "So, tell me about your talk with Sara."

Ryan took another sip, then set the glass down. She leaned back in her chair and adopted the expansive posture she always assumed when she was going to tell a story. Her chest stuck out and her head cocked a little bit to the side. "Like I said earlier, I made the right choice. But if I'd known what Sara was going to say, I never would have gone." She showed a sly half smile.

"More," Jamie insisted.

"Well, if I had to tell you what she said in just a few words, I'd say she kicked my butt."

"Really? Sara?"

"Yeah. Surprised the heck out of me. I went to see her because I wanted to talk to somebody who's known me for a really long time, someone who knows how I am about money. But I also wanted someone who wouldn't think I was crazy for not wanting a big pile of it set in front of me."

"And Sara didn't do that?"

"No, she didn't. She told me that I was mistreating you and that I had to change to be your partner."

"Really?" Jamie's mouth fell open.

"Yup. And hearing that from Sara, the one person I knew would be on my side, really knocked some sense into me." She took another sip of her drink. "I'm just going to have to suffer through being doused in dough. I'm sure all of the orphans living on twenty-five cents a day will feel very sorry for me." Her smirk was back in full force.

"That's not being fair to yourself. I know this is a continual adjustment for you. You're doing your best."

"Not really." Ryan's earnest face drew closer to Jamie's. "I haven't done my best. You've been incredibly patient with me, and I haven't made the effort to meet you halfway. I'm going to try harder."

Beaming, Jamie put her hand on Ryan's and squeezed it tightly. "Thank you. We've had a busy, traumatic, tumultuous year, baby, and I think you've done your best—even if you don't. But I would like to feel that I can spend some money and not have to apologize for it."

"Name it. What would you like?"

"Mmm… I'd like to travel." When she saw Ryan's eyes widen, she added, "Nothing big. I'd like to go to Pebble Beach for a few days. I want to get away so we can have some privacy."

"Living with the boys isn't great for you, is it?" Ryan looked both sad and resigned.

"It's fine. It's nice to be with your brother and your cousins. They bring a lot of life to the house. But I need time alone, too."

"I understand. We'll make plans to go away."

"I was thinking we'd go next week." Jamie shrank back, thinking Ryan might blow a gasket.

"Next week? That's so…soon."

"Yeah, it is, but we don't have any commitments."

Ryan held up a finger. "I have one, a big one. I want to make sure Jennie gets settled in summer school. Can we go after that?"

"When does she start?"

"Next Monday. Did I tell you I also made an appointment to talk to Robin Berkowitz that morning?"

"Nope. Why do you want to talk to your math advisor?"

Ryan's smile was guileless. "I want to start planning for the future. Robin might have some ideas that can help me focus."

"That's the last thing you need help with."

"I'm just reviewing my options. After I talk to her I'll spend a bit of time with Jen, then we can leave whenever you'd like." She grinned beguilingly.

"That's very flexible of you." Jamie leaned closer, saying quietly, "I want you to stay flexible so I can tie you into knots when we get to Pebble Beach."

They'd put the car in the restaurant's valet parking, and while they were waiting for it to be delivered, Jamie puzzled over why Ryan was always not just willing, but determined not to park on the street. "Why don't you mind spending money on valet parking? I'm always a little surprised when you don't want to hike a mile or two."

Ryan looked down. "One, when we go out, you always wear nice shoes, shoes that I can't imagine are comfortable to walk in. Two, if we ever had to run, you're at a real disadvantage. Sorry to be so pragmatic, but you just can't keep up with these long legs." She held up her hand and was just about to touch her third finger when Jamie interrupted.

Laughing, she said, "It's just a restaurant reservation. We can be a few minutes late. We don't have to sprint."

A pall of sadness that Jamie hadn't seen in quite a while settled onto Ryan's face. "I don't ever leave my car somewhere if I'm not confident I can run away from trouble." She put her arm around Jamie's shoulders and hugged her tightly. "I love going out with you, but you slow me down." She laughed just enough to make a small reverberation against Jamie's ear.

It took a second for Jamie to recall the time that Ryan had been gay bashed. She thought to herself how experiences like that changed almost every facet of Ryan's life. It hit her once again that they'd never look at the world in the same way. Even though a few remarkably bad things had happened to Jamie, they didn't color her world like they did Ryan's. From Jamie's perspective, she'd had more than her share of encounters with criminals and she was now basically home free. Ryan took those same experiences and convinced herself that any of them could happen again at a moment's notice. Given the choice, Jamie was glad for the way she dealt with trauma, but she was grateful that Ryan had the more cautious approach. Given her partner's penchant for having trouble find her, it was probably wise.

Their car was delivered and when they pulled away, Ryan took a wrong turn. "You should've turned right, honey."

"I don't mean to brag, but I think I could draw a map of this neighborhood from memory. I know where I'm going.'

"Where *are* you going?"

"To Berkeley. I wouldn't mind a little quiet myself." She turned briefly and locked eyes with Jamie's. "It's Saturday night. You know that increases the likelihood that one of our roommates will bring home some lucky girl. And even though I hate to admit that my father was right, it bugs the hell out of me to hear my brother banging the hell out of some woman." She looked like she was about to be sick. "Da said having dates over would lead to trouble, and he was right."

"I've never heard sex going on. Are you being serious?"

"Deadly."

"Where was I?"

"Sound asleep, princess. It happened last Saturday night. Conor got in late, well after we were asleep. You didn't stir, of course, but I got to hear the springs squeaking for a ridiculously long time. I hope the poor woman wanted to go at it as long as they did." She shivered, again looking vaguely ill.

"I'm really, really glad I missed that."

"I think I'd like it better if Kevin had the room above ours. Conor is one step too close on the relative scale for me to hear him having sex."

Jamie reached out and put a death grip on Ryan's arm. "If you can hear *him*..."

"Not to worry," Ryan soothed. "I don't hear voices; it's just the springs in the bed. That kind of sound travels down."

"Are you sure he can't hear us?"

"Pretty sure." Ryan thought of the extra insulation she'd forced Conor to put in around the heating ducts the previous year. "When we get back, I'll go up into his room and listen while you make your typical howls." She giggled, sparing a quick look at Jamie.

"I'll go upstairs. Your voice is deeper than mine and probably travels farther. I swear, if I hear one sound…"

"I'm with you on this one. Privacy is something I'm not willing to lose. I hated that Mia always knew when we were having sex."

Jamie let out an embarrassed laugh. "For some reason, that didn't bother me one bit. I actually kinda liked it."

"Really? That's…amazing."

"I wouldn't have liked it if she could hear anything specific. But she promised she could only hear vague shrieks and laughter. I guess I didn't like her hearing as much as I liked that we could be ourselves, that we didn't try to be quiet. We all trusted each other enough to know that Mia wasn't titillated by it."

Ryan shot her another look. "I wish I felt that way about my brother. He could easily block me out and think about you." For the third time that night, she looked as if she could easily have been sick.

They lay in bed, cuddling against each other to warm up. The temperature had dropped, and a light rain continued to patter against the roof, giving them a lovely bit of background noise.

"I'm going to make sure our trip to Pebble Beach is nice for you," Ryan said. She was lying behind Jamie and her breath was warm and moist against her ear.

"It will be. How could it be otherwise when you're going to be there."

"No. Really," Ryan said, sounding strangely intent.

Looking over her shoulder, Jamie said, "What are you getting at?"

"I'm still thinking of my talk with Sara. She reminded me that you've made a hell of a lot more compromises in the last year than I have. It's hard for me to keep that in my head, but I'm really going to try not to be such a taker."

"That's not how I'd describe you," Jamie said, chuckling. "You give too much, if anything."

"Not about some things. I'm going to make an effort to let

you do the things that give you pleasure."

"Like you?"

"Yeah," Ryan said, laughing softly. "Like me."

Jamie lay there, hoping Ryan took the hint. But she just continued to cuddle like a kitten. "I had a really nice time tonight," Jamie said. "Dinner was amazing, the wine was perfect and I got to look at your pretty face for a long time." She sighed, then took Ryan's hand and kissed it. "I just need one more thing to make it the perfect evening."

As if she'd been pinched, Ryan's hand started to move, roaming up and down Jamie's bare belly. "How about sex instead?" she said, a gentle laugh bubbling up.

"Oh, all right. You have such a one track mind!"

Ryan was conked out, flat on her back almost in the middle of the bed. Jamie reached out to turn off the light and Ryan's head lifted, eyes unfocused. "Go to sleep," Jamie whispered.

After smacking her lips together a time or two, Ryan tried to curl up against Jamie, letting out a mew of disappointment when she was given a shoulder rather than a smooth back. "Not sleepy?"

"Mmm, not yet." Jamie kissed her head. "Don't worry about me. You're zonked."

"No, I'm awake." It was almost funny. She blinked repeatedly, her eyes getting wider each time. "What's going on in that pretty head?"

Jamie turned and met her still-bleary gaze. "Nothing we need to talk about now. I'm just thinking."

Abruptly, Ryan sat up, then squished her pillow into a ball and used it as a backrest. "Talk to me." Ryan put an arm around Jamie and drew her against her body.

"It's nothing. Probably," she added, wincing when the word came out. "Really, baby. I'm worrying about something that I'm probably imagining."

Now Ryan was fully awake. Her voice was soft and low, and

when she spoke no one would have been able to refuse her. "Come on. Tell me what's up."

"I'm worried. A little worried...about sex."

Eyes wide, Ryan said, "We just..." She scooted down so she could see right into Jamie's eyes. "Wasn't it good?"

"Of course." Jamie kissed her tenderly, holding the contact for a long time. "It was wonderful." She took in a deep breath and said, "I'm worried. *Slightly* worried that you don't seem to initiate sex like you used to."

"I initiate," Ryan said defensively. "I do it at least fifty percent of the time."

Jamie leaned closer and gazed into Ryan's eyes. "You used to do it almost one hundred percent of the time. If I looked at you cross-eyed, you'd be on me. I really liked it that way," she concluded softly. "That's what turns me on, to have your limitless sex drive purring in the background all of the time."

Putting her hands behind her head, Ryan gazed at the ceiling for a few minutes. Jamie waited patiently, knowing it took her partner a while to process her thoughts.

"We've talked about this before. I thought it was okay now."

Jamie leaned in and kissed her gently. "I love our sex life. Once we get going there isn't a problem in the world. It's the getting going that I'm talking about. Your drive seems to have diminished. You don't have that..." she punched her open hand with a fist, making a loud smack, "drive any more. You're more like me."

"Oh God, not that!"

"Don't tease," Jamie said, her face just above Ryan's. "I want to know what's going on."

Ryan thought for another minute or two. "I'll admit that I'm not as obsessed with sex as I was." She ran her hand down Jamie's back and smiled warmly. "I've got access to the most gorgeous woman in the world. I don't have to find some inferior specimen, talk myself into her apartment, then into her pants..." She made a circular movement with her finger. "Et cetera. I can listen to my body and only make an overture when I'm really feeling it." She put her arm around Jamie's back and hugged her. "I'm feeling better than I ever have about sex. But it sounds like what's working for me isn't what's best for you."

Jamie shifted and rested her head on Ryan's shoulder. "What do we do?" It was hard, but she tried to keep the sadness out of her voice. This wasn't the worst thing in the world.

"I'll try to be more aggressive." Ryan used her most determined tone. "I was in a habit before, and I can get back into it."

Jamie gently patted her belly. "No, that's not the answer. If you're feeling good about sex, I want you to keep that feeling. I want each of us to be our best selves."

"But I want you to be perfectly happy." Ryan kissed the top of Jamie's head. "Perfectly."

"We'll figure it out. It'll take a little time, but we can do it if we talk about it."

"I promise to talk about it. Any time."

Jamie sat up and gazed into Ryan's beautiful blue eyes for a moment, then she kissed her longingly. "I love you. And I love you all the more when you listen to me and try to fix things that worry me. That's huge."

Chapter Four

When Jordan returned from her latest European trip, Mia was ready for her. In the few days she'd had alone, she'd packed up most of their stuff; the boxes were sitting in piles in the sparsely furnished living room.

"Going somewhere in a hurry?" Jordan asked, coming in the door with Toni, Jill, Ekaterina, and Makela.

"No," Mia lied, saying hello to the women she was itching to get away from. She accepted a warm hug from Jordan, then they went into their room. "Hell yes, I'm in a hurry," she whispered. "I would've been gone already if I knew anyone who could help. When you get home tomorrow night, we're outta here." She looked as pleased as it was possible for a person to be. "Now let's welcome you home by making love for the last time in this disgusting dump."

"Gosh, you sure do know how to get me in the mood." Jordan wrapped Mia in a tight hug and said, "I'm always in the mood when I'm with you. Let me take a quick shower and we'll have a proper goodbye for our disgusting dump." She was laughing to herself as she went into the hallway to claim the bathroom.

After Jordan went to practice the next day Mia dialed her parents' home number. "Hi, Mom," she said when her mom picked up.

"What softball game are you at now?" Anna Lisa said, clearly not in the mood to let their last fight die.

"I'm in Colorado Springs." Proud of herself for not rising to the bait, Mia repeated her mantra to act like an adult, even if she was alone in that endeavor. "Jordan and I are moving into a new apartment and I want to give you the address. If you want it."

"Why are you moving? Where'd you get the money?"

"I'll answer the first question. We're moving because it's too hard to have any privacy living with all of these other players. It's hard for Jordy to relax at night, and it's depressing for me to be in these bare rooms all day. It doesn't seem like home."

"It's not supposed to. It's a temporary place you might have to leave at any time. Did you have to sign a lease on your new place?"

"No. It's a furnished apartment, and we pay month to month." She was tempted to say that Catherine was paying the tab, but knew that would set her mother off.

"I don't see how you can afford that or why you'd want to. I've told you be—"

"Mom," Mia interrupted, "I don't mean to be rude, but I didn't call to ask permission to move. We're moving this afternoon. I just want to give you my new address."

"Do I get your phone number, too, or is that only for your friends?"

Mia could almost see her mother's narrowed eyes and feel their coldness. "We only have cell phones since we didn't want to spend the money to have a land line installed."

"Ooo, so now you're pinching pennies. Listen to me. It's important to have a real phone line. I saw something in the news about cell phones not being able to call your local 911."

"My phone works fine. I'll double check to make sure my service knows I'm in Colorado."

"I'm sure you'll do exactly what you want." She paused for a beat. "Don't you want to even ask about our vacation?"

"Okay. How was your vacation?" Mia was so tempted to add that she truly wasn't interested in the vacation she'd been prohibited from going on. Her mother got top honors on the shit list for disinviting her, given it was Mia's idea to travel to Switzerland together, but her brother was right behind for taking her spot. Tempting as it was to stir the pot, she didn't want to have another fight.

"Don't bother asking if that's all the enthusiasm you can muster."

Reaching the end of her rope, Mia said, "What do you want me to say? You're trying to goad me into a fight, and I'm not going to give it to you. I've had enough fighting. I'm tired." Even to herself she sounded exhausted.

There was a long silence, then Anna Lisa burst into tears. She cried so hard it took her a long while to catch her breath enough to speak. While she cried, Mia helplessly said soft words that she knew her mother couldn't even hear. "Don't cry, Mom. Please don't cry."

Finally regaining control, Anna Lisa said, "I don't know who you are anymore. You've changed so much that I don't feel like I know you. I miss the old you. I miss you so much," she said, starting to cry again.

The unusual display of what seemed like genuine sadness made her stomach knot. She didn't know how to respond, didn't have any idea how she *could* respond. It was absolutely true that she was different. But she felt she was growing up, which should have made her mother happy. At a total loss for words, she kept repeating, "I'm sorry, Mom. Please don't cry."

After taking a good long time to collect herself, Mia called Jamie, who, luckily, was available to talk.

Mia gave her the whole rundown, then said, "I don't know what to tell her. Isn't she supposed to want me to stand on my own? Isn't that the point of being a parent?"

"Yeah, I suppose that's the point, but I think it's hard for them too."

"My mom has spent the last ten years chewing my ass out

because I'm so immature and do such stupid things. According to her, all of my choices have been bad. But when I do something that any outsider would agree has some thought behind it, she gets even angrier. How do I reach her?"

"I'm not sure. I can't guess what's going on in her head. Would Peter have any ideas?"

"Peter can go fuck himself. If he hadn't taken my ticket, she would've had to deal with me. He screwed me over by taking my spot, and he didn't even have the decency to call me."

"Maybe he didn't know. Your mom might have told him she'd just come up with the idea of a trip."

"No such luck. He knew I was going, and he knew I was going to try to get her to delay the vacation. The jackass had a chance at a free trip, and he took it." She let out a soft moan. "I wish I knew how to get back to where my mom and I were just a couple of years ago. She gave me a hard time about things, but I never doubted she loved me. Now it's harder and harder to convince myself that she does."

Mia knew it was asking a lot, since Jordan was so tired after practice, but she had to get out of the apartment. Jill had a car, and even though she didn't offer to carry any of the boxes, she allowed them to use it.

Makela and Ekaterina were generous souls, and they helped take the boxes and wedge them into the small auto, managing to get many of them in. Jordan and Mia had to make about ten trips to get everything into the new apartment, but they had an elevator to their third floor place so it wasn't too arduous. Once they'd returned the borrowed car, they collapsed onto their new sofa and put their feet up on the substantial ottoman.

"This place is a little too much like a nice hotel room to seem like home, but it's so many times better than where we were I feel like I'm dreaming," Jordan said, her contented smile making Mia smile in return.

"I'm gonna have you on that counter," Mia said thoughtfully, pointing to the kitchen, "and on this sofa, and the ottoman, and on that chair, and, of course, the floor. Then we'll hit the bathroom and the bedroom."

Jordan turned her head and smiled. "Most people would *start* in the bedroom. That's one more thing I like about you; you don't stand on convention."

Chapter Five

Ryan had been trying to talk to her undergraduate advisor, Robin Berkowitz, since the day after graduation. But Robin had the good sense to go on a vacation with her husband, leaving anxious grads like Ryan to hold their questions until her return. Actually, there were very few students just like Ryan. The other people waiting for Robin's return were her grad students and a few worried undergrads who were undecided on their fall schedules. Most graduates who were not going on to grad school left campus on graduation day and only returned for football games, and that was only if they stayed in the Bay Area. But as Ryan proved so many times in her life, she wasn't average in many ways.

Robin's secretary scheduled Ryan for the first available slot, which was nine a.m. on the Monday Robin returned from her holiday. The professor was still working on her first cup of coffee when Ryan appeared, peeking around the doorframe. "I thought I'd gotten rid of you," Robin said, clearly teasing.

Ryan took that as an invitation to enter. She sat down on the chair in front of Robin's desk. "No such luck. I'm probably the kind of person who most teachers hate."

Laughing, Robin said, "Yeah. We all hate people with a lot of talent who work hard and never waste our time. That's all we talk about when we get together in the lounge."

"I'm not saying I'm difficult. I know I'm not, but I'm the kind who wants to pick your brain long after I should have made up my own mind."

Robin picked up a pencil and held it in both hands. She rolled it against her upper lip while appraising Ryan carefully for a few moments. "Still no idea of what you're gonna do next, huh?"

Sighing, Ryan said, "Oh, I have ideas. Too many ideas. That's the problem—I can't knock anything off the list."

"Give me the list again. I know it's a long one." She grinned unrepentantly.

Ryan held up her hand and ticked off items. "I want to be a firefighter and do swift water rescue, but Jamie's against it."

"Apparently Jamie's even smarter than you are," Robin said drolly.

"No doubt. I love chemistry, but not enough to focus on it."

"Then knock it off the list. Knock off the firefighting, too. You can't do that without your partner's support."

With her shoulders slumped, Ryan pulled both fingers back into a fist. She started again, letting her index finger pop up. "Bio. Love it."

"Enough to spend your career doing research and publishing?"

Making a face, Ryan shook her head. "I don't think I could teach. It's appealing, but I don't want to deal with all of the politics."

"Politics are everywhere. You can't escape them."

"True…" Ryan shook her head again. "I couldn't just do bio. I'd miss math too much."

"Then do math."

"It's not that simple." She scooted forward in her chair, fixing Robin with an earnest stare. "I don't want to sound like I have a God complex, but I want to do something important with my life."

"Don't we all? Especially when we're twenty-two."

"I'm twenty-five, and no, I don't think we all want to be of service. I want to do something that benefits the greatest number of people possible."

Not trying to hide her grin, Robin said, "How many people do you think the swift water rescue people plunk out of the water every year? I bet it's not ten."

Slumping back against the chair, Ryan scrunched up her eyes and rubbed at them with a fist. "If I can't do what I really want, I want to do something that benefits a lot of people."

"Good. At least you're able to be honest. Having the ability to see your foibles will help you make the right decision. What's wrong with math? You know you're damned good."

"Yeah, yeah, I love math and I know I'm gifted. But am I gifted enough to do something huge?"

"Huge as defined by whom? Other mathematicians?"

"No, as defined by…I don't know…history." Her voice had grown quiet when she said the last word.

Laughing again, Robin said, "Make no small plans, right?"

"Yeah, I'd say that's something I believe in. I want to do something that helps the world."

"Well, that could be math, but you've gotta get very lucky. To make a lasting impact, you've gotta do something practical, like work on a team that discovers a new way to do something big."

"Like what? I've had a hard time figuring out what that would be."

"Well," Robin stared at a point over Ryan's head for a few moments, "they couldn't have split the atom without math. Maybe you could work to discover a way to create non-polluting energy."

"Mmm." Ryan put her chin on her fist. "I'd have to work for the government or a big company and make sure I was on the right team."

"And make sure the other people on the team are as talented as you are. That's a big one. Politics comes into that, too. You know the energy companies don't want cheap power."

"Don't make me nuts. I'm doing that well enough on my own."

"Your main problem is that there's no guarantee that anything you do, no matter how well planned out, will make a big change in the world. Actually, the odds are very slim. You know how many people earn a Ph.D. in math every year, don't you?"

"Twelve hundred? Somewhere around there."

"How many of them get to do something that changes the world?"

"Two? Three?" Ryan said glumly.

"Maybe a few more, but not many. It's a big world, Ryan. It's also tough to change."

"Am I being really immature? Do I want something it's not possible to have?"

"You just graduated. You're supposed to be immature," Robin said, smiling warmly. "And what you want is possible; it's just not probable. It's a shot in the dark."

"Do you think I have the goods to be a great mathematician? I love pure math, and even though there's no practical application for most new proofs, I think I could be pretty happy working on them."

"You're twenty-five, right?" Robin started twisting the pencil again, moving it faster and faster. She set it on her desk and looked directly into Ryan's eyes. "You're a little long in the tooth. If you were obsessed with something, you'd have been working on it already. You also wouldn't be participating in sports."

Ryan let out a soft laugh. "I can hear the disdain in your voice."

Robin shielded her eyes with her hand. "Sorry to be so transparent, but I think you could have had a big career if you hadn't been dabbling in so many other things."

"I probably wouldn't even have a girlfriend," Ryan agreed.

"Maybe not, but you definitely wouldn't have been a double major. Math would be it for you, but since it hasn't been, I don't think it's gonna start eating up every moment of your time. An obsession isn't something you can switch on and off."

Ryan nodded. "Math's like a security blanket for me, but I

have a whole lot of other things that can completely capture my attention."

"Such as?"

"Well, if I wasn't so enmeshed with my family, I think I could be happy being a ski bum or a surfer." Her voice got softer and a satisfied smile covered her face. "Or snorkeling all day. I've never had a better time than when we were in the Bahamas."

"Snap out of it!" Robin teased. "I just got back from Cabo San Lucas and you're making my brain go right back there."

"Oh, shoot! I didn't even ask how your vacation was."

"Don't worry about it. You're not here for me; I'm here for you."

"Not any more," Ryan said glumly. "I've graduated."

"Free counseling for you. You're a special woman and I'd love to help you find a good fit."

"What about being a physician? Jamie thinks I'd be good at it."

"Yeah, I could see that. But not if Jamie's the one who wants it."

Ryan slumped down again. "Yeah, it's mostly her. I think I could get into it, though. I know I'd love the patient interaction."

"But…?"

"I'd rather do research to find a way to cure cancer or something." She gulped. "I can't believe how that sounded! I know I'm not going to be the one person to find a way to cure something that probably has a thousand causes. But I want the chance to do something big. Looking at kids' ear infections would be a nice way to make a living, but it wouldn't help me reach my goal."

"Got it." Robin took the pencil and tucked it behind her ear, but she immediately picked up another one and tapped it on the desk. "I've got one word for you. Technology."

Eagerly, Ryan nodded. "What about it?"

"I believe you can make a bigger impact in technology than you can in any other field. You still need a heck of a lot of luck, but you have the opportunity to make a bigger difference as an individual than in most other things. People who want to do something big are either going into technology or investment banking, and I don't see money as your big thing."

Making a sour face, Ryan shook her head. "Not my thing at all."

"So," Robin said, nodding in satisfaction, "here's a few scenarios off the top of my head. You could work in tech and make a new scanner that detects cancer no one has been able to spot. You could come up with a cheap computer that would let people in very impoverished areas have access to information they would never have otherwise. You could help make water cleaner, power cheaper, cars cleaner, sun less damaging. There are thousands of ways you could make a real difference. And you don't even have to have a Ph.D. It might help you get a good job, but you don't need it."

"Would getting a Ph.D. in math be a big help?"

"Mmm, not necessarily, but it wouldn't hurt. How much comp sci do you have?"

"Not much. Two upper division classes."

"Spend some time nailing CS. Really get into it and see if it sparks something in you. Get a masters or a Ph.D. if you find some research project you fall in love with, then go work for somebody big. Or somebody who's going to be big. But don't spend your life in a university if you don't love teaching and doing research. You'll feel trapped."

"Do you feel trapped?" Ryan asked, her eyes wide with concern.

"Not a bit. I love teaching, and this will still be a great job when we start a family—great benefits, time off, and a flexible schedule. Is that important to you? I don't know how you and Jamie have set things up."

"Having flexibility is important, but it's not critical." She fidgeted, not willing to tell Robin she'd be able to hire people to do a lot of things other people had to do for themselves.

"It's critical for me. My husband's a sweetheart, but he's not going to be a stay-at-home dad. I'm gonna have to do the lion's share."

"One more benefit of being a lesbian." Ryan held up two fingers as she grinned mischievously. "Two moms."

Chapter Six

Jamie was performing her favored morning routine; sitting outdoors drinking a latté and reading the newspaper. Around eleven she heard Maria Los' car pull into the drive, so she went into the house to say hello. Hearing clicking noises coming from upstairs, she went to Ryan's room and found her diligently scanning her computer screen. "When did you get home?"

Not tearing her attention away from the screen, Ryan said, "Ten, ten-thirty…not sure."

Jamie grabbed a section of her hair and gave it a sharp tug, then she sat down on the bed and stared at the back of her head. "You don't even tell me when you get home?"

Ryan didn't turn around. Her fingers danced on the keys as she continued to search for whatever was occupying her mind. "I'm sorry. Robin just told me some things and I started thinking about them, then I remembered they might start today so I wanted to see if there was one I could get into."

Jamie grasped the back of Ryan's desk chair and pulled until her partner could no longer reach the keys. Then she swiveled Ryan around so they were face-to-face. Grasping the arms of the chair with both hands, she held tight. "What are you talking about?"

Ryan turned her head, looking longingly at the keyboard. She faced Jamie again and said, "Robin thinks the best thing for me to do is to go into some form of technology. But to do that, I really need more computer science. Summer school starts today so I thought I'd—"

Jamie clapped her hands over Ryan's mouth, not letting her even speak the last words. "No way," she said decisively. "You are not going to summer school."

"But, Jamie," Ryan said as soon as a hand was removed. Immediately it was clamped down again.

"I understand without you saying another word. Robin gave you an idea about yet another field of study that you can focus your prodigious brain on. But we're not doing that this year. We agreed. And by 'we' I mean you and me. You're not going to back out of this, Ryan. We're taking this year off."

As soon as her hand moved Ryan struggled to make a point. "But..."

The hand clamped against Ryan's mouth again. "During this year you may consider—*consider* future fields of study, but you may not take classes in those fields or any other. Well, I would let you take a class in ceramics or glassblowing or carpentry or something for pure fun, but nothing career driven. You're going to spend this year learning how to relax."

She took her hand away and Ryan didn't speak for another moment. It looked as though she wanted to, but knew that whatever she said would not be appreciated. Turning back toward her computer, she systematically closed each of the windows she'd been working in. When she closed the last one, she put her computer to sleep.

Sitting there, facing away from Jamie for a few moments, the silence in the room was heavy. In the background they could hear Maria Los running the vacuum cleaner, but the sound seemed very far away. Finally Ryan turned around. She didn't look happy, but she didn't look as agitated as she had two minutes earlier.

"I understand what we agreed to for this year, I really do, but you have to understand that it's very hard for me to relax if I don't have a goal. I don't know what my next *goal* is." She got up and walked over to the window and settled herself onto the sill. "I guess you're not like this, but I have to have something I'm working towards. I structure my life around goals—some small, some large—but I *always* have one. If you won't let me do a little exploration into computer science, I won't know if that's something I should be working towards. That puts me right back where I've been, which is...aimless."

She looked so distraught Jamie felt her resolution begin to crumble. "I think I understand that." She turned toward Ryan and drew both of her feet up on the bed, sitting cross-legged, then leaned over a little and rested her elbows on her knees. "I think I understand how you are. But I'd like you to try to be a little different. I'd like you to try to truly relax for a change. I know it's something you've never done, but I think it would be good for you. So if you'll work with me at least through the summer, we can revisit this in the fall. How's that?"

Ryan's lips were set in a thin line. "I suppose I don't have any options. I agreed to take the year off, so I have to."

"I'm asking you for three months. You agreed to a full year, so cut me some slack."

"I'd like to, but I was in a different place mentally when I agreed to take the year off. I don't feel overwhelmed anymore. Now I'm itchy to do something, and I think taking some computer classes would keep me busy and let me see if this is the direction I want to take."

"When you say 'classes', what do you mean?"

"Well, there's three that I think could be helpful."

Jamie's eyebrows popped up. "Three? Did you say three?"

"Yeah," Ryan said, her voice very soft.

"How many days a week do these classes meet?"

Her voice was barely a whisper. "Two are on Monday, Wednesday, and Friday and the third is on Tuesday-Thursday."

"So you want to take a class every day of the week, while getting ready for the breast cancer walk, while keeping an eye on Jennie, not to mention tutoring her like you promised. And, of course, keeping me happy. Not necessarily in that order." She finally let a smile show.

"It's only three classes. I used to take five *and* work full time at the gym, and I still had plenty of time for a social life."

"You gave that up. Being in a relationship isn't the same as having a social life. I know it might not make much sense to you, but pleasing one woman is a lot harder than pleasing dozens for an hour at a time." She stretched her legs out, put her feet on the floor, and walked over to Ryan. Insinuating herself into the small space of her lap, she put an arm around her neck and nuzzled her face against Ryan's cheek. "I'm sorry I sounded so parental. If this is something you have to do, I'm certainly not going to stop you. But I would very much prefer that you didn't sign up for anything this summer. That's only three months."

Ryan sighed so heavily, she almost dislodged Jamie from her lap. "All right. I did promise, and I hate to go back on my promises."

Tickling under her chin, Jamie said, "Is there no part of you that's looking forward to having the summer off?"

Responding immediately, Ryan firmly said, "None."

Jamie got up and fondly ran her hand across Ryan's cheek. "You know I want you to be happy, but I've gotten burned several times letting you do things that I thought were too much for you." She ticked off the items on her fingers. "Basketball, starting softball while you were still playing basketball, and doing the math competition while you were playing a sport. I gave in every single time. I think it's your turn to give in to me." She bent and kissed Ryan's cheek. "Think about it. If you can't bear to relax, go ahead and do what you want. I'm not trying to guilt trip you, honey, and I know I'm asking you to change a big part of your personality. That's a lot, and if you can't do it I'll do my best to understand."

Ryan nodded, watching Jamie leave the room. She wedged her body into the window, getting her feet tucked against the far jamb and drawing in her knees until they almost touched her nose. She looked ridiculous, but she was better able to think when she was in a confined space. The breeze blew across her, bringing in the sweet scents of spring. Closing her eyes, she tried to think of what they could possibly do for three months. She knew Jamie could be happy reading, going on bike rides, and just hanging out. Just as certainly, she knew that would drive her stark raving mad.

Almost an hour later, Jamie peeked her head into Ryan's room, dismayed when she found her wedged into her window. "Ryan," she said, exasperated, "if it means that much to you, take your computer science courses. I'm not going to force you to have fun."

Ryan looked at her, blinking for a few seconds. "Huh? What did you say?"

Jamie walked over to her and put one hand on her shoulder and the other on her knee. Looking into her eyes, she asked, "Are you sulking, or thinking?"

"I'm thinking," Ryan said, her eyes filled with innocent question. "Why would I be sulking?"

"Never mind." Jamie kissed her on the temple, then walked over to the bed and sat down. "Do you want to talk about what you were thinking about?"

Ryan started to disentangle her long body from the window. Once she had her feet on the ground, she started to stretch, wincing occasionally. "Boy, I got stiff."

Jamie didn't comment, thinking most people would expect to be stiff after forcing themselves into a space the size of a large suitcase for over an hour.

Ryan got down on the floor and performed a series of stretches that had Jamie spellbound. While leaning over from the waist with her legs stretched out straight in front of her, Ryan waited until her head nearly touched her legs to start to speak. Her projection wasn't crystal clear, but Jamie heard her say, "I'm trying to make myself forget about all the stuff Jennie has gotten away with over the last month or two. I want to pick her up from summer school this afternoon, and I don't want to show how disappointed I still am in her."

Jamie studied the back of Ryan's head, looking at the neat twist she'd made with her hair. As she often did, she'd just whirled it around a few times and stuck a pencil through it, and somehow managed to make it look cute. Trying to force her attention back to the subject at hand, Jamie said, "She's pretty perceptive. Why not tell her the truth and be done with it?"

Ryan sat up and looked at her for a moment. "I don't know if that's a good idea. I don't want to be holding stuff over her head."

"Agreed, but you are, even though you don't want to be. I don't think it's a bad thing for her to understand she has some work to do to regain your trust."

Doing a few more stretches, Ryan was silent. Jamie placidly watched her, knowing she was thinking.

"You might be onto something there." She sat up straight. "I don't want her to feel like she has to beg to get back into my good graces, but it's probably good for her to realize her actions have repercussions."

Jumping to her feet, she put her arms over her head, looking as though she were trying to touch the ceiling. An inch of her belly was exposed and Jamie considered leaping for it, but she was a little conservative about their rough play ever since she'd broken her elbow. Instead, she crooked her finger at Ryan. When Ryan stood by the bed, Jamie wrapped her arms around her hips and tumbled her down so they were both lying on their sides. "Do you want to stay in San Francisco tonight?"

"I don't think so. If we're going to Pebble Beach in the morning, we might as well leave from here."

"So you're going to drive over just to pick up Jen? Seems like a long drive."

"Yeah, it is." Ryan thought for a moment. "Maybe I'll ride my motorcycle over, pick her up and take her to our house. I can help her get organized for her class, then drive her back to Oakland.

That'll give us more time together."

"Does she need my help with anything?"

"I'll ask, but I don't think so. She looked for the easiest class offered to go along with the math class I forced her to take."

"Well, please tell her I'm always willing to help. You know I'll go with you today if you want me to, right?"

"Of course I do. But you should probably stay here and decide what we should take with us to Pebble Beach. You're a fantastic packer."

"Practice makes perfect. Did you tell Sandy you were going to pick Jennie up?"

"Not yet, but it's on my to-do list. I still feel guilty about not telling her about Jennie hitchhiking and ditching school."

"Yeah, but I understand why you didn't. At this point it would just give her more to worry about."

"That's what I thought, too. Having eight teenage girls under your care is something I wouldn't wish on anyone."

Grinning, Jamie said, "What if we have octuplets?"

Ryan pushed herself up into a sitting position then looked back and gave Jamie a smirk. "We'll pick the cutest one and give the other seven to infertile couples. People will think we're incredibly generous. Ha ha ha!" She laughed loudly, almost sounding evil. "And the best part is, we'd be on TV and in all the magazines. You know how much I miss that." She put her hands around her neck as if she was strangling herself. Stumbling around the room, she then dragged herself through the open doorway, making it look as though someone were pulling her.

"Good luck!" Jamie yelled after her. "Let me know whether you'll be home for dinner."

"I will," Ryan's scratchy, choked-off voice replied.

Before she left, Ryan called Sandy and got permission to pick Jennie up, then she called the car service that usually fetched Jennie from school and told them they wouldn't be needed. After strapping the extra helmet on the back of her bike, she took off for San Francisco. The weather was still gloomy and gray, but it hadn't rained and the streets were dry.

Ryan had allowed plenty of time, so she drove slowly and concentrated intently on driving defensively. Even though she'd driven at or below the speed limit, she was still a few minutes early. So she got off the bike and went over to stand with the assortment of parents and nannies waiting for their kids.

The girls began to hurry from the building a few seconds after the bell rang. Most of them looked gleeful to be finished with at least one day of summer school. The procession of girls had slowed to a trickle and Ryan was beginning to worry that Jennie had spent her first day skipping, but the girl finally emerged, looking down at the ground, totally oblivious to the other kids. Ryan walked up beside her and tapped her on the shoulder. Jennie's head snapped up and it took a second for her eyes to connect to her brain. When they did, her face lit up in a bright smile and she threw her arms around Ryan. "Why are you here?"

"I couldn't bear the thought of you being in summer school without having a little bit of fun."

"Fun?" Her smile grew even brighter. "What are we gonna do?"

"I thought it'd be fun to go for a bike ride. There's not much traffic at this time of day; we can just cruise around the city."

"I'm ready!" Jennie started moving, even though she didn't know where to go.

Ryan pointed across the street. "Right over there, sport." Jennie ran across the street without looking to see if cars were coming, which made Ryan's stomach turn. She knew it wouldn't do any good, but she felt obligated to remind her, "You've got to take a peek to see if there's any traffic before you run across the street."

Jennie quickly removed the helmet from the back of the bike and secured it to her head. "Right, right."

Ryan took the girl's books and stowed them so she didn't have to hold them, then she got astride the bike and before she had time to tell Jennie she was ready, the girl was climbing aboard. They were allowed to wear regular clothing to summer school, so Jennie was wearing a pair of old jeans and a T-shirt. Ryan took off her own rain jacket and handed it to her. "You're gonna freeze without a coat."

"Nah, I'm fine."

"Put it on. If I'm cold, I can go by my house and get another one."

Jennie put on the jacket, which could have probably wound around her small body three times. Then Ryan turned on the engine and they took off, only speaking sporadically.

This was the way Ryan preferred to ride. When she had Jamie as a passenger, she usually got a running commentary on everything that Jamie saw that interested her in any manner. Jennie was usually quieter than Jamie, and she tended not to talk until she had thoroughly assessed a given situation. Ryan guessed that Jennie could tell she was still in trouble, and was keeping quiet just to be safe. But even though she was quiet, Ryan could tell her young friend was having a good time.

The part of the city they were riding in was so hilly that Ryan had to go up some of the streets at nearly full throttle. The three and four-story homes that lined the streets provided perfect acoustics for the roar of her Harley, and every time she gunned it, Jennie let out a whoop of pleasure. They drove around for nearly an hour before Ryan headed back to Noe Valley. When they saw a parking spot by the house, she instructed Jen to get off the bike so it would be easier to park. She managed to fit between a pair of cars, then the twosome walked up the stairs to the O'Flaherty house. As expected, the house was silent, Duffy now spending his days at Maeve's house when his mistress wasn't in town.

Ryan nosed around in the kitchen and found some cookies that her aunt had recently delivered, and a fresh quart of milk. She set out the cookies and poured a couple of glasses of milk and she and Jennie sat down at the dining table.

"Let's take a look at your math book and see what fun we're gonna have this summer." Ryan intentionally put on a goofy looking smile. Jennie pulled the book out and handed it to her, sitting quietly, munching on a cookie while Ryan looked through the text. "What did you go over today?"

"This is the same book I used last semester, and it's the same teacher, so we started up where we left off. I think it's chapter nine." She took the book back and paged through it. "Yeah. Right here. Do you understand this stuff?"

"Yeah, I understand this. Why don't you tell me what you went over today, but explain it in your own words."

Jennie looked at Ryan as if she were mad. "My own words? I don't have words for this stuff."

"Sure you do. You don't have to use math words. Try to explain what the big picture is behind this."

"Big picture?" Jennie asked dully.

"Yup. It might not seem like it, but you can explain this stuff. You just have to step back from it and try to see what they're trying to teach you."

"I have no idea what they're trying to teach me."

Ryan slapped Jennie sharply on the shoulder. "You will, buddy. You will."

Unable to contain her excitement, Ryan rubbed her hands together. "This is when math starts to get interesting. You don't have to memorize stuff. Take this first section here, where they're talking about imaginary numbers."

"I think all numbers are imaginary."

"In a sense that's very true." Ryan felt herself perk up at Jennie's perceptive comment. "They're all imaginary, in that you can't hold them or touch them. They're only real in your mind."

"Maybe *your* mind…" Jennie trailed off, looking down.

"Work with me here. Did you understand the concept behind imaginary numbers?"

"No. It's just another thing to memorize. I can memorize stuff if I try hard."

"Sure, sure you can, but I think it's easier if you understand why an imaginary number, or any other concept, is important. You know—like how you would use it in real life."

"Okay," Jennie said, seeming more engaged. "How would you use it in real life?"

"Well, I suppose the most common uses would be in engineering."

Warily, Jennie said, "I don't do any engineering."

"Not now, but you might someday. And you really need to have a good understanding of imaginary numbers if you want to be able to do differential equations. Engineers have to do differential equations all the time. It would be impossible to figure out the rate of growth of a function..." She saw Jennie's eyes glazing over.

"Okay," Ryan said, undeterred. "How about physics? You can't get anywhere in quantum mechanics if you can't state precisely where a particle is. You have to do a probability distribution of where its position in space most likely is, and you can only do that if you can use complex variables."

Jennie put her head down on the table and moaned.

Ryan's sighed. "I think I'm pushing you a little hard. For today, let's memorize this stuff."

After about an hour, Kevin and Dermot came into the house, dirty from work and hungry as always. Kevin snatched the entire container of remaining cookies and the two men sat at the table, stuffing their mouths like chipmunks.

"What are you guys doing?" Dermot asked.

"Ryan's helping me with my math homework," Jennie said. "Are you guys good at math?"

"Not as good as Ryan, but I'm pretty good," Kevin said.

"Not me," Dermot added. "I was always better in history and social sciences. Ryan dragged me through high school, even though she's younger than I am." He laughed hard at that, clearly not embarrassed in the least.

Jennie questioned the boys for the next half hour, asking about all sorts of topics, wasting time quite efficiently. Ryan allowed it to go on for a while, but then she said they were going to move downstairs to finish up. With regret, Jennie looked at the boys and followed along.

After they spent a long time working through problems that Ryan made up, she was confident Jennie was prepared for at least the next couple of days of class. But it had been a struggle to keep the girl's attention, especially after Conor came home. He had the TV on in his room and all three men were in there laughing and cutting up. To her credit, Jennie tried her best to pay attention, but it clearly wasn't easy for her.

"It's hard to concentrate with the boys making a racket, isn't it?"

"Kinda. But it's nicer than at my house. That place is crazy."

"How'd you get your work done during the year?"

"I went to Ms. Smith's most of the time."

Ryan looked at her blankly, with Jennie reminding her, "Jamie's mom changed her name. Remember?'

Ryan slapped herself on the head. "I'm a dope."

"Yeah. Right." Jennie laughed. "It's really quiet over there. I'd go up to the guest room, the one your brother's gonna make into the library. That one has the best view."

Ryan nodded, recalling Catherine mentioning that Conor and Kevin were going to start the renovation this week.

"There isn't a TV in there, and no radio either. Marta would come up every once in a while to check on me, but other than that I didn't have anything else to do."

"No other books?"

"Nothin'. It was like a room made to make people do homework. And there wasn't a bed, so I couldn't even take a nap." She looked slightly outraged as she listed the harsh conditions.

"Maybe we should meet over there."

Jennie eyes lit up. "That'd be cool. Your cookies were nice, but

Marta'd make me anything I wanted. I usually didn't even havta eat dinner when I got home. Her cooking is ten thousand times better than the crud I get at home."

Stifling a laugh, Ryan asked, "Does Sandy cook?"

"No. Some lady comes in to make dinner. Sandy's only got to watch us."

"Only that," Ryan agreed, thinking that was more than enough. "How are things at the house?"

"Eh. You know. Since Skylar left I haven't had anybody to hang out with. It's boring."

"How's your new roommate?"

Jennie shrugged, not commenting further.

"Trouble?"

"She doesn't speak a lot of English 'cuz she's only been in America for a year."

"I've forgotten her name."

"Sabrina." Jen shrugged again. "Shc doesn't like me much."

"Why do you say that?"

"We're really different. She spends half of the day putting on makeup."

Surprised, Ryan said, "Makeup? Really?"

"Yeah. She's got a girlfriend, Juana, who looks like a guy. Sabrina gets up an hour before I do so she can put all of this eyeliner and lipstick on. I guess she's trying to look good, but I think she looks like a freak."

"Huh. And she's gay?"

Jennie looked at her blankly. "I said 'girlfriend', didn't I?"

Scratching her head, Ryan sheepishly admitted, "I guess you did."

"You've gotta be queer to get sent to my house." She scowled, obviously irritated that Ryan wasn't keeping up.

"I'm sorry, buddy. I know everybody in your house is gay. I got confused by the makeup thing. That sounds…different."

Making a face, Jennie said, "She's real different. She's got a radio on all the time. In Spanish. She keeps it low, but that's just another excuse not to talk to me."

"Has she been at the home long?"

"No, not as long as me. She's two years older, and she's just counting the days until she gets out. I kinda feel bad for her, because she wants to quit school and live with her girlfriend, but she's not eighteen yet and the court won't let her."

Dismayed, Ryan couldn't find much to say. She knew it was hard for Jennie at the home in the best of circumstances, but not having a roommate to confide in had to make things more difficult. She was just glad that this girl would probably not be trouble like the previous roommate had been.

"Is everything okay between you and Pebbles?" It was hard for Ryan to say the girl's name without laughing, but the way Jennie had felt pressured was not a laughing matter.

Finally smiling, Jennie nodded. "Yeah, it's better. How did you get me moved without getting me beat up?"

"I promised you I wouldn't tell Sandy any details and I didn't. I said you and Pebbles were fighting, and I thought it was affecting your schoolwork." She held up her hands. "I didn't rat her out."

"Okay." Jennie nodded. "Well, Sandy got her into some volunteer program and she's usually gone until dinnertime. As long as I stay in the living room until bed, I hardly have to see her."

Ryan put her hand on Jennie's shoulder and gave it a squeeze. It hurt her deeply to have to send the girl back to a place where she always had to be on guard, but she knew that for the time being it was the best they could hope for.

After Ryan got back to Berkeley, she spent a long time telling Jamie all about her day.

"So Jen's new roommate spends all of her time putting on makeup?"

"Yeah. I met her when I dropped Jen off." Ryan pursed her lips, looking thoughtful. "She's from Guatemala and…" Ryan's eyes almost closed as she put her hands in the air and made a vague gesture. "I can't describe her. I'm obviously out of the loop because I've never seen a lesbian who looks like her." She smiled, looking a little abashed. "Not volunteering at the talk line is hurting my knowledge base."

Jamie placed a sloppy kiss on her cheek. "That's just how I want you—waaaaay out of the loop. Want me to go talk to her in Spanish?"

"Talk to her about what? Why she's not friendlier to Jen?" Ryan sat at a dining room chair and rubbed her eyes. "I think we'd better stay out of it unless Jennie wants us to do something. I don't want her to get the reputation of being a snitch or a whiner."

"No, that wouldn't be good." Jamie sat on Ryan's knee, hugging her briefly. "Where does the girl go to school? Is she a good student?"

"She goes to a high school for recent immigrants. I think they spend all day trying to learn English."

"So she's not anyone Jen could study with."

"Nope. I feel for the kid. Imagine how you'd feel if you moved to a country where you didn't speak the language and then got kicked out of your home because you were gay. Then, on top of that, you had to share a room with someone two years younger. That's a big gap, even if they both spoke Spanish."

"Let's try hard to stay on top of things. It sounds like Jen needs us more than ever."

"I'm afraid you're right. I think I'm going to start meeting her over at your mom's house after school, or have her driver bring her over here. It's too noisy at my house."

"Were the boys home?"

"Yeah, and they were watching something on TV and stomping their big boots on the floor. It sounded like someone was herding cattle."

"Mom would love to see us more, so that works for me."

"Me too." She patted Jamie on the butt. "Let's get dinner

rocking. I only had three cookies this afternoon."

The next morning, Ryan poked around, having trouble finishing her little tasks. Jamie was used to the way she fussed, knowing it was all part of her dislike of any form of travel—no matter how much she truly wanted to go somewhere. Still, it could get aggravating, especially when she had an agenda.

"Honey, you don't need to unplug all of the lamps. Maria Los will be here tomorrow afternoon, and she'll keep an eye on things."

"I'd better take another peek in the refrigerator. I don't want to come home to spoiled food."

"You cleaned every plate last night. We've got nothing but some cheese I'm aging." Jamie clapped her hands together. "Let's go!"

"Maybe I should put the trash bins out now…"

"Maria Los knows when they go out. She also knows what goes into each one. She's been doing this all year, baby. The world doesn't change just because we're going to be in Pebble Beach."

"I know, I know," she said absently, as her eyes scanned the room, looking for hazards that would jump up and destroy the house the minute they headed south.

"Come on." Jamie grasped her arm and tugged her towards the front door. "I'm driving."

"My car?" Her brows rose.

"Uh-huh. You're too scattered. You can relax and watch the scenery." Ryan followed along, not commenting. Jamie knew she preferred driving, but today she was going to be a passenger—hopefully a compliant one.

Traffic wasn't horrible, and they got onto I-880 without too much trouble. Ryan was doing her usual—backseat driving while trying to stop herself—but Jamie was able to focus and make her own decisions. After about an hour, she got into the left lane and passed a couple of slow moving cars.

"You need to stay to the right," Ryan said. "The turnoff for

156 is coming up."

Jamie turned and gave her a smile. "Did I ever tell you my first long drive was down to Pebble Beach?"

"Uhm…no."

"Well, it was. I was fifteen and my dad let me drive down. So I've been doing this for seven years."

Ryan gave her a wry smile. "Is that your polite way of telling me to shut up?"

"Uh-huh. I know where I'm going, sweetheart."

"Uhm…you just missed the turnoff, so you might want to re-think that." Ryan pointed helpfully to the exit they'd just whizzed past.

"I didn't miss it, because I'm not taking it."

"You might have some super secret way of getting to Pebble Beach, but if you do, I can't imagine what it is."

"I know where I'm going, and I truly don't need help."

"Have it your way." She made an exaggerated show of letting her seat recline, then turned her attention to Jamie. "I'll just stare at you while you lead us into the wilds of California. Should I call my family to say goodbye?"

Jamie reached over and gave her a playful slap on the leg. "If you don't stop picking at me, you're going to be walking home, so you can see them much, much later tonight."

"I'm just enjoying the trip," Ryan insisted. "I'm looking at one of California's great natural beauties. You."

After a while, it became clear they were going to continue down 101. Ryan reached over and ran her hand down Jamie's leg, saying softly, "I have a sneaking suspicion we going to meet up with the AIDS Ride people."

"Bingo!" Jamie said, holding her hand out for a high five. "We won't be able to do anything formally, but I've got an idea."

"Your ideas are always super, so lead the way, Jamers."

They drove for a long time, spending the time recalling highlights of their own ride. They passed King City, the site of the second night campground, but Jamie kept driving. They pulled over to a well-marked rest stop not far from the Salinas River, just a narrow bit of sluggish water at this point. The stop was no big deal, simply a place to pause and get out of the sun for a few minutes, and Ryan recalled she'd always been toast by the time they reached it. Your excitement made the first two days go by pretty fast, but now that you were well inland, far from the cooling breezes of the Pacific, you realized you had four more days to ride and you began to question your own sanity.

About a dozen volunteers stood under big umbrellas, waiting for riders. Jamie and Ryan walked over to them, with Jamie saying, "How's business?"

One of the guys looked at her for a second, his head cocked. "We're not selling anything. This is a rest stop for a charity bike ride."

"I know. We did it last year." She reached out for Ryan and put an arm around her waist. "This stud's done it every year, but I'm a neophyte."

"Oh, cool," the guy said. "I've never done the ride, but I've volunteered a couple of times. This is the most exciting thing we have around here all year."

"I bought some treats," Jamie said. "When I was riding, all I wanted was chocolate, but they kept giving us healthy things. Do you mind if I use your table to set out some of the stuff I bought?"

"Be my guest," he said. "Only about a dozen riders have come through so far, so I hope you've brought a lot."

"I did," she said, grinning that knowing smile that Ryan loved.

Groups of riders started to arrive after about a half hour of waiting in the heat, with only the dirty, dry wind providing any comfort. Karen Joncas, one of Ryan's former tent mates was in one of the first groups, and they kissed and hugged and slapped each other on the back so hard Jamie was afraid she was going to have to find an ER for her partner.

Karen was much gentler when she hugged Jamie, saying, "I can't believe you've nailed this one down for a whole year. Hasn't she driven you crazy?"

Jamie released her and put her arm around Ryan. "Yes, she drives me crazy, but I do the same to her. That seems fair."

"Why aren't you guys riding this year? I was really bummed when I didn't see you at the opening ceremonies." She put her hand on Ryan's shoulder and said, "Was it because of all of that stuff that happened to you over Christmas?"

Ryan spoke up before Jamie could brush the question off, her usual tactic, given how much Ryan hated to talk about the carjacking. "Yeah. Pretty much." She took a breath. "I was in a bad place when I had to make the decision. Jamie talked me out of riding, and I'm glad she did. I needed some time to relax and get my feet back under myself."

Jamie mentally rolled her eyes. If Ryan had been relaxing this year…

As if Ryan could see her silently scoffing, she added, "I'm sure Jamie doesn't think I rested much, but compared to what I would have had to do if I'd started to train, I was on easy street."

"You should have come over to the ceremonies, buddy. We would have all loved to have seen you."

Ryan shook her head. "I couldn't make myself do it." Jamie watched a flicker of pain pass across her face. They'd both known the ride started on Sunday, but neither had mentioned it. She'd learned that Ryan didn't like to bring up troubling topics, and generally thought it best to let her choose which ones to bury.

"Well, I'm glad you made it down today. This is a hell of a drive for you, isn't it? Why not pick us up in Santa Cruz?"

"Oh, I'm involved with a kid I kinda mentor and she needed some support yesterday."

Karen shot Jamie a look. "She mentors kids?"

"Don't ask. She'd be a volunteer firefighter if they'd let her." She gave Ryan a rough hug. "She has unlimited energy—until she falls flat on her face."

"That's sounds about right," Karen agreed. "I'm riding slower this year since I don't have to keep up with her." She slapped Ryan's shoulder again. "But I still miss you."

"I miss you too. We'll be back next year. We're doing the Breast Cancer Three Day, but I know I won't get the same boost I do from this."

Karen draped her arm around Ryan's shoulders and gave her a shake. "Like walking three days is taking it easy."

"She won't even train," Jamie said, ducking when Ryan tried to grab her. "She's a beast!"

"Speaking of beasts," Ryan said, leading Karen over to the table filled with chocolate Jamie had bought at a shop in Berkeley that hand-made all of their goodies. "Jamie's decided to satisfy the little devil inside every rider who's sick of energy bars. Name your chocolate, and it's here."

They spent a good two hours at the rest stop, with Ryan making her way through the tired riders, handing out candy from a tray they'd fashioned. She'd met some of her old friends, and, as usual, made some new ones by the time their treats were all gobbled up. There was about a ten minute gap where no new riders reached the stop. "We'd better get going," Jamie said. "We've got a lot of backtracking to do."

Once back in the car, Ryan turned it on and cranked up the air conditioning, turning all of the available vents towards herself. "Damn, it's nice to sit in an air conditioned car. When are they going to have the ride in January, where it belongs?"

"Probably never. But we'll be out there next year, sweating our butts off with everyone else."

Ryan turned to give her a love-filled look. "Have I told you today how lucky I am to have found you?"

"Nope. But I saved you a piece of chocolate, so you can tell me now." She pulled the dark chocolate mint patty from her pocket, glad she'd had the foresight to wrap it carefully. "It's a little gooey, but I can't imagine that will bother you."

"Gooey's my favorite," Ryan decided, yanking it from Jamie's hand and taking a big bite. "I love you enough to share this." She held it temptingly in front of Jamie's nose.

"I'm good. I get enjoyment out of watching you eat."

"That's nuts, but I'm glad for it. One more sign that we're made for each other." She leaned across the car and placed a long, sweet kiss on Jamie's lips. "As if I needed another one."

On Wednesday morning, a chilly, damp breeze was coming in through the open window, but Jamie was wrapped in a pair of warm arms and an even warmer body pressed against her from shoulders to butt. Everything about the tableaux was perfect, and she knew it was going to be a good day. Ryan was probably awake since it was hard to maintain such a tight hold while sleeping. Jamie wasn't sure what signals she gave off, but Ryan always knew the moment she woke. A few soft kisses started at her hairline and stopped at the base of her neck.

"Good morning," Jamie purred, while rubbing languidly against Ryan's body. "It's going to take a lot of effort for me to stay this happy all day long."

Ryan bent her knees and tucked them behind Jamie's so that they were now touching from shoulders to toes. "Let's stay right here all day, then we don't have to worry. We always have a good day in bed."

"Fantastic idea." Jamie started to peel herself away, playfully slapping at Ryan's grasping hands. "I need a quick bathroom break. Have you already showered?"

"Yep. I also had a fantastic breakfast of stale crackers."

Jamie reached behind herself and patted Ryan's belly. "I was afraid we'd get down here too late to shop."

"That's my fault. If I hadn't dawdled…"

"We're on vacation, honey. We don't have to be on a strict schedule."

Jamie got up and went into the bathroom, deciding to take a

shower while she was there. It only took a few minutes to match Ryan's cleanliness, and when she went back into the bedroom she smiled at Ryan, lying on her back, stark naked. "You're obviously cold. Your nipples are like rocks." She sat on the edge of the bed and sampled various selections of chilled skin.

"I like to get cold so you can warm me up."

Ryan looked so ridiculously adorable that Jamie almost let a detail slip her mind. "You're distracting me from my business." Picking up her cell phone, she pulled a number from the address book and waited for a moment. "Hi, it's Jamie Evans. Yes, it has been a while."

Ryan looked up at her with a completely puzzled expression.

Patting the cold skin on her hip, Jamie continued, "We need to stock up for the day."

Now Ryan's puzzled expression disappeared and she nodded.

"We need some bread, whatever you have that's fresh. Sure, a baguette is fine. A quart of whole milk, a pound of sliced turkey, if it's fresh, some cheddar cheese, and a dozen eggs. Also a whole chicken, some mushrooms…" She paused, then nodded. "Yes, crimini are fine. And a couple of pounds of baking potatoes and a green vegetable. Whatever's fresh. No, that should do it. I'll order more when we're settled. I only need enough to get us through the day. Just let yourself in. Thanks very much." Hanging up, she smiled at Ryan's perplexed expression. "You said you wanted to stay in bed." She dove for the mattress, pulled the covers over both of them, then rubbed her warm hands all over Ryan's cold body.

"So somebody's gonna come over here while we're in bed?"

"Yeah. We use that service. We did it when we came for our honeymoon."

"I was so stunned by the entire production that I have very few memories of the details." She wrapped Jamie in her arms, making her squeal when Ryan's cold parts met her warm ones. "That's one thing I remember, there was a lot of shrieking going on."

"It'll take them an hour to get here." Jamie's voice was low and soft, a little slower than usual. "Why don't you think of something to while away the time?"

Laughing, Ryan said, "You sound like a vamp from an old movie."

"That reminds me. We probably have fifty classic movies on DVD. We should watch some of them. That's a nice way to spend a rainy afternoon."

Ryan grabbed her and pushed her onto her back. With a hand on each of Jamie's shoulders, she loomed over her and tossed her hair so that it framed her face beautifully. "If you'd rather watch a movie than stay in bed, the honeymoon is definitely over."

Blinking, Jamie said, "What's a movie?"

Two hours later, both Ryan's libido and belly had been fed. One of Jamie's appetites had recently been more prodigious than Ryan's, but she was pretty sure her partner would fulfill any and all desires during their stay.

With Ryan's head in her lap, Jamie carefully braided hanks of her hair for no particular reason. They'd both been quiet for a while, content to just be together.

"It's hard for me to believe that we've been together almost a full year," Ryan said. "We're well into the 'and they lived happily ever after' period."

"We are? I thought that started on your wedding day."

"Nope. That starts when you really get together. And we really got together a year ago."

"I suppose I don't mind being in the 'happily ever after' phase. Does that go until 'last woman standing?'"

Chuckling softly, Ryan said, "I'm planning on going together. If it looks like I'm failing and you're still doing well, I'm taking you with me anyway."

"That's just how I'd like it." Jamie continued with her project, having constructed at least twenty braids on the left side of

Ryan's head. "It's a good thing we're not leaving the house today. Your hair is gonna look crazy."

Ryan pulled away and rolled onto her belly, bracing herself with her forearms so she was facing Jamie. "I forgot about the resolution I'd made."

"What's that?"

"I decided that we should go out for every meal. There are lots of restaurants down here you like, and I don't want you cooking on your vacation."

Jamie put her hands on Ryan's cheeks and cupped them briefly. "You're such a sweetheart. But I don't cook because it's a chore; I like it."

"I know that, but you also like to go out. We're only gonna be here a few days, so I thought it would be a nice treat for you."

"I bought things for dinner tonight, and they'll spoil if we don't eat them."

"Then we'll roast the chicken for lunch." Ryan's expression was almost plaintive.

"What will we do with a pound of turkey?"

"Appetizers." She laughed. "You know me. I'll snack on it. Come on, let's go out for dinner."

"Fine," Jamie said. "But I'll have to buy you something to wear. You only brought shorts and jeans."

"No problem. We can go shopping after lunch." Jamie rested the back of her hand on Ryan's forehead, feigning concern. "No, I don't have a fever." Ryan stuck her tongue out. "I'm being well behaved."

"You certainly are. I know I always say I like bad girls, but maybe I like well behaved girls better."

After lunch, which Ryan insisted on preparing, they got into Jim's classic Mustang and took it over to Carmel. While walking down the length of the main shopping street, Jamie made note of any place that looked promising and when they reached the terminus, she said, "I'd like to try two places. Can you tolerate that?"

"I'd like to go to one—the skate and surf shop right up there." Ryan pointed to the most garish looking store on the entire street. "I'll make you a deal. You go to the two stores you like and buy anything you want; I'll go to the store I want and buy myself a pair of flip-flops that won't look stupid with nice clothes."

Jamie was fairly sure flip-flops of that caliber had never been invented, but it was a struggle to get Ryan into anything other than running shoes, so a pair of flip-flops was probably an improvement. "You really want me to buy whatever I want? Anything at all?" The mere thought was intoxicating.

Ryan nodded. "Anything at all. Just make sure we can return things that don't fit."

"So if it fits, you'll wear it." It was impossible to contain her suspicions.

Holding up her hand as though she were taking a vow, Ryan said, "On my honor."

After their shopping expedition, the swimming pool called to them. Spending a moment to observe the joyful expression on Ryan's face, Jamie was certain that her partner was never happier than when she was swimming in the nude. She was at her most playful, acting just as silly as she did when they had Caitlin. This was the part of Ryan that had been an infrequent visitor since the carjacking, and Jamie was happy beyond expression to have her back.

They played like a pair of otter pups, chasing each other around the pool, wrestling playfully. Neither one actually swam much, which puzzled Jamie—but she was careful not to make a point of it. To the best of her knowledge, Ryan hadn't done anything even vaguely aerobic all day, and she couldn't remember the last time a healthy Ryan had skipped a day of exercising. But there was no sign of the ridiculously determined athlete in this smiling, naked woman who looked like she was focused only on having fun. The last thing Jamie wanted to do was break the spell.

"Lie on your stomach and put your hands out in front of you," Ryan instructed. "I want to see how aerodynamic I can make you by pushing you around by your feet."

"How will I breathe?"

Ryan huffed out a long breath. "It's silly questions like this that frustrate scientists." Her serious mien disappeared and she jumped out of the pool to go to a teak locker on the deck. As expected, the locker was filled with toys, one of them a child's snorkel. It had been around since Jamie's youth, and Ryan jumped in, tested it and found it still acceptably watertight. "Here you go."

Jamie put it in her mouth, stretched her arms out in front of her, and floated on her stomach, waiting for Ryan to take over. For the next half hour, Ryan pushed her around the pool, adjusting the angle of her head, her arms, the tilt of her hands and the way she clasped them together. Finally Ryan stopped and flipped Jamie over onto her back, where she floated peacefully.

"I could do a lot better job with fiberglass, but I think I got you at a pretty good angle." Her pleasure with her accomplishment was comical. Even when playing a meaningless game, Ryan had to have a goal. Pulling her legs up in front of herself, Ryan lazily turned onto her back, then grasped Jamie's hand. They floated around for quite a while, neither talking. Finally Ryan sighed and said, "This is the life."

It was the most positive thing Ryan had ever said about the Evans' way of living, and Jamie felt strangely optimistic that Ryan might one day get over her enmity towards wealth and leisure.

After they'd been in the water so long their fingers started to prune, Ryan got out and pulled a few bath sheets from a tower of them. Looking childishly playful, she went outside without a word. Unable to resist, Jamie jumped out of the pool and followed her, parading around, wet, naked and dripping.

Ryan stretched one of the big towels out onto the lush green grass and pointed at it. "Why don't you lie down right here and relax in the sun for a few minutes." She put her hands behind her back and gave Jamie a supremely innocent smile.

"There's only one towel. Where will you be?"

Ryan pointed at the two that were still folded. "It's all taken care of. Just lie down now."

Knowing something fun was in the offing, Jamie compliantly lay down.

As though she'd just now noticed this, Ryan said, "Hmm, your skin is awfully fair. You could get burned lying in the sun naked." She shook out one of the towels and placed it over Jamie's head, extending it to her knees. "That's much better."

"Ryan, there's a towel over my face."

"Hmm, what to do? I don't want the towel over your face to annoy you, but I also don't want you to get burned. Maybe I can think of some way to distract you."

Jamie saw this coming from a mile away, but she was the last to complain about the obviousness of the game. Ryan positioned herself somewhere below the end of the towel and gently spread Jamie's legs apart. Starting with a knee, kisses and gentle licks flicked the water droplets away, slowly and deliberately making progress to an obvious goal. Jamie used her hands to tent the towel up so it wasn't directly on her face. Her skin really was fair enough to burn in the time she expected this activity to take, so she placidly lay there under the fluffy cotton and let Ryan work her magic.

Chapter Seven

On Wednesday, Jennie walked over to Catherine's house as soon as her classes were finished. Even though school was out every day at noon, she'd told Sandy not to expect her before eight p.m. Staying away from the group home as much as possible was her intent, and she'd planned carefully.

Going to Catherine's after school was a perfect way to kill at least four hours. If she was lucky, Catherine would invite her for dinner, letting her stay in the city until she absolutely had to get home. And if she didn't get a dinner invite, she could wander around Oakland until eight, looking for a friend from her old neighborhood.

No matter when she went home, she was determined never to have to eat with her roommates. That pledge was slightly less firm than the one she'd made never to be alone in the house with Pebbles, but it was still important. She knew that Ryan wouldn't like her wandering around for a few hours every afternoon, but she had to protect herself. There was only so much even Ryan could do.

There'd been no evidence that anyone knew Ryan had gotten involved in getting her a new roommate. Even though most of the girls in the home were okay, a couple of them were always looking for trouble. And finding out someone had complained about another girl could get her butt kicked all across Oakland.

She got to Catherine's at about twelve-thirty. As always,

Marta answered the door with a welcoming smile. "Come in, come in. I've been expecting you." She put her arm around Jennie and gave her a brief hug. "What would you like for lunch? I can make anything."

Jennie thought for a minute, then said, "Can you make me a hamburger?"

"Of course. I was just going to make lunch for Conor. He's here working on the house, you know. You two can eat together."

"Cool. I'll go up and see what he's doing."

Jennie dropped her book bag by the front door and dashed up the stairs. Conor was alone, doing some demolition of the walls in Catherine's proposed library. He wore big, clear glasses and a pair of earmuffs to protect his eyes from dust and his hearing from the noise. A gigantic electric saw was buzzing through drywall when Jennie poked her head in.

He turned off his saw and smiled broadly. "Look what the cat dragged in." His voice was atypically loud, then he took off his earmuffs. "I was just going to have lunch. Are you joining me?"

"Yeah, Marta is making me a hamburger."

"Run down and tell her to make me the same thing. I don't want her to have to go to too much trouble."

Jennie smiled at him. "She likes to go to trouble. She's one of those people who likes to be busy, and she hardly ever cooks for Ms. Smith."

He nodded. "My father and my aunt are just like that. They're not happy if they're not busy. I've never understood it," he said, chuckling. "Do you want to help me out today? I could always use a demolition assistant."

Her eyes grew wide, "I'd love to."

"What are you doing here anyway?"

"Oh." A guilty look stole over her face. "I'm supposed to be doing my homework. I have to go to summer school."

"I had to go to summer school almost every year, since I always managed to screw something up. What are you taking?"

"One really sucky math class and one really fun drawing class.

It's not too bad. Ryan's trying to help me get organized so I can be better in math."

"I'm pretty good at math. If you need any help, I could take a peek."

She wasn't sure why, but having Conor offer made her feel a little shy. "Okay. If you don't mind."

"I don't mind a bit, kiddo." He put his saw on the floor and unplugged it, then removed his glasses and flicked the dust out of his hair and off his shirt. "Let's go down and eat, then you can do your homework. If you have any free time, you can help me out. I've got to get finished with the demo today because my cousin's coming tomorrow to start rewiring the place."

They walked down together, with Jennie trying to get past her discomfort. Conor was a lot like Ryan, but he was a real guy. That made it kinda weird.

As she usually did, Marta left the room while they were eating, despite their pleas that she stay. Once she'd gone, Jennie said, "If I'm here alone, she'll stay, but if Ms. Smith is here, she won't. It's like she doesn't think it's allowed." Her stomach felt tight when she thought about the way Marta acted. "I hate that she acts like she's a servant."

"Well, she is." She must have made a face, because he jumped right back in. "I don't mean anything bad by that. That's just the way she sees herself fitting in. She certainly isn't a member of the family, even though Jamie and Catherine think of her that way. I think it's really tough to live in somebody else's house when you're an employee."

"Do you think she *has* to work here?" Jennie asked plaintively.

Conor was chewing and he waited until he'd swallowed to reply. "I'd say this is one of the best jobs for a cook anywhere in the world. She does next to nothing and has a fantastic house to herself almost all of the time. I don't think you have to feel sorry for Marta. But a lot of those kids she looks after down in the South Bay have a tough life."

"Why? The South Bay's nice."

"Not for them. It's no fun to be born into a third world country and that's where most of those people she mentors come from. We've got a lot of problems here, but we don't have anything near the problems they have south of the border."

"Have you been there?"

Conor smiled and shook his head. "Not really. I've been to Mexico, but only for fun. Most of the guys I work with are from Mexico though, and they all grew up a lot poorer than I can even imagine."

"My new roommate is from Guatemala, but I don't know anything about her."

"Did you just meet?"

"No, she's been at the home for a while but she doesn't speak very much English." She shrugged. "She doesn't like me."

"How do you feel about that place?"

"The group home?"

When Conor nodded, Jennie looked down at her plate and used her fork to play with her coleslaw. Finally she said, "I don't know. I never get yelled at or hit, so that's good. But sometimes I'd rather be home. Even when my mom's mean, she's still my mom. You know?"

"I know. I guess it'll never be home for you."

"No, it's not home. They give you meals and there's a TV, but I'm not friends with anybody. Since I started coming over to San Francisco to go to school, I'm not really one of them. And I get nicer stuff than everybody because of Ms. Smith. That pisses some of them off."

"How does it piss them off?" Conor asked, his eyes narrowing.

"Nobody really says anything," Jennie said quickly. "But I'm surprised I still have my computer and the other stuff Ms. Smith bought me for Christmas. A couple of them take anything that's nice and ruin it, just so you can't have it."

"How do you protect your stuff?"

"I have a backpack and I keep my computer and drawing stuff in it. I keep it with me *all* the time. I even take it into the shower with me. That's the only room with a lock on the door."

Conor looked down and focused on his meal. He looked like he was gonna say something but was too mad.

"It's not bad. Don't tell Ryan."

"I won't tell her anything." He gave Jennie a half smile. "Sometimes you have to be careful with what you tell Ryan. If you tell her something is bothering you, she'll figure out a way to fix it. Even if you don't want her to."

Jennie smiled up at him. "I already figured that out."

Jamie's legs were too weak to walk, so Ryan had to sling her over her shoulder to find someplace to escape the sun's strong afternoon rays. The pool-house was the closest place, and they went back inside to reconnoiter.

They lay together on a chaise longue, with Jamie absently playing with Ryan's hair. "I don't think it's possible to be happier," she whispered, her eyes bright.

"Tell me why you're happy. I want to make sure I can replicate anything I've done to get you there."

Enfolding Ryan in her arms, Jamie nuzzled her face against her chest. "Everything you've done has made me happy. You're treating me like it's my birthday. Not that I'm complaining."

"It takes getting away for a little while to remember how busy we've been. When I have a spare second, I'm always concentrating on you."

"How about you? Are you having as much fun as I am?"

Ryan stretched her arms out and yawned. "Yeah, I'd say I'm digging this. Great weather, great house, great food, great girlfriend. Just flip the order of those things and you've got a recipe for perfection."

"I was so busy shopping for you that I didn't see what else you bought today. Do you have any new toys?"

"Nope. I just got sandals. I had to go to a normal shoe store for 'em, but I survived."

Lifting her head so she could get a good look at Ryan, Jamie asked, "You didn't want anything else? Not even from the surf shop?"

"Oh, there were four or five things I've been thinking of, but I didn't bite."

"What's on your wish list?"

"There's nothing I need, but I've been looking at getting a longboard." She wrinkled up her nose. "The dudes at the store weren't interested in talking to me, so I bagged it."

"Why weren't they interested?"

"They were very dudey dudes. A lot of skateboarders don't think women can skate."

"Screw 'em."

"That's my motto. If I'm not feeling the love, I'm not spending my money." She didn't add that she'd had no intention of actually *buying* a new skateboard. Parting with money was harder now that it had ever been, but she wasn't going to share that difficulty with Jamie. She'd have to learn how to deal with her money, and she was going to have to figure it out for herself.

That night, without a raised eyebrow or word of complaint, Ryan put on the dress Jamie had bought her. Normally Jamie wouldn't have been so bold, but Ryan had given her carte blanche. It was short, so short that it seemed like a foot of Ryan's thighs were displayed. That was an optical illusion—those lovely legs just so tantalizing that they caught and held the eye. The dress was markedly feminine, made of a delicate, light blue print fabric with a plunging neckline. Jamie was one hundred percent sure this was something Ryan would never have picked for herself, but since getting her into dressy clothes was always a fight, she'd decided that she might as well make the fight worth the reward. And when she saw Ryan in the dress, she knew she would put up a very good fight to see her in this outfit more often.

"Does this work?" Ryan ran a hand over her breast, showing

that she was braless.

Jamie tried not to leer too obviously. "It does for me." The neckline went to a V in the middle of Ryan's sternum, and any bra she owned would have shown. "I can offer an easy solution." She went to the dresser and sorted through the top drawers, murmuring a quiet, "Ah-ha," then walked back over, holding a pair of flesh-colored disks. "Nipple covers."

Ryan took the silicone pads in her hand. "Weird." She explored them carefully. "How do they stay on?"

Jamie took one and warmed it between her hands. "Body heat, which you always have plenty of." She slipped the dress from Ryan's shoulder, applied the cover to her nipple and smoothed it down so it adhered. "No adhesive. Cool, huh?"

Ryan tentatively brushed her fingers over her nipple, unable to make it harden and pop the cover off. "I might wear these every day."

"No way. I love seeing those hard nipples. I just don't want everyone else to see them, which they would through this thin fabric."

Once both covers were in place, Ryan did a slow spin, making the fabric flare out around her thighs. Smiling seductively, she lowered her voice to its sexiest register and said, "Good?"

This was the attitude that Jamie was unable to resist. It was clear that Ryan knew she was a good-looking woman, and equally clear that her knowledge of this fact was just that—a fact. Ryan was never overly invested in her looks, and that made her rare preening all the more adorable.

Jamie put her hands on Ryan's hips and held her at arm's length, devouring her with her eyes. "I've never seen a more beautiful woman. If you were a bad tempered jerk I'd still be lucky to have you." She giggled at the mere thought.

"I'm sure you're wearing some old rag you've had since you were in high school," Ryan said with a straight face. "But you look delicious in it."

Jamie kissed her tenderly, letting her tongue run over the

shiny lips to which Ryan had just applied gloss. "Let's go to a drive-through, grab a burger, and get back here."

Ryan held her in her arms and chuckled. "First, we dine."

Following behind Ryan as they were shown to their seats, Jamie studied her, seeing how she altered her gait to walk in a dress. The change wasn't dramatic, mostly because Ryan had been able to find a pair of vaguely dressy sandals that showed just a narrow band of black leather. Since she didn't have to wear heels she was able to walk in close to her normal fashion, but Jamie noted that her stride was a little shorter and her hips swayed slightly more than usual. For a change, it didn't annoy her when every man in the restaurant discreetly followed Ryan with his eyes. They were only human.

They'd only been home a short time before Ryan got a devilishly hungry look in her eye and proceeded to slowly remove Jamie's clothing as they wandered through the first floor. The energy that poured off her was incandescent and by the time she was fully naked Jamie was ready for anything. Surprisingly, Ryan picked her up and put her on the bar in the den. It seemed like an odd place, but once Jamie's legs were wrapped around Ryan's shoulders they could have been in Buckingham palace and she wouldn't have noticed the Queen having tea…in the nude.

Ryan stood in the bathroom the next morning, applying the finishing touches to her ponytail.

"Honey?" Jamie called out groggily.

Ryan popped into the room. "Ready for breakfast?"

Jamie sat up and rested her weight on an elbow. "You're bright eyed and bushy tailed."

Turning to twitch her butt, Ryan said, "Let's eat, and then go play golf. It's a great day for it."

"Golf?" Jamie's expression was one of pure joy. "You really want to play golf?"

She asked the question the way a child would ask if they were really going to Disneyland. Smiling broadly, Ryan said, "I already called and got us a tee time. Can you be ready in an hour?"

Jamie leapt out of bed, stopped to give Ryan a quick kiss, then headed for the shower, singing a happy tune.

They spent the afternoon swimming again, but just like the day before, Ryan didn't do a single serious lap. She was behaving like a normal person on vacation, stunning Jamie more with every passing hour. When they were done playing in the pool, Ryan brought out a chilled bottle of white wine and a pair of glasses and they sat out in the warm afternoon sun to enjoy it. Ryan kept her chair in the full sun while Jamie found shelter in the shade of the building. Ryan had her feet on Jamie's lap, and by the time they were finished with their first glass of wine, she was determinedly trying to flick Jamie's nipple with her big toe. She had a playful look on her face and when Jamie got up and excused herself to use the restroom, Ryan followed right behind her. Jamie used the bathroom in the pool house with Ryan standing outside, scratching on the door like a dog.

"As soon as you get out here, I'm going to throw you over my shoulder and make you my woman!"

Jamie was laughing out loud, finding the way Ryan made these pronouncements hilarious. It was clear she meant what she said, but the way she said it was so silly, so un-Ryanlike, that it tickled her funny-bone.

Since it was clear Ryan meant business, Jamie quickly showered off, always trying to give her partner a clean canvas upon which to work. She opened the door and posed in the doorway, trying to look seductive. "Where do you want me?" she asked in her sexiest voice.

Ryan leaned over and grasped her around the thighs, then stood up, letting Jamie dangle down her back. As Ryan headed for the closest bed, she kept turning her head to take big, playful bites out of Jamie's butt. "I'm not sure where I'm going," she said, laughing at herself, "but I sure am in a hurry to get there."

By six o'clock Jamie was loved out. She lay on the pool-house guest bed with her head hanging off the edge. "We should have eaten before we came to bed. Now I'm starving and I don't want to wait until a decent hour to have dinner. You didn't make reservations anywhere, did you?"

"No, but I have plans."

After a quick trip to a gourmet food shop, Ryan drove Jim's GTO to the spot where they'd performed their unofficial wedding ceremony a year earlier. The weather was perfection. For a change, the wind was blowing from the land toward the sea, making it unseasonably warm and dry. As they looked down at the shore, they saw that everyone within their view had a camera. Even the locals wanted to memorialize such a nice evening.

Ryan had re-chilled their wine, and Jamie poured some for them while Ryan got busy opening the little containers they'd bought. They were each working, not paying much attention to their position and they wound up on their knees, almost facing each other.

Ryan held her glass in one hand and touched Jamie's face gently with the other. "Here's to us," she said, her voice rough with emotion. "Here's to every glorious day we've had together, and the inglorious ones too. I wouldn't trade any one of them for the world."

Jamie clinked her glass against her partner's, then each took a sip. "You are my life, Ryan O'Flaherty, and the day I met you put me on a new path that I will forever be grateful for."

"We both did pretty well for ourselves."

Ryan was smiling so sweetly that Jamie had to put her glass down and settle Ryan's on the ground as well. They wrapped each other in tender hugs and started to kiss, completely forgetting how hungry they both were. Soon they were lying on their sides, gently exploring each other's mouths, as though that were the only destination in their universe.

When the sun set, the wind changed, chilling them both in a matter of minutes. They hurriedly packed up their things and started for home, with Jamie spreading cheese on crackers and popping them into Ryan's open mouth. "You're going to lose five pounds if I don't start feeding you."

"I haven't missed a meal yet. I'm not convinced I'm gonna miss this one, either," she said. "It's just a little delayed."

"Do you want to stop somewhere and get something more substantial?"

"No. I've come to like eating fruit and cheese and bread. It's really starting to grow on me. Just don't think we can ever get away with this if any of my brothers or my father are around. No matter how much fruit you have, it's just a snack."

They had one more day of vacation and Ryan began the day just as she had the previous one. "Golf?" she asked as soon as Jamie opened her eyes.

"Are you sure you want to play again? We could go to the ocean. You could go surfing."

"Nope." Ryan didn't look even vaguely interested. "Now that your arm is okay, you need to get back into golf shape. And even though I'm never going to be in golf shape, I can certainly improve my game if I put my mind to it."

Batting her eyes, Jamie said, "Are you sure you're not just doing this for me?"

"Nope. It's not as fantastic today as yesterday, but it's still darned nice. I can't think of many things I'd rather do than be outside with you."

Jamie put her feet on the floor and walked over to revel in the warm hug she knew Ryan would have for her. "You are a most excellent girlfriend."

That evening found them at the most exclusive restaurant within thirty miles. Jamie had to use her father's name to get a table, but it was worth it. Ryan looked magnificent in the very thin, black, V-necked sleeveless sweater Jamie had bought her, along with slim fitting white slacks. Ryan hadn't even complained when they had to go to a local seamstress to have the slacks altered to fit. Even though it was a rush job, the seamstress had been happy to make the alterations, and even happier with the tip Jamie gave her.

When they were shown to their table Ryan didn't even open her menu. As their server approached, she said, "Will you order for me?"

"Sure. But what would you like to drink?"

Placidly, Ryan said, "Whatever you think I should have."

Jamie took her at her word and ordered as she would have before they'd met. Paying no attention to prices, she tried to find what would best pair with the wine she had her eye on, a vineyard she was very fond of. The sommelier came by and agreed that the wine she was interested in would be a great companion to the West Coast oysters but that it might be too acidic for those from Japan. Ryan sat there looking interested, but not offering her opinion.

When Jamie had made her decision, she sat back in her chair and smiled at her partner. "I don't know why, but I really like ordering for you. I think it's cool that you sit back and let me do it."

"That's what makes a good marriage. You need to do the things that you like to do, and I need to do the same." Ryan leaned over and whispered, "One thing I really like, and I think I'm pretty good at, is getting my tongue right into that little spot…"

The sommelier re-appeared, hovering just out of hearing distance, waiting to pour the wine. Ryan sat up and nodded at him so that he approached. "We'll get back to that point a little later," she said with a wink.

Ryan let Jamie get all the way upstairs, but as soon as she started to undress, Ryan swooped up behind her and took over.

Neither of them had had too much to drink, but the wine had loosened them up. Not that Ryan could get much looser than she'd been. She grabbed the blanket from their bed and took it, and a couple of pillows, as she grasped Jamie's hand and headed downstairs. There she opened the door to the glass paneled patio.

Even though there was decent illumination from the moon, there was very little to see in the darkness of the night. Ryan had obviously taken that into account. She urged Jamie to lie down on the chaise, then she put the pillows on the ground and knelt on them. As Ryan started to kiss her way to her favorite spot, she said, "Look up at the stars. If you counted every one of them, they wouldn't be a fraction of a percent of how much love I have for you."

Letting out a soft sigh, Jamie said, "I don't care if nine tenths of what you say is bull, I love to hear it." She laughed, the sound turning into a giggle when Ryan started lapping her thighs like a playful puppy.

The plan was to get going early in the morning so Ryan could go by and check on Jennie again. She got up early once again and made a hearty breakfast, which Jamie was allowed to enjoy in bed, capping three days of pampering.

They both ran up and down the stairs at least seven times, trying to make sure they hadn't forgotten anything. While Jamie did one final search, Ryan loaded their bags into the car.

In Catherine's office, Jamie found Ryan's omnipresent date book next to the laptop. Ryan had obviously used some of her early morning time to check her mail. The book was open, and practically begging to be looked at. As usual, Jamie's curiosity got the best of her and her eyes focused on the bold handwriting. In one-inch tall letters, Ryan had scrawled across two pages: "Don't be so self-involved."

Jamie wanted to close the book, but she couldn't make herself. In smaller print, underlined, was "Go out for meals." Her heart sank, and then she felt as if she'd been kicked in the gut when she read the next words: "No real exercise!"

She was heartsick. Ryan had been doing only what she thought Jamie would like. She was "behaving" the way she thought she should, not simply being herself.

The last words, written in red, hurt the most: "Initiate lovemaking." "Initiate" was underlined several times.

Jamie sank down into her mother's desk chair, wondering what part of their trip had been genuine. Was it all just something Ryan had to write down in her calendar? Was none of it what she felt in her heart?

Ryan called from the first floor, "Are you ready?"

Jamie went to the door. "I need a few minutes. Is that okay? You could go check the pool house to make sure we turned everything off."

"Okay."

She heard Ryan walk across the entryway, then saw the light on the keypad by the door blink, showing she'd left the building. Jamie went back into the office and sat down, staring at Ryan's reminders. The last one should have been obvious. "Don't complain about spending money or buying stuff. *AT ALL!*" Jamie had known something was up with that, but the rest of the items had her flummoxed.

Her thoughts were a mass of confused messages. Ryan's love was beyond doubt, but what if the other things were more like obligations? She sat there quietly, thinking back over the past three days.

Ryan wasn't particularly good at hiding her feelings, and Jamie was certain she would've noticed if any part of the trip had been a strain. She was certain they'd had fun when they were golfing, and just as certain that Ryan truly enjoyed their meals out. No one could make up the kind of enthusiasm she'd exhibited for those expertly prepared meals. She'd been witty and flirty and intensely observant during them, asking perceptive questions about the food and the wine. Ryan just wasn't the type to do that if she wasn't truly curious. And even though she tried to hide it, Jamie could tell that Ryan got a certain amount of pleasure while strutting around in her new dress, even though it was clear she was most interested in attracting Jamie. And even if she had to remind herself to initiate lovemaking, there was no pretending in her excitement or her enjoyment. You couldn't make that stuff up.

Looking back, Jamie realized it wasn't that Ryan was faking it—she clearly wasn't. But she also wasn't being fully authentic. She needed to remind herself to do the things she thought she should be doing.

Was that so bad? Of course not. Having a woman love you enough to make you feel like the world revolved around you couldn't ever be considered a negative. But it would be so much nicer if it came from the heart, rather than the head.

Jamie stood up and slapped the book closed, deciding that the spin she put on the situation had a great deal to do with how she felt about it. Ryan was a list-maker. That's just how her brain worked. They'd had the talk about her not initiating sex, so she made a note to do better. She was trying—trying hard. And any woman who would complain about such a generous, loving act was a fool.

It was time to give Ryan a break. To stop asking for every little detail of their lives to be perfect. The poor lamb was such an over-achiever she'd always be making lists if Jamie continued to harp on things. Ryan needed a break—a break from every form of test—especially tests of her love.

Chapter Eight

They got back early enough on Friday afternoon to go by Catherine's house and check on Jennie and her progress. Jen had not only kept up, she'd even managed to finish her homework for Monday.

"Tomorrow I'm going to go work with my cousins on that apartment building we bought," Ryan said. "And Jamie's going to go with her mom to look at some places to have our wedding reception. Would you like to join one of us?" She waggled her eyebrows up and down a couple of times as though Jennie's answer was pre-ordained, which, in fact, it was.

Jennie gave Jamie a quick look and said, "What you're doin' sounds like a lot of fun, but I'd rather go with Ryan, if that's okay."

Ryan looked shocked. "I was sure you were going to want to go with Catherine and Jamie. I guess I don't know you as well as I think I do."

"Did you really think that?" Jennie asked, looking at Ryan with puzzled confusion.

"Nah. I had a pretty good idea you'd rather hang out with the guys. Can Jamie and I give you a ride home now? We're going to go over to Berkeley to check our mail and take care of a few things."

"Sure. Let me call the car guy and tell him he doesn't have to come."

After Jennie made her arrangements, they all went up and said good-bye to Catherine and Conor, then left for Oakland. For a change, Jennie was there in time for dinner, and Sandy was just starting to round up the girls to get ready for the meal. Jennie's new roommate, Sabrina, was sitting on the front porch, giving off a world-weary vibe much older than her seventeen years. When Ryan went in to talk to Sandy about having Jen with her for the next day, Jamie stayed outside. In Spanish, she said, "Hi, my name is Jamie. I don't think we've met before."

The girl looked at her, then looked away, saying nothing.

"Jennie's my friend and she tells me she's your new roommate."

Not looking back, Sabrina said, "So?"

"So nothing. I was just trying to be polite."

Frostily, Sabrina said, "Maybe you could butt in again and I could have another person in my room."

"I didn't butt in," Jamie said truthfully. She didn't add that Ryan had. "Do you have a problem with Jen?"

"Yeah. I don't want her or anybody else in my room. My girlfriend doesn't like it."

Jamie spent a moment trying to hide her shock and think of how to respond. It hadn't dawned on her that it didn't really matter if you were talking about heterosexual or homosexual couples; at this age, they were all trouble. "Were you the only girl who was living by herself?"

Sabrina looked at her and her expression slowly turned into a haughty smile. "After Juana got finished kicking Josie's ass, I was. If she ever sees Jennie around, she'll kick her ass, too. Lucky for her, Jennie doesn't go to our school."

Jamie thought that it was lucky for Jen on many levels that she didn't go to that particular Oakland high school. "If you honestly think Jennie is in trouble, I'll talk to Sandy about seeing if we can move her."

"She's not going to put her back with Pebbles, and she's got the only single now. Nobody else wants to room with Pebbles either. She's crazy."

"So Jen either has to stay with you and risk getting beaten up, or stay with Pebbles."

She didn't finish her thought so Sabrina finished it for her. "And get raped." She laughed, the sound so bitter and cold that it sent shivers down Jamie's spine.

Jamie felt like beating her head against the porch, but it seemed like that was what the young woman wanted, so she tried to act cool. "I guess Jennie had better take her chances with getting her ass kicked. But you should remind your girlfriend that Ryan's been kicking ass for a very long time."

"Juana is in a gang. Does your girlfriend carry a knife?"

The casual yet bitter way she said this made Jamie quake. She had to force her voice to be calm. "She doesn't need to." With that she got up and went into the house, hoping she and Ryan could leave without her grabbing Jennie, throwing her into the car, and never returning.

After reporting on Sabrina's comments, they rode home in silence. Glumly, they sat together in the living room. "What do we do?" Jamie asked. "We can't leave her there."

Ryan dropped her head into her open hands and rubbed her face against them, a clear sign of frustration. "It'll be a cold day in hell when the court awards custody of a fifteen-year-old lesbian kid to a lesbian couple in their twenties." She shook her head. "And don't forget that we wouldn't get much support from our families if we tried. Da made it clear I wasn't ready for a fish tank."

Jamie patted her. "Not true. But he's right about us not being the right people to parent Jen. She's way past our experience level."

"Jennie's mom clearly doesn't want her, and even if her dad wanted her—which I don't think he does—his wife and Jen are like oil and water."

"So what do we do?" A dull, throbbing ache had started

behind her eyes. "We can't supervise her every minute."

"I know, I know." Ryan leaned back on the sofa and let out a heavy breath. "I'm out of ideas. I just hope she stays out of trouble at the group home. If she has to go back into the system..." She didn't state the obvious. Jen had run away from every placement she'd ever been in.

They went into the kitchen and started to prepare dinner, both of them quiet and introspective.

"I've known Jen for less than two years," Jamie said reflectively. "Can you imagine how much more invested you'd be in your own kids? God." She shivered. "The responsibility must be overwhelming."

The next morning Ryan rode her motorcycle over to Jennie's home. She went in and talked to Sandy, making sure she didn't mind having Jen ride on the back of the bike. This was purely to make up for her oversight of the other day, when she hadn't asked. Luckily, Sandy didn't have a problem with it so long as Jennie wore a helmet. Properly protected, they got on the bike and went over to the Mission District, site of the O'Flaherty family project.

Most of the cousins had been working on the house every available weekend since they'd bought it, but they were still deep in the demolition phase.

The building was fairly unique for the neighborhood—built as three generous full-floor apartments. But over the eighty years of its life it had been remodeled and chopped up. They'd gotten a pretty good set of working plans from their architect and were happy with them, but to turn the little rabbit warrens into apartments that would be desirable enough for yuppies to rent was not a small task. There was a rickety staircase barely hanging off the back of the building, entry doors shoved into hallways, bathrooms jammed into corners that had never been properly plumbed, and such a mess of electrical wiring that all of the boys were surprised the place was still standing.

The neighborhood was gentrifying so quickly they were all sure they could make a nice payday if they did a good job, but having only two apartments to rent wasn't ideal.

The place had obviously been a nice building when it was new, and some of the details were impressive, particularly the chamfered ceilings and moldings on the first floor, where Tommy and Annie would live. But as you went up, the quality deteriorated. The top floor was a wreck, and Conor had warned they might have to rip out the floor and start over. That was a task no one was looking forward to.

Ryan and Jennie got to work removing drywall from a room that had clearly been added sometime in the last thirty years. As per Jamie's instructions, they both wore respirator masks so they wouldn't inhale anything toxic. Ryan showed Jen how to use a screwpull and hammer to pull off the drywall and remove any exposed nails, then they put on their safety glasses and got to work, each paying close attention to her task and not speaking for several hours.

At the end of the day they were both dirty, dusty, filthy messes, and when Jamie and Catherine came to the job-site at about four o'clock, the workers were too tired to muster up much enthusiasm for the Smith/Evans women's tale of their difficult day.

"We went to three different places, and none of them was quite right," Jamie said. "Canapés and steak and fish and then cake. It was terrible," she said, putting on the drama for Ryan's sake.

"That doesn't sound that hard to me," Jennie said seriously.

Catherine laughed. "I think you two should come over to my house for dinner. Marta can get you all fixed up with anything you'd like, and Jamie and I can sit and watch you, since we're too stuffed to eat another bite." There was a twinkle in her brown eyes and it drew a weary laugh from both Ryan and Jennie.

The fledgling tradeswomen were too dirty to go directly to

Catherine's, so they stopped at the O'Flaherty house to clean up before dinner. Conor wasn't home, so Jamie found some of her smallest clothes and set Jennie up to shower in Conor's room. When Jamie went back downstairs, Ryan was dawdling and hadn't yet taken off her clothes.

Jamie went up to her and put her hands on Ryan's hips, looking up at her with a devilish smile. "If Jennie wasn't here, I'd peel those dirty clothes off you and have my way with you in the shower."

"I think I'm too tired, anyway." She placed her hands on Jamie's shoulders and looked at her somberly. "I'm so glad we don't have kids. You still have to watch Jennie as close as Caitlin."

As Ryan's hands slid down her arms, heading for her waist, Jamie danced away saying, "I don't want to have to send my clothes to the dry cleaner. In my fantasy, I take my clothes off first."

"It always surprises me that such a clean woman likes it when I'm filthy."

"I'm sure it's just because you're so butch when you look like a laborer. I find women who work in blue-collar and no-collar jobs much sexier than the ones who look like they never break a sweat."

Ryan turned for the bath, chuckling to herself as she went. "Damned lucky for me."

Ryan wasn't particularly surprised to see her brother at Catherine's. He was trying to squeeze in the renovations on the library while keeping up with his regular job, and the only way to get both done was to skip work on the apartment building. The rest of the cousins understood, as they all would have done the same thing if a job for a family member had popped up, but the whole thing didn't sit right.

She was surprised, and a little annoyed, to find Conor in the kitchen with Marta. While leaning against the counter, he was in the process of swiping a carrot right before Marta was ready to chop it.

Marta playfully slapped his hand, then turned and said to Ryan, "Your brother is the only person I've ever met who eats more than you do."

Ryan walked over and slugged him on the shoulder, making him wince and rub the spot.

"What was that for?"

"Marta wanted to do that, but she's too polite." Ryan ducked her head down and kissed Marta on the cheek. "Don't encourage him. It's like feeding a stray cat—you'll never get rid of him."

Laughing, Marta said, "Oh, I like him. When he and Jennie are here, I actually get to cook."

"Yes, but it's not your job to cook for him." She gave Conor a narrow eyed scowl. "He's supposed to be an adult, and he can fend for himself."

He glanced sideways, saw that Marta wasn't looking, then flicked his fingers hard across Ryan's cheek. She flinched and blinked to get the tears out of her eyes and was about to pop him one when she remembered where she was. Instead of a punch, she merely glared at him. Conor wore the same happy look he always had when he'd gotten one of his siblings good and knew they couldn't retaliate. She'd seen that superior look thousands of times, and was fairly sure he'd seen the same look in her eyes on an equal number of occasions. To avoid temptation, she opened the refrigerator and took out a beer. Staying away from Conor, she sat on the other side of the kitchen island and watched Marta work.

"I can't tell what you're making, but it looks good."

"I am making paella. Your brother was nice enough to go to the market and get some sausage."

"It's nice to know he's not totally useless." Ryan gave Conor a sickeningly sweet smile.

Jamie and Catherine entered the room, followed closely by Jennie. Jamie put her arm around Ryan's shoulders. "Drinking again?"

Ryan took a long sip, then handed the bottle to her partner. "Beer is a good analgesic. My shoulders are stiff. The stuff you do in the gym never replicates physical labor."

"You're not too tired to go for a walk, are you?" Jennie asked, looking hopeful. "I've got a lot of catching up to do."

Dully, Ryan looked at her. "Catching up for what?"

"Didn't your aunt tell you? I'm gonna do the breast cancer walk with you guys."

Ryan's eyes grew wider and she snuck a quick look at Jamie, who didn't seem to be aware of this development. Ryan took another drink, then sheepishly said, "No, my aunt didn't tell me, and I wish she would have. There's a problem, Jen. You've gotta be sixteen to do the walk." At Jennie's crestfallen look, Ryan said, "I'm really sorry, but you have to have a physical and you have to prove your age."

Disconsolate, Jennie sat on the stool next to Ryan. She let her head fall until it rested atop Ryan's shoulder. "I'm too young for everything."

"Could she volunteer?" Conor asked.

Ryan shot him another scolding look. "No. She's technically old enough, but she has to be with an adult, and we're all doing the walk."

"I'm not," he said. "Hey, Jen, do you want to volunteer with me?"

The girl looked at him as if he'd just tossed her the keys to his truck. "Really? That'd be awesome. We could be there and hang out and not have to do any training."

Ryan smirked, making eye contact with Catherine. "Two of a kind."

After dinner, Ryan, Jamie and Conor all went back to the O'Flaherty house. Jamie was wearing a nice pair of shoes because of her outing with her mother, so Ryan dropped her off at the house on her first swing around the block to look for parking. On only her second loop she found a spot and started to jog home.

About a block away from the house, she saw Conor getting out of his truck. Quietly sneaking up behind him, she bent down and gave him a chop across the back of both knees, making him fall against his open door. Her maniacal laugh echoed down the street as she took off running.

Conor stood up and closed his door. "Truce!" he shouted. "No paybacks."

Ryan slowed down, then turned and tentatively approached him. "When have you ever called for a truce?"

"I'm getting old. Besides, I wanna know why you're pissed off. I knew I had to ask you when Jamie's not around so you'd tell me the truth."

They started walking to the house and she tried to put her concerns into a cogent statement. "I didn't handle it very politely, but I meant what I said. It's not fair to hang out there and expect Catherine and Marta to feed you."

"What's it to you? Marta's not kidding. She really does love to cook, and she gets bored. I'm hungry after working, so it works out."

"You shouldn't do anything there that you wouldn't do at a relative's house."

"If I was working on Uncle Francis' house and they were getting ready to have dinner, they'd ask me to stay, and I would."

Ryan knew he was telling the truth, but it still bothered her. She wasn't sure what he was up to, but she was fairly certain he was nosing around Catherine, and that was absolutely forbidden as far as she was concerned. She was sure Catherine had too much sense to date Conor, and equally sure Conor was dumb enough to picture himself sitting pretty in Pacific Heights.

She knew she sounded cranky, and didn't even try to mask it. "How long are you going to be working on the library? There's an awful lot of carpentry work that needs to be done at the apartment building."

"I know that," he said tiredly, "but I promised Catherine I'd do this long before we bought the building. I can't put her off for as long as it'll take us to fix that place up."

"I'll come by and help you. The sooner you're done, the sooner we can make some progress on the big project."

"Don't bother. I've done the demolition, and Kevin has finished most of the electric." He put his arm around her and gave her a surprisingly loving hug. "Keep going to the apartment building. You're really helping out there."

"Okay. I will." They continued their walk towards the house. "I'm just worried the cousins will make me take a share of the profits if I work too much. You know how crazy they are about everyone being equal."

His body language changed. She felt it in the tension of the arm that was still around her shoulders. He was hiding something. Ryan studied his face in the streetlight. Then it hit her. "Is Catherine paying you?"

"You know how she is. She wouldn't let me do it unless she paid me. She had some other guys come out and give her an estimate, and she insists on paying me that much."

"Okay, fine. I know she's pretty insistent about things like that. So you can take the money she's paying you and put it into the fund for the apartment."

He jerked to a halt. "What? Are you shitting me? I'm killing myself working two jobs!"

"Doesn't matter. It's not fair to spend your spare time working on a side project that you get paid for when the rest of the family is working on the apartment building. It's just not fair."

"You can't make me do that. And if you tell, you'll look like a snitch. Everybody hates snitches."

She turned and locked onto his angry glare. "If you don't share, you're a cheat." Patting him sharply on the cheek, she took off for the stairs. "Live with that, bucko."

The next morning Ryan lingered in the shower, letting the hot water hit the stiff muscles in her shoulders. After getting dressed, she went upstairs to find Jamie starting to make a pot of coffee. Lunging for the can, Ryan grabbed it from her before she could open it.

"What in the hell?"

"We're going out for coffee. If you're not into going, I'll go alone and bring some back for you." She shook the can. "Don't ever use this."

"Ryan, what in the heck is wrong with you?"

She could hardly keep the disgust from her expression. "I'm not saying who, but one of the boys played a prank the other day, and they used this coffee."

Jamie looked at the can, and said tentatively, "What could you do with a coffee can?"

"Trust me, you do *not* want to know." Ryan put the can down as though it were a live grenade. "I can't believe those pigs didn't throw it out." She walked into the dining room and picked her wallet out of the bowl. "Do you want to go with me?"

Looking at the can, Jamie said, "I wanna know what they did."

"Trust me, you don't. It'll only make you think less of them."

"Come on. It's no fair to keep secrets."

"We live with a couple of them now. The more you know, the more you'll hate it here." She gave her a charming smile. "They're not like humans."

"I was engaged to a man, you know. I realize they have their quirks."

"Jack was a Homo sapien. The boyos…not so much." She started for the door. "I'll bring you a latté. Back in a few."

She walked out the front door, counted to five, then walked back inside, catching Jamie starting to pry the lid off the can. She approached her guilty looking lover, took the can, and put it in a garbage bag. "You asked for it, so I'll tell you. One of them opened the can and farted into it. Then he put the lid back on, took it and handed it to the other one, saying, "Does this coffee smell funny to you?"

Making a disgusted face, Jamie said, "What happened?"

Chuckling, Ryan said, "I don't know what it is about coffee, but it's one of those things where you stick your nose into it and breathe in deeply. He got a full dose." She was laughing, but she tried to make herself stop when she saw the look on Jamie's face.

"I might vomit."

"That's why I didn't want to tell you. If you'd just walked away from the can, everything would have been fine. You have no one to blame but yourself and your curiosity."

"Which one did it? You've gotta tell me."

"If just one of them was a deviant, I'd tell you. Problem is, everyone but Brendan and Rory would do the same thing if he had the chance. Trust no one," she said leaning over and whispering.

"That's just not human," Jamie said, shaking her head as she walked back towards their room.

Chapter Nine

After an early dinner on Monday night, Jamie went downstairs and found Ryan mumbling to herself as she stood in front of her open closet.

"You don't have to get dressed up. I bet most of the guys will wear jeans."

"The women won't," Ryan said, sounding grumpy. "We're the only gay people, I don't want to look like the stereotypical butch."

Jamie stood behind her and tucked her arms around Ryan's waist. "What's the matter? When Poppa suggested taking this marriage preparation class, you seemed like you were in favor of it."

"It wasn't really a suggestion." Ryan turned around and put her hand on Jamie's cheek, giving it a soft pat. "Your grandfather made it pretty clear he wouldn't marry us if we didn't participate."

Jamie shrugged. "I think it's a chance for us to get to know each other better. I've been looking forward to it."

"That makes one of us."

Parking was always difficult around the church, so they decided to take the bus. Actually, they had to take several buses, and even though they thought they'd left plenty of time, they arrived at eight o'clock on the button. To Ryan, that meant they were late, even though they were precisely on time. As soon as they saw Jamie's grandfather, Ryan started apologizing, but Charles waved her off and gave each of them a welcoming hug and kiss.

"We have a bigger group than I expected," Charles said. "Five couples have signed up. I think that will make for some interesting discussions." He led them to a nicely appointed sitting room next to his office. "I think we're all here," he said, and eight pairs of eyes landed on Jamie and Ryan. "This is my granddaughter, Jamie Evans, and her fiancée, Ryan O'Flaherty."

Both of them nodded to the group and Charles quickly introduced everyone else. When they were all seated, he started the meeting with a prayer, then asked each couple to talk about how they met and how long they'd been together. It was a good icebreaker, and by the time they were done, all of the couples looked like they felt comfortable with one another.

Charles got up and handed a packet of papers to each of the participants. "If you have friends who've taken this course, I'm sure you've heard about the survey."

The quiet laughs and nodding heads showed that everyone but Jamie and Ryan knew what he was talking about.

"When we first started using this questionnaire, I was very doubtful about its effectiveness, but I've become a believer." He glanced at Jamie and Ryan. "Many people describe this as a compatibility survey, but I think that's inaccurate. I think it's better viewed as a discussion enhancer."

Ryan raised an eyebrow while quickly scanning the first page of the survey. "Or an argument enhancer," she said, skeptically.

"It can be that," Charles admitted. "But the survey covers a lot of things that couples might not experience in the early years of their relationship. For example, if one of you feels strongly that earning money is the most important thing, while the other feels that money is the root of all evil, now's a good time to work through that."

All of the participants were paging through the survey and Charles said, "Spend some time filling this out. When you're finished, I'll have someone go over them and score them." He caught everyone's gaze and added, "Truthfully, I've never found the score to be predictive of your compatibility as a couple. As a matter of fact, I'd ignore the score completely. What matters is that you take the survey home and spend some time talking about the items where your views differ significantly. Remember, the survey is only intended as a way to bring up difficult topics you might not otherwise discuss."

He left them to work, and when he came back half an hour later, everyone but Ryan was finished. Nine people stood by a small table snacking on cookies and drinking coffee, while one was still deep in concentration, her dark hair shielding her face from view as she leaned over, her face just a few inches from the paper.

Charles went up behind her and touched her gently on the back, making her flinch noticeably. "I'm sorry, I didn't mean to startle you."

She looked around, seeing that everyone else was finished. "I'm almost done. Can I have another minute or two?"

"Sure. Take your time." He walked over to the table and chatted with the other participants. Several minutes passed without her finishing, and he finally went back over and said, "There's no right answer. I'm sure you've done most of it."

He reached down and started to take the paper, but he had to tug it away from her firm grasp. "It's okay," he said soothingly.

He took hers and all of the other surveys and left the room for a minute. When he came back, they all took their seats again and began to talk about their plans for raising children in the faith. Just before ten, a woman knocked and came into the room, handing Charles the surveys. He didn't take the time to look at them, just quickly handed them back to their authors. "Take my advice and look these over carefully. Again, the score isn't important. What matters is discovering the areas where you have disagreements so you can figure out ways to reach an accord."

Everybody got up and spent a few minutes saying goodbye to

one another. After bidding Charles goodbye, Ryan led the way to the corner, then surprisingly turned away from the bus route and headed for the nearest bar. "Where are you going?" Jamie asked.

"I can't wait an hour to see how we did." Jamie gave her a look that questioned her sanity, but that didn't change her path. Ryan opened the door to a dim bar and they found a table for two in an even darker corner. "What'll you have?" Ryan asked.

"This doesn't look like the kind of place that has a good wine selection, so I'll have an Amaretto sour."

Ryan blinked a couple of times, looking like she was going to say something, then went to the bar and ordered Jamie's drink, and an Irish whiskey and water for herself. When she got back to the table, she set the drinks down and went and collected every unused candle she could find. Taking her seat, Ryan looked at the papers still on the table. "I can't believe you didn't even look at those yet. Have you no curiosity?"

Jamie gave her a catlike grin while she took a sip of her drink. "I listened to my grandfather. These are supposed to be discussion aids."

"Ha! This is a test. Let's see how we did." She held the papers up to the dim light, then smiled broadly and slapped them against the table. "We did great! We're *very* compatible. That's the top category." She put the papers down on the table and took a celebratory drink.

Jamie picked up Ryan's test and started to look through it. "I can't imagine what took you so long, the questions weren't difficult."

"Well, first I answered them without thinking much, then I went through and tried to think like you think. I had to change a bunch of stuff."

Jamie looked at her, marveling at the satisfied smile on her lovely face. "Are you insane?"

"What? *What?*"

"It's not a test." She rolled up the papers and smacked Ryan on the head with them a couple of times.

Ryan covered her head with her hands while complaining, "It's always a test. They lie to you and say it's not, but it is. Everybody knows that."

"We should use this to discuss things we disagree on. The point is not to get a higher score. Nobody's judging us." She sighed heavily and rested her head on the table for a second. "Everything isn't a competition."

Ryan reached across the table and tugged on a lock of Jamie's hair. "We got a really good score, so now we can talk about it."

Jamie looked at her for a few seconds. "I can't tell whether you're being serious or not. Do you really not know it's counterproductive to cheat on a self-assessment?"

Ryan grinned, looking like she'd just heard a hilarious joke. "You can't cheat on a *self*-assessment. It's not possible." When Jamie's eyes narrowed, Ryan's smile dimmed. "I didn't play around *just* to get a good score." Again her grin didn't spur Jamie to smile back. "Look," she said, her frustration showing, "this kind of thing isn't for me. I'm never going to be completely candid in front of strangers. Our relationship is none of their business."

Jamie sat back and stared at Ryan, flabbergasted. "You're kidding."

"Not a bit. I love your grandfather, but he doesn't need to know our issues either. No one does."

Slapping the survey papers on the table, Jamie said, "Are you serious about this whole thing?"

"Thing?"

"Getting married. I'm getting a lot of vibes from you that tell me you're not really into it."

"Of course I am! You know how much I want to be married to you. I just don't want to spill my guts in public."

"Fine," Jamie said tiredly. She started to carefully read Ryan's answers. After just a moment, she looked up at her skeptically. "You're familiar with the Episcopal church's doctrines of faith?"

"No, but you are. And I know you believe in them." She smiled. "That's cool with me."

"Sweetheart, that's not the point." She said each word slowly, carefully. "The purpose of this exercise is for us to discuss our faith. We're asking my grandfather to marry us in a religious ceremony. He's not acting as a Justice of the Peace."

Now scowling, Ryan said, "I thought we wanted him to marry us because he's your grandfather. That's kinda how I've been proceeding." She worked her teeth over her lower lip for a few seconds. "I feel a lot more comfortable not having God and the Church involved in this. Your grandpa has civil powers too, right?"

"If you're asking whether he has the *ability* to marry us under the laws of the state of California, then yes. But that's not what I want. Anybody can do that. You can send away for a certificate and get a license to marry people. I want to be married in the Church, and I want to swear to God that I take you as my spouse."

Ryan nodded, her eyes darting to focus on the table. "Uhm, then we're gonna have a problem. I'm drifting farther and farther away from believing in God—at all. I wish that wasn't true, but it is."

Jamie stared at her, open-mouthed. The seconds ticked away, with her finally saying, "I knew you had doubts…"

"They've grown bigger." She took a drink and set the glass down carefully. Knitting her hands together, she gazed at Jamie.

"Any follow-up on that?"

"Sure. If you're interested."

Jamie leaned forward until they were nose to nose. "We're talking about our marriage. Nothing is more important to me."

"Okay, okay." Ryan leaned back, a frown settling on her face. "After the carjacking, I spent a lot of time thinking about God. I don't remember the moment it happened, but we were down in Pebble Beach at the time." She looked thoughtful, introspective. "It got clear in my head. A loving God wouldn't put us through everything we go through as humans, and I can't even begin to consider a hateful God." She shuddered, and reached for her drink, taking a healthy gulp.

Jamie reached across the table and took Ryan's hand. She put both of hers around it, cradling it for a moment. Not looking up, she said, "I thought you'd taken theology classes."

"I took two at USF. Why?"

"Mmm, I don't want this to sound harsh, but the way you put it makes it sound like you're looking for a God who's sitting up in heaven and looking down at us, laughing when we fall."

Frowning, Ryan said, "I don't think my views are that simplistic."

"I'm not putting you down, I'd just think that someone like you would have a sophisticated view of creation, something more liberal."

"If you think that my view of creation is simplistic, what've you got? You've told me you believe in God and that Jesus was his son. That's pretty old school."

"Not really. I don't mean 'son' like Brendan is to your father. And I don't mean 'God' as a being. I fully admit it's too big a concept for me to explain what God might be, much less what he truly is. When we talked before I was making a more general point."

"That's not how I recall it. I distinctly remember you saying God wasn't a theory for you, and that you believed Jesus was his son."

Frustrated, Jamie closed her eyes for a second. When she opened them she spoke slowly. "It's very, very hard to talk about belief. So much of it is beyond words. It's hard for me to say what God is to me."

"But you believe in him." Ryan's skepticism was apparent.

"I believe in a creative something that's beyond words. It *was* before anything else existed. It's beyond my understanding in every way." She took Ryan's hand and lightly tapped it on the table, her eyes fierce with certainty, "but I believe."

"I don't." Ryan looked sad, almost tearful. "I wish I did. I was happier when I was a kid and believed in everything they taught me at school."

"But you grew up, and your views have to grow up too."

"That's twice you've basically said I'm immature in this area. I'm not crazy about that."

Jamie looked down and shook her head. "I'm not explaining myself well. How about this? How can you prove your thoughts exist?"

"Can't."

"Right. How can you prove you exist?"

"Can't."

"I agree. We *think* we exist, but it's not so easy to prove. God's like that for me. I believe in a creator as much as I believe in the creation. They're entwined for me, even though I can't prove either one."

"That *can't* be enough to consider yourself a Christian."

Laughing, Jamie said, "It's plenty. I believe that Jesus was special in some very important way. It's impossible to explain his godliness, but I believe in his teachings. I very much want to follow his example."

"But you don't have any doctrine in there." Ryan was becoming more playful. She pulled on Jamie's ear and tried to look inside it.

"Coleridge said something like 'Christianity is a life, not a doctrine.' That's how I feel. I'm trying to follow Jesus' precepts. I think that's plenty of bona fides to call myself a Christian."

"That's enough for your grandfather? Does he know you're not into the whole 'God up in heaven' part?"

"Yes, honey. He knows. And I didn't say there isn't a God in heaven. I just don't know how to define God or heaven."

"That can't be right." Ryan's dark head shook. "He can't go along with that."

"He can. We've talked about this since I was a little girl. In fact, he gave me most of the books that have helped me form my beliefs."

"Huh." Ryan took the last sip of her drink. "Maybe I should read some of those books."

"They're all in Berkeley. I can tell you which ones have most influenced me."

"I'm sure I'm not going to come to any great revelation by August. It's June already. What does that mean for our plans?"

Looking completely befuddled, Jamie quietly said, "I wish I knew."

The next morning, even though she was feeling a little sluggish, Ryan laced up her running shoes and started off for a jog. Jamie was still dead to the world, but Duffy was ready and eager to accompany his mistress. Ryan had kept to her pledge of staying a little closer to home on her runs, and the dog seemed well able to keep up with her now. They stayed pretty close to home, zigging and zagging along and across familiar streets. It wasn't intentional, but Ryan found herself cruising in front of her father's fire station. To her great surprise, he was sitting in front of the firehouse drinking a cup of tea. The second the dog saw him, Duffy took off in Martin's direction with Ryan gamely following along.

As the dog jumped onto Martin's lap and covered his face with licks, Martin was barely able to say, "You'd better learn to get a handle on this pooch. He's remarkably ill mannered." It was clear he was teasing, since he was roughly running his hands through Duffy's coat.

"He's not so bad. He just loves his grandfather."

"I would love to be hung with that moniker, but I'd prefer it be for a human. I figure that you and Jamie should have that well in hand within a year or two at the most."

Ryan sat down on the tiny swath of grass that ran along the side of the driveway. She unlaced a shoe and tried to get her sock to lie properly. "We went to our first marriage preparation class last night. I haven't checked this morning, but I'm not sure Jamie still wants to marry me."

Smiling fondly at her, Martin said, "What terrible thing did you do this time?"

"For a change, I didn't do anything stupid. I thought we did really well because they rated us as very compatible. But there are two areas that we didn't score well in and Jamie seems to think they're critical."

"Do you care to discuss them, or is this just between the two of you?"

"The two of us, Charlie, and four couples we've never met before last night. Apparently in the next class we're going to discuss our surveys and talk about how we plan on working through any problems we have."

She made a face, one that Martin had seen many, many times. "It won't do to already have your dander up about this. If Jamie thinks there are issues, you'd do well to pay attention to her."

"I know we have some things to work on—I assume every couple does—I'm just not crazy about working on them in a group of strangers. I also don't think you have to have everything settled before you get married. Who'd ever do it if you had to have every potential problem worked out first?"

Martin laughed, nodding his head sagely. "Truer words were never spoken. But Charlie seems like a very thoughtful man, and if he didn't think there was any benefit to this class, he wouldn't have urged you to do it. So, what are the big issues that Jamie wants to work on?"

Looking a little concerned, Ryan said, "I guess they are pretty big. One is religion and the other is money."

"From what I've heard, those are the two biggest issues for most people, especially if they're marrying outside of their own faith."

Ryan chuckled at that, thinking that the differences between the Anglican Communion and the Catholic Church were relatively minor. Still, her father had a point. "Jamie's been an Episcopalian since the day she was born. She'd really like her grandfather to marry us as an Episcopal priest. Ideally, I'd believe the same things she does, but I can't say that I do. I'm willing to overlook the differences, but it really troubles her."

"Well, it would be the same thing in the Catholic Church. You can marry a non-Catholic, but you have to pledge to raise your children as Catholics."

"They don't want me to sign anything. It's Jamie who feels that way. She'd like our kids to be Episcopalians, and she'd like me to be one also." She pulled her knees up and rested her chin there, looking forlorn.

"I've been worried about this," Martin said. "I know you have your issues with the Church, but leaving it for another is a very big decision."

Ryan merely nodded, having decided long ago that she didn't want to share her ebbing faith with anyone in her family. This was one area where she thought keeping her own counsel was the only way to go. "The religion issue isn't a small one, but the money issue is much bigger."

"We've talked about this many times, darlin'. It's none of your business how Jamie spends her money."

"This is about more than that. We kind of had it out last night after we got home. Both of us put our cards on the table and said what we really wanted. It turns out that Jamie wants to live like she's always lived—have a very nice house, travel, go out for expensive meals, have someone clean our house and wash our cars. The whole enchilada."

"I assume that's an expression. I can't figure what an enchilada has to do with anything."

Laughing softly, Ryan said, "Yes, that's an expression. It means she wants everything."

"And what do you want, my shy and retiring girl?"

Ryan could feel her discomfort growing. "I don't want anything to change. I'm ridiculously happy. We're spending most of our time in the city and I can walk to see anybody in the family, including Catherine. Everything is just like it used to be, with the exception of your being gone, which does put a major crimp in my happiness."

"Do you think I wanted to leave my home? Your aunt has a

lovely place, but it's not mine. I don't like having Conor in my bedroom, and I don't like having to come down the street just to have breakfast with my family. But this is what Maeve wanted, and it's more important to me to have her happy than to have my silly little needs be primary."

He got up from his chair and put his teacup on the pavement. Approaching his daughter, he held out a hand and helped her to her feet. After putting his hands on her shoulders, he stood still and looked into her eyes for almost a minute. "Are you sure you're ready to acknowledge that Jamie's needs are as important as your own?"

"Yes! I'd do anything for her, Da."

"You've proven you'd risk life and limb for the girl, but that need doesn't arise very often. What happens every day are the small compromises. Those are what matter in a marriage."

"You don't ask many questions that you don't already have an answer to. Do you think I'm ready for marriage?"

"No, I don't," he said frankly. "You *will* be in the not-too-distant future, but if I was in charge, I'd urge you to wait. You haven't been in enough relationships to know what it takes to make one work."

Ryan pulled away from his loose embrace and moved back a foot or two. "I think I've sewed enough wild oats. I know Jamie is the woman for me."

"I have no doubt about that, and that's not my point. Just knowing who you want to be with isn't everything. *How* you'll be with that person is what makes a marriage. The fact that you have so little experience in this area troubles me. It doesn't trouble me enough to think you won't be successful, but if I were setting the date, I'd push this one out."

"It's nice of you to finally tell me," Ryan said, her annoyance overtaking any discomfort she'd felt.

"You never asked me, darlin'. As I said, if I were confident you were doomed to failure, I would have spoken up. I know you'll have a successful marriage, I simply think you could use a little more seasoning. And even though I wasn't wild about the idea of your not working or going to school this coming year, it does seem like a lovely time to focus on learning how to be in an intimate relationship."

"So you and Mama had this all worked out before you got married?" There was an edge to Ryan's voice that she rarely showed her father.

"No, we didn't. We had no experience in being in a relationship, and we didn't have much experience in being intimate, either. That first year or two felt like we were always tiptoeing around, waiting to step onto a land mine. You can do it that way if you wish, I'm just recommending a less tumultuous journey."

Having let herself really listen to her father's advice, Ryan nodded slowly. "I think I understand what you're saying. And I think it *would* be easier if we had some of these things worked out. But we're going to be together while we work them out, so I don't really see the difference. Things were different for you and Mama. You didn't live together before you were married."

He laughed soundlessly. "That's the honest truth. We barely held hands. I know it's different for you, Siobhán, but in some ways it's not different at all. I'm just trying to help you make your life a little easier in the long run, but I'll understand completely if you ignore my advice." Martin reached out and pulled her into a hug. "I promise that I'll never say I told you so if you have troubles." Releasing her, he smiled and said, "And you will have your troubles, everyone does, but I know you'll get through them. Even if you get married before you resolve any of your concerns, I know they won't be fatal. So set things up however you want. I'm on your side."

"That means the world to me, Da." She leaned into him and took another hug, then pointed at the chair and his tea cup. "I've gotta admit, I was amazed to see you sitting out in front of the firehouse."

"The whole crew left at four. No word on when they'll be coming back, so I don't have a soul to cook for."

"I could use a good breakfast," she said, waggling her eyebrows.

Recognizing that she was teasing, Martin slapped her on the rump. "The day I use city resources to feed my own family is the day I should be fired."

That afternoon, Ryan swung by Catherine's house to check on Jennie's school work. It was still early and Conor hadn't arrived, so they were able to do their work in peace. The only interruption was Marta coming into the dining room to lure them from their focus with cookies.

Jamie and Catherine had been out visiting caterers, and they returned to Catherine's house just as Ryan and Jennie were finishing up. "It was another tough day," Jamie said, dropping heavily into Ryan's lap. "How much cured salmon and fennel can one woman be expected to eat?"

"What's cured salmon and fennel?" Jennie asked.

Catherine replied, "It's an hors d'oeuvres that every caterer in town seems to have on their menu this year. It astounds me how similar all of the offerings are."

Jamie kissed Ryan on the cheek. "How long have you two been at it?"

"Not too long. About two hours, I guess."

Jamie made eye contact with Jennie. "Two hours for a summer school class? Do you really have that much homework?"

Ryan discreetly pinched her and said chidingly, "We're trying to get a system down."

"I'm an idiot," Jennie said. "Ryan acts like this is the easiest stuff in the world, but it's not for me. I don't understand what a system is, much less what's in it."

Patiently, Ryan said, "This is all building blocks. If you make sure you have a good foundation, each incremental part is just a slight stretch."

"I wasn't very good in math either, Jen. Just memorize what you have to memorize and don't take any more courses than you have to." Jamie giggled when Ryan pinched her waist. "I'm being serious," she said to her partner. "Not everybody can be good at every class. Jennie's more like me, but she's a lot more talented than I ever was in art."

Jennie beamed at her. Catherine walked over and sat down next to the girl, moving the textbook so she could look at it. "I'm glad Ryan's here for you, dear. I can read the English words that surround the equations, but after that I'm lost."

"You could all do this if you just took it easy and made sure you understood each step," Ryan said. "This is just algebra two. These are the bare basics."

"Not for us," Jamie said. "I haven't given a second thought to algebra one or two since the day I finished those classes. Don't worry about it, Jen."

Looking a little ill, Jennie said, "Ryan's making me take another math class in the second summer session. It's gonna be harder than this one."

Sounding like a nursery school teacher, Ryan said, "It's not harder, it's more fun!"

They were all in the kitchen chatting with Marta, who had convinced everyone to stay for dinner. Catherine's phone rang, and she went into the other room to take the call. She came back in after a few minutes and said, "Your Aunt Maeve is on the phone, Ryan. She thinks tomorrow morning would be an ideal time to go for a ten-mile walk. Are you two free?"

"Yeah, I don't think we have anything planned. It's supposed to be a nice day. Are you up for it, Jamie?"

"Sure. As long as we can stop for coffee after a mile or two." She was smiling at her mother, but when she turned her gaze back toward Ryan, she noticed Jennie sitting there, looking forlorn.

After dinner, they went into the living room, where Catherine turned on the stereo, choosing a bright, calming CD of Vivaldi pieces. "I'm very happy with the job Conor and Kevin are doing," Catherine said, as she settled next to Jennie on the sofa. "It's been wonderful to have handy people in the family."

"They're glad to help," Ryan said.

"Are you in a big hurry?" Jennie asked, looking at Catherine.

"No, I'm not. Why do you ask?"

"'Cause Conor's working so late at night. Marta said the neighbors came over yesterday to complain when he was hammering."

Catherine's brows shot skyward. "They did?"

Ryan gave the girl a pointed look, but Jennie was oblivious. "Yeah. I thought you made him stay."

"No, I'm not pushing him. He said he wanted to get it done as quickly as possible." She looked at Ryan. "Is he working too hard?"

"Nah," she said, blithely. "He's young."

Catherine persisted. "When does he go to work in the morning?"

Ryan didn't answer for a moment, hoping she wouldn't have to tell the truth.

"What do you mean in the morning?" Jennie asked. "He does something before he comes here?"

"He has a regular job," Jamie explained when she saw that Ryan wasn't going to step in. "He's doing this in his free time."

Jennie looked unconvinced. "Why doesn't he do this on the weekends? He looks tired."

"You know, he does," Catherine agreed. "Maybe I should talk to him about slowing down and doing this solely on the weekends."

Ryan shook her head. "That won't work. It'd take him months, and he can't let the cousins wait that long. They need him for a couple of projects on the apartment building."

Sternly, Catherine said, "We're going to have to make some adjustments. I'm not sure what to do, but I won't have him working too hard. He needs his rest." She looked at her watch, then added, "And so do you, Jennie. Perhaps you should call for your ride home."

The girl looked around the room, clearly hoping that someone had a better idea, but she eventually got up and went to the phone, asking the service to send someone.

Catherine turned to Jamie. "Why don't you and Ryan spend the night? I brought some of your clothes from Hillsborough, and Ryan's dressed appropriately for a walk. You might be able to help get me up as early as Maeve likes to go."

Ryan shrugged, so Jamie said, "That'd be great. Our first night in your new house. Do you have a guest room set up?"

"Two," Jennie said, looking like a sad, lost puppy.

They all stood at the front door watching the dejected teenager carry her oversized book bag to the curb. "I'll see you tomorrow," Catherine called.

Jennie turned and gave her an earnest but lusterless smile. "Okay. Goodnight, Ms. Smith. Goodnight, Jamie. Goodnight, Ryan."

As the car departed, Catherine looked at her guests and said, "Who feels like an ogre?"

Both Jamie and Ryan held up a hand. They walked back into the living room and Ryan said, "Sometimes she breaks my heart. I wish we could have her stay here or at our house more often, but Sandy doesn't think it's a good idea to make a habit of that. And as my father has reminded me, we have to trust Sandy's judgment. She's the one who has experience dealing with kids like Jen."

"That doesn't make it any easier to see that pathetic little face," Catherine said. "She gives me a look sometimes that makes me feel like I'm having all the fun and she's being forced into some sort of gulag."

"If that means 'prison,' she kind of is," Ryan said, shaking her head.

Chapter Ten

A few days later, Jamie was standing on the tee of the eleventh hole at the Olympic Club when her phone rang. She made a sheepish face and ran over to her bag to extract her cell. "I should know to turn this off before I play golf," she grumbled. "The guys on the next hole just shot me a look like I unleashed a sack full of groundhogs onto the course." She answered on the fifth ring. "Hi, Mom. What's up?"

"Hello, dear. I was wondering if you and Ryan would like my tickets to the symphony tonight."

"Maybe. Why can't you use them?"

"Conor and I are going over some sketches he's made. I'm not sure how long it will take, and I don't want to have to rush. Plus, I don't have anyone to go with." She laughed softly. "Sometimes I wish my seats were up in the second balcony. Then I wouldn't know so many people who'd whisper about me if I were alone."

"If you really want to go, I'm sure Ryan wouldn't mind if I went with you."

"That's very sweet of you, but I think Conor and I might need a long time to cement these plans. They're playing Mahler's Fifth, and I know you're a fan."

"I'm a huge fan," Jamie said, her excitement starting to bubble. "Hold on a sec." She put the phone on mute and said to Ryan, "You've made me happy by playing golf today, wanna keep it going by taking me to the symphony tonight?"

"I was so hoping you'd ask," Ryan said with a wry grin.

That afternoon, when Conor knocked on Catherine's door, she answered quickly, her smile betraying her impish mood. "I have a surprise for you."

Quizzically, Conor entered to find two strapping young guys sitting uncomfortably on Catherine's sofa. He walked into the room to hear Catherine say, "Miguel and Fernando just completed a program in basic carpentry. They're going to be your assistants."

He looked from Catherine to the two men several times. "Assistants?"

"We'll do everything you don't want to do," Miguel spoke up. "Miss Smith wants us to give you more time to do the hard stuff."

Once more Conor gazed at Catherine, unable to keep the smile from his face. "You sure are full of surprises. I never know what you're going to come up with next."

An hour before the symphony was set to begin, Ryan finished dressing. She was using a lint brush to clean off her black suit when Jamie emerged wearing a lovely dark green satin cocktail dress with a heavy cream-colored silk wrap around her shoulders. "You look fantastic," Ryan said, drawing out the word. "Really, really great."

"Thanks. You do too, sweetie."

Saluting, Ryan said, "I'm reporting for duty."

"It's not a uniform." Jamie kissed her cheek, then rubbed the spot with her thumb to remove the faint lipstick mark.

"I wear it every time we go out, so that's what it feels like."

"Not every time. Just in the city. When we're someplace warm you have three complete ensembles."

"Then I'm all set for when we move to Eleuthera."

Jamie just smiled at her. She knew Ryan would move to Eleuthera shortly after she stopped loving math.

As Catherine had intimated, the dress code at the symphony varied wildly. Many people in the upper levels dressed as they would to attend a Giants game, but people in Catherine's section would not have been out of place at a state dinner at the White House.

To Ryan's surprise, they weren't anywhere near the orchestra. In fact, they weren't on the main floor. Their section was surprisingly small, only three rows deep, but they were right in the center of the auditorium. "Why aren't we down there?" Ryan asked quietly after they were shown to their seats.

"That's the orchestra," Jamie whispered back. "Mom doesn't like sitting down there; she likes to be up in the loge. I agree with her. The music travels really nicely here. Sometimes it can sound a little muddy in the orchestra."

Ryan leaned back in her seat and raised an eyebrow. "You sound like you know a lot about this."

With a haughty smile, Jamie said, "I know plenty. I've been coming to the symphony since I was…oh, four years old."

"This is my first."

Jamie tried to keep her mouth from hanging open. "You've never been to Davies Hall?"

"Or any other symphony place."

Amazed at this revelation, Jamie said, "I thought you went to the symphony last year with Tracy."

"Nope. We went to the opera. I sure hope this is better." She gave Jamie a sly smile.

"I'll tell you what. If you don't like this…no, if you don't *love* this, I'll go to any event you choose for paybacks. Any kind of goofy sports thing or science thing—you name it."

"There aren't a lot of science events for spectators, so you're getting off easy, but I'll take the bet. What do you get if you're right?"

Looking smugly self-assured, Jamie said, "Music is its own reward."

The guest conductor that night was Finnish, and he led a pared down orchestra in three short, very modern pieces. They weren't really to Jamie's taste, but they were interesting and very different from the norm. Some of the instruments seemed to have been created just for the piece, with several looking more like contraptions than something you'd find on the stage of the symphony. Nonetheless, the audience was used to more modern music and their generous applause showed their approval.

As soon as the last notes were played, Jamie nudged Ryan and they got up and exited their section. "Follow me," Jamie said. She took off, scampering up a wide staircase until they got to the top level where she pulled a card out of her purse while leading Ryan into a small, beautifully decorated room. Flashing her card at the beefy man who stood at the door, she led the way to an empty bar and ordered a glass of champagne for herself. "For you?" she asked Ryan.

"I'll have the same."

Jamie pulled out cash and paid for their wine, leaving a generous tip, then she hustled Ryan right back out of the room. They passed a bar in the main gathering area that already had thirty people waiting in line, breezed past them and went out onto a balcony, where Ryan stared open-mouthed at the beautiful view of City Hall.

"I had no idea…"

Jamie clinked their glasses together and they each sipped their champagne.

"Not bad," Ryan said.

"I'm surprised you got champagne. I know that isn't your favorite drink."

"It's fine."

"Why didn't you order what you really wanted? They have a full bar."

Scowling slightly, Ryan said, "I saw all of that champagne sitting out and I figured that's all they had."

"No, dear. You can have anything you like. They could even

make you a Mai-Tai."

Ryan tilted her head back and said, "Where's that warm air coming from? I know it's not natural."

"Too true. I can't ever remember having a warm night in San Francisco in June. I'm sure it's happened, but not to me." She pointed up at the vents behind them. "No one would ever use these balconies if they didn't have those blowers."

Thoughtful for a moment, Ryan said, "We should get one of those for the house."

The balcony was soon filled with their fellow concertgoers and they watched people come and go. "A lot of gay guys here," Ryan said. "Don't see many lesbians, though. Oh, there's a pair."

"A lot of gay men love the symphony. Duh," Jamie teased, laughing.

Ryan bent her head and kissed Jamie on the cheek. When Jamie tilted her face upward, Ryan delivered another kiss to her lips. "If there aren't many of us, we have to make a more obvious showing."

They had to hurry to get back to their seats, and the concertmaster was just tuning the orchestra when they sat down. "I'm having a nice time, but so far, no love," Ryan whispered. "I'm already thinking of what sporty thing I'm gonna drag you to."

Jamie gave her a friendly pat, still looking very confident. The conductor took the podium and a solo trumpet let out a long, almost plaintive note. Jamie shifted her gaze to see her partner looking alert, her eyes scanning the entire orchestra, anticipating what would come next. By the time the full orchestra entered into the piece Ryan was leaning forward, her elbows on her knees, chin in hand, eyes fixed on the orchestra.

This symphony was one of Jamie's favorites, by one of her favorite composers, and she was sure she'd played a CD of the work at home several times. But she knew there was nothing quite like being at a live performance.

One of the things Jamie most liked about Mahler was how he had one foot in the classical period and the other taking sometimes tentative and sometimes bold steps into the modern. Another favorite characteristic was the way he used percussion in innovative ways. She laughed softly when Ryan jumped as the percussionist snapped a whip, making a sound she was sure Ryan hadn't expected.

The piece was long, lasting over an hour, but at the last measure, Ryan jumped to her feet and applauded lustily. She turned to Jamie, looking slightly stunned as she said, "Don't you ever get tired of being right?"

Ryan talked like a magpie on the way home. Jamie was fairly sure they were the only people to leave prime seats in Davies Hall and head for MUNI, but she knew how much Ryan hated taking cabs. They stood on the platform, with Ryan peppering her with questions.

"It reminded me of physics. I can't even say why, but there was something about it that was so…" Her eyes were focused on something in the distance, and she eventually shook her head. "I can't describe it, but I have the same feeling when I'm really getting into a problem in physics, trying to keep track of where everything is and how it could possibly be moving, and what other possibilities there are." She let out a breath. "Some of it sounded familiar, but not much of it. It was a totally unique experience. I can't wait to come back."

"I know I've played the CD. I'm sure you've heard it."

Ryan shrugged. "Every time I hear something classical, I kind of ignore it. I've gotta stop that."

"I love listening to my CDs, but they don't hold a candle to a live performance, especially by a big symphony like this."

"They almost ran out of room! I think they had every kind of instrument I've ever heard of. And there were a couple I've never seen before."

"Maybe the English horn? Or the bass clarinet?"

"Maybe. What was that really big thing? The lady who played the bassoon played it."

"Oh, that was the contrabassoon. They play that fairly frequently in symphonies, but you don't see it anyplace else."

"It was ultra cool. Do you think I could take lessons on that?"

Jamie just smiled at her. When Ryan went from liking something to believing she could do it, it was a sure sign of love.

Ryan was still prattling away when they walked into the O'Flaherty house at eleven o'clock. They made eye contact when they crossed the threshold and heard cheering coming from Conor's bedroom. Duffy ran to meet them, gave them a look that said "come on!" then ran back. Doing the dog's bidding, they went in and found Conor, Kevin, Tommy, and Declan watching the Giants game. Tommy was still in his firefighter's uniform, obviously just having gotten off work.

"Great game, guys," Conor said. "Grab a beer and join us."

Ryan shot a brief look at her elegantly dressed lover, then said, "We've gotta go get changed. Maybe we'll come back up." She moved into the room enough to see that the game was in the top half of the ninth inning.

She and Jamie headed downstairs, and when they got there, Jamie said, "You can watch the game if you want to."

Scoffing, Ryan said, "I have no intention of going back upstairs. But if I gave them any indication I wanted to be alone with you, then I'd have to put up with the teasing." She put the back of Jamie's hand to her lips and made exaggerated kissing noises.

Laughing, Jamie said, "That's about how it goes here at Alpha Alpha O'Flaherty."

"Do you hate it?" Ryan asked, uncertainty coloring her voice.

"Not a bit. I think I'm adjusting very well." She moved next to Ryan and put her hands around her waist.

"You're adjusting to my life so much better than I'm adjusting to yours. My father and Sara both pointed that out to me very sharply."

"Don't worry about what other people tell you." Jamie looked up into Ryan's eyes with undisguised love. "I'm the only one you need to listen to, and I'm very happy."

Smiling at her, Ryan removed the wrap that covered Jamie's bare shoulders. She slipped out of her own jacket and put both garments on the bed, then she took Jamie's hand and led her over to the loveseat, where they both sat down.

"What did you call the part of the symphony that was so soft and beautiful?"

"That style is usually an adagio, but I think Mahler calls it something different. I can look in the program."

"No need. I just want to make sure you knew what I was referring to."

"I do. It's the part that almost brings tears to your eyes, right?"

Smiling widely, Ryan said, "Exactly!" She took Jamie's hands and held them loosely while she gazed at them. "When that started to play, I was hearing the feelings that I have for you set to music."

She tilted her chin, embarrassed that she was tearing up. "It's hard for me to describe, but that music was love. It brought up every tender feeling I have for you, and they are legion." She lifted her head and locked eyes with Jamie. "I don't tell you enough how utterly and helplessly I am in love with you. It's so much more than attraction or desire, even though I've got plenty of both. My love for you is a part of me now, as much as my love for my family. I know I have a long way to go before I'm the partner you deserve, but I'll never stop trying to be better."

Green eyes glistening with tears, Jamie slipped her hand along the back of Ryan's head and pulled her close. When their lips were almost touching, she said, "I love you with all my heart."

They kissed, their lips barely touching, the softness of the skin sending chills up their spines. Jamie emitted a sensual purr and Ryan shifted to pull her in tighter. Jamie's hands went to Ryan's head and her fingers slid through the cascade of ebony hair, making Ryan shiver at the delicious sensation. Ryan mirrored the gesture, gently scraping her fingers all along Jamie's scalp.

Pulling away just a few inches, Jamie whispered, "That feels so sexy."

"I'm just getting started." The cocky, self-assured grin that always shot Jamie's desire into the stratosphere was firmly in place.

"If symphonic music makes you feel like this, we're getting a subscription."

Chapter Eleven

As was becoming the new habit, Catherine appeared at the O'Flaherty house late on Sunday afternoon. Since she was incapable of coming empty handed, she brought several bottles of wine and a tray of delectable looking antipasto. Ryan greeted her at the door, relieving her of her burdens.

"If I'd known you'd class up our Sunday dinners so much, I would have invited you the day we met," Ryan said, bending over awkwardly to kiss Catherine's cheek.

"I doubt I would have accepted back then. To be honest, you frightened me a little." She laughed, partly at the statement and partly at the stunned look on Ryan's face. "It wasn't you," Catherine assured her as they went upstairs. "I'd built things up in my mind to the point that I'd decided you had some Svengalian hold over my little girl."

Walking into the room in time to catch the end of her mother's comment, Jamie said, "She did. She does." Moving up alongside Catherine, she kissed her cheek. "I'm glad you could come, Mom. Ryan and I have decided that you're now on the 'call if you're not coming' list. If we don't hear from you, we'll expect you every Sunday."

"Yeah," Ryan said as she returned to the kitchen. "We cook so much extra for you!"

"I'm going to match your appetite one of these days," Catherine called back, rather than walking into the kitchen, something she was slowly adjusting to. "Walking all over the city has given me a heartier appetite than I've ever had in my life."

"I'm making iced tea with a little lemonade," Ryan said. "Want one?"

"I'd love one." Catherine looked at Jamie and said, "My mother would turn over in her grave if she heard me speaking to someone in another room."

Smiling, Jamie said quietly "I know. But you'd look stupid being the only one getting up and going from room to room to have a conversation."

"It *is* a lot easier." Catherine laughed devilishly. "Mother will have to deal with it." She squeezed Jamie's knee. "And you, my dear, have to deal with sending out announcements. You're getting married in seven weeks."

Grimacing, Jamie said, "That's gonna be tough."

Catherine cocked her head, looking at her for a few moments. "But you have to. It's rude to ask people at the last minute. I haven't talked to your father about this, but I'm sure he'll have a long list of people to invite. You can't ask members of Congress to keep their schedules clear for the entire month of August."

"I know, I know." Jamie stood up and started for the kitchen, then turned back and just stood there, looking unsure of herself.

"What's up?" Ryan said, appearing with three glasses of tea-monade, as she called it.

"Invitations," Jamie said, wrinkling up her nose.

Ryan sat down and took a drink. "Well, don't you normally tell people where to come?" She looked over the edge of her glass, a faux innocent gaze directed at Jamie.

"Yes, wise guy, you do." She sat down and let her head drop, her longish hair falling forward. "I know I've screwed this up, but I haven't found any place that's right. I just don't want to settle for something I don't like."

"To be fair," Catherine said, "all of the best places are gone. But we've seen a couple of halls that would have been all right."

"I don't want 'all right,'" Jamie pouted. "I know what I want, and I haven't seen it. I haven't seen anything close."

"We'd better send out 'save the date' cards at the very least," Catherine said. "You're going to invite your cousins, aren't you? They'll need to make travel arrangements."

Dryly, Jamie said, "They aren't the types to book early to save money."

"Your cousins on your father's side are."

"Eww. I forgot about them."

Ryan sat there watching, wondering how anyone could forget her only first cousins.

Slapping her hands on her thighs, Jamie declared, "We'll just have to scale it down. Maybe we'll only have immediate family. We could tell everyone on Friday and have it on Saturday, right here in the yard."

Both Catherine and Ryan stared at her. "But that's not what you want," Catherine said.

"No, but it might have to do. I don't want to send out invitations if I don't know where we're going to be, so we'll just wing it."

Catherine met Ryan's eyes. "Is that all right with you?"

"Well." She cleared her throat and took a quick look at Jamie. "I've been looking forward to a big party. I want to invite all of my old buddies. But if we wind up winging it, I guess that's okay."

Catherine looked at both young women; both appeared disappointed. There was clearly more going on than Jamie's inability to find a venue, but she had no idea what the problem might be.

The next evening Jamie and Ryan sat quietly at their marriage preparation class. The goal for the evening was to have each couple talk about one of the areas where the survey indicated disagreement. Neither woman had brought up the class or their differences since their blowout of the week before. It seemed as though each was waiting for the other to broach the subject.

They'd maintained their usual interactions in all other areas, which was also odd. Typically, when something was bothering one of them, it spilled over into every area. But this was different, for reasons neither could guess.

It was late when it came to their turn, and Jamie surprised Ryan by bringing up a topic she thought they'd dealt with.

"I'm worried we're going to have a tough time reaching an agreement about our religious life," Jamie said quietly.

"Do you want to give us some background?" Charles asked. He made eye contact with Ryan, who took the cue.

"My family has been Catholic ever since Saint Patrick drove the snakes out of Ireland," she said with a faint smile. "But I've found my faith in God lessening a little more every year. Jamie," she said, reaching out and grasping her partner's hand, "has a strong faith, and I think she worries about having kids and giving them inconsistent messages."

"Is that true?" Charles asked, looking at his granddaughter.

"Of course that's part of it. But we won't have kids until we have that worked out." She cast her glance around the room, but it was clear she was actually addressing Ryan. "I'm more concerned about the present."

"You are?" Ryan interrupted. "What about the present?"

Jamie still didn't look Ryan directly in the eye. She focused on the bookshelf behind and to the left of Ryan's chair. "We're getting married in seven weeks, and I plan on swearing to my God that I'll be your partner until death parts us. It seems as if that's something you can't do."

Without waiting for Charles to give her the green light, Ryan said, "I guess you're right. But that doesn't mean my word isn't good."

Jamie finally made eye contact. "I know your word is good. That's not what I'm worried about."

"What are you worried about?'

As though there were no one else in the room, Jamie faced the topic head on. "I'm worried that you don't support my faith."

Ryan's eyes flew open wide. "What?"

"Every time we go to church, we automatically go to St. Phil's. I don't mind going there, but I'm not Catholic. I feel much more comfortable in the Episcopal Church, and since you don't seem to believe in any of the tenets of the Catholic Church, it puzzles me that we still go there."

Ryan was clearly stunned. Her mouth hung open, and she didn't say a word. Charles stepped in. "Have the two of you had a chance to discuss this?"

"No," Jamie said. "Not this particular thing." She looked down at the ground, seemingly a little embarrassed. "We should have talked about this before tonight."

Ryan no longer looked stunned—she looked angry. "We sure should have!"

"The purpose of the survey was to show whether there are any issues that you might not have gotten around to considering yet. I think it's done that for everyone," Charles said. "Next week we're going to discuss raising children in the faith. It sounds like Jamie and Ryan have gotten a head-start on the rest of us, but we'll catch up." He smiled at the group and stood up, with everyone following suit.

Ryan got up quickly and grabbed their jackets. She was waiting impatiently by the front door when Jamie finally joined her.

"Wanna go back to that bar again?" Ryan said.

"No thanks. Let's walk home."

Without even saying a formal goodbye to Charles or the other participants, they walked outside into the clear, dark night. It was a nice evening, but because of the brisk wind, they both needed their jackets. They headed towards Noe Valley, Ryan looking aggravated as she strode along with her hands shoved into her pockets.

Jamie struggled to keep up with her partner's long stride, finally grasping her sleeve and pulling her to a stop. "I'd like to walk home *with* you, not a quarter-mile behind you."

Ryan took a long breath. "Why did you spring that on me in front of all of those people?"

"Those people? Those people are the ones we chose to have these discussions with. I didn't make an announcement at the Giants game."

Ryan looked like she was about to say something sharp, but she hesitated for a moment and then started to walk more slowly in the direction of home. "You know how I feel about telling things to strangers. We'll never see those people again."

"Maybe that's part of the problem. I'd like to get to know some of them. Have you noticed that they all know each other?"

"Why is that?" Ryan looked a little puzzled. "Do all Episcopalians know each other?"

It was a small attempt at humor, but it was better than nothing. "They know each other because they're all members of the church. When my grandfather said he thought it was important for us to be members for two years before we were married, he was referring to things like that."

"Yeah, that's nice. But I don't need any more friends. I can't keep up with the ones I have."

"*I* need more friends," Jamie said quietly. "I like talking to people about faith and about hope and how to live morally in this crazy world. I want to start going to my grandfather's church, and I want to go to some of the classes they offer. I want to be involved, just like your family's involved at St. Phil's."

"My family doesn't do that kind of thing," Ryan said dismissively. "Well, we do the volunteer stuff, but not the religious stuff. It's more social for us."

Quietly, Jamie said, "I know. That's a nice aspect of having a faith community, but it's not what I'm after. I want to talk about the difficult issues and have people with more experience give me advice."

"Why didn't you ever say this before?" Ryan's tone was still sharp, and it was clear her feelings were hurt. "You made it sound like I drag you over to St. Phil's."

"That's not how I feel. When we first got together, I had the distinct impression you got a lot out of attending services. I went along with you because you felt so comfortable there and it was nice to go with your family. But I'm *not* comfortable. I honestly think your pastor would rather we didn't attend, and that's a major turnoff."

Ryan waved her hand in the air. "Don't listen to him. He just wants things to be easy. It's easier for him if nobody complains about a couple of lesbians showing up. He thinks it's his church, but it isn't."

"It *is* his church. He has the authority to decide who can take communion."

For the next few moments, the only sound was their heels hitting the sidewalk. It felt like the silence before a storm—the storm brewing inside Ryan. When she spoke again, her voice was low and full, and she spit the words out precisely. "What did he say to you?"

Jamie had hoped to avoid this discussion, but it was unfair to keep to herself. Trying to sound as though it weren't a big deal, she said, "Someone must have mentioned to him that I wasn't Catholic."

Sharply, Ryan barked, "So what?"

"I've been going to communion. You told me it was fine." Jamie could feel the anger and heat coming off Ryan, and she put her hand on her arm to try to soothe her. "It's okay. I know you think it's fine, but he doesn't. He said it's the same as if I were a Republican and tried to vote in the Democratic primary."

"What the fuck?"

"It wasn't a great analogy, but I understood his point. Taking communion implies I agree with the doctrines of your faith, and I clearly don't."

"It's almost the same. So you don't think the Pope is the boss. No big deal."

Stopping in her tracks, Jamie said, "It *is* a big deal. I think it's wrong to prohibit women priests; I think it's wrong to exclude gay people from important roles; and I don't believe it's really the body and blood of Jesus Christ. I think it's a metaphor."

"Of course it's a metaphor!"

"Then you might want to join me in the Episcopal Church." Jamie smiled, but her smile wasn't returned. She put her arm around Ryan's waist, but it was clear Ryan was in no mood to be placated.

"I'm gonna have to go over there tomorrow and rattle his windows one more time. He can't get away with treating you like that."

"Yes, he can! Why do you want to get into a fight over this? You're clearly culturally Catholic, but that's about it."

"That's all anybody is! Nobody who thinks about it for long believes all that crap."

"I know you're wrong about that, but it's almost beside the point. If you care, why don't you join a group of people who want to change the church? Put your anger to some good use."

Ryan waved the idea away dismissively. "I don't want to waste my time doing that. That's like an ant trying to move a boulder. The church is getting more and more conservative, and it's gonna take a long time for that trend to change."

"Then let it go. I've been trying to get something out of St. Phil's that I don't think is there. I don't mind going with you when you want to go, but it's not giving me what I need."

"Fine." Ryan sighed heavily. "I really would like to get my father and go over there and give old Aloysius Pender a good tongue lashing. But I won't do it if you don't want me to."

"You can do what you want. I'm not going to attempt to go to communion again. I don't think he can prohibit me from entering the building, so I'm good." She laughed again, and this time she got a mild smile from Ryan in return. "I think you might be on thin ice, though. Even though you're Catholic, he can decide you aren't eligible for communion. A lot of bishops around the country are prohibiting Catholic lawmakers who support abortion rights from receiving it."

"Don't remind me." Ryan shoved her hands deeper into her pockets and mumbled something to herself. Jamie didn't ask her to repeat it, knowing that her mumbled comments were indecipherable for a reason.

It was still fairly early, but Ryan was lying on the bed, hands laced behind her head, eyes unfocused. Jamie had put on a sweatshirt and flannel pajama bottoms, and she and Duffy lounged on the loveseat. She patted his soft, curly coat, running a hand down his back while he leaned against her, always wanting more. "Are you angry with me?" she asked after a long silence.

Ryan raised her head and looked at her for a moment. "What?"

"I asked if you're angry with me."

"About what?" Ryan's head fell back down to the pillow.

"About anything. What's on your mind?"

Ryan raised her knees and crossed one ankle over her other leg. She started doing some stretching exercises that Jamie realized were calculated to relax her mind as much as her legs.

"I'm not angry. Definitely not angry."

Waiting a beat but not getting any additional information, Jamie said, "What's going through your mind? I know something is."

With a grunt of exertion, Ryan pushed on her knee, stretching her hip out. "I'm wondering how many other things bother you that you keep secret." She lay back for a moment and added, "And I wonder what message I'm sending that you feel like you have to keep things to yourself."

"I like the way you phrased that. Having that attitude shows why we're ready to get married."

"Huh?" Ryan's dark head shot up again and she stared at Jamie quizzically. "We just spent two hours telling a bunch of strangers we're not ready."

Waving her off, Jamie said, "Don't be silly. We did no such thing. We have things to work out, but every couple has them.

We've only been together a year, you know. We've barely started to get to know each other."

Head still elevated, Ryan said, "Really?"

"Definitely." Jamie waved at her again, and Ryan put her head down. "You know, the fact that you've never been in a long-term relationship has given you a…warped view of how things are." The head popped up again. "I didn't mean that as a put down; it's just an observation." Ryan nodded, but she looked a little suspicious when she dropped her head. "You haven't had to work out small things with another person. If something wasn't right, you moved on to greener pastures."

"You always say that doesn't bother you."

"It doesn't. I'm just saying that it takes a while to get used to being in a relationship. We're going to have some rough sledding."

"It never snows here. The sledding is super smooth."

"You're a funny little monkey, but you're not going to distract me." She went over to sit next to Ryan. "I know it can be a pain in the butt, but we need to keep talking about the little issues that come up."

"I know." Ryan nodded somberly. "I just wish we could do it in private."

Jamie pinched her cheek. "Not to worry. We'll have dozens and dozens and dozens of things to work out all on our own. This is just the appetizer."

Her lower lip stuck out for a second, then Ryan said, "I've lost my appetite."

Chapter Twelve

On a lovely Friday night in late June, Conor stretched and took a look at his watch. To his surprise it was after eleven p.m. He'd come over to Catherine's after work, then he'd chatted with Marta and graciously allowed her to make him a couple of quesadillas for a snack before he got down to business.

Catherine had come home at five, and had rushed around getting ready for some sort of gathering. He barely registered her leaving, since he was intently measuring a wall with many blips and dips from moldings and windows. He'd measured the entire place several times, but Catherine had made a few substantive changes, making him recalculate the entire wall for a different purpose.

After he was finished, he allowed Marta to make him dinner. When it was just the two of them, she would sit down at the table and eat with him, which always made the evening fun.

He could have gone home, but something about the wall was bothering him. When Marta came into the proposed library to see whether he needed anything before she retired for the evening, Conor was sitting on the floor, a sturdy clipboard on his lap and a mechanical pencil in his hand. He was roughly erasing something and started when she entered. "Hey, what's going on?" he asked.

"I'm going to bed now, and I wanted to make sure you didn't need anything. You have a key to lock the door, correct?"

"Sure do. I'm good, Marta. Thanks a lot for making such a nice dinner for me. I haven't had a better dinner or a better dining companion in a long, long time."

"You're a sweet talker, Conor. How you've escaped marriage this long is a mystery."

He chuckled. "I'm too young to think about marriage. I'm not even thirty."

"Your sister is younger and she will be married in a short while. I think you could manage it."

"Maybe," he allowed, grinning rakishly, "but I'm not as easily managed as my sister."

Catherine walked past the library on her way to her bedroom, managing to muffle a scream when she reached inside the room to turn off the lights and heard Conor's deep voice from behind the door.

"I can't work in the dark."

"Conor! You scared me half to death. What are you doing here this time of night?"

"Honestly? I didn't have any plans for the evening so Marta and I ate together. I was going to head home, but I kept thinking about what you wanted to do around this window, and something wasn't sitting right." He walked over to the wall. Extending his index finger, he pointed alongside the window. "I think wooden shutters would look good in here, but we won't have enough clearance to open them. How about shades? Maybe a Roman shade? We could put up a nice box valance to hide them."

Catherine put her hand around Conor's arm and gave it a squeeze. "You're the best carpenter I've ever worked with. You're as serious and thorough as your sister is, and that's saying a lot."

"I taught her everything she knows," he said, grinning. "So, what do you think about the shades?"

"I need to sleep on it. I had my heart set on wooden shutters. Why won't they fit?"

"They'll fit. You just won't be able to open them fully to clean the windows. There won't be enough clearance here," he indicated with his hand where the problem was, "for them to fold back."

Pointing at the same area, she said, "What if they were mounted from the center and folded from outside in?"

"That would look strange if you ever wanted them open for anything other than cleaning, but it would technically work. I don't know of any place that makes them that way, so that's another hurdle."

She looked completely unconcerned. "I'm sure there's a custom cabinet maker in the city that could do it if we chose to go that way. But I'll see if I can conjure up the image of Roman shades. That would obviously be easier."

"It would. But after working with you for a short while, I've come to realize you're not very attracted to the easy way."

Laughing, she said, "Don't tell anyone my secret. Would you like to sit on the balcony and have a nightcap?"

"If you'll join me."

"I will. I was going to change clothes first, but I suppose I don't need to."

"Not on my account," Conor said, furtively assessing the dark violet, form fitting dress she was wearing.

Catherine went downstairs to get their drinks and when she returned Conor had fired up the propane heat lamps. It was almost seventy degrees and there wasn't a cloud in the sky, but he knew she got chilled at any temperature under eighty. She handed him his drink and sat down in the chair perpendicular to his.

"To good carpenters," she toasted, clinking glasses together.

He took a drink, then asked, "Did you have a nice night?"

"It was nice enough. I went to a small fundraiser for the opera."

"My buddies," he said, grinning widely.

"Indeed. You know, I was a little worried about spending most of my time here in the city. I was afraid I'd be lonely. But I've saved so many hours by not having to drive down to the

South Bay after events like this that I'd prefer it—even if I was lonely."

"Are you?" he asked, concern radiating.

"No, I haven't been. Having the girls so close has made all the difference."

"That's really nice to hear. Where was your party?"

"Not far from here—just on the other side of Pacific Heights."

"Do you mind going to things like that alone?"

"Well, I think I'd always prefer to have an escort so long as he or she wanted to be there. In most couples, it seems as if only one person loves the opera. The other one usually has the look of a hostage." She chuckled lightly.

"Did Jim enjoy opera?"

She sat quietly for a few moments, considering the question. "He certainly never complained. He'd never been before we met, but he was interested enough to ask a lot of questions and read a number of books to give himself some background. Still, I rather doubt he goes now."

Conor took another sip of his drink. His eyes were dark and his voice was a little lower when he asked, "How about Giacomo?"

She hadn't thought about him all night, and hearing his name made her heart rate pick up. "It's in his blood. Truly, he knows much more about it than I do. If you give him the opportunity, he'll launch into his Pavarotti imitation with absolutely no trepidation."

"But he's not here." Coldly, he added, "And he never will be."

He didn't say another word, and Catherine didn't comment. It was tiring having almost everyone opposed to Giacomo, but that was something she was going to have to live with. "It's a silly saying, but true. You can't always get what you want."

As though he'd been waiting for her to say exactly that, he launched into what seemed like a prepared statement. "There's no reason in the world you can't get what you want. What's on your list of requirements?"

She thought for a few minutes, with the sound of the propane heaters providing ambient noise. "My requirements are probably the same as those of most women. I want someone who's interested in me, attentive, loving, someone with a good sense of humor, and someone I would miss when we were apart."

"That's not a very difficult list. There's probably thirty thousand guys in the city alone who would love to have a chance."

Catherine laughed, letting her head fall back onto her chair-back. "I think you overstate, but even so, I have to be attracted to the person. And I believe I've gotten harder to please."

"Maybe that's part of the problem," he said earnestly. He leaned forward in his chair and rested his forearms on his knees. "I think you have an image of the type of guy you think you belong with."

"Everyone does."

"Everyone probably does," Conor agreed, "but I think we'd all be better off if we expanded our view. If you're only looking for guys who are in your tax bracket, that's gonna take those thirty thousand guys and cut them by ninety percent."

Smiling at that, Catherine said, "I'd be perfectly comfortable dating someone who didn't have a lot of money. The tough part is finding someone who doesn't have money who's comfortable being around it. Just look at the trouble your sister has with it."

"She's weird," he said, waving a hand. "She thinks money makes you evil."

"A lot of people do. But I think men have more trouble with it than women. Particularly a man of my age."

"Why limit yourself to men your age? You're only forty. You could easily go out with a guy who was…like thirty. Younger guys wouldn't be as intimidated by your money."

Still smiling, Catherine said, "I must admit I reveled in going to that first opera benefit on your arm. Half of the women there wanted to trade places with me; the other half also wanted to, but were afraid to admit it."

Looking even more determined, Conor leaned forward and said, "Then why not give something like that another chance? I hate to see you spending so much time alone when I know there's someone right here in San Francisco who would love to be with you."

Catherine leaned back in her chair and let her eyes drift up to the sky. A few stars were visible and she thought about the constellations, trying to remember which ones were in the sky in the early summer. Letting her mind wander, she considered Conor's words. A younger man, one without much money, right here in the city… It hit her right in the solar plexus, as though someone had physically knocked the wind out of her. Conor was talking about himself.

She was afraid to raise her head and meet his eyes, afraid to speak and have her voice betray her. Forcing herself to maintain a lighthearted tone, she said, "What constellation is that right overhead?"

He leaned back and looked up, then shook his head. "I have no idea. I'm not much for the stars."

Desperately trying to think of a way to tell Conor the truth without hurting him, Catherine's brain went into overdrive. She was almost at a loss when she thought of something that had happened on her recent trip. "I hope you know how much I appreciate your concern for me—I know it's deeply felt—but I have what I want. I just don't have enough of it."

"Isn't that the same as not having it?"

"No, I don't think so. There are many things I hold more dear because of their rarity. Giacomo is like that. Rare and elusive. The last time we were together, we were sitting outdoors late in the evening. He'd rented a lovely house for us on an island, and when we looked up at the sky, the stars were so profuse they took my breath away. Giacomo was holding my hand and he started telling me about some of the constellations, about the Roman gods and the ways in which some of the constellations had been created. Then he told me how he would rearrange the stars for me."

At Conor's muffled snort, Catherine smiled. "I know it sounds silly, but that's the kind of man I'm attracted to. Jim was a practical fellow who tried to be what I wanted, but he never reached my soul. Giacomo has the soul of an artist, and he touches that same part in me. I always had to wait for Jim to catch up, but I have to try and catch up with Giacomo. That's an irresistible turn-on for me," she sighed, intentionally revealing the sensual longing she felt. "We're incredibly well-matched in every way."

"Every way?" His eyebrows rose.

It wasn't easy to force herself, but she made her voice as sexy as possible. "*Especially* that way. I'll admit I haven't had a lot of experience, but I can't imagine a more satisfying physical relationship. A few days with Giacomo satisfies me more than a year with any other man."

Conor swallowed, his Adam's apple moving noticeably. "*Any* other man?"

"Yes. I've met hundreds of men in my life, maybe thousands, and I've never met anyone like Giacomo. Yes, I wish we could be together more, but for him, I'll take what I can get."

After a long silence Conor put his glass up to his lips and drained his drink in a few gulps. "He's a lucky guy. I hope he knows that."

"Oh, he does. He realizes how rare it is to find someone who understands you at the level we communicate on. Once you have that, Conor, it's unfair to yourself to settle for less."

"Yeah, I can see that."

The dejection was clear in his voice, but Catherine was confident Conor would get over his feelings for her...whatever they were...quickly. And she was equally certain his ideal mate was waiting for him somewhere other than her balcony.

Less than a half hour had passed. Just long enough for Conor to drive like hell and park his truck illegally, but close to the house. Work-boots thumping on the floor, he went to his closet and took out his tuxedo, and his navy blue blazer. Turning, he threw them into a heap, the blazer missing the bed and falling to the floor. Next were two suits, but this time he carried them closer before throwing them atop the tux. Then he walked to the other side of the room and went through his chest of drawers, pulling out a couple of sweaters and at least six ties. Back to the closet, he started going through his shirts, boxed from the laundry. The cardboard tore like tissue paper in his hands, and he kicked the box high into the air after he'd freed a pair of shirts.

"What in the fuck?" Ryan said, standing in his doorway, sleepy-eyed and disheveled.

"Go back to bed."

His gruff tone almost made her comply. Almost. She walked into the room and started picking up his things, acting as if he hadn't said a word. "You're making too much noise for me to sleep." She bent to pick up the blazer, laying it neatly on the bed. Not facing him, she said, "Wanna talk?"

"No. I'll be quiet. Go back to bed."

She turned and looked at him, seeing his eyes bright with what she guessed was rage. Rage at his clothes? She looked at what lay on the bed—everything new, everything expensive. This had to be his bounty from Catherine. "What happened?" She made a space for herself and sat on the bed. "Come on."

"I'm rearranging my closet," he snapped. "I said I'd be quiet."

Making her voice as gentle and understanding as she could, Ryan looked him in the eye. "Tell me. What happened between you and Catherine?"

"What do you think happened?" he sneered. "Everybody was right. Happy?"

Getting up and approaching him, she put a hand on his cheek, still looking directly at him. "I'm never happy when you're in pain."

He pushed her hand away, then thumped noisily into the overstuffed chair in the corner. By the time he sat down, there were tears in his eyes. "God damn it!" he groaned. "She'd rather be alone fifty weeks of the year than give me a chance."

"Oh, Conor." She sighed, hating that she'd been right about his intentions. Walking over to the edge of the bed, she sat down. "I'm sorry. I really am."

"Why?" His eyes showed anger as well as embarrassment. "Da told me to stay away and you wanted to but didn't get the chance. You both love to be right. Celebrate!"

She reached forward and patted his leg. "Never at your expense."

Her gentleness and patience finally wore him down. He leaned forward and dropped his head into his hands. The light shone on his black hair, now long enough to show some of its natural wave. Standing next to him, she put her hand on his head and stroked it tenderly. "Tell me what happened."

A rough sigh emerged. "Catherine would be happy with me. We have such a good time when we go out. She loosens up and acts like she's having the time of her life." Pain-filled blue eyes looked up at his sister. "Why's she shutting the door on me?"

Ryan was pretty sure she knew. Even if Catherine were wild for Conor, she wouldn't give in to her feelings. There was no way she'd work so hard to have a good relationship with Jamie and risk it by dating a member of the family. But more than that, Conor simply wasn't sophisticated enough for Catherine. He was a great guy, but he was a *guy*. He was sophisticated for a twenty-nine year old carpenter, but Catherine needed much, much more. She was all about music and art and culture. And given what Ryan had learned about Giacomo, she had what she needed. But Conor didn't need to have that rubbed in.

She sat down on the bed and said, "Look, if things were different, Catherine would probably love to go out with you. I think you read her signals right."

He looked at her sharply. "What do you mean?"

"There's just no way she can be with you, Con. My being with Jamie has screwed that up for you." She put her hand on his knee. "I'm sorry."

"You really think that?"

Nodding slowly, she said, "She's probably afraid, too. She's not much of a risk taker. Being with you would be pretty out there for her. I just don't think she's that wild."

Showing a touch of vulnerability, he asked, "You don't think that guy's better for her than me, do you?"

"Nah." She leaned over and kissed his head. "You'd be great for her, but she's a little old for you. I know you want to have kids, and she's over that."

"People her age are having kids all the time. They need a little help sometimes, but she's got the money to have the best doctors in the world."

"Yeah, but she doesn't want a baby. And you're way too young to give up the idea of having your own." Slapping his back, she added, "I think things were off just enough to make her not willing to take a chance. And that sucks for you."

"Yeah. It really does."

He dropped his head again and she placed another kiss on it. "I won't tell Jamie about this. Promise."

He nodded, and when she got to the door, he quietly said, "I know you won't. Thanks."

The next day was Saturday, and Ryan and Jamie spent the day walking along Twenty-fourth Street, the main shopping venue for Noe Valley. The O'Flaherty Fourth of July party was on Monday, and they had lots of shopping to do. They went into the grocery store, the bakery, the small farmer's market, and any other store where Jamie saw something cute. Ryan had to admit it took a lot longer to run errands when she was with Jamie, but she was more than willing to trade efficiency for such pleasant company.

When they got home, Ryan was going to grab Duffy and take him for a long walk while Jamie started dinner for whomever was home, but Ryan's phone rang and she looked at the display.

"Huh," she said and sat down on a chair in the living room. "Hey, Chloe. What's up?"

Jamie spent a moment trying to place the name, then realized Chloe was the math major who Ryan had spoken to a couple of times. She was also the woman Jamie was unreasonably, unaccountably, irrationally jealous of.

Ryan put a leg over the arm of the chair and wedged her phone into the crook of her neck, clearly settling in for a chat. "No, I'm not busy. I can talk."

Jamie's eyes met Duffy's, who was dividing his attention between his mistresses, trying to see if one of them was going to engage him somehow. "You were supposed to get a walk," she said to the pooch. "Maybe after dinner." As if he could understand her, he followed her into the kitchen, abandoning Ryan to her conversation.

Jamie was making a spring vegetable risotto, one of Ryan's favorites. She knew the men of the house wouldn't find it filling enough, but she went up to Kevin's room to see if he was interested anyway. As always, he was sprawled out across his bed, sound asleep. On the way back to the kitchen, she stopped by Conor's room and put her ear to the door. Quiet snores were all she heard. It was almost a waste to seek the boys out. If they were in their rooms, they were asleep. Assuming they'd want to eat even if the entree was just an appetizer for them, she went back into the kitchen, waving back at Ryan who wiggled a couple of fingers at her.

Since she was using five different vegetables, it took a while to peel, chop, dice, and slice. And the risotto had to be stirred almost the entire cooking time. So an hour passed with her working intently, singing to herself and occasionally tossing Duffy a carrot, his favorite vegetable.

When the rice was ready she went into the living room and heard Ryan say, "Does your mom like it there?"

"Dinner's ready," Jamie announced, making Ryan jump in surprise.

She turned and held up a finger, asking for another minute. Jamie went to rouse Kevin and Conor, and by the time she got back, Ryan was saying, "No, not a problem. Give me a call whenever something comes up. I'm glad to help."

Ryan went into the kitchen and washed her hands, saying, "That was that math major I met who Robin's advising."

Jamie was transferring the risotto to a serving dish. "Yeah, I figured. I heard you say her name."

"She's trying to decide if she should apply to work with Dr. Chen in the fall. Thought I might know something about him."

As Jamie brushed by, she said, "Are you going to take Duffy out later?"

"Sure." Ryan followed behind and put her hand on Jamie's waist, leaning over to give her a kiss. "Thanks for making dinner. It looks great."

When Jamie didn't acknowledge the compliment, Ryan moved so she could see her face. "Something wrong?"

Sharply, Jamie said, "I thought you were going to take the dog out. I can't cook and walk him at the same time."

Kevin and Conor approached from different directions, and they both veered off and headed for the kitchen when they heard the tone of Jamie's voice.

"Who wants something to drink?" Conor asked, even though there were water glasses set out already.

"Anybody want a beer?" Kevin called out.

"No thanks," Ryan said. She narrowed her eyes briefly at Jamie, then sat down. For the rest of the dinner hour she spoke to Kevin and Conor only, never even glancing in Jamie's direction. As soon as she finished her last bite she jumped up and started cleaning the kitchen.

Kevin started to get up to help, but Ryan said, "I'm good. I know you guys are probably still hungry. You can take off if you like."

Conor still had some rice on his plate but when Kevin headed for freedom, he dropped his fork and joined him. "See you guys later," he called, all but running for the door.

Ryan worked quickly, her job made easier by Jamie's habit of cleaning up after herself as she cooked. When she was finished, Jamie was still sitting at the table, idly picking at the remains of her dinner. Duffy had been next to Ryan, always hoping something would fall from a plate, but now he ran to Jamie's side, nuzzling against her leg. She reached down and petted him, speaking softly and sweetly. Ryan walked past them, heading for the front door. Duffy's head jerked up when he heard his leash jangle. He bolted for the door, and just before she left, Ryan called out, "We'll be back later."

Jamie sat there for a moment in silence, then broke down in tears, resting her head on her forearms as she cried, lost and lonely and thoroughly befuddled.

After a good long walk, Ryan sat on the chaise on the deck, watching the few visible stars and waiting. She wasn't sure what she was waiting for, but she wasn't up to going inside yet. Duffy was anxious, jumping up every time someone drove down the street below. He hated having his people apart, and he always knew when there was even an undercurrent of tension between them. Ryan soothed him, feeling better when she sent some love his way. When she heard Conor and Kevin coming up the street, she and Duffy dashed inside and went downstairs. They found Jamie sitting on the love seat, one of her journals in her lap.

Ryan took a look, trying to discern whether it was safe to talk, but Jamie beat her to it.

"I've been going over my journals for the last year."

Tentatively perching on the arm of the love seat, Ryan said, "Yeah?"

"Guess how many times we've had fights because of my jealousy."

Ryan wasn't sure whether it was a rhetorical question, but she took a guess anyway. "About ten?"

"Nope. Twelve. One for every month."

It was tough to read Jamie's mood, so Ryan didn't try. "It seems more like two or three in a hunk, then a month or two off." She looked down and saw several journals under Jamie's leg. "How many have we had because of my jealousy?"

"Just one that I could find. You were pretty grouchy about Chip on our honeymoon."

Smacking her fist into a hand, Ryan glowered playfully. "I shoulda clocked him."

"He really *was* looking to go out with me, while I get mad at you for nothing at all."

"Kinda true." Sensing it was safe, Ryan slid from the arm onto the seat, trapping Jamie's foot for a moment. "It's getting old."

A few tears leaked out. "It is for me, too. I just don't know how to stop."

Patting her leg, Ryan sighed. "I don't have any ideas either."

They sat there in silence, with Jamie crying softly. After a while, Ryan said, "I'm not going to cheat on you. That's all there is to it. If you don't believe me, we really should consider couples therapy or something, because I don't want to get married with this hanging over my head."

Her tears fell harder and Jamie threw her arms around Ryan, hugging her fiercely. "I hate myself for being jealous. I truly hate myself."

Ryan stroked her side soothingly, kissing the top of Jamie's head. "That's not going to help, baby. I don't know why you do this, but getting angry with yourself isn't the answer."

"I was okay when Chloe called. If you'd just answered a quick question, I could've gotten past it. But when I heard you just chatting…I wanted to rip the phone out of your hand. I despise that girl, for no reason other than she's cute and has great hair. Why am I like that?"

"I don't know. But I can't change my personality to avoid making you mad." Her voice took on added certainty. "I won't." She continued to pat and stroke Jamie, after a few minutes adding, "I did that for a while, and it didn't work."

"When…what did you do?" Jamie looked up at Ryan, eyes red-rimmed and swollen.

"If you're going to be monogamous, you have to avoid temptation. My father told me that, and he's right. I knew I had to do that, but I started getting carried away."

"How? I didn't notice anything."

"It was mostly with Mia," Ryan said, shaking her head. "I know that she's really into Jordan, and I know she's a very good friend to both of us, but I found myself avoiding being alone with her."

Turning in her seat, Jamie stared, slack-jawed. "That's what she meant!"

"What?"

"Mia told me you were acting weird around her."

"It wasn't weird," Ryan said defensively. "Well, maybe it was a little weird. But sometimes she looks at me like I'm…on display." She looked adorably embarrassed and Jamie hugged her tightly. "Well, I was trying to be really safe, so I'd practically run away when she'd do that."

Finally laughing, Jamie said, "You don't have to worry about Mia. She does that to everyone."

"Not to you."

Thoughtfully, Jamie nodded. "She thinks of me like a sister. But she thinks you're sizzling hot, 'cause you are."

"It was making me uncomfortable because I didn't want you to think I was encouraging it, so I tried to avoid it completely. Which was impossible!" she said, exasperated. "One night I was doing pushups and she was lurking around, watching me. That's not right."

"That's just Mia. Don't let it bother you."

"It wouldn't if I knew it wouldn't bother *you*. I've had aggressive girls check me out before. I can handle Mia."

Jamie stroked her partner's cheek lovingly. "I promise I'll never be jealous of Mia. She's harmless. You know there's no distance between her thoughts and her actions. She's like a little kid who asks pregnant women why they're fat."

"Did she *have* parents?" Ryan asked, a half smile showing.

"You've met them. They didn't do a good job of teaching her self-control in many areas, but I love her, and I know you do too."

"I do. But I love you more, and I want to get to the bottom of this. It can't keep coming up again and again. It's too destructive."

"I know," Jamie moaned. "What can we do?"

"Let's go to church tomorrow," Ryan said, seemingly from out in left field. "Maybe we can get a free counseling session out of your grandfather."

"It's a deal. Now can we put this aside for the night?"

Ryan picked up an imaginary object, then turned to put it on the floor next to the love seat. "Done."

After the service on Sunday, they didn't have to work hard to convince Charles to join them for lunch. As always, Jamie let him pick the restaurant, and he chose one of his old favorites not too far from Nob Hill. Charles tended to like the kind of fare Martin and his brothers liked—simply prepared protein with potatoes and possibly a green vegetable. That wasn't Jamie's idea of good eating, but her grandfather didn't eat many meals out and she wanted him to have what he liked.

After they'd all ordered, Charles flicked his gaze from Ryan to Jamie. "I'm always a little worried when people in the marriage preparation class want to meet with me for a talk."

"You have good instincts," Ryan said with a half smile.

"It's nothing bad, Poppa." Jamie snuck a quick look at Ryan then added, "Maybe it's a little bad."

"Tell me what's going on. I know you were both taken aback by the results of your surveys."

"We were, but the problem isn't that we have disagreements, it's that we don't know how to solve them," Jamie said.

Grinning, Charles said, "That *is* the hard part. During our class, you talked about your differing levels of religious faith. Has something else come up?"

"Yes," Jamie said. "A couple of things." She looked at Ryan. "Do you mind?"

"I'll talk." Ryan scooted to the edge of her seat and looked at Charles. "We've got three big issues: fidelity, money, and religious faith. I think we understand each other's position, but that isn't helping us make any progress."

"I'm surprised to hear that fidelity is an issue," Charles said, frowning. "But that's true for the majority of couples, so don't feel that you're alone."

"No, no," Ryan said hurriedly. "It's not an issue in actuality. The problem, in my view, is that Jamie can't trust me one hundred percent, and I'm not willing to live with less than that."

"Is that how you see things?" he asked Jamie.

"That's definitely part of it. But it's not so much that I don't trust Ryan and more that my jealousy gets in the way, even though it's usually unfounded."

"It's *always* unfounded."

Jamie's mouth contracted into a small pout. It was an expression Ryan had seen many, many times, and it was usually the harbinger of an unpleasant conversation.

"Not always," Jamie said.

Ryan stared at her fiercely. "How so?"

Sighing, Jamie said, "This is another conversation we've had many times, and we've never come to a real peace over it." She sat there for a moment with both Ryan and Charles' full attention. "We don't agree on the strict definition of fidelity." Her eyes shifted nervously in Ryan's direction. "When I bring this up, it sounds like I'm on my moral high horse, but I don't feel that way. Do you understand, honey?"

Ryan nodded, looking weary. She turned to Charles and said, "When I was single, I went out with women who were in committed relationships. When Jamie and I were first together,

I told her that I thought what I'd done was wrong and I deeply regretted it." She shrugged, looking embarrassed. "I really believed that at the time, but the more I thought about it, the more I had to acknowledge that my original feelings really hadn't changed. I didn't think it was wrong when I did it, and I still don't." She paused. "That worries Jamie, and I can see why."

Jamie reached out and grasped her hand. "You can? That's the first time you've ever said that."

Ryan gave her a hesitant smile. "I'm evolving."

Charles reached out and put a hand on each woman's arm. "I'm entirely confident you two will have a long, happy marriage, but I think we all made a mistake in trying to have the ceremony this August. There's a reason we want people to be together for two years, and it's a good one."

"But you agreed we'd been through so much this year our time together has been the equivalent of a much longer relationship," Jamie said.

"I'm evolving too." He smiled warmly. "If you two are determined to have your ceremony in August, I won't fight you. But it's not what I recommend. I've married an awful lot of people, and the happiest relationships are the ones where the couple has been working on their issues for quite a while. There are no shortcuts to finding resolutions."

"Do we have more issues than most people?" Ryan asked, looking atypically vulnerable.

Charles laughed. "Not by a long shot. Two or three big issues is the minimum I've seen. You're lucky that you like each other's families and you don't have children from previous relationships. Those two can be fatal."

"I like some members of Jamie's family better than others," Ryan said, her eyes twinkling with mischief.

"That's perfectly understandable. Do you want to talk about postponing, or do you need time to talk about it alone?"

Jamie looked at her partner and almost simultaneously they nodded their heads. "I think we should wait," Ryan said.

"I do too. We didn't even talk about her money issue, Poppa, and it's not insignificant."

"Knowing Ryan a little bit, I think I can guess what your money issue is. Everyone believes you can't have too much money, but coming into a lot of it is difficult to adjust to."

"It sure is for me," Ryan said. "And that drives Jamie nuts."

"Not nuts," Jamie demurred, "but it gets a little old. Kind of like my jealousy."

Looking at Charles again, Ryan said, "I think we've both known we're rushing things. We still don't have a place for the wedding and we haven't sent out invitations. I think we might have been subconsciously sabotaging our plans."

"Mom and I have looked at a dozen places and none of them seem right," Jamie said. "It feels like there are too many decisions to make in too short a time. I've been putting off decisions I would usually make pretty quickly, so I guess you're right. As always," Jamie said, smiling at her partner.

The server approached with a large tray and started placing dishes in front of each of them.

"So, we'll just leave the date open?" Ryan said.

"How about same time next year?" Jamie suggested. "We'll have been together two years, and if we're not ready by then—"

"That works for me," Ryan said, cutting her off before Jamie had to say the unthinkable. "And I'd like to be more involved in the planning. It's not fair to ask you to make all the decisions."

"After lunch we'll go back to my house and I'll check the schedule," Charles said. "At this point it should be pretty open."

"And if we still don't think we're ready to get married, we'll just have a big party on that day," Ryan said, smiling devilishly. "I'm sure it'll be at a gorgeous place, and all of our friends will be there, so we should be good to go. Par-tay!"

They ate their lunch, chatting about the busy wedding schedule Charles had for the summer. They were waiting for dessert when Jamie looked at Ryan and said, "Does it make sense to get married at all?"

Rolling her eyes, Ryan said, "That's a crazy question. We just have a few—"

"No, no, I didn't phrase that right. What I mean is, why have a ceremony? What will it give us that we don't have?"

Ryan took a quick look at Charles. "Uhm…it'll be a church wedding. That's what you want."

Jamie also sought Charles' gaze. "But something about it seems off."

He reached across the table and put his hand over hers. "Tell me what you mean."

"Well, if Ryan and I had the same beliefs, it would be something we were both doing. But if I'm the only one making a vow to God…"

Ryan looked more than a little aggrieved. "I can't lie, Jamers."

Jamie grabbed her hand, shaking it quickly. "I don't want you to. That's my point. Getting married isn't legal, and if we're not doing it for religious reasons, it *is* just a big party."

Making a face, Ryan said, "That's how I've been thinking about it. I already promised that I'd be your spouse. That's all the counts for me."

Charles said, "Would you feel different if the state recognized your marriage?"

Ryan shrugged. "I guess." Then she nodded more firmly. "Yeah, I would."

"That's always an option," Charles said. "It won't be long."

Jamie looked unconvinced. "I'm not ready to get on the schedule for next year. Let's see what happens."

"Is that okay with you?" Charles asked Ryan.

"I guess." Ryan peered at Jamie carefully. "Yeah. I guess it is."

The day was fine and the breeze off the Bay was calming, a perfect day for a walk from Nob Hill to the Noe Valley. Jamie and Ryan left the restaurant holding hands, but that was their only form of communication for much of the walk. They were only about ten blocks from home when Jamie said, "How are you feeling about all of this?"

"Not great. I think it was the right decision, but I'm a little off." She gave Jamie a sad smile. "Do you know what I mean?"

"I think so. I feel like we've failed, at least a little bit, and that's depressing."

"Yeah. That feels right." Ryan's shoulders rose and dropped, then she tossed her hair over her shoulder and got a partial look at the Bay. She turned fully, then stopped. "I'd feel a heck of a lot worse if it wasn't such a beautiful day." She took in a big breath of the clean, dry air. "I always think the air's going to smell like salt, but it never does up here. I wonder why that is."

Jamie took her hand again and the two of them stood on the sidewalk, their weight back on their heels to balance the steep incline of the hill. There wasn't another person in sight, a very common phenomena on the far side of Nob Hill.

Ryan said, "I can't imagine living anywhere else. When I look at that bright blue bay and feel the wind whipping my hair around, I feel like I'm just where the universe wants me to be." She turned her head and smiled when Jamie's eyes met hers. "I love all the foggy days because it makes the beautiful ones so much more special." She put her arm around Jamie's shoulders and hugged her close. "That's how I feel about the women I was with before you. I was vaguely unsatisfied with every woman I ever spent a significant amount of time with—until you. They were fog. You're the sun warming my face."

Jamie turned so she could get both of her arms around Ryan's waist. They stood just like that, holding each other tenderly. They were both gazing at the Bay, watching sailboats tip and bounce and glide along, great white sails snapping.

"You know what I'm thinking?"

"Yep," Jamie said confidently. "We should ask your brothers if they want to join us."

Ryan flinched. "I was thinking we should make love."

"Yikes! I saw all of those beautiful sailboats and thought we should grab a bunch of people and go sailing." She gave Ryan a squeeze. "You must have thought I was mad."

"That would've made it one hell of a day. We decide to put off our marriage, then you want to drag a couple of my brothers into the bedroom with us." She shivered, clearly unable to get the image out of her head. "Then I'd have to tell those strangers in our marriage prep class about it. Hey," she said smiling brightly, "can we drop out?"

"No," Jamie said, playfully biting the end of Ryan's nose. "We cannot drop. As a matter of fact, I'm gonna make you take it every six months for punishment."

Knowing she was teasing, Ryan stuck her tongue out. "Well, since we're not gonna have sex with my brothers, maybe we should go sailing alone and make love out on the bay."

"We could. I just thought you'd like to be around your family today."

"How many people can that boat hold?"

"A lot."

They started to walk again, with Ryan saying, "That just reinforces how ready we are to be married. You know me better than I know myself. I'm a little upset, and being with my family doing something fun is the best thing in the world to cure that."

Jamie gave her another fond squeeze. "Lovemaking tends to have a good effect on your mood too."

"How true that is. But we can easily do both. We just have to do them in order."

They ended up sailing with Brendan, Maggie, Conor, Kevin, Frank, Donal, Tommy, and Caitlin. It was the first time aboard a sailboat for everyone except Brendan, Maggie, and Conor, and only Caitlin was completely without fear. Even though Ryan had only been sailing a few times, she took it upon herself to encourage the others as well as give them a very stern safety talk.

Conor butted in to say, "The first time she went sailing, this big thing hit her," he slapped his hand against the boom, "and knocked her right into the water."

Ryan not so gently patted his cheek while the others laughed. "Should I tell everyone who was driving the boat?"

"They're not interested in that part. But I bet every one of them is thinking about what you looked like being tossed around like a doll."

"It wasn't funny, Conor," Jamie called out from behind the wheel.

"It wasn't then; it is now." He looked at Ryan and shrugged while she reciprocated with the exact same gesture. "She still doesn't get us," he said.

"She's trying. You've gotta give her credit for that."

Maggie had been sailing many times on Lake Michigan, so after ascertaining that she really did know what she was doing, Jamie turned the wheel over to her. The landlubbers were doing well, sitting around the cockpit getting ready to make fun of Brendan, whom Maggie was going to teach how to steer. Jamie could have stayed with them but she was drawn towards the bow of the boat where Ryan sat. Caitlin stood between her legs holding on to the lifelines, the lowest of which was just about eye level for her.

The water was choppy, as always, and Jamie had to hold on to various stays, sheets, and pieces of hardware to get to the bow of the forty-five foot yacht. Just as she started to sit down, they hit a trench and the boat came up to meet her butt. "Yow!"

Ryan turned. "Are you okay back there?"

Jamie scooted up behind her partner, wrapping her legs around her from behind. "Yeah. I just sat down a little faster than I expected to. Do you think Annie would approve of Caitlin being up here?"

Ryan smiled devilishly, the sun glinting off her teeth. "Doesn't know. Won't hurt her."

"You *do* have a good grasp on her, don't you?"

Ryan turned around even further and frowned. "I'm kind of fond of the kid." She leaned to the side, letting Jamie see she was holding on to the loop at the top of Caitlin's life jacket with one hand, while the other encased a chubby thigh.

"I couldn't see from here." Jamie rested her chin on Ryan's shoulder until another sharp dip made her teeth snap together hard. "Damn! I'm taking a beating today."

"Dan! Dan! Dan!" Caitlin shouted over the waves, bending at her hips with each repetition.

Ryan gave Jamie a superior look. "Bang!" she said loudly the next time the boat slapped against the sea.

"Ban! Ban! Ban!" Caitlin shouted, joyous at the thrill.

Salt spray hit them all in the face and Caitlin sputtered for a few seconds, but she didn't let it ruin the moment. Every time Ryan or Jamie made a noise or cried out, she mimicked them, turning around occasionally to make sure they were having fun too.

"That is the most reckless kid I've ever been around," Jamie said. "What will she be like when she learns how to ride a bike?"

Somberly, Ryan shouted over the baby's screams, "If she's anything like me, they should never teach her to ride."

Even though she hadn't discussed it with Jamie, Ryan decided to tell the group their news. "None of you have to put on a suit in August. We've decided we're not ready to get married."

"I can give you some tips for the honeymoon, if that's what you're worried about," Frank said, smirking.

"I think I've got that covered." Ryan gave him a sickly smile. "We've just run out of time. It's rude if we don't send invitations out this week, but we still haven't found a good place to have the ceremony."

"When will you have it?" Maggie asked.

"We don't have a firm date," Jamie said. "But we'll give

everyone plenty of notice."

"I've been amazed you've been planning on having it this year," Maggie said. "Having a big wedding is a full time job."

"We bit off more than we could chew," Ryan said, putting her arm around Jamie, looking very relaxed as they sat next to each other in the cockpit.

"Speaking of chewing, when do we eat?" Conor asked. "Let's get shakin'."

Jamie was back at the helm, and Ryan got up. "I'll start bringing the food up." She slipped past her cousins to go to the galley. Conor was sitting the closest and he got up and followed her.

"What gives?" he asked immediately.

"'Bout what?" She started rooting through the bags they'd brought from the deli.

"You know what." He was unloading as fast as she was. "What's with the wedding? I don't buy the excuse that you're too busy."

Leaning back and looking at him with a smirk, she said, "You don't buy it, huh?"

"Nope. Something's wrong or you wouldn't put it off. I know you."

"I'm sure you do." She smiled again, knowing that it looked forced. "But we waited too long to get started."

"If you really wanted to get married now, you'd do it at Catherine's and just call people to invite them. Marta could provide a wedding reception with ten hours notice."

Ryan started to argue, then decided it didn't make any sense to lie to Conor. If he didn't believe her, he'd make up his own reasons. "Okay." She put her hands on the counter and took in a breath. "We've got a couple of big issues we haven't worked out yet. We could get married now, but Charlie thinks we should wait."

"How long?"

"Don't know. We might wait until it's legal."

"That'll be years!"

"Yeah, it could be."

"What're your issues? They must be bad."

"No, they're not too bad. Probably the same ones everyone has."

"Past girlfriends?" he asked, raising an eyebrow.

"No, not technically, but Jamie'd like it if I'd been with as many women as she has." She chortled softly as she tried to hold onto the counter while putting the antipasto on a tray.

"Elvis has left that building."

"Yeah, I know. And that's not really the issue. It's much more complex than that." She faced him and looked into his eyes. "We're fine, Con. We're over the moon about each other and that's not going to change." She squeezed his shoulder. "We're just trying to be mature about this and take our time."

"Are you sure?" His blue eyes, so like her own, stared, unblinking.

"Positive. I'm disappointed, but I think it's best."

He went back to work, neatly arranging sandwiches on a rectangular tray. "So, is it the *number* of girls?"

"No, it's not like that. She's just..." She took in a breath. "To be honest, she's got some doubts about whether I can be faithful."

He stopped abruptly and stared at her. "Are you shitting me?" he asked loudly.

"Shh! Keep it down." Ryan looked up to see if any of the others heard him. "Why are you so shocked?"

"If you promised her you were going to hop on one foot for a year, she could bet the fuckin' farm on it. When you make a promise, it's done." He clapped his hands together. "I'd be worried about her if I was you. She's the one who comes from bad stock." His cheeks were flushed and he looked like he was about to spit.

Ryan put her hand on his shoulder again and spent a moment feeling the indignation that radiated from him. Unable to stop herself, she wrapped her arms around him and hugged him tightly. His hands hovered tentatively above her back, then slid down and encircled her.

"I can't stand to have anyone cut you down. You don't deserve that. Ever," he said hotly.

Pulling away, Ryan smiled at him, fighting the tears that threatened to come. "Mam would love that you always look out for me. She'd rest easy."

He misted up as well, wiping his eyes with the back of his hand. "I promised her I'd always look out for you, and my word is as good as yours."

"I know that." She leaned forward and kissed his bristly cheek. "Jamie's not cutting me down, far from it. She knows she doesn't have anything to worry about. But finding out about her dad's past has been hard for her. It's made her suspicious of promises."

He shrugged. "Maybc. But Jim's a class-A dick. That didn't just start in the past year. Jamie wasn't able to see what was right in front of her eyes." He went back to work once again, adding, "You might want to think about *that* while you're thinking."

Ryan busied her hands, but her head lingered on Conor's comment. She didn't want to admit it, but he had a point. One that she'd considered many times. If Jamie had been so sure her father was a great guy, what did that say about her judgment?

They were one of the last boats back for the night. It wasn't fully dark, but it was close when they'd finished putting on the boom cover and battening the hatches. Caitlin was asleep, so worn out she didn't notice being handed off from Ryan to Tommy on the dock. They'd come in three cars, and Jamie and Ryan were alone in Jamie's car on the way home.

"How are you feeling now?" Jamie asked, noting her partner's serene face.

"Great. Really great. We've gotta go sailing more often. It's crazy having this boat just sit there."

"You're right. We've got the time, let's get over here every week."

"I'm down with that."

"Hey, just because we're not getting married now doesn't mean we should skip the honeymoon."

"We had that," Ryan said, smiling at her. "Pebble Beach, just a couple of weeks ago. Did you forget already?"

"You know I didn't." Jamie reached over and pinched Ryan's thigh. "But that wasn't a honeymoon. That's our 'making love' anniversary. I want to take you to Ireland for our honeymoon—even without the wedding."

"Yeah." Ryan sighed. "I need to go. My grandparents are having their sixtieth anniversary in a couple of weeks. If we'd gone for our honeymoon, we would have been able to have a delayed celebration with them."

"So? What do you say?"

Ryan sat up straighter. "About what?"

Jamie took a quick look at her. "About going to Ireland."

"I agree. We need to go."

"When?"

"You want me to decide that now, just in the blink of an eye?" She sounded nearly outraged.

Laughing, Jamie said, "It's not that big a deal; it's just a trip. I could be ready to go tomorrow."

"Tomorrow? I'm stressing out about Sydney, and that's not for weeks!"

"We should go before Sydney," Jamie said seriously. "We're not back from there until October."

"Oh, no," Ryan said, her voice high and wobbly. "I couldn't possibly do that. We'll have to go after Sydney."

"When?" Jamie asked again.

"Soon. Don't worry about it; we'll go soon."

Jamie cast a quick glance at her, seeing Ryan start to chew on her lip, a sure sign of anxiety. "You don't have to decide today, honey, but we do need to go. I *want* to go."

"Yeah, yeah, me too."

Jamie was fairly sure that falser words were never spoken.

Chapter Thirteen

The Breast Cancer Walk foursome had gotten into the habit of going for a walk a couple of times a week on the mornings that Jamie and Ryan were in San Francisco. Maeve and Catherine went without them if they weren't there, but when the four of them went together they went further, and at a faster pace, which was exactly what they needed to be ready.

One morning, after they'd walked Maeve back to her house, Catherine proposed that they all keep going to Pacific Heights.

"I think I need some extra work. Since I haven't been playing tennis frequently, I've let things slip. I fear I'm slowing Maeve down."

"My aunt has been a walker for years," Ryan said, "and she pushes Caitlin around the hills of Noe Valley almost as easily as I do. But you're keeping up, Catherine. I don't think you're going to have difficulty with this walk at all."

"I need some work on hills, so I'm going to start walking over to pick Maeve up instead of driving."

"And it's good for the environment, too," Ryan said. They kept walking, approaching a fairly steep hill. They were all quiet as they climbed, and it took Catherine a minute to catch her breath after they crested it.

"Well, I made it. But I think there are two more between here and my house."

"At least two," Jamie said. "When I first started coming over here to see Ryan, only her irresistible charm kept me coming back. These hills almost sent me right back home."

"We can take the bus home," Ryan said, smiling sweetly.

"You just say that because there isn't a direct bus, and you know I won't want to change three times to get home."

"That might have played a part in my decision-making process before making the offer." She put her arm around Jamie's shoulders and gave her a squeeze

"I know what would make the time fly by," Catherine said. "Ryan and I can have an argument."

Ryan stared at her, clearly puzzled. "Do we have many arguments?"

"No, but I don't often try to give you money."

"Money? Why would you want to give me money?"

"Because of the enormous sums you saved me by urging me to get out of tech stocks. I was clearly overly invested, a scheme the so-called experts pushed me into."

Ryan waved her hand. "That was just dumb luck. The person who convinced me was my father, so you can try to get him to take a cut." She laughed. "Good luck with that."

"That's not true," Catherine said. "Your thesis, or your project—whatever you call it—told you very clearly that the market was too high and it was time to sell. Don't act like that didn't happen," Catherine said, waving her finger near Ryan's face.

"No, it happened. But I kept thinking that I was wrong. It was just a projection, and those are wrong so often it's not funny. It was really my father who made me step back and look at things in a way that an outsider would. I think that's probably part of the problem with professional investing; you get so caught up in it that it's hard to step back and say 'this is ridiculous.'"

"Well, I know I'll never get your father to take any money, I thought I might have better luck with you."

"Tell your mother how that went for you," Ryan said, winking at Jamie.

"Do you really want me to tell her?" Ryan nodded, and Jamie turned to meet Catherine's expectant smile. "When Ryan and I were playing the stock market game, I was convinced that we both knew what we were doing. Since I had some extra money, I invested it, but I opened two accounts—one in my name and one in Ryan's. I did well, but Ryan did even better. She's more of a gambler than I am."

Ryan interrupted. "Only if I think it's a game. I'm not very darned reckless when it comes to real money."

"How much did you make? Or is that an incredibly rude question?"

"Too much," Ryan said. "So much that I was insufferable for a couple of weeks. Jamie was about to put me in a steamer trunk and send me packing."

Jamie took her hand and linked their fingers together. She looked up at Ryan with undisguised affection. "You weren't that bad. You felt as if I'd tricked you, and, in a sense, I had."

Laughing, Ryan said, "It wasn't 'in a sense'. You *did* trick me. But I can understand why you did it and your motives were good. So eventually I decided to stop being an ass, even though I'm still having a tough time getting acclimated to having a bank account balance with all of those zeros in it."

"I suppose that means you won't take my money?" Catherine asked, her eyes twinkling just as Jamie's often did when she was teasing.

"No, I don't think so. But feel free to take whatever you'd like to share with me and give it to the AIDS Ride. Jamie already made a contribution, but I still feel bad that I didn't ride this year."

"That's a good idea," Catherine said. "I'll make a donation in your name."

Ryan started to nod, then she said, "Would you make it in my cousin Michael's name? Seeing his name in print helps keep him alive a little bit for me." She was smiling, but as always when she spoke of Michael, her smile was diluted with sadness. "Michael

Brendan Driscoll. Twenty-eight short years on this beautiful planet."

A few days later, Catherine and Maeve were walking through Golden Gate Park when Maeve asked, "Have you spoken to Giacomo lately? You haven't mentioned him much."

"I haven't?" Catherine looked briefly puzzled. "I suppose I don't talk about him as often as I think about him." She laughed. "No one would be able to stand it."

"Do you speak to him often?"

"Fairly often. Two or three times a week. I haven't told him this, but I'm considering selling my apartment in Milan."

"Really? Why would you do that? Isn't it difficult enough to see him?"

"Yes, but I don't like seeing him there. I love Italy, and part of the reason I bought the apartment was to be closer to the art scene. And of course I love going to the opera in Milan. I've also been known to go to a runway show or two. But since I've taken up with Giacomo, I'm not as comfortable there. I'm on his turf, and I think I'd be happier seeing him someplace more neutral."

"I assume you have someplace in mind?"

"I do. I think I'm going to buy a place in New York. I've always wanted to spend more time there, and it appeals to me more than any place in Europe right now."

"But how will that help—"

"Giacomo frequently has to go to New York. It's about a six or seven hour trip for him and roughly the same for me. I think it would be good for us to have a place that could be ours, together."

"It sounds like you've given a lot of thought to this."

"I've given it *some* thought. Meeting in a neutral place feels like it will be more of a vacation for both of us."

"How do you think he'll feel about it?"

"My guess is that he won't like it. Actually, I'm fairly sure he won't. Ideally, he'd like me to visit every month, but I'm not going to do that. Even though he and his wife have what I suppose one would call an open marriage, having me in town that frequently could be destabilizing. And even though I've done a number of things that I know are wrong, I will not be a more active party to helping their marriage dissolve."

"How would this be different?" Maeve looked interested, but also confused. "You'd still be seeing him…he'd still be married."

"All true. But I think it would be better if I let him make his trips to New York for business. I think he'd be less tempted to be away from home as frequently as he would if I were to visit Milan as much as he wants me to." She had a wry smile on her face as she added, "Having an affair isn't as easy as it looks on television."

"Are you really having an affair? It hardly seems so, given that his wife not only knows about your relationship, but approves of it."

Catherine still wore a faint smile, but it was tinged with sadness. "I can call it anything I want, but I'm in love with a married man. I think that's the textbook definition of an affair."

They continued their walk but Catherine was uncharacteristically silent. Tentatively, Maeve said, "I didn't upset you by asking about Giacomo, did I?"

"Of course not. I'm happy to talk about any part of my life with you. I hope you feel the same."

"I do. It surprises me, but I find myself telling you things I wouldn't tell some of my oldest friends."

Beaming a smile, Catherine said, "I feel the same way. Every once in a while you find a friend you know you can trust, someone who understands you. And when you find someone like that, you need to hold on tightly."

"I agree. I'm very glad Jamie brought you into our lives."

"I am too. You have no idea how glad I am."

Catherine threaded her arm around Maeve's and they walked on, arms linked but words very rare. They'd gone over a quarter mile when Catherine sighed and said, "There are so many times I wish things had worked out between Jim and me. I know Jamie was happier when we were a family."

Eyes wide, Maeve said, "I wouldn't have guessed you'd say that. Ever."

"Just a thought I have sometimes. I suppose my feelings center mostly around Jamie. I know how hard this has been for her."

"That's probably true, but it's not fair of children to ask that their parents' feelings never change. I know what it's like to be in a loveless marriage, and I wouldn't wish that on the devil himself."

"I wouldn't say Jim and I had a loveless marriage. As a matter of fact, I frequently find myself missing him."

Maeve stopped in her tracks and stared at Catherine. "You've shocked me twice today. Are you serious? After how you talk about Giacomo, I assumed Jim never crossed your mind."

"No, he crosses my mind all the time. In an ideal world I'd have an amalgam of the two of them."

Smiling suspiciously, Maeve said, "Now, how would that work?"

Catherine's eyes danced with interest as she made up her imaginary man. "I'd have Giacomo for romance. Being with him is almost like being in an opera. He professes his love for me with all the passion of the love-struck tenor."

"Oh, my," Maeve said, giggling. "I can't imagine what that would be like."

"It's divine," Catherine said, almost swooning. "And he can be so poetic. He doesn't have many practical bones in his body." She chuckled softly. "If we lived together I can't imagine we'd accomplish a thing."

"I bet that wasn't true with Jim."

Catherine laughed. "He's the antithesis of Giacomo. He's practical and prudent, and he knows exactly what his next step is going to be."

"That's how he seems. I don't know him well at all, but he seems very practical."

"Completely. Sometimes it's for good and sometimes it's for evil, but he's planning the next step while taking the first. There's a part of me that's attracted to a man who's a strategist. And even though he wasn't an art lover, he was a very good companion at the hundreds of benefits and openings and exhibits that I took him to over the years."

"That's hard to get a man to do. Did he complain?"

"No. Never. And he didn't act like he was just doing it to make business contacts or to get his face in the paper, although I'm sure that was part of it. He's a curious person by nature, and he wanted to know more about art and music and other cultural things he'd never been exposed to."

"He sounds like a good partner," Maeve said thoughtfully.

"He was, in many ways. If I'd been enough for him, he would have easily been enough for me."

"It's a pitiful shame, that's what it is. I can't imagine not finding you attractive enough or interesting enough to hold his attention."

"Thank you for the generous compliment, but I'm not sure, in retrospect, that I was lacking. I think many powerful men are powerful because they have so much desire, whether that's desire for power or fame or notoriety. Sexual desire seems like it's part and parcel. I think that for Jim it was more of a game than anything else. It's a way for a man to feel that he's still on top."

"I'll never understand it myself. I suppose it's just not something within my experience." Maeve laughed, the sound so filled with happiness that it made passersby smile at her in return. "All I know is that my second marriage so far surpasses my first that it's hard to believe it's the same institution. I hope you can find what I have with the delightful, charming, albeit not very powerful Martin O'Flaherty."

"If he had a single twin, I'd throw myself at him," Catherine said, giggling.

Chapter Fourteen

It was a warm, bright summer day in San Francisco, the kind of day most tourists expect to find on their visit to the city. Sadly, the reality rarely met the expectation, and most tourists shivered through their visit. When the day was in fact summery, the natives basked in the sun like seal pups along the piers. People left work early, took long lunch hours, called in sick, and did whatever they could to enjoy each drop of sunshine.

After spending an hour tutoring Jennie at Catherine's house, Jamie and Ryan stepped outside and both breathed in the clean, clear air. Jamie said, "Let's walk over to the Marina and hang out for a while. It's too nice a day to be inside."

"I was itching to be outside the whole time Jen and I were going over her algebra. Don't think I didn't know you were upstairs on that fantastic balcony."

Jamie grinned unrepentantly. "I've got nothing to add to the math discussion, and she doesn't need help with her art class." She patted the small canvas shoulder bag she carried. "I've got a good book with me, so you can plunk me down anywhere and I'm happy."

"You know," Ryan said, "I've gotta admit I'm a little surprised by how much you read. You're really a bookworm."

"I am, but it goes in spurts. I didn't get to read anything fun this past year so I'm making up for lost time." She took Ryan's hand and did a stutter step to synch their strides. "I'm surprised by how little you read, but I'm taking my acceptance of that as proof of how much I love you. I could never have imagined partnering with someone who doesn't read for fun, but it's working out pretty darned well."

Ryan turned and grinned at her. "No complaints here."

They walked on, cresting a good-sized hill before the Bay opened up in front of them, making both of them sigh with pleasure. "Could this be any prettier?" Jamie asked rhetorically.

"Why would anyone choose to live anywhere else? When we traveled for Cal, I'd be on the bus looking around and thinking 'How can people live here? No hills, no water, cold weather.' Why bother?"

Jamie smiled at her, thinking that Ryan's list of comparison cities was woefully small, but she decided not to comment on that. "It's crowded enough. If every summer day was like this, we'd have a million more people trying to cram in."

"Too true."

As they went down the hill towards the Marina, Jamie said, "How's the enforced relaxation going? You haven't been complaining."

"How long has it been? A month?"

"Seven weeks on Monday."

"No!"

"Yep."

"Hmm." Ryan's gaze settled on the Bay, its calm blue serenity letting her mind wander to consider the past few weeks. "I'm surprised by how fast it's gone. I thought I'd be hellishly bored."

"How could you be bored? You're up running every morning with Duffy. You swing by and see Caitlin almost every day. Then you drag me over to the apartment building to do something simple that the boys graciously leave for me." She squeezed Ryan's hand and chuckled when Ryan tried to look like she didn't know what Jamie was talking about. "Then it's off to my mom's to work with Jennie for an hour or two."

"You forgot our long walks. We've put a lot of miles under our belts."

"I haven't forgotten." She laughed. "Well, I've forgotten all of the early morning walks. You know I don't function until eight a.m."

"You like the evening walks better, don't you."

"Yep. Much, much better. I like to walk in the dark with just you." She leaned heavily against Ryan's side, making her tilt to the left.

"I like that too, but my aunt's in bed by the time you really like to go out."

"True. But I'm in bed when she really wants to go. Why does she win so often?"

It was obvious she was teasing, but Ryan commented anyway. "You know you can sleep in and have me go with you at night."

"I know, but I like to hang out with the group. And I know it's better for me to get up early and get going."

"We like having you."

"Does your aunt know you go running most mornings before we walk?"

"Not sure. I'm not gonna make a point of telling her." She tapped Jamie's head. "Don't go volunteering the info."

"Not a word. I know that's your time to think."

"Yep. Time to clean out the pipes. So, are you happy with your time off?"

"I'm happier than I've ever been in my life," Jamie said, smiling so contentedly that Ryan almost choked up just looking at her. "Lots of time with you, time with my mom, not running from one house to the other, no practices, matches, games, studying. It's sweet!" she exclaimed at high volume.

"Nothing you need to tweak?"

"Not really. Eventually I'd like to make some friends over here, but that's about it."

"Friends?" Ryan asked as though Jamie had said "toasters". "Why do you want friends?"

They were near the wide swath of Marina Green and Jamie led the way, stepping around or over dozens of sunbathers, parents with their kids and other assorted humans. She found a decent sized space and plopped down on the ground. When Ryan joined her she said, "You've got more friends than anyone I've ever known. We rarely go out that you don't run into someone who acts like you're their *best* friend."

"Yeah. I know a lot of people."

"But you never *see* them," Jamie said pointedly. "You never call anyone, you never invite anyone over. What's up with that?"

Ryan lay back on the short grass, shifting around until she got comfortable. "Hmm. Why don't I call anyone?"

Her feet were on the ground and she crossed an ankle over a knee then put her hands behind her head. Jamie could see her eyes follow one of the more colorful kites that was skittering across the sky.

"I'm not sure why I don't. I guess I've never had the kind of free time to commit to doing something at a certain time." She turned her head and made eye contact. "Know what I mean?"

Jamie lay down perpendicular to Ryan and rested her head on her partner's hip. "I guess I do. You didn't have a minute to yourself last year."

Ryan shifted her hip, making Jamie's head bounce. "I was busier before I met you. I worked twenty hours a week when I was taking a full course load and playing a sport at USF."

"Well, you have some free time now. Do you want to reconnect with some of your friends?"

"Mmm." Ryan was speaking slowly, and Jamie could tell this topic wasn't really reaching her. "Maybe."

"Just maybe?"

Threading her fingers through Jamie's hair, Ryan started to give her a light head rub. "I'm not sure my old friends are the right people to hang with."

"Because?"

"Oh, you know…they're kinda…mmm…"

"People to sleep with?" Jamie teased.

"Ha. Funny. No, not really. But they're all pretty specific. I have AIDS Ride friends, I have workout friends, I have friends from USF, obviously I have people I used to sleep with. They're all...you know...specific."

"So you never had any couple friends?"

"Not many. I mean, I do, but no one I've ever done anything with other than the thing I knew them from."

Jamie sat up. "Are you speaking English?"

"Yeah." Ryan smiled at her. "I knew couples from the AIDS Ride, but I never had dinner with them or anything. And I trained some couples, but I didn't hang out with them."

Lying down again, Jamie said, "Then I guess we'll have to make some new ones."

"Do we hafta?"

Sitting up again, Jamie looked at her partner carefully. "Why don't you want to?"

"We've got the lads and your mom. Isn't that enough? Any night you want to go out, someone'll go."

Jamie let the thought of having dinner at a nice restaurant with five or six cousins roll through her head. She couldn't get the image to focus properly, probably because none of the boyos liked anything more formal than tacos. And taking her mother to a lesbian club was just as jarring. "Wouldn't you like to go dancing sometime?"

"Dancing?" Ryan was quiet for a minute. "I was just thinking about dancing with you at the bar in Berkeley. I've had serious foreplay that wasn't that hot." She chuckled, making her belly move up and down. "I'm in. Any time."

"I'd like to go with other people. That's a lot more fun, isn't it?"

Ryan resumed her lazy head rub. "I guess. But I'm content to be with you alone. Dancing, moving against you, feeling how warm your body gets, how you smell." She let out a sigh. "I don't need another soul."

"You're very sweet, but I'd like to hang out with people we're not related to once in a while. Any objections?"

"No. Whatever you want, babe, I'm up for it."

"Hey, how about Sara and Ally?"

It took even longer for Ryan to reply this time, and her response was less than enthusiastic. "Sure. Whatever. Just tell me where to be and I'll be there."

"I'm happy to try to make some friends at church. You're the one who says she wants Sara and Ally in her life."

"I know." Ryan's shoulders rose and fell. "I do."

"You could show a little more enthusiasm, honey."

She smiled wanly. "I'd rather see Sara and Ally than any of the people from our marriage class." Her lip twitched, nearly curling with disdain. "They're not my type."

Jamie decided it was too nice an evening to go home and cook so they walked over to a landmark vegetarian restaurant in Fort Mason. Ryan had never been there and she didn't want to be indoors, so Jamie went in and got carry-outs. They sat on a nearby bench to watch the water while they ate.

Ryan poked around in the big bag, looking suspicious. "I can't tell what anything is. What should I eat first?"

"Whatever you want. It's all locally grown vegetables. Good for you."

Taking out the cartons, Ryan opened each and set them between them. "Just vegetables, huh?"

Smiling at her reticence, Jamie said, "Yep. I'll go get more if you're still hungry."

"No, this should be enough," Ryan said as she looked carefully at the four and a half pounds of local bounty. "We can get ice cream on the way home."

Jamie smirked at the serious look on Ryan's face, then started to eat a tart beet salad. "Mmm, yummy. Try this." She loaded the fork and held it in front of Ryan's mouth.

"Good." She chewed thoughtfully. "Really good. Goat

cheese?"

"Yeah. Goat cheese, orange segments, onion, chives. Tasty."

Ryan took a bite of a crisp pizza with tomatoes and roasted potatoes, nodding her head as her eyes closed. "Terrific. You have superb ideas."

The next afternoon, while Ryan and Jennie were belaboring a math problem, Jamie and her mother were sitting on the balcony. They were both wrapped in blankets and the heat lamps were blazing. "Nice day," Jamie said, trying to stop her teeth from chattering. "I think I prefer yesterday."

"Wait until October. We'll have many days like that."

"True. Sometimes I miss the South Bay's weather. How about you?"

"Not too often. After three or four days of fog, I sometimes go down to Hillsborough just to warm up, but I like the city much more than I expected to."

"I'm glad you're here. And I'm especially glad we're able to see each other so often."

"I'm a little surprised you've been at home so consistently. I thought you'd travel a little now that your time is your own."

"If it were up to me, we'd have taken at least two trips so far this summer. I suppose I've got to make plans and not let Ryan stop me."

"Does she try?"

"No, not really. Those big blue eyes stare at me while she pouts, but I can't give in."

"What's the issue? Does she simply want to stay home?"

"Yep. For some reason, she hates to travel for fun, but she didn't ever complain about taking a bus across Oregon to play softball. She's an eternal conundrum."

"Does she actually refuse to go? That doesn't sound like her."

"No, she's not the type to refuse. Her trick is to put me off. I want to go to Ireland, and she said she'd go later in the year, after she has time to plan."

"Plan?" Catherine blinked. "Plan what?"

"Nothing!" Jamie's frustration showed clearly. "She doesn't want to go and she thinks I'll give up asking if she delays long enough. So I'm going to make my plans and let her decide whether or not to come. By the way, if you go to Rhode Island in August, I'll go with you. Ryan won't like it, but I can't be a homebody like she is."

Looking slightly worried, Catherine said, "I can't see you staying in one place for long, but I also can't see Ryan traveling as often as you'd like."

"She doesn't need to go as often as I'd like. I've been nowhere…absolutely nowhere since we've been together. Going on two or three trips a year isn't asking for too much in my opinion. I'll give up ten trips that I'd like to take, so she only has to go on two or three she doesn't want to make. That's fair," she said with certainty. "We've both got to give."

"Just because it's fair doesn't mean it'll be easy."

"No," Jamie said, rolling her eyes. "I suppose it won't."

"Well, I won't be taking you away to Rhode Island. I told Uncle David we wouldn't be able to come because of your wedding."

"Uhm…won't he wonder when he doesn't get an invitation?"

"I'll let them know about the cancellation soon—just not soon enough to have to visit. Even though it's only once a year, it seems much more frequent!"

Early the next morning, Ryan arrived at a run-down Victorian home in the Castro, just a few blocks from the O'Flaherty manse. She'd volunteered to help Conor with some demolition work that needed a careful hand, and when she tapped the horn Conor came out. She handed over the breakfast she'd stopped to buy for the crew, and he handed it off to a guy who'd walked out with him. Ryan took a bite of her breakfast burrito, then nodded towards the building. "The place looks like crap."

"Yeah, it is crap. But it'll be fantastic when we're done. The owners are cool. A couple of gay guys. One of them's an architect and he's remarkably easy to work with."

"Architects aren't usually your best friends."

"Right-o. But when the architect is his own general contractor and actually has to pay the bills, that seems to make them more realistic." He hitched one dark eyebrow up and down, making Ryan smile.

"What's the other guy do?"

"Designer. One of those guys the old ladies in town take to social events."

Tactfully, she didn't mention that was the role he had been filling for Catherine recently.

"I'm damned glad these guys aren't pains in the butt. It's bad enough working two jobs. It'd kill me if I was working for jerks."

She slapped her hand onto his thigh. "I can help you out any time you need it. I've got more free time now than I've had since I was out of diapers."

He looked thoughtful, then said, "It's probably best to have you helping at the apartment building. The OFC is suffering."

"OFC?"

"Frank's creation. O'Flaherty Cousins. I like it."

She nodded. "Me too. I guess the Driscoll brothers and Jamie lose out to the masses."

She spent the next three hours ripping treads and headers and stringers apart with a claw hammer and a cat's paw. As Conor had mentioned when he proposed the task, he was going to reuse as much of the wood as he could, meaning she had to be careful to preserve the materials while destroying the integrity of the construction. The work was very dirty since the staircase had to be at least seventy years old, and she felt as though seventy years of dirt was stuck to her sweaty body by the time Conor came to get her for lunch. "Roach coach is here. Are you hungry?"

"I'd eat anything that would stop moving long enough, but I think Jamie's gonna come by and bring me something. I sure hope she hurries. I've never been so hungry."

She went back to work, unable to stand to watch the others eat when she was so famished. She checked her watch again and again, angry with herself for not telling her partner that work crews always liked to eat early.

Right at noon Jamie approached the house, and tried to decide if the outside stairs were safe to climb. They were wooden and had lost most of their paint years before. Now it wasn't clear if they still retained nails. Avoiding the trash that had accumulated during the day, she stepped inside and walked around until she found her lover, or at least a reasonable facsimile. This model came in a tan color that really didn't suit her, and Jamie hoped that the poor woman could get a ride home in Conor's truck. Love had its limits.

To Ryan's glee, Jamie had made a trip to her favorite burger joint, procuring a double chili cheeseburger, chili fries, and a chocolate malt.

"Wash your hands and we can go outside and eat."

"No water," Ryan said, shaking her head. "Porta Potties are outside, but the sinks in them haven't been filled recently."

Jamie stared, flustered.

"I've got an idea," Ryan said, leading the way outdoors.

Conor and another man approached a few minutes later, both laughing at the sight of the neat, clean blonde woman dangling chili-coated French fries into her grimy partner's mouth.

"Hey, guys," Conor said, "this is Andrew Harris, one of the owners of the house. Andrew, I'd like you to meet my sister, Ryan and her partner, Jamie Evans. Ryan's helping us out today, and, as you can see—Jamie's helping Ryan."

Ryan brushed the dirt off her hand as best she could before she extended it. "Glad to meet you, Andrew. Conor's been raving about the place so much I wanted to see it for myself."

"I haven't seen much," Jamie said, "but I'd love a quick tour if you have the time."

"I'm glad you could both come," he said with a friendly smile. "And I'd love to take you on a tour. Any chance to show off my baby. Are you interested in Victorians?"

"I always have been," Ryan said. "And since Conor's been working on them, my interest has grown. It's always been my dream to get a place in Noe Valley and renovate it."

"That's a tough dream to realize now," Andrew said, referring to the skyrocketing housing market.

"Not for them," Conor advised. "Jamie's loaded."

Ryan punched him in the arm as she smiled over at Andrew. "He's so discreet."

"For over a year, Rick and I looked at every property in the city. I'm not sure why, but recently there have been a lot more units coming on the market. I'd suggest that you start looking soon if you want to have a place to live within two years."

"Wow. That long, huh?" Ryan said.

"Sure. If you want to renovate, it might take a year to find what you want, and at least a year to get it where you want it."

"I suppose that's true," Jamie mused. "Maybe we should stop being so casual about it and really get to work."

"Do you have an agent to work with?"

"We do," Jamie said. "My mother just bought a place and she loved the guy she worked with."

"Then give him a call and start pounding the pavement. I hope you two find exactly what you're looking for."

As Andrew walked away, Conor shot his sister a glance. "I didn't know you were interested in renovating."

She nodded. "We've been talking about it more and more lately. I mean, we've always known that we wanted to come back to Noe after we graduated, and since we both love old homes it just seems like it would be a cool thing to do."

"I'd love to have you guys over here. Maybe we could find

you a big old Victorian. This one will have over three thousand square feet when we're done. That's just big enough for you two and a few rug rats."

"Seems awfully big," Ryan said, looking up at the three-story structure.

Conor and Jamie's eyes met and they shared a smile behind Ryan's oblivious back.

"Hey, Pig Pen," Conor teased three hours later as he tried to see his sister's eyes.

Ryan had tied a bandana around her nose and mouth to block the waves of dust rolling into her face, and her safety glasses were foggy with condensation from her efforts. "Yes?" she answered pleasantly.

"I just got a page from home. I assume it's Jamie."

"Thanks." She found her supervisor for the day. "I'll be back in a few, Carlos," she called out as she jogged from the building. She stood outside of Conor's truck for a moment, peeling off her flannel shirt and using it to beat the dust from her jeans as best she could. Removing her baseball cap, she bent from the waist and ruffled her fingers through the hair that had fallen from her braid. Then she took off her glasses, earplugs, and bandana, hopped in and dialed as she rolled down the windows to let in the cool afternoon breeze.

"Hi, I just wanted to see if you need an afternoon snack."

"Aww, you're the best, Jamers. I'd take you up on it, but we're about a half hour from finished."

"So soon?"

"You've obviously never taken a staircase down. I feel like it's Friday."

"Poor thing. I'll walk down there and we can go home in the BMW." There was a pause before she added, "I'll bring a sheet to cover the seat."

"So what did you think?" Jamie asked as she got her partner

arranged on the sheet. "Do you want to forget about grad school and work construction?"

"To tell you the truth, I really could do this full time," Ryan said reflectively. "It's kind of like a sport. You're all on the same team, you've got a common goal, and it's easy to define your progress. I like it a lot."

"Well, I don't know anyone who would look better in a flannel shirt with the sleeves cut off so I could see those biceps, and faded jeans with big, steel-toed boots. You know my motto, 'As long as I like the outfit, you can do it.'"

Ryan laughed at her requirements. "I think I'll stick with the academic track. Even though construction is fun, I feel like I've been hit by a truck. I'm gonna go home and soak in the tub until I prune."

"Maybe your spouse could be persuaded to give you a nice massage."

"Mmm…it feels good just to think about it," she sighed, sinking into the leather surface while she dreamt of Jamie's soft hands roaming over her body.

"Don't forget, we agreed to go out to dinner with my mom tonight."

Ryan groaned pathetically. "You might have to cut my meat, but I'll go."

Jamie thought her grumbled comment was "the things we do for love" but she thought it wise not to press Ryan at that moment.

Chapter Fifteen

They met Catherine at a place on Market, not too far from each of their homes. Ryan was fixated on using as little nonrenewable energy as possible these days, so she convinced Jamie to walk. It was about a mile away, not far at all when one wore the proper shoes. As they walked, Jamie grumbled about just that.

"I don't know why someone can't design a shoe that's attractive and comfortable." She stuck her foot out in front of herself and looked at it critically. "I hate these shoes. They only look good with slacks, and I prefer to wear a dress when I go to a nice restaurant. Slacks are just too casual." Looking at Ryan's black slacks, Jamie made a face. "Except on you, of course."

"Right," Ryan said, smirking. "Well, I think you look nice, but I guess I'd agree that you look better in a dress."

"You can do more with a dress. Shoes, jewelry, purses, scarves—lots of ways to change the look."

Ryan squeezed her hand, smiling warmly. "I never thought I'd partner with such a girly-girl, but I like it."

"Might as well, you're stuck with me." Jamie waved her engagement ring under Ryan's nose, smiling when Ryan acted like the stones had temporarily blinded her.

While they ate, Jamie regaled her mother with a fanciful tale of Ryan's disheveled state at lunch. "No, really, Mom," she said, putting her hand over Ryan's mouth. "She wanted to eat a chili burger with hands so filthy her fingerprints were obscured."

Ryan pulled her hand away. "I had on gloves for the first hour or two, but they were too unwieldy. I should have had deerskin or something more flexible."

"Do you enjoy that kind of work?" Catherine asked.

"I do. I talked to Conor a little today and we agreed that I could be partially happy doing renovation work."

"Partially?" Catherine asked.

"Yeah." Ryan ducked her head, looking embarrassed. "I've never found anything that could satisfy me full time. I have a short attention span."

Jamie put her arm around her and squeezed gently. "She's too modest to say her brain's too big to light on one thing. She needs something to engage all of the parts of her personality, and she's having a heck of a time finding that elusive career path."

"You'll get there," Catherine said, patting her hand. "I know you won't give up until you find something or several somethings that fulfill you."

"I wish I had your confidence."

"You'll get there," Jamie echoed. "In the meantime, we can get busy with house-hunting. Will you help us, Mom?"

"Absolutely. I'm in a house hunting mood right now, as a matter of fact."

Ryan raised an eyebrow. "You just bought your house. Are you looking for another?"

"Not here," Catherine said, her smile dimming as she shot a quick look in Jamie's direction. "I might look in New York."

"New York?" Jamie asked, brow furrowed.

"Yes. I think I'll sell my Milan apartment and find one in New York. I've seen all that Milan has to offer."

"What about…" Jamie trailed off, knowing she didn't have to mention Giacomo's name.

"New York is roughly equidistant between San Francisco and Milan. I'd like to spend more time in the galleries there, and Giacomo would be a fabulous tour guide. He travels there four or five times a year for business, and I think it would work out better for me than going to Milan."

"Interesting," Jamie said, sipping from her water glass, thoughts of her own house hunting forgotten.

The next day Ryan rapped on the door of Catherine's house and tried the knob. It was open, and she stepped inside, calling out, "Anybody home?"

"I'm here," Jennie replied from the dining room.

Ryan sauntered in, stopping in her tracks when Jen looked up at her. "What happened to you?"

Jennie's lower lip was red and swelled out half an inch. "Nothin' much." She held up a test, showing that she'd received a B+. "Good news!" she said, her smile making her mouth look worse.

"Yeah, that's really good news." Ryan walked up behind her and took the test in her hand, reading over Jen's answers. Then she put it down and squatted until their heads were on the same level. "What happened to your mouth?"

"Nothin'. You know how it is. You're just messing around and you catch an elbow or something. I bet you've gotten hit in the mouth a bunch of times."

Carefully, Ryan tugged on the edge of Jennie's lip, pulling it down. "Did it bleed a lot?"

Eyes wide, Jennie nodded. "A ton. Sandy put some ice in a washcloth and held it on there for a long time. It finally stopped bleeding, so we didn't have to go to the ER."

"So you were home when you were messing around?"

"Uhm…yeah. I was home."

"In the house?"

"No. Outside." She scuffed her chair back and got up. "I'm gonna get some more milk. You want some?"

"Sure."

Ryan sat down in the chair next to Jennie's and waited patiently. The girl returned in a couple of minutes and said, "I have no idea what happened in class today." She pointed at the title to a new chapter in her math book. "Can you explain this stuff in English?"

Ryan spent a moment looking at the chapter, then said casually, "Sure. What happened with your lip?"

"I *told* you. It's nothing."

"I believe you. I just want to know what happened." She bumped her shoulder against Jennie. "I'm really nosy."

"You are," Jennie agreed, reluctantly smiling. "Fine." She took a breath. "I was outside listening to my music when this other girl tried to take my player. She just wanted to look at it I guess, but I didn't want her to. I grabbed it back and we started to wrestle for it. My mouth must have hit her shoulder or something. It like *gushed* blood, and got all over her. Ha-ha," she added, with no sympathy.

"Huh. Who was the girl? Anybody I know?"

Jennie looked down, and clearly made an effort to sound casual. "Yeah. That Pebbles idiot."

"Mmm." Ryan touched her lip again, flipping it against her teeth. "Hit her shoulder, huh?"

"Yeah."

"Look me in the eye," Ryan said.

Jennie slowly complied. She gazed into Ryan's eyes for a few moments, and it was clear it made her uncomfortable.

"Tell me again how it happened."

Jennie gave her a murderous look and slumped down into her chair. "I was outside, sitting on the porch." What Jennie referred to as a porch was really just a poured concrete slab with one step down to the scraggly back yard.

"Yeah."

"That asshole came up from behind. I didn't hear her 'cause I had earphones on."

"Got it."

"She flopped down behind me, put her big, stupid head on my shoulder, and grabbed my boobs."

"Oh, shit," Ryan muttered.

"I shot my elbow into her gut and she punched me in the mouth. I *did* bleed all over her," she added proudly.

Ryan put an arm around Jennie's narrow shoulders and pulled her in for a hug. Jennie soaked up the affection, but she seemed remarkably composed.

"I'm really sorry, Jen. I wish…I wish you didn't have to put up with this kind of stuff."

"S'okay." She sat up and started thumbing through her book. Her voice was resigned when she said, "I'm used to it."

"Why make up a lie about it?"

"'Cause she's on thin ice. If Sandy reported this, they'd send her to the Youth Authority."

"Maybe that's where she belongs."

Jennie met Ryan's eyes and stared at her hotly. "Nobody belongs there. It's like a cage where you put dogs before you kill 'em."

That brought Ryan up short. She dropped her head into her hands and tried to think of something, anything to make Jennie feel safe. But she didn't have a thing to offer. Finally she said, "Do you want me to get involved?"

"No. You can't fix this." She pushed her book at Ryan. "Just tell me what this stuff says, okay?"

Jennie's driver arrived at five to pick her up. Catherine had been out, and she drove down the street just as Ryan was starting to walk home. "Hi there," Catherine said. "Want a ride?"

Ryan approached the car and leaned into the open window. "Think Marta would like to cook for us tonight?"

Looking surprised, Catherine said, "She'd love to. Just the two of us, or Jamie, too?"

Making a face, Ryan said, "It's hard to get rid of her. She'll probably find me. We may as well go pick her up."

"Get in, you tease."

Ryan opened the door and hopped in. "Did you have a nice day?" Catherine was dressed very casually: pale blue cotton slacks, and a white shirt, with a blue and white striped sweater draped over her shoulders.

"Very nice. I went down to Hillsborough to work on my garden."

Her clothes were pristine, not a hair out of place, and her manicure was flawless. Ryan didn't ask what kind of gardening left one looking so good, mainly because she was fairly certain Catherine always looked wonderful. "Did you get a lot done?"

"I'd say so. I had some fall bulbs planted to replace some annuals that weren't holding up well. Then I had a few rose bushes transplanted. I have to watch one section of the garden carefully or the roses can get mildewed."

"Ah, so your gardener was there today?"

Catherine paused a second, then said, "He's there every day, dear. Monday through Friday, that is. He has his own home." She laughed a little at that.

"I guess you can keep a guy busy."

"My parents had two full-time gardeners. They had a little less land than I have, but a much bigger garden. My father had a greenhouse just for his orchids."

She sighed heavily, and Ryan could almost see her reminiscing about her family home.

"It's too bad Jamie doesn't remember your dad much."

"And my mother not at all." She pulled up in front of the O'Flaherty house. "Should I park?"

"No. Jamie's always ready to go." She winked at Catherine. "Just like her mom."

As predicted, Jamie walked down the stairs with Ryan just a few minutes later. She scooted into the back seat of the coupe, kissing Catherine on the cheek as she did. "Ryan thinks this counts as taking me out to dinner, and I think you should dissuade her of that notion."

"Ryan," Catherine said in a stern voice, "take your poor fiancée out once in a while."

"That's exactly how often I take her out," Ryan said, grinning unrepentantly. "And since we're not getting married for at least a year, I can treat her badly for ten or eleven months and still pull it off."

"Incorrigible," Catherine teased.

"Jamie claims to like my incorrigi..." she trailed off. "Is there a word for that?"

"Do you mean a noun form?" Jamie asked.

Ryan waved a hand. "Never mind. If you two want to go out, I'm game."

Catherine squawked, "I couldn't go out looking like this!"

Ryan looked down at her own jeans and golf shirt, then took a quick glance into the back seat, noting Jamie's pressed chinos, green print blouse, and braided leather belt which perfectly matched brown tassel loafers. "My bad," she said. "I've got a reputation in this town and I can't be seen out with you two looking like yesterday's rubbish."

They went in and gathered in the kitchen around Marta, who was very pleased to have a couple of hearty eaters present. After going through her provisions they settled on the menu, then went up to the balcony to have a drink. Catherine convinced Ryan to try a Campari and soda, and after a couple of tiny sips she looked up and smiled. "I think I had this once. It's odd, but good. Bitter and refreshing."

"Precisely. I love it as an aperitif."

Ryan raised the tall glass. "Whatever," she agreed, taking another sip.

"You're in a playful mood," Jamie said.

"I know. I shouldn't be, but I kind of am."

"Why shouldn't you be, dear?" Catherine asked.

"It's Jen." Ryan took another sip and spent a moment thinking of how to explain what had happened. "She and her nemesis got into a scrap."

Catherine gasped, putting her hand over her mouth.

"I wish that's all it was. Pebbles grabbed Jennie's breasts and

Jen hit her. Pebbles slugged her in the mouth, giving her a fat lip."

"I won't stand for her being there another minute!" Catherine said, getting up from her chair.

Ryan tugged on her pant leg. "What are you going to do with her?"

"I'll figure that out after I get her away from that girl!"

"It's not that easy, Mom," Jamie said, looking a little ill. "We can't just take her away; she's a ward of the state."

Catherine sank into her chair. Clearly upset, she looked from Jamie to Ryan. "We've got to do something. We've got to."

"It's complicated by the fact that Jen didn't tell Sandy what really happened. She said they just had a fight. So Sandy's got both of them grounded for two weeks. Jen can't stay out past six."

"Why would she lie like that?" Jamie asked.

"Because Jennie's a nice person. Pebbles will get sent back to the Youth Authority if she's acting out sexually with the other girls. They have a zero tolerance policy for that."

"She should have thought of that before she touched Jennie."

"I agree," Ryan said, "but I'm not sure Pebbles is all there, if you know what I mean. At best, she seems slow. She's one of those kids who don't know how to interact with other people. The kid has no friends, and her mother doesn't want her back. She'll be very lucky to graduate from high school, if you ask me."

"Still…" Catherine said. "That's no excuse."

"No, but I hate to be the one to send her back to be warehoused. The last time I talked to Sandy about Jen not liking Pebbles, Sandy said Pebbles was one of the saddest cases she's worked with. I got the impression that Pebbles' parents don't like her, and she's a total outcast at the home."

"But is it safe to have her around other girls if she can't control herself? Maybe she needs more supervision."

Ryan shrugged. "She probably does. But it's hard to find the perfect situation for everyone."

"There has to be a way," Catherine insisted.

"Sure. They could send her to the Youth Authority, but Jennie acts like that's the seventh level of hell."

"Do you think that's true?" Catherine asked.

Shrugging, Ryan said, "I'm not sure I know enough to have a valid opinion. I know the social workers work their butts off to do what they can, but they have a bunch of girls they can't place. To them, Pebbles would seem pretty harmless."

Catherine's eyebrows shot up.

"She doesn't threaten Jen with a weapon," Ryan said, "and she only hits her when provoked. There are girls at Youth Authority who'd set you on fire for looking at them the wrong way."

Her whole body shivered as Catherine took a deep breath. "I feel sorry for Pebbles; I feel sorry for all of the children in that system, but Jennie's not ruined—yet. We can't let her get so traumatized that we lose her."

"I know, I know." Ryan sat back and took another drink. "I agree we have to do something. I wonder if Sandy would allow us to pay for Pebbles to see a good psychiatrist."

"I'm happy to do that," Catherine said. "I'll pay to send her anywhere that can help her." She leaned forward again. "But I won't have Pebbles frightening or hurting Jennie. We can't save everyone, but we have a chance with Jennie and I won't stand by and see that chance slip away."

After dinner, Ryan and Jamie decided to walk home, even though Catherine tried to talk them into accepting a ride. They were barely out the front door when Ryan said, "I've never seen your mom so determined. I'm proud of her."

"Yeah." Jamie smiled up at her partner. "I am too. Now we just have to decide what we can do."

"I'll see how I can finesse Sandy. I'll tell her that I'm worried about Jennie's temper and ask if there's a way to make sure she and Pebbles are separated all of the time."

"That's a sucky solution."

"I know, but it's all I've got for the moment." They walked the rest of the way in silence, each thinking of ideas only to quickly shoot them down.

The next day, Sandy was welcoming a new girl to the group home and she told Ryan that she couldn't make time to speak to her before five o'clock.

They decided to talk to Sandy without letting Jennie know. The girl was understandably anxious when they got involved, and they didn't want to make things more difficult for her.

Catherine agreed to wait until Jennie was finished with her homework and then drive her back to Oakland. That way, Catherine could call Jamie to warn her when they were close.

Since they had the larger part of their day free, Jamie and Ryan decided to go over to Berkeley and go sailing. The day wasn't as beautiful as either of them would have liked, but it was still brisk and breezy, a perfect day for Jamie to impart some of her sailing knowledge to her partner. Ryan was, as expected, a good student, eager to learn the arcane, fanciful names for everything connected to the pastime. They were out for a solid five hours, and as they left the Marina, Ryan said, "Why does sailing make me so tired?"

"I'm not sure, but it makes me tired too. But all we've got time to do is run by the house and check our mail, then go over to Oakland."

They were met at the Berkeley house by their entire staff. Ramundo and Esteban, the gardeners, were working diligently, with Maria Los and Zaragoza, the car washer, helping out. It was actually quite comical, watching four people working on a lawn the size of a postage stamp, but Ryan didn't see the humor in it. Once they were inside the house, she said, "We're paying that woman to come here three times a week and dust." She bent down and ran her hand along the wooden floor. Looking at it carefully, Ryan said, "There's not a speck of dirt. I think she washes the floors three times a week. She's gonna wash the varnish off! And the windows are so clean, I'm surprised we don't have birds flying into them."

"I'd be happy to have her come to San Francisco. Kevin and Conor's rooms could really use a good cleaning and I'm not going to do it. She'd probably get lost, but over time she'd figure out how to get there. She's quite resourceful."

"Nah. I don't think they'd like it, and I don't really like Maria Los in the house when I'm home. It reminds me of how lazy I am." She gave Jamie an unenthusiastic smile. "It just seems silly to have her wasting her time."

"Okay." Jamie sat on the edge of the big table by the front stairs. "Suggest an alternative."

"There's the obvious one."

"Nope. I'm not going to fire her. It's not her fault we're staying in San Francisco more than here."

"How about just laying her off? We can bring her back if we come back here full time."

Jamie looked at Ryan curiously. "What does she do for money when she's laid off? For someone who's always had to work, you sure don't have much empathy for a woman who has to support herself in a new country."

Clearly affronted, Ryan sputtered, "I have plenty of empathy. But nobody ever gave me a cushy job so I could go to school. She could get a job cleaning for somebody else. That's what I'd do if I were her."

"Well, you're not her, and I'm not going to break my promise. She wants to work, Ryan, why else would she be outside on her hands and knees deadheading the flowers? She could easily sit on her butt inside. We'd never have known the difference."

Looking chagrined, Ryan said, "I'm never going to like having someone clean my house. It makes me feel like I'm using her."

"She's using us to get money to eat and have a place to live. Think of it like that." She leaned forward and grasped Ryan by the waist, pulling her close. "I know this isn't your thing, but I'm going to keep them all busy—one way or another."

When they got to the group home, it was clear Sandy had had a trying day. She was too polite to state her feelings, but she looked as though she wanted to tell them to get lost. Sighing, she said, "Let's go out in the backyard to talk."

They went out the back door and crossed the pathetic yard to sit on a poorly maintained picnic table under an orange tree badly in need of pruning and watering. In her usual no-nonsense way, Sandy slapped her hands on the tabletop and said, "What do you need?"

Ryan jumped right in. "I'm worried about the fight that Pebbles and Jennie had. It doesn't seem like it was very serious, but Jennie's got a real temper and I hate to see her get in more serious trouble because of it."

"They're both grounded for two weeks, Ryan. I'm not gonna change that."

"I don't want you to; that's not why we came. I want to know if you can think of anything that would make sure they keep their distance."

"Look," she said, tiredly, "Jennie is the one with the temper. Pebbles is just… She comes on too strong and kids hate that. You can tell from a mile away that she's desperate to be their friend. Once someone gives off that vibe, the only people who want to be close to them are the ones who want to exploit them."

"Yeah," Ryan said, nodding. "I'm sure that's true."

"I know Jennie dislikes Pebbles, but you could help by making her see that Pebbles just needs some understanding." She put her fists to her eyes and rubbed them. "It pisses me off that every one of these kids has been where Pebbles is right now, and still none of them will give her a break."

Ryan made eye contact with Jamie then turned back to Sandy. "What's Pebbles' home situation?"

"The father is in and out. There are half siblings from each parent in the house. The mom has an on and off drug problem. Two of the younger kids are already in the system. Pretty common story."

"And nobody from her family visits her or talks to her?"

"Her grandmother on her father's side acts like she cares a little bit. She's from somewhere else…New Guinea?" She puzzled over whether that was the right place. "Samoa?"

"Does the grandmother speak English?" Ryan asked.

"Yeah. I got the feeling she might take Pebbles if she had any money. She seemed worried about her, and she was affectionate—something I don't see a lot of."

"Does she live around here?"

"Yeah. I don't remember exactly where, but she came to visit once and Pebbles said it took her most of the day on the bus to get here." Sandy laughed wryly. "Given how screwed up the bus system is, she might be as close as San Leandro."

They sat in silence for a couple of moments, then Jamie said, "Do the girls clean the house?"

"Yeah. Why?" There was an edge to Sandy's voice.

"The young woman who cleans our house has some free time. If you need help, I could pay to have her do some of the things you don't have time for."

"No thanks. I think the house is clean enough. Besides, the girls need to do jobs to give them some responsibility." She looked around at the desolate landscape. "Have you got a gardener?"

They went back in through the house and Jamie got to meet Pebbles, who was sitting in the living room watching TV. She was a very big girl: tall, stocky, and seriously overweight. She was probably mixed race, but it wasn't obvious what the mix was. Her hair was kinky, a muted orange color, and just long enough to not be able to style in any attractive way. Her vacant expression would easily lead one to believe there was not a lot going on inside her head.

When they got outside, Jamie said, "Well, I've got another

job for the gardeners, but nothing for Maria Los. Maybe I'll just have her tag along with them."

"Yeah," Ryan said, giving her a smirk. "I've been worried sick about those gardeners."

"We can't save the world, honey. But we *can* take a little bite whenever we can. I've got four people I'm going to help succeed in this country." She pinched Ryan on the nose. "Whether or not you approve."

They decided to go back to Berkeley and leave Jamie's car there so Zaragoza could wash it. They were sitting around waiting for Catherine when Ryan said, "What's the name of the church on the next corner?"

"I think it's the First Presbyterian. Why?"

"I'm gonna call over there and ask them if they have cars that need washing or houses that need cleaning. If Maria Los wanted to be a gardener, she probably would have been one by now."

Jamie smiled as her partner went upstairs to make the call. Ryan might talk tough, but she wouldn't have the heart to force Maria Los to do something she wasn't prepared for. Luckily, Ryan would now think of ways to utilize their human capital, saving Jamie the trouble. It was a victory for all involved.

Catherine arrived by six thirty and she was noticeably distressed. "That poor little girl," she said, dropping inelegantly into a chair. "Her lip was swollen and she just didn't act like herself. We had a long talk on the way over here and even though she denied it, I got the impression that she's afraid of Pebbles."

Ryan was leaning up against the table in the hallway, her arms crossed over her chest. "I think Jennie can take care of herself in most situations, but I know she's worried. I think she's afraid Pebbles will do something again and she'll go nuclear on her and wind up in jail."

"What are we going to do?" Catherine asked.

"We got a shred of good news," Jamie said. "Sandy says that Pebbles has a grandmother who lives somewhere in the area.

Maybe we could find some way to have her get custody. Pebbles is almost sixteen. If we could support her until she's out of high school, we could get her out of the group home and keep her out of the Youth Authority."

"She and her grandmother can move into my house in Hillsborough," Catherine said decisively. "I'd gladly send her to Jamie's prep school."

Jamie spent a millisecond trying to see Pebbles fitting into the elite prep school, where Jamie herself had been far from the wealthiest student. "I think Pebbles would be better off staying in Oakland. She apparently doesn't have any friends, but she could probably use some stability."

"I'm going to try to get in touch with her grandmother and see if we can work something out," Ryan said. To Jamie, she said, "Would you ask your therapist if there's anything that can be done for a kid who's socially maladjusted? Pebbles needs someone who cares about her, someone who can give her some clues about how to behave. I'd do it, but—"

"No way," Jamie said, her tone leaving no question about her seriousness. "You've got all you can handle."

Smiling, Ryan said, "That was going to be the end of my sentence. Thanks for saving me the breath."

"You have to admit you have a bad track record when it comes to overcommitting," Catherine teased.

Ryan nodded, a half grin on her face. "I have so much free time this summer, I feel like I could take on ten or fifteen new projects. But if I go to graduate school next year, I'll be swamped again. And I'm pretty confident that helping poor Pebbles would be a full-time job." She shook her head. "The first thing I'd do is ask her if she wanted to change her name. When you look like her, and your name is Pebbles, you're begging for trouble."

The next afternoon, Ryan and Jamie went over to Catherine's. When the pair walked in the front door and said hello, Jennie eyed them nervously. "Why are both of you guys here? Did Sandy say something yesterday?"

Jamie walked over to her and rubbed her hand across Jennie's pale hair. "It's nice to see you, too."

"Why were you there when I wasn't? The other girls teased me all night."

"I'm sorry about that, kiddo. We thought we could have a chat with Sandy and not upset you. Guess that didn't work." She offered a quick hug. "Is my mom home?"

Now looking terrified, Jennie said, "You need your mom, too? What did I do?"

Ryan put a hand on her shoulder and rocked her back and forth in her seat. "Nothing. That we know of." She leaned over and kissed Jennie's head. "We just want to talk about your living situation."

Jennie sank down into her chair. "It sucks."

"We know that part. We wanted to talk about some specifics."

Catherine walked into the room and greeted her guests. Ryan said, "I was just telling Jennie that we want to talk about the group home."

Catherine sat down right next to the girl and Jamie and Ryan moved to the other side of the table and took their chairs.

Ryan began, "I want to make sure you know how seriously we all take what happened between you and Pebbles. There's no excuse for her touching you that way, and we're working together to make sure it doesn't happen again."

Jennie said grumpily, "She'll just do something else. She doesn't know what she's doing half the time anyway."

Catherine sat up a little straighter in her chair. "Does she do drugs?"

"Nah. She's just a gluffer."

"Gluffer?" all three of them asked, almost in unison.

"She huffs," Jennie said. She mimed holding a bag and putting it over her nose and mouth and inhaling deeply. "Head cleaner."

"Does Sandy know about this?"

Two confused sets of eyes looked at Ryan. "What are you two talking about?" Catherine asked.

"Apparently Pebbles abuses inhalants."

"Not just *apparently*; I've seen her do it. Dozens of times. She's high most of the time." She cocked her head, looking at Ryan curiously. "You couldn't tell?"

Looking slightly embarrassed, Ryan said, "I thought she was just slow."

Jennie laughed, but Catherine and Jamie were still watching the exchange in confusion.

"Inhalants?" Catherine asked.

Jamie said, "Like sniffing glue?"

"She likes Whip-Its, but they won't let her into the grocery stores around us because they caught her stealing stuff too many times. Most of the time she has to use gasoline."

"I feel like I'm going to be sick," Catherine said, "and I'm not even sure what we're talking about."

"What's a Whip-It?" Jamie asked.

Showing far too much knowledge about the topic, Jennie said, "You take an aerosol can, like one for whipped cream, and you tilt it and breathe the noz in."

Astounded, Catherine said, "What is noz and what does it do to you?"

Jennie shrugged, but it was clear to everyone that she knew, probably from first-hand experience.

Ryan said, "Nitrous oxide, laughing gas. It gives you a pretty short high. You're euphoric for a few seconds, then you're groggy for a little longer."

Jamie almost volunteered that she was familiar with nitrous oxide from Mia's adventures, but she caught herself before revealing that information to Jennie.

"Gasoline makes you high, too?" Catherine asked.

Again Jennie shrugged and Ryan got up to go over to her side of the table. She crouched down so they were nose to nose. "If you've been sniffing gasoline…"

Jennie held both hands up. "I swear I never have. I swear it, Ryan."

"That can kill you, Jen. Easily. I'm being one hundred percent honest with you. Noz is bad, but gasoline is deadly."

"It smells bad, too. Pebbles used to make me throw clean clothes to her outside the window so Sandy wouldn't smell her." She made a face. "Half the time she throws up after she does it. She's *so* disgusting. I think Sandy likes her just because she washes her own clothes. She doesn't know Pebbles does it so she doesn't stink up the house and get caught."

Ryan stood and started to pace back and forth across the dining room. "Why didn't you ever tell us this?"

Sulking, Jennie grumbled, "You don't do that to people."

"What's your new roommate doing, lighting herself on fire? Sword swallowing? Whatever it is, I'm sure we won't find out until she kills herself or you." Ryan was so agitated, her cheeks were flushed and her eyes were like lasers as they scanned around the room.

"She doesn't do anything bad." Jennie swallowed. "Nothing that can hurt *me* at least."

"Oh fuck." All of the fire went out of Ryan and she grabbed a chair and slumped into it. "This can't go on."

"I'm doing the best I can," Jennie said, her eyes filling with tears. "I'd get my ass kicked bad if I told what they were all doing."

Catherine leaned over and wrapped Jennie in her arms. She shot a disapproving glance at Ryan as she murmured soothing words to Jen. "It's going to be fine, dear. We'll help you get through this."

Ryan got up and stood behind the pair, putting her hand on Jennie's head. "I'm sorry, buddy. I just get so worried about you." She ruffled her hair. "You know how much I care about you, don't you?"

"Yeah," Jennie said, the word muffled by Catherine's embrace. The girl stayed just where she was, looking like a wilted flower that slowly gained strength after a good rain. Finally she sat up and rubbed her eyes. "I'm trying to be good, but it's hard."

"You're doing your best," Ryan agreed. She went back to sit by Jamie.

"What can we do?" Catherine asked Jennie. "How can we help you?"

"Can you get rid of Pebbles? She sucks bad, and Sandy's always on her side."

"I think Sandy feels bad for her. It doesn't sound like Pebbles has any friends."

Jennie scowled. "She's a huge asshat who takes your stuff and eats your food and grabs you if she thinks she can get away with it. And she can! She takes the food right off my plate the second nobody's watching her."

"We'll figure something out, Jen," Jamie said. "I know you don't want to tell on your friends, but if anyone is doing anything dangerous…"

"Just Pebbles," she insisted. "I've seen her light a cigarette while she's got a cup full of kerosene in her hand. "

"Okay!" Ryan said brightly, standing up and clapping her hands together. "Who feels better?"

Looking at her through hooded eyes, Jennie said, "You said to tell you."

"I'm glad you did. It just makes me want to put each of you on your own separate island." She walked over and chucked Jennie gently on the arm.

"What are you gonna do?"

"I'm trying to make contact with Pebble's grandmother. I haven't had much luck, and Sandy says she can't help because of privacy issues."

"I'll get the number for you," Jennie volunteered. "I know where Pebbles keeps her important stuff. She's got numbers and addresses in a notebook."

Ryan shrugged. "Go for it. Just don't set anything on fire while you're looking."

They had a snack together in the kitchen, with Jamie, Ryan and Catherine having some guacamole and chips while Jennie had a couple of tacos and a quesadilla. "Pebbles can't get my food here," she said, happily munching away.

"We'll try to make sure that doesn't happen at the house, either," Catherine said.

"It's not too bad most of the time. Two of the girls aren't bad at all. I wouldn't want to be friends with them or anything, but they're not horrible."

"A glowing endorsement," Ryan said, wryly. "How are your school buddies?"

"They're good. I talk to them, but I haven't really seen 'em. I'd never have them over to my house, and I don't want them to know I have some guy pick me up in a black car, so I can't go to their houses."

"Have they asked you, dear?" Catherine asked.

"Sure. But I just don't think I can swing it."

"When you're not grounded, you can have them come over here. Marta and I would love to entertain your friends."

Jennie smiled for a moment, then her expression collapsed into another frown. "How could I explain who you were?"

"Hmm, you could say I was your—"

"Tell the truth," Ryan said, "Catherine's your friend. She lives close to school, so you come over here to avoid the bad traffic going back to Oakland. It's lots easier if you keep things as honest as you can."

Jennie smiled the way she often did when she thought Ryan was being naïve. "Yeah, that works great."

By the next afternoon Ryan had the phone number for Pebbles' grandmother. She sat at her desk in her bedroom in San Francisco and carefully dialed the number. "Mrs. Muliutufaga?" she asked, grimacing at the way she had probably mangled the name. It was only after she had ascertained that this was in fact Pebbles' grandmother that she realized she had no easy way to explain who she was or why she was calling.

Jamie went downstairs and saw that Ryan was still on the phone. When she saw her partner nodding and talking with her hands, she knew things weren't going well since Ryan usually only used her hands to talk when her words weren't getting the job done.

"I understand that, ma'am. I'm sure you *have* had a lot of people make promises to you, but if you'll let me come and visit you…" She turned around in her swivel chair and made a face. "No, ma'am. No, I don't, ma'am. Okay. You do that, and I'll call you back." She hung up and said, "I'll save you the dissertation and just say that she's going to call Sandy to see if I'm as crazy as I sound."

Jamie came over and sat on her lap. "What's going to happen when Sandy tells her you're crazier than you sound?"

Ryan dropped her head against Jamie's shoulder. "Everybody loves a comic," she mumbled.

Chapter Sixteen

After dinner that night Jamie and Ryan decided to go on their never-ending quest for great ice cream. They wanted to go by Catherine's house at some point, but neither of them knew of any good spots in Pacific Heights, so they decided they'd have to keep walking until they found one. Given how determined Ryan was when she was really fixated on something, Jamie decided they'd better stop by her mother's first, just in case they had to leave the county to complete their quest.

It was around eight p.m., and when they got close to the house they saw Conor tossing his heavy tool belt into the passenger seat of his truck.

"What did you talk Marta into making you for dinner?" Ryan asked, coming up behind him and slapping him on the back.

He turned around, looking tired and not particularly happy. "Nothing. I've got too much to do to spend my time eating. I'm gonna go get something now."

"We have lots of leftovers," Jamie said. "Go on home and you can watch the Giants on TV."

He smiled gratefully. "Best offer I've had all day." He walked around to the driver's side and gave them a halfhearted wave before getting in the idling truck and taking off.

"I wonder why Marta didn't try to get him to eat dinner," Jamie said.

"No idea."

They went into the house and Marta directed them to the upstairs balcony. It was a lovely, remarkably warm night, but Catherine still had her heat lamps on. After saying hello, they all sat down.

"Well, I had to use every bit of my Irish gift for gab, but it looks like I've talked Pebbles' grandmother into taking her to Samoa for a visit."

Catherine cocked her head, looking puzzled. "That's nice, dear, but how does that help?"

"I'm simply trying to get us a little breathing room. The grandmother doesn't work, so she's got the time to go for a nice long trip. She's living with one of her sons and his family, and it sounds like she hates it."

"Is that why she hasn't tried to keep Pebbles with her?"

Frowning, Ryan said, "I got that impression. She doesn't speak great English, so we were both guessing at what the other had to say."

"Do you know what language she speaks?" Jamie asked. "Maybe we know someone…

"I think Samoans speak…Samoan?" Ryan chuckled. "I could take all I know about Samoa and put it into a flea's belly-button."

Jamie piped up, "I don't know much more than you do, and Samoan isn't one of my languages. But if Pebbles is out of the picture for a while, we can concentrate on figuring out what we can do for the long term."

"I've been thinking about this a lot," Catherine said. She shifted forward to sit on the edge of her chair. "The solution is for me to petition the court for custody of Jennie."

Ryan and Jamie exchanged startled looks. "Would you really do that?" Jamie asked. "That would fix everything, but…"

Looking pleased, Catherine said, "It's not how I envisioned my life at this point, but I love that child and I can't stand to see her mistreated."

Jamie was almost giggling with excitement but when she

turned and saw the look on Ryan's face, her smile died. "What's wrong?"

"It would be very difficult to get custody, and it would take a long time."

"Don't you think it's a good idea?" Jamie persisted.

Showing just a nanosecond of annoyance, Ryan said, "Of course I do. It would be an awful lot of work, but it would be great for Jen. I'm just worried that by the time we get it all settled, Jennie will have aged out of the system."

"Oh, Ryan, don't be such a pessimist. We have a United States senator at our disposal. That's another good reason to get moving on this. We've only got a couple of months until Jim's back home."

Ryan stood up. "We're going in search of fantastic ice cream. Want to go with us?"

"No, but thank you. I'm going to sit here and make plans. Now I'm almost sorry I'm turning the second best bedroom into my library. That would have been a fantastic place for Jennie." She inclined her head toward the living space. "Is Conor still here?"

"He was leaving just as we came in," Jamie said. "I was surprised Marta didn't feed him."

"Mmm. I'm sure she tried."

It looked to Ryan as though Catherine knew exactly why Conor wasn't staying for dinner. She felt a quick, short burst of anger, then immediately reminded herself that this was one area where she couldn't favor Conor. Catherine had done the right thing in rebuffing him, but it was hard to ignore years of conditioning to always be on her brother's side.

Once they were outside, Jamie opened her mouth to speak but Ryan forestalled her. "I think it's fabulously generous of your mother to want to help Jennie, but I don't think she has any idea how difficult it would be."

Clearly annoyed, Jamie said, "Did I really turn out that

bad?"

"That's hardly what I'm saying. You weren't dropped onto your parents' doorstep when you were going into your sophomore year of high school."

"I realize that—"

"There are many sides to our little friend," Ryan interrupted. "And Jennie consistently shows her most angelic one to your mom. I'm not saying she's not a great kid, because you know I think she is, but you also know she does exactly what she wants, and your mom would have to be on her toes every minute. That would be a huge adjustment for her."

"Mom's not stupid; she saw what happened when Jennie wanted to go to your softball game. She'll figure out a way to make it work. And she's got Marta to help her."

"I know Marta was a ton of help when you were a little girl, but we should probably ask if she's willing to do it again. That was twenty years ago." Ryan could have brought up the fact that Jennie had easily slipped away from Marta's care just a few weeks ago, but she didn't want to belabor the point.

"Even if my mom didn't have a clue, it would still be better for Jennie to live somewhere where she was wanted. If nothing else, my mom could afford to send her to the best shrinks in town if she screws her up any worse."

Ryan didn't answer. She just put her arm around Jamie's shoulders as they continued in their search for the perfect ice cream.

The next morning, Catherine and Maeve were out for an early morning walk, bundled up against the chilly temperatures and the damp July fog. They were in Golden Gate Park and the morning air was redolent of redwood bark and the humus that had just been spread around the beds of the rose garden.

"You'll never guess what I'm considering doing," Catherine said.

"Then I won't try. Just tell me."

"I'm thinking of asking the court for permission to get custody of Jennie."

Maeve stopped dead in her tracks. "Custody? Full-time custody?"

"Yes, full-time. Things aren't going well for her, and I'm concerned for her safety."

They started walking again, but much more slowly this time. "Is she in danger?"

"In many ways, yes. There are only eight girls in her group home, but it's impossible for one person to keep track of that many teenagers."

"One person?"

"There are more than that, but one woman is in charge. Someone comes in to cook and there are different women who come in overnight and weekends, but Sandy has the authority, and she's the one the girls go to for permission and guidance. I think she does a very good job, but it's just not enough. It's nothing like a home."

"I can imagine that's true, but why now?"

"Jennie's been having trouble with one of the other girls. As you can imagine, they're a pretty troubled bunch. It's nothing horrible; it's simply stressful for her and makes her feel unsafe. She's such a sweet child that it tears at my heart to see her so troubled."

They were walking arm in arm and Maeve gently squeezed Catherine's. "You're a good soul. Jennie's lucky to have you."

"I'm lucky to have *her*. She's given me a new perspective by letting me see how lucky I am. I don't think it will be easy, in any sense, but Jim has been quite enthusiastic and he's promised to call in any favors he can to help me if I need it."

Maeve hated to immediately think the worst of Jim, but so far he'd earned every bit of suspicion she could muster. "He thinks your getting legal custody of Jennie is a good idea?"

"Surprisingly, yes. I spoke to him before I left the house. He's very much in favor of it."

"Isn't that interesting," Maeve said thoughtfully. "Interesting indeed." Silently, Maeve wondered how this could benefit him. He might have been a good fellow, as Jamie insisted, but he'd certainly hidden his selflessness very, very well.

Jamie woke on Saturday morning to find Ryan's side of the bed cool. "Honey?" she mumbled groggily.

"Right here." Ryan got up from her desk chair and went to sit on the edge of the bed. Several soft kisses on Jamie's bare neck and back had both of them purring with pleasure.

"Get back in bed," Jamie demanded.

"Can't. We're taking Cait to the park. Did you forget?"

"This early?"

"It's eight o'clock. That's not early."

Opening one eye to see if Ryan was teasing, Jamie realized she was perfectly serious. "Is she at home?"

"No. Da and my aunt have her. Tommy's working at OFC today and Annie's on the seven a.m. shift at the hospital." Ryan tickled Jamie's side. "I told Da we'd be by early to mind the baby. They want to be off to get the messages," she said this in an Irish accent that sounded very much like Martin's.

"The messages." Jamie giggled. "After all these years, they still don't say 'errands.'"

"Would you start saying 'messages' if you moved to Ireland?"

"Point taken. Why don't you go get Caitlin? I'll lie here and think about getting up."

Ryan placed a few wet kisses across her forehead and cheeks. "You're a lazy girl, but I love you. We'll bring you breakfast, even though you've done nothing to deserve it." Ryan gave her a last kiss and bounded up the stairs, leaving Jamie to wonder for a few moments about her prodigious energy before she contentedly fell back to sleep.

When Ryan hurried up the stairs to her aunt's house, Caitlin was at the storm door, slapping it with her hands, calling out her version of Jamie's name, "May-me! May-me!"

Ryan opened the door and caught Caitlin in her arms. "Why is she your favorite? Hmm?" She kissed the baby until she squealed with delight, then they went into the kitchen where it seemed her father and aunt spent the majority of their time. Indeed, they were at the small table by the window, still sipping tea and reading the paper.

"Where's your best half?" Martin asked.

"Does anyone notice I'm here?" She bent to kiss her father, then her aunt. "Caitlin only notices Jamie's absence too." She sat down, with Cait on her lap. "What's on your agenda for the day?"

"Nothing too unique," Maeve said. "It's lovely to have Marty home on a Saturday, and I plan on enjoying every moment. We thought we'd start by going to Ferry Street for the market."

"Oh, cool. Get us somc stone fruit, will you? I like everything with a pit."

"Of course. Anything else?"

"No. I just like to have fruit around for snacks. Jamie's in charge of everything else and I never know what she's gonna cook."

"Kevin says he's been exposed to a whole array of dishes he's never had before," Maeve said.

"Kevin isn't very experimental on his own," Ryan agreed. "But he eats whatever's put in front of him."

Laughing, Maeve agreed. "My boys have always been good eaters."

Caitlin began to struggle, wanting to get moving, and Ryan started to get up to leave. But Martin put a hand on her leg. "Let the baby go for a moment. We wanted to talk to you and now seems like a good time."

Ryan's immediate reaction to any overtures of serious conversations was, as always, dread. "What's wrong?"

"Nothing. For the love of Mike, nothing is wrong. We want

to talk about Jennie."

Ryan made a face, then put the baby on the floor. Caitlin got under the table and started clambering around their shoes. Ryan took a look under the tablecloth, watching her sing a song to herself as she studied Martin's and Ryan's respective laces. "Odd kid," she teased.

"Well," Martin began, "your aunt and I have discussed this at great length. We're agreed that Catherine would be taking on too big a job to get custody of the girl."

Ryan tilted her head back. "Thank God. I've been thinking I was the only one who felt that way."

"You know how much we both love Catherine," Maeve said, "but Jennie's not an easy child. If she were, she wouldn't be in the position she's in now."

"Agreed," Ryan said. "Catherine hasn't been there when she runs away or gets caught smoking grass. She also hasn't had to chase her through Oakland in the middle of the night when she's on the corner with a bunch of drug addicts and prostitutes." She shivered at the memory.

"So what's to be done? She's can't stay where she is," Martin said firmly. "She's not safe in that place."

"She might be," Ryan said. "We're close to getting the girl who's causing the trouble out of town for a few weeks. Her grandmother's taking her to Samoa, their family home. We're hoping Pebbles likes it and will want to live there. She clearly could use a fresh start."

"But who will take *that* girl's place?" Maeve asked. "You don't wind up in a group home because you're well behaved."

Ryan shrugged. "It happens. Not often, but some of the girls are just throw-aways because they're gay."

"Ahh, but who can go through that and be well behaved?" Martin asked. "It's hard enough to be a teenager these days. Having your parents throw you out of the house has to send a child half off her rocker."

"True. But what do we do? You've clearly pointed out that

Jamie and I aren't equipped to handle her."

"No, but we are," Martin said, the gravity of his tone reflecting the seriousness of the issue.

"You?" Ryan looked from her aunt to her father. "You'd do that?"

"I think we have to," Maeve said. "Neither of us anticipated having a teenager appear on our doorstep, but we can't let the girl be lost."

Ryan nodded, then looked down at Caitlin, busily playing with shoes. "You've got very kind grandparents, kiddo." She smiled at her aunt. "But you've got your hands full. Caitlin's going to be more work for you now that she can get into everything."

"True. But Jennie could help out with her."

Scratching her head, Ryan said, "I'm not sure about that. For short periods of time, maybe, but Jennie has a lot to learn about taking care of herself before I'd trust her with the baby."

"Jennie's a lovely child," Martin said. "She just needs some consistency."

"I agree. But giving it to her will take an awful lot of work. Are you sure you want to spend a good part of your lives doing that?"

Martin sighed. "No, it's not what we want. But someone has to do it, and we're the most able."

Ryan reached down and snatched Caitlin from under the table, hoisting her into the air. The baby stuck her arms and legs out, begging to have Ryan make her into an airplane. Ryan stood and swooped her around the room, making jet sounds. When her arms were tired, she tucked Caitlin under one of them and started for the door. "Let's keep kicking the idea around. Maybe we should have a family meeting."

"All right," Maeve said. "Let's have dinner at the house." Ryan kissed each of them goodbye, then headed for home, already planning the confab.

The meeting was planned for the following Friday evening,

the first night everyone involved was available. Mid-week, Ryan got the news that Pebbles and her grandmother would be flying to Pago Pago on the weekend and would be gone until school began.

"Woo-hoo!" she shouted when Sandy called with the update. She ran through the house to find Jamie. "Good news! Pebbles is out of the equation until school starts. We've got a little breathing room."

"Thank God," Jamie sighed. "I hope it's a tropical paradise and Pebbles loves it so much she insists on staying."

"Me too, as much for her sake as Jen's. Being with her grandmother might straighten her out a little bit."

"Couldn't hurt," Jamie said. "I hope."

Chapter Seventeen

In Colorado Springs, Mia was happily ensconced in their new apartment, playing homemaker while Jordan chased her dream. But when Jordan came home one Monday night in July, Mia knew something was wrong as soon as she stepped in the door.

"What happened?" Mia demanded.

Jordan dropped her bag and walked into the kitchen where Mia was preparing an early dinner. She sat down on a stool and let her hands dangle between her legs. Taking a breath, she said, "The coaches made a cut this morning. We were all on the court together on Saturday, but there was one less outside hitter this morning."

"Which one?'

"Ekaterina."

"Ekaterina! What happened? It's July the…" she looked at the calendar on the wall, "twenty-third. The next cut was supposed to be August first."

"It was supposed to be. I guess they figured we weren't tense enough, so they added in another level of anxiety." She dropped her head to her arms, resting on the counter before her. "If I wasn't so worried about being caught, I'd try to get some Valium or something. I'm so nervous, my stomach's upset most of the time."

Mia put down her knife and went to stand behind Jordan. Offering the only support she knew how to give, she wrapped her in a tight hug and held on.

The next day, afternoon practice was about to start when Toni came up beside Jordan. "One less person to worry about, huh?"

"Uhm, I guess so. But I didn't think she was the weakest of the six of us."

Toni slapped Jordan hard on the butt. "No, she wasn't." Grinning evilly, she went to take her position, leaving Jordan feeling like vomiting from anxiety.

As soon as practice was over, Jordan jogged over to Toni to catch her before she had a chance to leave. "What did you mean when you said—"

"Shh," Toni interrupted. "It's not safe to talk here. Come over to the apartment."

Jordan glanced at the clock on the wall. "Mia's usually making dinner by now. I don't want to keep her waiting."

"Then forget about it. It's no big deal."

Toni started to walk away but Jordan dashed to catch her. "Can I call you?"

"Not tonight. I'm gonna take a nap and then go out. Maybe we could get together tomorrow."

Jordan knew she wouldn't be able to get a moment's rest until she knew what Toni knew. "Can I come over now?"

Smiling seductively, Toni said, "Sure. You can give me a ride. We'll beat the other girls home and we can talk in private."

Jordan shivered when she entered their old apartment. There was something so transient about it that she wondered how she'd been able to stay there for as long as she had. They went directly into Toni's room and she closed the door.

"I'll turn on some music so the other girls don't know you're here."

"Why do we have to be so secretive?"

"Because you're competing against them." Toni gave her a look that indicated her surprise at Jordan's naiveté. "To have winners, you have to have losers."

"Yeah, I know, but I feel like I'm in this with all of the other outside hitters. I liked Ekaterina. God," she let out a breath. "She came here to college and got citizenship just so she could make the team. She had so much invested..."

Toni tapped Jordan's forehead. "Wrong, wrong, wrong."

She started to take off her warm-up suit, acting as though she were alone. That wasn't unusual behavior for her, but it still discomfited Jordan. The room was so small there was nowhere to hide, and she felt stupid facing the wall, so she sat on the bed and averted her eyes.

"The only thing you have in common with the other two rookies," Toni continued, "is that you all should want the other two to go home. Their loss is your gain." She picked up a bottle of lotion and started rubbing it into her arms. "Taking so many showers is killing my skin."

"After lunch you said that Ekaterina wasn't the least talented outside hitter. What did you mean by that?"

"Just what I said. She's better than Makela, and pretty comparable to you. So you can thank me for helping to get rid of her." Toni sat down on the opposite side of the bed and continued to massage lotion into her muscular arms.

"What you mean by that?" Jordan was so shocked by her statement that her naturally high voice went up even higher, making her sound shrill.

"I talked to the coach."

"About what?"

Toni turned and looked at her. "I know you're not stupid, but you're sure acting it. I did a little politicking for you. I figured if we got rid of Ekaterina sooner rather than later, Makela can go next. That will let him make an easier cut at outside hitter and he can make the tough decision about which libero to keep."

"And you think he listened to you?" Jordan shook her head. "I didn't mean that like it sounded. I'm just surprised he'd take advice from a player."

"Well, not from just any player. He listens to a couple of us.

We go way back, you know. He trusts my judgment; he knows I understand what it takes to have a team rather than a bunch of good players." She turned around again, facing away from Jordan. Bending her arm behind herself she held out the lotion. "Will you put some of this on my back?"

Mechanically, Jordan did as she was asked, the ramifications of Toni's information flying around in her head. She hardly noticed when Toni pulled away and got under the sheet.

"Why don't you join me?" she asked, breaking Jordan from her reverie.

"Do *what*?"

Holding the sheet up in invitation, as well as displaying her very attractive naked body, Toni said, "You don't want the other girls to see you leave. You already told Mia you're gonna be late, so slide on in and grab a…nap."

The words were relatively harmless, really quite benign, but the way Toni stressed the last word and held Jordan's gaze made her immediately jump to her feet. "I've got to go," she said, totally flustered.

Patiently, Toni said, "I told you not to let the other girls see you here. They'll know we've been talking, and I don't want them to know I have coach's ear."

"They won't know that. Why can't we just be talking?"

Sighing, Toni said, "Nobody just talks at this point in training camp. It's like a reality show, Jordan. You have to be plotting how to get the other people off the island."

"That's not what I'm good at. I need to focus on playing as well as I can."

"That's a given. Everybody has to do that, even me, and I'm a lock. But you have to do more. You have to make your alliances." She held the sheet even further away from herself. "Come on and lie down. No one needs to know. There's no better stress reliever."

In seconds, sweat covered Jordan's body. She had no idea whether Toni was telling the truth. Maybe she really did have their coach's ear, but it didn't matter. She had to get out of this room, and she had to go now. With whatever presence of mind she could summon, she decided to look clueless rather than sick to her stomach at the thought of having sex with Toni.

"I really wish I could, because I'm really tired. I told Mia I'd just be a few minutes, and I don't want her to call and…wake us up." Jordan hurried towards the door, turning the knob and sliding out before Toni could protest.

Jordan sat right outside their new apartment, talking to Ryan on the phone. She'd gone over the entire incident three times but she still needed reassurance. "Are you *sure* she was hitting on me?"

"Pinning you to the bed and ripping your clothes off would have been the next step. What she did was inexcusable. You've gotta go to the coach and report her."

"For what? She's not on the coaching staff. There's no rule that says you can't try to get your teammates to have sex with you. Besides, they'd believe her over me if she's as close to the coach as she says she is."

"She's an asshole, and she'll probably do it to somebody else if you don't stop her."

"Don't put that kind of pressure on me right now," Jordan said, her voice shaking. "I've got fifteen years of work riding on this. Besides, she hasn't shown any interest in any of the other girls. I don't want to be cold, but everybody else is gonna have to look out for herself."

"Don't worry about it. That was just my gut response. You *do* need to take care of yourself right now, and you need to keep Mia away from Toni, 'cause she'll kill her, and I'm not kidding."

Jordan knew that she was completely inept at hiding her feelings. She only hoped she could make Mia think she was upset about what she'd learned from Toni, rather than what Toni had offered. Her first mistake was going into the apartment with a fake cheerful smile.

"Honey, I'm home."

Mia walked into the living room and cocked her head. Coming up to stand right in front of Jordan, she said, "Something's not right. That smile doesn't match the rest of the package." She took a moment to give Jordan a sincere welcome home kiss, then she backed away again, her intent brown eyes roaming over Jordan's face and body. "I can't tell if you're nervous or excited or frightened." She ran her hand across Jordan's cheek. "But whatever it is, you're about to explode."

"Dammit! Ryan might give good advice, but it never works."

Mia took Jordan by the hand and led her over to the sofa, then she gave her a push and Jordan flopped down. Straddling her lap, Mia rested all of her weight on Jordan's thighs. "You're bigger than I am, and you're stronger, but I don't think you can get up from this position unless I let you. And I'm not letting you up until you tell me the truth. You're trying to hide something from me, and you're horrible at it."

Jordan looked up into Mia's eyes and knew she had to get it over with. "It turns out that Toni talked to the coach and convinced him to get rid of Ekaterina to make the competition easier for me."

Mia raised one eyebrow dramatically. "She's no humanitarian."

"She's not." Jordan looked down, staring at the stripes on Mia's shirt.

Chucking a finger under Jordan's chin, Mia tilted her head up. "Tell me what happened."

Sighing in defeat, Jordan said, "She just told me that's what she did, and she told me that I needed to make alliances. She said it wasn't enough to play well."

"At what point did she proposition you?"

She said it so calmly Jordan thought they all might escape without bloodshed. "After she told me that. She said we should take a nap together."

Looking puzzled, and still calm, Mia said, "A nap? She

wanted to take a nap?"

"Yeah." It took Jordan a few seconds to get the rest of it out. "She was naked and lying in bed, and she said nobody had to know. She said it would be good for me." She gulped. "Ryan says that was a threat."

Her eyebrows twitched together just once, then Mia got up and went into the kitchen. When she emerged she was holding her car keys, striding for the door. Jordan jumped up and blocked her way, fighting to keep her balance when Mia tried to push past her.

"Stand aside," she said, still as calm as before.

"No!" Jordan put her hands alongside Mia's face and forced her to look at her. "You can't go over there."

"Watch me."

Mia hit Jordan with her hip, almost knocking her over. As Jordan struggled to stay upright, she wrapped her arms around Mia and wrestled her to the sofa. But Mia wasn't going down without a fight and she tried to slither away, forcing them both to the ground.

"You'll get me thrown off the team," Jordan pleaded. "Please don't kill her."

"I'm not gonna kill her," Mia scoffed. "Killing's too easy. I'm gonna make her *wish* I'd killed her." She kicked her legs, trying to free herself, but only managed to have Jordan roll on top of her.

"Please torture her after I make the team or get cut. I'll help you torture her then. Really." Her face was red and veins throbbed on her temples. Slowly, Mia released her hold.

"I have to do something," she growled, now sitting up. "I've got to get rid of some of this energy or I can't be responsible for my actions."

"We could go for a run. Or you could wear my Supergirl outfit and rock the house."

Jordan wore a playful grin, but Mia didn't return it. She got to her feet and headed for the bedroom. "We'd better go for a run first. If I put on your Supergirl outfit right now, you'll never walk again."

Ryan had been at the OFC all day, using her staircase demolition experience to replicate what she'd done for Conor. Jamie had been willing to go, but Ryan tactfully suggested there were better ways for her to spend the day. Jamie was always a joy to be with, but she wasn't the right person to demolish an apartment building. And finding jobs for her to do at this point of the project was too time consuming to be worth the effort.

When she returned home, Ryan was covered with dust and grit; the only thing clean about her was her white socks, which had been covered by her work boots.

Jamie pointed at the bathroom. "Get in there immediately." She jumped up and went with Ryan. "Actually, get in the tub. This grit is so fine, it'll be easier to wash it down the drain than vacuum it up."

"Aren't you glad I didn't make you come with me?"

"Obviously." Jamie started to peel Ryan's clothes off her, one layer at a time. "Who was there?"

"Sean and Seamus. Brian stopped by and stood around talking until Sean told him to get lost."

"I'd say Brian is your least favorite cousin."

Eyes wide, Ryan said, "Why would you say that? I don't have a least favorite. They're all fine."

Jamie reminded herself it didn't matter how much a part of the family she was, she would never be allowed to criticize any of them or imply that some were higher on the food chain than others.

"My mistake. I've been on the phone with Mia. Big news."

"Jordan called me yesterday and told me about the cut."

Jamie pinched her. "Why didn't you tell me?"

"Jordan didn't tell me to."

Rolling her eyes, Jamie pulled the shower curtain closed and sat down on the toilet while Ryan started the water. "Well, Mia is in quite a state. You know that woman Jordan used to live with? Toni?"

"Yeah."

"She apparently made a major play for Jordan and Mia's plotting how to kill her. Jordan had to physically restrain her from doing God knows what."

"I didn't see Mia's picture in the news today so I guess she didn't go through with it."

Jamie pulled the curtain aside, in order to see Ryan's face. "You don't sound surprised by any of this."

Ryan caught her look and mustered a reasonably innocent smile. "I'm surprised by everything."

"Good. Then be surprised by this. I'm gonna go see Mia tomorrow. Are you going with me?"

"Tomorrow! You can't go tomorrow."

"Sure I can. There are plenty of seats available. We leave here at ten and we're there by noon."

Ryan rinsed off the rest of the soap and turned off the water. "You act like it's no more complicated than going to the grocery store."

Grinning, Jamie said, "I think it's *less* complicated than going through the produce aisle at the Berkeley Bowl."

"It's not funny. I can't just pick up at the drop of a hat and go."

"Yes you can. You choose not to, but you can."

"I thought it'd be cool to go on August the fifteenth. That's when they announce the final team. If Jordan makes it, we'd be there to celebrate. If she doesn't, we're there to bring her home."

"I think that's a fantastic idea. We can go again then."

"Aw, Jamie."

Jamie wrapped her arms around Ryan's damp body. "I know I'm mean to you, but I appreciate your putting up with me."

"I *really* don't want to go."

"I didn't expect you to. Actually, I was just asking to be polite.

Can you take me to the airport in the morning?"

Slightly dumbfounded, Ryan said, "You're really going to go without me?"

"I'm going to go, honey. I'd like to go with you, but I'm going with or without you."

"Fine. I'll go. It's gonna screw up the week, though. We're supposed to have our meeting about Jennie on Friday."

"We can reschedule it."

Ryan took her towel and ran it briskly over her head. She went out into the main room, mumbling, "Not everybody's schedule is as flexible as yours."

When they were actually on the plane the next day, Ryan's mood was much improved. Jamie had come to the conclusion that making the decision about traveling was much harder for Ryan than actually going. As a courtesy, Jamie had booked them economy class seats. It wasn't her preferred means of travel, but if Ryan was going to be flexible enough to go, Jamie thought she had to be flexible enough to sit in the back.

It was a relatively small plane, two seats on each side of the aisle. They'd been in the air long enough to have soft drinks and some strange snack mix delivered when Jamie said, "Remember the other week when we talked about you and Mia?"

Ryan eyed Jamie's unopened snack mix, then grinned when Jamie automatically handed it to her. "We talk about Mia all the time."

"No, when we talked about how you were bothered by her sometimes."

"Yeah, I remember."

"I just want to make sure you know that I would never be jealous about you and Mia teasing each other or anything. I hope you can really be yourself with her."

"I can be. I'm not sure what was going on with me, but whatever it was, I'm over it."

Jamie leaned over and kissed her cheek. "Good. They're both

really tense, and I hope having us around for a few days might take Jordan's mind off her worries. And when Jordan isn't as worried, Mia's a lot happier."

"As it should be."

They'd had only one relatively minor argument over their travel plans. Jamie had decided that it was too inconvenient to have Mia drive all the way to Denver to pick them up at the airport, so she hadn't told her they were coming. Ryan found the whole thing crazy, arguing that people loved to go to the airport to pick up their loved ones. But Jamie knew Mia well enough to know that she'd like nothing more than having her friends turn up on her doorstep.

It was almost four o'clock, and from their frequent phone contact, Jamie knew that was right about when Jordan got home. Jamie was paying the shuttle driver while Ryan went up to the entryway to search for their friends' names on a board. She was turning around to see if Jamie was on her way when Jordan appeared from around the corner.

"Boomer!"

Ryan heard her nickname, then nearly fell to the ground when Jordan literally threw herself at her. Jordan landed mostly on Ryan's back, her arms wrapped around her shoulders. When Jamie turned to see what the yelling was, she saw Jordan's feet kicking out behind herself while she dangled from Ryan's back.

"You're killing me!"

Jordan dropped to the ground then gave Ryan a hug from behind, burying her face between her shoulders. "You guys rock," she murmured.

By the time Jamie reached the pair, Jordan had released her hold on Ryan. Then she gave Jamie a remarkably un-Jordanlike welcome. She hugged her so tightly Jamie's feet came off the ground, then she put her down and kissed her innumerable times. "I'm *so* glad to see you guys. You couldn't have come at a better time."

Jamie looked over at a grinning Ryan, stuck her tongue out at her, then mouthed, "Told you so."

The neighbors didn't call the police, but Ryan wouldn't have blamed them if they had. When Mia saw them come in, she grabbed Jamie and they jumped up and down, shrieking for what seemed like hours. Ryan guessed there were words among the gibberish that was coming out of them, but she understood none of them.

When Mia was finally exhausted she stumbled over to Ryan and said, "Kiss me."

Ryan did, showing her the same level of affection she did for all of her close friends. Then she wrapped Mia in her arms and hugged her until she struggled to get away.

"Jamie and Jordan are right here. Keep it on the down low," Mia said, giggling.

"It's not easy, but I'll try to behave."

Mia grabbed Jamie by the hand and pulled her into the living room, where they both sank down into the spacious L-shaped seating area. "Can you believe how nice this place is?" Mia asked. "You've gotta take a bunch of pictures and show your mom."

Ryan and Jordan strolled over to the seating area and sat down more purposefully. "I can't believe you didn't tell us you were coming," Jordan said. "But it's really cool that you surprised us."

"I think it's really cool I didn't have to go to the airport and get you," Mia said, smiling sweetly at Ryan.

"Obviously, Jamie made our arrangements," Ryan said. "If I'd made them, it'd be twenty-one days from now, since that's when the best fares are, and you would most definitely have had to come to Denver to pick us up."

"Denver? Why didn't you fly into Colorado Springs?" Jordan asked.

"We would have, but the flight I wanted was booked," Jamie said. "I would've had to get up at dawn to make the one that was still available."

Ryan stared at her, open mouthed. "You told me there were no flights."

Smiling demurely, Jamie said, "There were no flights that *I* was going to be on, and I didn't think you wanted to go separately."

Mia and Jamie went into the kitchen to finish preparing dinner, and Jordan leaned back with her arms stretched across the sofa. "Pretty nice, huh, Boom? Our women are cooking and we get to put our feet up."

"I'm really quite able to cook, but Jamie prefers to do it all. Now that we're spending so much time together, I think it's a way for her to have her own space."

"Mia does it solely to save money. She doesn't have any love for cooking."

"Maybe she does it because it'd be hard to get the kind of food you need at a restaurant."

"No, not really. A lot of the locals treat meals like science experiments. There are lots of healthy places to choose from, but they're expensive."

"Good food *is* expensive. That's why fast food is cheap. So, talk to me about this latest cut."

"It was fucked up." She shook her head. "We're at sixteen players now, and we're going down to fourteen by next week if they stick to the schedule." She put her hands around her throat and acted like she was choking herself. "The pressure's about to kill me."

"I can't see how keeping you guys under the gun constantly is supposed to help your play. When's your final cut?"

"In three weeks. August fifteenth. We're gonna be somewhere in Asia when we have to get down to the final twelve. I guess they'll take the last two girls they cut and stick them on a plane for home."

Ryan waited a beat to see if she was kidding, but the look on Jordan's face showed she was deadly serious. "Where are you going to be?"

With a half smile, Jordan said, "I hope I'm gonna be somewhere in Asia. We start in Macau. If I make the next cut, I'll be on a plane ten days from now."

"And you're gone for how long?"

"Almost four weeks. The tournament's in Macau, Thailand, Taiwan, Malaysia, and China. The finals are in the Philippines. Gruesome schedule," she added.

"Damn. I'm glad Jamie talked me into coming now. I was planning on coming to celebrate with you when you made the final cut."

Smirking at her, Jordan said, "Or put me in a straight jacket and take me home."

Ryan shook her head. "No way. You've made it this far, no one's gonna stop you now."

As soon as Mia and Jamie got into the kitchen Jamie whispered, "Where's the rest of Jordan?"

Mia draped herself dramatically across the counter. "I'm gonna be so glad when this is over. All of her beautiful curves… gone! I didn't know you could take a body that fantastic and turn it into something so hard. You can't tell when she has her clothes on, but you can see her veins. When we're having sex, I see all those veins and tendons bulging and it freaks me out."

"She really does look different. She's still gorgeous, of course…"

"Yeah, of course. She can't help being gorgeous. I'm using this time to get ready for what I'll do when we're old. When we have sex, I close my eyes and think about how she used to look." She laughed impishly, but it was clear she was partially serious.

"Is it really that different?"

"You know I'm like a dude. I'm all about the visuals. I love her as much as ever, but I don't get hot when I see her naked anymore. She has to make a move or we have to kiss. Before, I could just see her and have to have her. That's over. And I hope to God it's temporary."

"Take it from me, her curves can come back. Ryan's have come and gone twice, and they're just as good as they ever were."

Mia sighed. "When Ryan hugged me, I wanted to keep hanging on. She feels so springy. I miss flesh."

"Yeah, she's back to perfect. I'm still trying to lose three pounds. All the walking we've been doing should take care of that eventually."

"You look hot and you know it." Mia put her arms around Jamie and hugged her tightly. "You're the best friend I've ever had, and I hope you know it. Having you come here now is absolutely fantastic."

"There's no place I'd rather be."

By the time they all sat down to dinner, it was as though they'd just picked up their usual evening meal from Berkeley and plopped it down in Colorado Springs. Everything was exactly the same: Mia teased everyone, Jordan placidly watched, Jamie tried to be the voice of reason, and Ryan was the butt of most jokes. The menu was less festive than what they were used to, but that was in deference to Jordan's training restrictions.

Ryan said, "Since we're not rushing to get married, we've decided to put our energies into finding a house."

"Awesome." Jordan nodded her approval. "I wish I could help you. There's almost nothing I like better than looking at houses."

"Are you looking for a house?" Mia asked, holding her arms far apart. "Or a house?" She moved her hands together until the distance between them was the size of a shoebox.

"Somewhere in the middle," Jamie said.

Ryan piped up, "I think we're gonna go pretty big. We'll probably sell the house in Berkeley. You guys don't mind living in the city, do you?"

"We get to come?" Mia asked brightly.

"Of course." Ryan leaned back and smiled, likely thinking about having her little family together once more. She didn't see the look she was getting from her partner, but luckily no one else did either.

Jordan and Mia offered their bedroom, but their guests would not hear of it. "You need your space and your bed, Jamie insisted. "You don't want to get a stiff back from sleeping on the sofa."

"But I'll wake you up in the morning."

"I wanna get up when you do," Ryan said. Turning to Jamie, she added, "Jordan's pretty sure she can get me in to practice by telling her coach that I'm considering trying out for the team."

"Then maybe Mia and I should sleep in the bedroom, and you and Jordan can sleep out here so you don't bother us when you get up."

"That's fine," Jordan said, always amenable.

Mia grabbed the sleeve of her T-shirt and started tugging her towards the bedroom. "She's teasing, baby. Pay no attention to the mean lady."

When they were ensconced on the sofa bed, Jamie rolled onto her side and propped her head up with her hand. "Can I ask a favor?"

"Sure. Anything."

"Would you check with me before you invite anyone else to live with us permanently?" She batted her eyes and smiled.

"Am I in trouble?"

"Of course not. I just think we should make decisions like that in tandem."

Looking a little puzzled, Ryan said, "Don't you want them to live with us?"

"Depending on the kind of house we get, that could work out. But getting a place that could accommodate two master suites is going to make house hunting a lot tougher."

"We don't need master suites. As long as we have two bedrooms and two baths, we'd be good to go."

Ryan had such a sweet, good-natured smile on her face that Jamie was incapable of disappointing her. "You're right. It won't be that hard to find a place. But I still want you to tell me if you invite anybody else."

Ryan kissed her on the forehead. "You've got a deal."

Before the crack of dawn, Jordan came out and very quietly put her hand on Ryan's shoulder. "Still wanna go with me?"

By way of answer, Ryan slipped off the edge of the sofa bed and started gathering the clothes she'd laid out the night before.

"You're awfully easy to wake up," Jordan whispered.

"Firefighter genes."

As Jordan predicted, it was quite easy to get an all-access visitor pass for Ryan. In general, passes of that sort were almost impossible to obtain. But a couple of the coaches had seen Ryan play at Cal, and were fans.

For most of the day, Ryan sat in the stands and watched intently. The team did a variety of drills, all of which were more difficult than any Ryan had ever been subjected to. It seemed that the coach's goal was to work the team to failure, and he did a good job of it. No matter how good a job a player was doing on the drill, she stayed out there until she wasn't able to successfully complete it. Ryan hadn't had any experience with coaches who used that technique. It wasn't the type of thing you could get away with on a girls team, and even many college players would have just given up. But these women wanted to be on this team so badly, Ryan understood his thinking. She didn't agree with it, but she understood it. He was trying to make them use all of their reserves in order to enhance their skills. She thought that might work in some instances, but not in this short a timeframe. It was the kind of thing a coach could do with a stable roster and a couple of years—not, in her opinion, a changing roster and a few weeks time.

After the morning drills, Jordan was scheduled to work out with free weights until lunch. Ryan was able to join her, and the strength coach worked them out together. By the time they were finished, Ryan was toast.

"I couldn't do this," she said, dragging her way behind Jordan in the lunch line at the cafeteria.

"It didn't start out this intense. If it had, there wouldn't be anybody left."

"If I worked out that hard on a regular basis, I'd look like a guy. Jamie'd hate it."

"Mia doesn't like it either. Either that or the honeymoon's over, but she's not on me like she used to be. I miss it," Jordan said longingly.

"Have you talked to her about it?"

"No." Jordan grabbed two bananas from a basket. "We're still having sex a lot; she just doesn't tackle me when I'm walking through a room."

"Huh. That's what Jamie says about me. Maybe I'd better talk to Mia and see what's going on with us."

"Don't do that. I don't want her to know I talked to you about this. She might get embarrassed."

"Yeah," Ryan said with a smirk, "Mia gets embarrassed awfully easily."

Minutes after Ryan and Jordan left for the training session, Mia joined Jamie on the sofa bed. She scooted around, trying to get comfortable. "This ain't great." Jamie stuck her arm out and Mia curled up alongside, resting her head on Jamie's shoulder. "Much better. Much much better."

Jamie ran her fingers through Mia's curls. "Your hair has gotten so long. It looks great."

Mia purred like a kitten as she moved her head around to receive more contact. "Jordy loves it so I guess I'll keep growing it out. How about you? Going to let yours go?"

"I suppose so. Ryan wants to see it long. I'm at a critical juncture. Another inch and it's gonna look messy."

"You'll have to suck it up and get through it. But your hair's super great when it's long. I couldn't believe when you cut it. When we were first at Cal, you were the only girl with good hair who had it short."

Jamie chuckled softly. "And I'm sure you checked every girl out."

"New school. Gotta scope out the talent."

"How about Colorado Springs? Are the girls pretty here?"

"Haven't noticed," Mia said through a yawn. "When you've got the best looking girl in the world, it's a waste of time."

Their nap lasted until eight, but neither had the motivation or the desire to get out of bed. "So," Jamie said, "what are you going to do to this Toni person?"

Mia lay on her back, legs crossed at the knee, hands behind her head, a contented, dreamy look in her eyes. "I have so many ideas. And some of them are epic, truly epic, James. But I can't do any of them until after the Olympics. If I maim and mutilate her now, it could hurt Jordy's chances, and I'd never risk that." She laughed evilly. "If I'd gotten out of the house the other day, I can't say what I would have done, so I guess I *might* be willing to hurt Jordy."

It was a gorgeous summer day, with sparkling clear skies of a blue hue almost indescribably pretty. They didn't have a car, but they had the day to themselves, and Jamie's bank account to support any endeavor. "Let's do something you never get to do," Jamie suggested.

Dryly, Mia said, "I lie by the pool and listen to music, I make dinner every evening, I watch Jordy act like she's not falling asleep the minute dinner's over, and most nights I get lucky. Everything that's not on that list is something I never do."

"Is any part of this good for you?"

A surprisingly sincere smile illuminated Mia's face. "Every part. This is where Jordy needs to be, and I need to be with her."

Jamie called her mother for recommendations, and after just a few minutes conversation, she had an agenda. "Mom says the Broadmoor has a really good spa. Have you been there?"

Mia looked at her for a few long seconds. "What part of 'I

don't go anywhere' don't you get?"

"I thought maybe you went for drives when Jordan wasn't working. She gets a day off, doesn't she?"

"Usually. But I just drag her down to the pool so she gets a little color in her cheeks. If we were still living in that other dump, she'd look like she had a terminal illness." She put both hands on Jamie's shoulders and shook her gently. "Your mother saved my life. She really saved my life. I was going mad over there."

"Let's hop in a cab and go have a decadent breakfast, then hit that spa."

"If I had any pride, I'd try to convince you to just hang out here until the girls get home. Luckily, I don't have even an ounce of it." She threw both arms around Jamie and hugged her. "I swear I would love you just as much if you were broke, but I really love your money."

Giggling, Jamie said, "Don't tell Ryan, but that makes two of us. Being rich rocks."

They had a breakfast that contained more sugar and fat than Mia had eaten in months, given that she stuck close to Jordan's diet. "I don't know what's got my head buzzing more, the Mimosa or the French toast. Whichever it is, I want more."

Jamie was carefully reviewing the list of services the spa offered. "Here's what I want: a hot stone massage, a swim in the lap pool, then lunch, then this cool shower thing with eighteen heads, then a pedicure and a facial." She handed the card to Mia. "Pick your poison."

Without glancing at the card, Mia said, "You're the expert. I defer to your superior experience."

An hour later, they lay face down on comfortable chaise lounges by the indoor lap pool. It was too nice a day to be indoors, but Jamie didn't want to have to slather herself with sunblock. The other guests weren't as sun-phobic, so she and Mia were the only people by the pool.

"This is so cool," Mia said. "It's like having our own private pool." She laughed for a second. "What am I talking about? This isn't nearly as nice as your pool in Pebble Beach…or Hillsborough, for that matter."

"True. But I don't compare things like that. That's one of the many things I'm learning from Ryan."

"Besides cunnilingus?" Mia teased.

"Yep, although that's the *best* thing I've learned. I try really hard to enjoy what I'm doing no matter where I am. I've got so many nice things it's silly to try to replicate them. Whenever I leave home, I'm probably not going to be as comfortable."

"I agree that Ryan's been the best thing that's ever happened to you. If I were you and I had to choose between being dirt poor and having her, or rich and having just about anyone else, I'd take her."

Jamie laughed. "Anybody else in the *world*? I'll have to think about that."

Mia picked up a hand and made a gesture like she was going to swat Jamie, but her reach didn't extend that far and she let it drop. "Ryan's perfect for you. You couldn't do any better."

"Too true, but she's been a little shaky in the perfection department." Jamie turned over so she was lying on her side. "Her sex drive has diminished to a human level, and I'm not loving it."

Mia mirrored her posture and they looked at each other with alarm. "Damn, I hope Jordy doesn't feel that way about me!"

"Double damn! Ryan better not be slacking off because she's not as attracted to me as she used to be!" She reached down and pinched the fat that no one else would have noticed. "Maybe I only turn her on when I'm in perfect shape. Breaking my elbow really screwed me up."

"You're on drugs. You look fantastic, James. Tell me how she's slacking off and I'll give you a diagnosis."

"Well," Jamie said thoughtfully, "she swears she's not slacking off, and it *is* a pretty subtle difference, but she's not as ravenous as she used to be. She hops to it if I make any overtures at all, but she used to be like a pot on a simmer."

Mia nodded. "That does sound like me. But you look as good if not better than you did six months ago, so it's clearly not that. What does she say when you ask her?" She giggled. "And don't say you haven't asked her. You two can't let anything fester."

"Of course I asked her. She said she's never been in a relationship where she could relax and be herself."

"And being herself means being less…ravenous?"

"Something like that."

"I hate to say it, James, but there's a chance she's being honest. The girl was like a wild mustang before she met you. Don't you think you change once somebody gets a saddle and bridle on you?"

"But I don't want her to change." Jamie tried not to pout, but she knew she wasn't doing a good job of it.

"I'm not sure your vote counts. She might just be trying to adjust to life in the stable."

"It wouldn't be a big deal if I didn't want her to always make the first move, but that's what really turns me on."

"I'm not like that, but I could see how that'd be hard to finesse." She was quiet for a few seconds. "How to get her to always make the first move, while secretly directing her to do your bidding…" Mia tapped her chin with her finger a few times. "That's a tough one, one that women have been wrestling with since Adam didn't realize Eve had a kinky side only the damn snake knew about."

When Jordan and Ryan got home, their girlfriends were waiting for them—relaxed, rejuvenated, and smelling sweet. After they were properly greeted, Mia said, "We're going out to dinner, girls. You have half an hour to get ready."

Jordan looked at Ryan and said, "I get to shower first." She dashed for the bathroom, chuckling to herself.

Mia shook her head. "You'd think you'd be quicker at that,

having grown up with three brothers."

Ryan sat down next to Jamie, looking a little abashed. "I've always been slow."

A long search on the Internet led them to try a Thai place that had gotten very good reviews. After ordering, Mia said, "This was a great idea. There were twenty things Jordy could have had. We're going to have to go out more often." She made a face. "If I could get a job, we could go out all the time."

"By the time you get through the application process, you'll be gone," Ryan said. "I think you'll have to put your job-hunting on hold until after the Olympics."

Mia rolled her eyes. "I never thought I'd be complaining about not working, but it's really boring just lying around all day."

Jamie reached over and tried to put her hand over Mia's mouth. "Don't tell Ryan that. She hasn't figured that out yet."

"I'm not getting paid," Ryan admitted, "but I've done more than my share of work on the apartment building."

Jamie smiled sweetly. "She's doing my share, too. I'm only trained to set tile, and we're a long way away from that."

After dinner found them back at the apartment, with Jordan lying down on the sofa, her head in Mia's lap. She was trying to stay awake, but it was clearly difficult for her.

"If you two could see how hard Jordan works," Ryan said, "you'd be amazed. It doesn't make sense that their coaches are trying to kill them less than two months before the Olympics, but that's the only thing I can figure."

"Makes us stronger," Jordan mumbled.

Mia put a hand on the side of her lover's face and patted her gently. "You're strong enough." Jordan gave her a half smile and was asleep in moments. Mia continued to stroke her, keeping her hand moving as she talked. "Did you notice that my Jordy's the only one who's all skin and muscle?"

"Yeah, I did. That girl from Stanford looks just the same as she did in college. Sweet," she said grinning. "Jordan says the nutritionist worked with each of them to figure out what type of body they had and how to maximize its potential."

"And they decided they needed a stick figure?" Mia retorted crossly.

"No. Jordan's not very muscular so they decided to get her as light as possible. I know she's not enjoying all of the restrictions, but her vertical leap's much better than it was at Cal. From what I saw, she's the best jumper on the team."

"I hope it pays off for her, because my girl has really suffered." She stroked Jordan's side possessively.

"It hardly seems fair. Jordan's pale and skinny and you look absolutely fantastic." Ryan looked Mia up and down, leering, and Mia tossed her hair, letting her curls bounce. Smiling slyly, Ryan said, "Beautiful hair, nice tan, perfect weight. You oughta stop time, 'cause you can't get any better lookin'."

Mia slapped at her, leaving a handprint on her leg. "It's about time you noticed," she huffed.

Ryan leaned over and put her chin on Mia's shoulder, in much the way Duffy did when he wanted someone's sandwich. "Who wouldn't notice you?"

"Jamie, your girlfriend is hitting on me." Mia giggled as she pushed Ryan's face away.

"I don't mind. It's all in the family. If we all live together, I figure we'll get around to swapping one of these days."

Ryan sat up and straightened her hair. "Yeah, that sounds like us. Anything goes."

They went to bed at nine, ridiculously early from Jamie's perspective, but Mia and Jordan had been getting up at five for months, and staying up until nine was actually a little late for them.

Ryan was already in bed when Jamie came out of the bathroom. She went to her bag and found the pajamas she'd brought. Ryan watched her put on the pale green camisole-style top and satiny boy-cut panties. "You brought that to wear around other people?"

Jamie turned and gave Ryan a perfectly innocent look. "I knew what the setup was. I just wanted to have something on in case Jordan had to come running through here at some point. Mia has seen me in far less," she added.

"Still," Ryan looked her up and down, "that's more like lingerie."

"Huh." Jamie looked down at herself and noticed her hard nipples poking against the filmy fabric. "I guess it is." She walked over to the sofa bed and bent down to give Ryan a quick kiss. "I'm gonna stay up and read a while."

Ryan patted the bed. "There's a lamp right there. You can lie next to me."

"The chair's more comfortable. I'll come to bed pretty soon." Jamie crossed the room and sat sideways on the chair, draping her legs over one arm.

The room was completely quiet for a few minutes until Ryan's fully awake voice said, "Do you have to kick your legs like that?"

"You can hear that?"

"No. I can see it."

"I have a solution. Close your eyes."

"I can't afford to."

"Want to clue me in on your plans? Do you have to be somewhere in the next few minutes?"

"No, but I'm really beat. If I close my eyes, I'll fall asleep."

"Isn't that the general idea?"

"Not when you're lolling around in that outfit." She smacked her lips. "I've gotta have me some of that."

Jamie innocently pointed at herself. "Of this?"

"Yep. You look good enough to eat."

Wrinkling up her nose, Jamie said, "Kinda crass, but I'll take it as a compliment."

"You definitely should. Everything I said about Mia goes double for you."

"I appreciate that, baby, but I don't think I'm comfortable having sex out here in the open."

"They've got a door." Ryan sat up and pointed, as though Jamie couldn't see it for herself.

"I know, but the bathroom's out here. I don't want to be in the middle of having fun and have one of them come out to use it."

Scowling, Ryan lay down. "Next time, will you wear something that covers you up a little more? That's just brutal."

"Yes, dear," Jamie said, grinning happily. "I'll try to look worse in the future."

"That's all I ask. Just a little humanitarian aid."

Ryan closed her eyes and Jamie sat in the chair, gazing at her for a few minutes. Maybe Ryan *was* more like Mia than Jamie had guessed. If she needed sexy lingerie to keep her on a low boil Jamie was definitely up to the challenge. No one loved wearing nice lingerie more than she did, and if Ryan got hot looking at it everyone would be happy.

The four friends spent the next day lying around the outdoor pool, chatting and playing in the water. Jordan was either eating or sleeping much of the day, and by the time she was ready to go to her late afternoon walkthrough, she looked more like herself. Her color was better, she looked well rested, and she had a little fire in her eyes. Mia left to drive her to the gym, and as soon as the door closed Ryan was right next to Jamie, saying, "We've got half an hour. Wanna do it?"

Jamie looked up at her, blinking. "Did I miss something?"

"Yeah. You missed having a really good time with me last night."

Putting her hand on Ryan's belly, Jamie said, "Ahh, that's right. And you want to make up for that missed opportunity by jumping on me without any warning?"

"You've been warned." Ryan leaned over and put her hands on both arms of the chair Jamie was sitting on. "Come on," she urged. "I can make it worth your while."

Jamie stroked her face gently. "I'm sure you can, but I don't know if I can get going that quickly."

"Sure you can." Ryan leaned over and tried to place a kiss on Jamie's mouth, but the mouth moved just enough to have the kiss land on a cheek.

"Don't be disappointed, but I'm not in the mood for fast and furious right now. You should have told me earlier so I could have been fantasizing about you."

Ryan stood up, looking a little surprised. "Are you really saying no?"

"I'm not saying no; I'm saying not this minute."

"That's the same as no."

"Uhm…then I guess I'm saying no."

Ryan dropped down into a squat. "You never say no."

Jamie touched her tenderly, stroking her cheeks and sweeping her hair off her shoulders. "I don't want to say no, but this isn't an ideal situation. I can't relax knowing that Mia could come back and catch us."

"She's caught us before," Ryan said, a hopeful note in her voice.

"I know. And neither of us liked it."

"We could go into the bathroom and lock the door."

"Honey," Jamie soothed, "it sounds like you really need a release. Why don't you go into Mia's room and have yourself, as you say it. I'll tell her you're taking a nap."

Shaking her head, Ryan stood up. "I don't want a release. I want you."

"Technically you want me *and* a release."

"Yeah, I suppose that's true. But we're gonna be here for two more days. Are you really saying I've gotta wait that long?"

"We both do." Jamie got up from her chair and put her arms around Ryan, then tilted her head and kissed Ryan tenderly. "We can let our desire build up and really rock the house when we get home."

"We'd better go to Pebble Beach." Ryan put her arms around Jamie and kissed her like she was leaving for a year. When she pulled away, they were both flushed and slightly out of breath. "The neighbors are much farther away there."

Jamie watched as her partner went into the kitchen. Maybe a combination of sexy underwear and occasional denial was the key. She was more than willing to try whatever it took to get this eager, hungry Ryan back on a regular basis.

They went over to the gym a little early to show Jamie the facilities. She was suitably impressed, and they poked around the campus, with Jamie commenting, "It's like a nice university where everyone's an athlete."

"Yeah," Mia agreed. "I would have gone to class a lot more if my fellow students had looked like this."

Jamie tugged on a lock of Mia's hair. "I thought you didn't look anymore."

"I'm talking about the past. If people had looked like this *before* I met Jordy, I'd have taken extra classes. Now? I don't notice a thing."

They sat in the stands at the crowded gym, Mia and Jamie prattling away while Ryan watched every point like she might be called on to save it.

"Hey, I forgot to tell you who wants Jordan to pose for them," Mia said during the first game, which the USA was winning handily.

"Who?"

Mia's eyebrows waggled up and down. "Playboy."

"What?"

Jamie's voice was so loud it pulled Ryan from her trance. "What?"

"They asked Jordan to pose for Playboy," Jamie said.

Ryan frowned briefly. "Naked?"

"Yeah, but they wouldn't show her va-jay-jay."

"Nice." Ryan went back to watching the game, flinching when any U.S. player missed a return.

"Are you cool with that?" Jamie asked.

"Sure. Why not?"

"Mmm, I don't think I'd like Ryan to do it. That's a little too objectifying for me. I'm the only one who gets to objectify her like that."

"It doesn't bother me. I'm not sure she's gonna do it, though. She's sick of modeling."

"Then why consider it?"

"They won't say this publicly, but the federation wants her to do it. Any publicity for volleyball is good."

"Still…" Jamie trailed off. "She wants to be an architect, not a volleyball player. Doing something like that could hurt her in the future."

"Or get her an interview anywhere there are guys," Mia said, smirking.

In bed that night, Jamie played with Ryan's hair while they talked quietly. "I don't think Jordan should do Playboy," Ryan said. "That's how people would refer to her for the rest of her life."

"You have a point. Mia says it'll get her an interview anywhere, and she's probably right, but at what cost?"

"Who else is doing it?"

"A woman who does the high jump, a pole vaulter, a swimmer, and somebody else. No one I've ever heard of."

Ryan shook her head, pulling a large hank of hair from Jamie's grasp. "I wouldn't do it. I hope Jordan asks my opinion."

"You won't say anything if she doesn't?"

"Nope. It's only my business if she asks me."

"Hmm. I was just thinking that I'd like a photo shoot of you. Would you pose for me?"

"For you? Of course. I wouldn't want to do it for another photographer, though. I don't think I could relax."

"Cool. Let's see about renting equipment again and doing it."

"Will you pose for me?"

“Uhm…sure. I’d feel weird, but you could calm me down.”

“You know…” Ryan flipped onto her side and slid up to lie next to Jamie. She got very close and whispered into her ear, “It would be pretty cool to have everybody see how smokin’ hot you are and know I’m the only one who got to touch you.”

Jamie turned and saw the sparkle in Ryan’s eyes. “That’s all true. Only you will ever touch me that way.” She kissed Ryan briefly. “But not tonight.”

The next evening the foursome began their goodbyes long before the taxi was scheduled to pick them up. As they often did, Mia and Jamie drifted in one direction, Jordan and Ryan in another.

“You looked great last night,” Ryan said, repeating her congratulations on the win. “Just keep doing what you’re doing.”

Looking a little embarrassed, Jordan nodded. “I know I’m playing well. If the only thing they go on is who’s peaking—I’m in.”

Ryan clapped her on the back. “Good for you. You’re sharper than the veterans. That should count.”

“I don’t think it will. I’m afraid I’m gonna be the last cut. I think he’ll keep three vets and the Wonderkid from Stanford.”

“You can’t know what your coach is thinking, but it’s possible he’ll go with experience. And you’ve got more experience than the kid from Stanford.”

“Yeah, but she’s got all the press. That matters too. It’s not just about the sport.”

“It never is,” Ryan agreed glumly.

On the flight home, Jamie rested her head against Ryan’s shoulder and tried to sleep. She was almost out when she remembered something. “Oh, I forgot to tell you, I wrote Mia a check to pay for her to go to that tournament in Asia.”

Ryan jumped so abruptly that Jamie’s head bounced and

hit fairly hard when it landed back on Ryan's shoulder. "Sorry!" Ryan whispered.

"What's wrong?"

"I told Jordan I'd pay to send Mia. That's the first time I've ever offered to pay for something huge and now I don't have to." She looked painfully disappointed.

Rubbing the sore spot on her head, Jamie said, "You pay Jordan; I'll tell Mia to use the check for a bunch of dinners or something else to break the monotony. I want her to have some good memories of this year."

"Okay. But it's not the same." She still looked put out.

"We're gonna be home tonight," Jamie reminded her. "Guess what we get to do?"

Ryan's smile was full and bright. "I'm gonna start fantasizing right now to save time. I can't wait."

Jamie held Ryan's hand and put her head back down. Everything was right in her world.

Chapter Eighteen

They'd gotten home from Colorado around midnight, both too tired to get to their deferred lovemaking. The next morning the phone rang at eight, with Martin giving them their marching orders for the day. The whole extended clan was gathering in Golden Gate Park for Ryan's Aunt Deirdre's fiftieth birthday party, and Martin couldn't stop his micromanaging, even though they'd shown their competence in making potato salad for a crowd.

When Ryan hung up, she seemed a little grouchy. "My father says the potatoes won't boil themselves."

"There's no rush," Jamie said. She curled around Ryan's body and closed her eyes.

"He's upstairs."

"Oh, fuck. We've gotta change that lock."

Hours later, Jamie was helping Francis tend one of four barbecues, while Catherine and Maeve instructed Jennie in the art of laying out a buffet for nearly a hundred guests. Ryan stood on the edge of the softball field, talking on her cell phone, while her brothers and cousins yelled at her to hang up and get behind the plate. "I'm coming," she growled, hanging up. She glared at Brendan, who was standing at the plate waiting to bat. "I was on the phone for two friggin' minutes."

Brendan didn't respond, he just made eye contact with Maggie, who was next up. She shrugged her shoulders, indicating her puzzlement about Ryan's obviously bad mood.

Ryan called out to Declan, who was pitching, "Let's go! Everybody was in such a damned hurry when I was on the phone. Look alive!"

When the game was over, Ryan walked over to Jamie, who was lying on a blanket reading a book. Caitlin was lying right next to her, curled up and sound asleep. With a gentle smile, Ryan folded her legs under herself and sat down gracefully.

"I can't resist a couple of pretty girls." Her smile was brief and she said, "Why didn't you tell me you saw Ally the other day?"

Jamie blinked, then nodded. "I forgot."

Ryan didn't say a word. She just continued to stare.

"I was walking down Market and she was on her way to the gym. We crossed paths." After a silent beat, Jamie added, "What's got you in such a mood?"

"I'd like to know when you've extended invitations to people. I hate being out of the loop."

"Loop? There's a loop?" Jamie didn't know what she'd done, but it was clearly enough to tick her partner off.

"Yeah. There's a loop. You want to hang out with other people and you're obviously fixated on seeing Ally and Sara." Her eyes were like blue steel and her strained tone indicated she was only keeping her voice quiet because of the baby.

Jamie sat up and stared right back at her. "You're angry about something, but it isn't anything I did. Why don't you do a little self-examination and come find me when you're in a better mood. I'm not going to let you ruin this party for me." With that, she stood up and strode away, leaving Ryan and a soundly sleeping baby.

She wanted to run after Jamie, but that would have required asking someone else to keep an eye on Caitlin. That would have been easy to do, but she didn't want to explain herself to anyone, so she lay down on her side and watched the child as she slept. There was something so peaceful and restful about watching

Caitlin's chest rise and fall that Ryan eventually put her arm around her and allowed her own eyes to close. She let her mind wander to that tranquil space between wakefulness and sleep, trying to get a read on her mood and her temper. A half hour later, when Caitlin began to stir, she picked her up and cuddled her, letting her wake slowly. Finally the girl opened her eyes wide and said, "May-me?"

"Jamie's around here someplace, punkin. Let's go find her, okay?"

Their group was so large that it was spread out far beyond the space they'd been allocated. Ryan went to the four corners of the clique, asking if anyone had seen Jamie. Some of her Aunt Deirdre's people confirmed the last sighting, saying she'd passed by quite a while earlier, heading for Lloyd Lake.

"She was trying to find a place to finish her book," Deirdre's brother said. "She's a studious girl, isn't she?"

"Yeah, that's her," Ryan said, smiling. She put Caitlin on her shoulders and took off, telling the child, "She's also studiously avoiding me. I've been a bad girl, Cait. Can you say 'bad girl?'"

Caitlin slapped at Ryan's head, calling out, "Bad!" as they cantered down the path. The lake was only a quarter mile away, just far enough for Ryan to get winded by the addition of Caitlin's weight. She slowed down and scanned the small lake carefully, finally seeing her partner sitting on the stairs of a facsimile of a Greek facade. It was an odd piece of architecture, just plopped down by the pond, but the structure provided a bit of shade. Jamie had positioned herself to use the shade to shield her book. As she approached, Ryan called out, "Are you speaking to us?"

Jamie looked up and smiled broadly at Caitlin. "I'm always happy to see my favorite woman." She held her hands out and Caitlin started to squeal and fight to get down. Ryan put her on the ground and Cait ran in her halting way and tumbled into Jamie's arms as if she hadn't seen her in months. Jamie swept her up and put her in her lap, kissing her golden hair and pink cheeks.

"Are you my favorite woman?" she cooed. "Or is that big baby behind you my favorite?" She finally looked at Ryan. "Are you still being a baby, or have you come to your senses?"

"Senses." Ryan sat down and put her elbows on her knees, then dropped her head into her hands. "I'm sorry."

Jamie reached out and scratched her back. "S'okay. What's got you cranky?"

"Ally called while we were playing softball. She wants to know if we want to go to a club tonight. You wanna?"

"Of course not."

Ryan turned quickly. "Why not? It was your idea."

"No, it wasn't. Ally asked if we'd like to do something and I said I'd love to. But not if you're gonna throw a fit at the mere idea." She braced her head on her hand. "You know, you don't always have to do what other people want you to do. It's okay to be selfish sometimes, especially about something that really bothers you."

"It shouldn't bother me," she grumbled.

"Don't be silly. You had very close, but very different relationships with these women, and if being around them upsets you, you should cut bait. You don't even have to explain. Just say 'no' a few times and they'll stop asking."

Ryan sighed and let her head drop. "I want to have a relationship with both of them..." She trailed off weakly.

"Does it bother you to see them together?"

Broad shoulders moved up and down. "I dunno."

"What about seeing them singly? You seemed to like being able to go talk to Sara a few weeks ago."

"I did."

Ryan let out another dramatic sigh, one so filled with feeling that Jamie hid her smile behind Caitlin's head so Ryan wouldn't see her.

"I think we should go out together. I'll see how much it bothers me—then I'll have a better idea about whether to see them again or not."

"Okay," Jamie said, a concerned expression on her face. "What are we going to do?"

"Ally wants to go to a club. I'll try to make sure it's someplace we can talk."

Caitlin had reached the end of her bonding period and climbed out of Jamie's embrace, heading for the water. Ryan jumped to her feet and ran after her, catching her just before she walked right in.

"I'm having the children," Jamie called. "That baby only shares twenty-five percent of your genes and even that's too many!"

Conor was still car-sitting for Jim's Range Rover, and Ryan tried to convince him to give them a ride to SOMA. When Ryan suggested he and Kieran might be able to use the car to help them procure dates at one of the clubs, Conor's enthusiasm rose dramatically.

When they walked down the street to get in the long line, Jamie reminded her partner that they'd not gone dancing since they'd become lovers. "You took me to bars when I couldn't have you," she teased. "That was so backwards. You'd get me all hot and bothered and then take me home."

"Well, tonight I still get to take you home," Ryan said, smiling, "but I get to stay with you. Much better arrangement all around."

"My first time at a real gay club. I'm excited."

"This place isn't exclusively gay. It's actually a funny mix, but I thought it would be a place where we could talk and dance and even sing."

"Sing? It's a karaoke place?"

"No, not that kind of singing. I'm telling you, it's an odd mix."

As soon as they went inside, Jamie worried Ryan had chosen the wrong kind of place. They were in the middle of a fairly typical bar, with lots of good-looking, young gay men. The music was loud, and the place was dark, not the kind of environment for conversation. But Ryan placed a hand on her back and urged her to continue walking, guiding her into a much roomier, brighter, quieter area in the back of the building. There were a number of tables and sofas scattered around, and Ryan immediately spotted Ally and Sara seated on a sofa in the rear corner of the room. They walked over and greeted their friends, kissing each before they sat down on the sofa that Ally had pulled over and placed at a right angle to the one on which she and Sara lounged.

"I'll go get drinks for us," Ryan said, not even waiting for Jamie to respond. As she backed away, she said, "Refills?" to Ally and Sara. Ally held up her glass of what looked like sparkling water and lime, and Sara shook her head.

Still searching for a drink she could sip that wouldn't have quite the kick of Irish whiskey, she decided on Cosmopolitans. "Well, aren't you an adult tonight?" Jamie teased as Ryan handed her the drink.

"Just fits with the atmosphere," Ryan said, and moments later her comment became more understandable. A man in a tuxedo took a seat at the piano and began to play, running through a variety of show tunes until someone called out a favorite. He launched into "I'm Just a Girl Who Can't Say No" to the delight of the audience, many of whom knew the words and sang along.

"Jesus, this is a gay man's version of heaven!" Jamie laughed. "Good looking guys, strong drinks, and show tunes."

They spent a long while observing the crowd and occasionally singing along. The music and crowd noise made the women lean close to each other to converse. Jamie was trying to say something to Ally, and she finally had to go sit on the arm of her sofa to be

e

heard.

Sara took the opportunity to do the same with Ryan. "How are you holding up? Are you making progress with the money issue?"

"Kinda." Ryan shrugged. "It's gonna take a while to get used to each other's habits. This relationship thing isn't as easy as it looks."

"True enough."

Ryan looked up at her. "You've got a cat-that-ate-the-canary smile. What's going on with you?"

It was dark, but not dark enough to hide the blush that crept up Sara's cheeks. "Nothing. We're just getting along really well. You've got six months on us; we still think this is all fun and games."

"Ahh."

Ryan's stomach did a flip, but she forced herself to acknowledge the feelings behind the discomfort. Two women she was interested in, probably loved, had rejected her, and she was never going to like it. But Jamie was the right woman for her and letting old jealous feelings creep up on her was just childish.

"We're still having a lot of fun," Ryan said with a smile, "so don't be scared off."

Sara moved to sit right next to Ryan. "Did I ever tell you that Jack Townsend is in my department?"

Ryan leaned back, the familiar name adding to her unease. "How is old Jack?"

"Ooo." Sara chuckled. "Jealous?"

Smiling slightly, Ryan shook her head. "Not much. I don't have good feelings for him, but I didn't meet him under the best of circumstances."

Tentatively, Sara said, "Were you and Jamie…while they were still together?"

"No!" Ryan said, loud enough for both Ally and Jamie to look in her direction. She shrugged her shoulders. "No," she said, this time much more quietly. "But Jamie was struggling with her orientation, and he thought I was pushing her in my direction." She pushed her hair back over her shoulder, an old habit that she used to give herself a second to think. "I would have thought the same thing if I was in his position, so I should cut him a break."

"He's a nice guy. I think you'd like him."

"He might be nice, but he must also be as dense as a rock to let Jamie get away." She shook her head quickly. "Who knows? Maybe he couldn't have stopped her from leaving."

"Hard to say," Sara said thoughtfully. "You've got to be strong to go against the grain. Jamie must have really loved you to break off an engagement to a guy like Jack." She gave Ryan a sad smile and held her gaze for a moment. Just then Ally reached over and grasped her hand, and Ryan tried to suppress the tendril of jealousy she felt when she saw it.

"You look like you need another sparkling water," Sara said as she eyed Ally's empty glass. "Be right back."

Jamie got up when Sara did. "I need to visit the rest room. Be back in a few."

Jamie took off, and, as was her habit, Ryan watched to make sure she made it to her destination. Sara was dawdling, trying to find some bills in her small purse. When she left the table, two pairs of eyes followed her. Ally stopped surveying before Ryan did and when the blue eyes turned back to meet Ally's gaze, Ryan realized what she'd been doing.

"Is this gonna work?" Ally asked softly, putting an arm around Ryan and hugging her.

Ryan sighed heavily. "I think it can." She looked at Ally helplessly. "I'd watch you walk away too. I was very, very attracted to both of you, and it's gonna take a while to remind my body that we don't go there anymore."

"I understand that, and it doesn't bother me, but is it worth it?"

"Yeah, I think it is. I'm just a little jealous…of both of you." She frowned. "I'm jealous of you for having her and I'm jealous of her for having you. It's fucked up!"

Ally gazed at her for a few moments, then stood and extended her hand. "Dance with me," she said quietly.

Surprised by the invitation, Ryan nonetheless got up and took Ally's hand. When they reached the dance floor, Ally slipped an arm around her in a very familiar fashion. They had danced together on many occasions, although all of them had been at Ally's apartment. The touch was so evocative of their many couplings Ryan started to get lost in the memories. She had to consciously remind herself that they were not now, nor would they ever again, be lovers. She forcefully distanced herself from the sensuality of the experience and just enjoyed the easy familiarity they had with each other, feeling her mood lighten as she did so.

The next song began, the beat lively and quick. "Not for me," Ally said decisively, leading Ryan back to their seats. "If I can't touch a woman, I don't see the sense in dancing." She gave Ryan her most wolfish smile, which always made Ryan giggle.

Ryan caught Jamie's gaze and twitched her head, indicating the small dance floor by the piano. Jamie immediately got up to join her.

The pianist was playing a medley of love songs, and Jamie melted into her partner's strong, sure embrace. "God, you dance well," she murmured, feeling Ryan lead her body effortlessly around the space.

"Lots of practice in Ireland," Ryan said with a chuckle. "Granny had us dancing when we were just tykes. Aisling and I were always in demand at the church socials."

"I think that's so cute," Jamie said, snuggling closer. "How're you doing? Are you having a good time?"

"Yeah. I'm pretty relaxed. It didn't even bother me much to dance with Ally."

"Did you two go dancing often?"

"Mmm…yeah, we danced together a lot," Ryan said, leaving it at that.

"Who led?" the teasing voice asked.

"Ha ha." Ryan clutched Jamie tighter, spun her around forcefully and dipped her, lowering her so far that Jamie's head went past horizontal. Ryan pulled her back into her arms and whispered hotly into her ear, "My days of being a frail little bottom are over. It's all top, all the time."

Jamie laughed, but didn't respond, letting Ryan have whatever illusions she cared to keep.

Sara had danced with both Ally and Jamie, and she finally got around to taking a turn with Ryan. As they moved together, she tilted her lips so they were close to Ryan's ear. "I'm in love."

Ryan didn't answer immediately. She let her body move to the slow beat of the music, Sara moving with her, following her lead seamlessly. "I had a feeling." Ryan moved back a few inches and flashed a smile.

"Are you cool with that?"

"Want the truth?"

Sara stiffened noticeably. "Yes, I do."

"I really try to be mature. I try to make the adult choices and decisions, because I know they're the right way for me to live. But every once in a while, I want to be a three-year-old and get what I want. I feel a little like that about you and Ally."

"Explain how you mean that. I don't think I get it."

"It's like when I used to visit Aisling. She and I were together constantly during the summer, and we had a marvelous time together. But when I'd come home, she'd write to me about what she was doing, and I'd always get jealous. I wasn't there…I couldn't play with her…but it still bothered me that someone else was filling my role. I was the one who should be playing with Aisling—no one else."

"And I'm Aisling?"

"You both are. I want both of you to stay single so I never have to confront my jealousy." She drew Sara closer, placing her hand low on her back to pull her in. "It's immature and selfish, and it's not how I want to feel. I'm completely satisfied with and permanently committed to Jamie. This jealousy is truly stupid."

Sara sighed and wrapped her arm tighter around Ryan's torso. "I understand the feeling," she admitted. "It's still hard for me to see you with Jamie, even though I know we can't be together."

Ryan leaned back in Sara's embrace. "It's going to be hard to get through this transition, but I want you in my life and I want you to be happy. That's what matters."

"Thanks," Sara said softly, nestling her head against Ryan's neck. "I appreciate that you're honest with me."

"It's the only way we'll get through this. It's not going to be easy, but I think it's worth the discomfort."

"Being your friend is worth everything I have," Sara said, hugging Ryan tenderly as the song finished.

Ryan took a turn standing in line for drinks, and she'd just carefully balanced four bottles of water in her grip when the bartender delivered another Cosmopolitan. "Compliments of the lady at the end of the bar," he said.

Scanning the crowd, Ryan spotted a woman she'd gone out with a few times while she was attending USF. Name…name…name…she thought as she tilted her head and smiled. She held up a finger to indicate she'd be over to chat and turned to deliver the water, when it was taken from her by her partner.

"Don't you have to go thank someone for the drink?" Jamie asked, her voice betraying no emotion at all.

Ryan grimaced slightly. "I can't remember her name. It was a nice name, very attractive and a little unusual…" She shook her head. "It's just not coming to me."

"Want me to handle it for you?" Jamie cocked her head in question. "I'll tell her you're not allowed to come out and play any longer."

"Thanks," Ryan grinned. "I appreciate the offer, but I think I'll handle it myself." She started to walk away, but turned and grasped her partner's shoulder. "Is that okay? I mean, if you want to go with me…"

Jamie touched the tip of her nose. "Of course it's okay. I don't really get much pleasure out of seeing you with women you used to date, so go be polite."

Ryan blinked at her and said, "We're with the two women who meant the most to me. Doesn't that bother you?"

Smiling again, Jamie said, "Not really. It's the ones whose names you don't recall that bother me." She shrugged. "Just one of my quirks."

Giving her a sad smile, Ryan nodded. "I'll just be a few." She walked down the bar, holding the drink in her hand. As she approached, the name came to her and she said, "Hi, Darien. It's been a long time. Thanks for the drink."

"I'd ask how you've been, but I think I know. Jamie's much prettier in person than that picture the TV news kept running after your…event."

"That was her high school graduation picture. Some jerk from her school obviously sold their yearbook to a media outlet."

Darien placed a warm hand on Ryan's arm. Her lips curled into a gentle smile, and Ryan remembered their time together as being particularly enjoyable.

"How are you, really? I've thought about you a lot since Christmas but I didn't want to call." She made a vague gesture with her hand. "I wasn't sure you'd even remember me."

"Of course I do," Ryan lied. "I'm doing well. I don't think I could have gotten through it all without Jamie. It took me a while to figure this out, but having a partner makes life so much better."

"Partner, like life partner?" Darien gaped. "Really? I mean, I knew you two were together…"

"Yep." Ryan lifted her drink and took a sip, the soft lights of the bar catching the fire in her ring and nearly blinding Darien.

"Wow," she said as she grasped Ryan's hand and took a long look at her ring. "Is this from her?"

"Yes. We're engaged," she said with an attractive blush stealing up her cheeks.

"I didn't think you were the type," Darien said, shaking her head in surprise. "I guess I should have hung in a little longer, huh?"

A wide smile settled onto Ryan's face as she recalled she hadn't stopped seeing Darien, Darien had stopped seeing her, deciding that she wanted a relationship rather than casual sex.

"You never know," Ryan agreed. "I didn't think I was the type to get serious, but Jamie's convinced me otherwise. How are things going for you? Did you graduate?"

"Yeah. I'm going for an MBA at USF this fall. Got a few more years of school ahead of me. How about you?"

"We're both going to take the year off." Ryan smiled warmly, feeling a strange glow of satisfaction when she stated this fact. "I wanted to keep going, but Jamie convinced me we'd had too much stress this year. After we're a little more centered, we'll make some decisions about the future."

"I always thought you'd wind up being a doctor," Darien mused. With a playful grin, she added, "You'd be the world's best gynecologist."

Ryan chuckled. "You never know, but that's not how I'm leaning. Actually, I shouldn't say that. All of my options are still open at this point." She smiled wryly and added, "Except for the fire department's swift-water rescue squad. After jumping into the Bay, I've decided that isn't for me."

"I remember you talking about how much you wanted to be a firefighter," Darien said fondly.

"Yeah. But we've decided that I probably wouldn't live to get my pension. Being in love changes how you feel about things like that. Now I don't need to seek thrills all of the time."

"For someone who's not looking for thrills, you're doing pretty well at finding them."

"This is true." Ryan smiled. "Thanks again for the drink, Darien. It's good to see you, and feel free to call if I'm ever in the papers again." She looked up and folded her hands towards the heavens. "Please God, no."

Darien laughed. "You'd better get back before your girlfriend comes looking for you."

"Oh, she knows where I am. She sees all."

"Does it bother you to have someone supervising you? You were practically phobic about your independence."

"She doesn't supervise me," Ryan said, beaming a grin. "She just loves me."

"Cute woman," Jamie said when her partner sat down next to her.

"Yeah," Ryan agreed. "Very cute. Nice, too. Smart, fun to be around, good sense of humor. Kinda wry."

"Why'd you stop seeing her?"

"Didn't. She stopped seeing me."

Jamie laughed. "That's a switch!"

"I've told you many times that I got shot down every once in a while. Darien was more mature than I was. I think she thought I was a little juvenile in my habits."

Jamie's eyebrows popped up and down as she decided, "I think you're pretty darned mature now. What happened?"

"You happened," Ryan said, her eyes losing their playful look and becoming focused and intent. "You helped me see that just being sexual with people was immature. Now that I have real intimacy with you, all of those other hookups seem so superficial. They were a waste of my time, for the most part."

"Don't think of it like that. Those experiences were part of your growing up. They served their purpose." A seductive fire started to burn in the clear blue eyes, and in seconds Jamie felt herself being drawn in.

"You're my only purpose now," Ryan said as she leaned in for a kiss.

Jamie expected a quick brush of lips, but she got much more. She could feel the power and passion start to build just under the surface of Ryan's placid demeanor, and felt her body quickly respond. Before she knew it, her arms were locked around Ryan's neck and her lips had parted, welcoming Ryan's warm tongue into her mouth.

When they finally moved apart, Jamie stared right at Ryan's luscious lips, unable to tear her focus from them. "This wasn't a good idea," she managed to get out. "We haven't had a chance to burn off anything that built up in Colorado."

"You're the one who fell asleep on me last night."

"You're the one who took a shower. I couldn't make myself

stay awake that long, even though I really, really tried." Jamie delivered one quick kiss. "I was ready this morning, but someone's father and his potatoes were not to be denied."

She put her arms around Ryan's neck, still looking at the beautiful lips, watching how lovely they looked when they moved. She couldn't resist; she had to kiss Ryan again. Their lips merged and soon Jamie was being held tightly as Ryan sucked and nibbled on her sensitive mouth.

Ryan pulled back and took a deep breath, her face just an inch from Jamie's. Her eyes were unfocused but they burned with desire, causing a tightening in Jamie's gut.

Ryan's voice was husky and low when she said, "I'm about one kiss away from throwing you down on this couch and having you."

Jamie smirked inwardly, watching Ryan walk right into her trap. Saying no just a couple of times had sparked Ryan's libido, and no one was happier to see it than Jamie. She kissed her again and found herself once more pulled into Ryan's magnetic aura. They kissed as though they'd been apart for a year and were only able to see each other for a few minutes before being separated again.

They finally pulled apart slowly, with Ryan leaning in for one last quick kiss. She was almost panting when she said, "We need to leave now."

Ryan's breath was hot and moist as it caressed Jamie's cheek, and she impulsively pulled Ryan in for another long, torrid kiss. When she released her, Ryan's eyes were even more unfocused, her mouth slightly open.

"Leave," Ryan said again, insistently, her eyes not straying from Jamie's mouth.

"We can't leave while Sara and Ally are dancing in the other room. We have to be polite."

"Then you'd better dance with me. God knows what I'll do to you on this couch if you kiss me again."

The pianist in their section was playing yet another romantic ballad. Jamie decided that rubbing up against Ryan's sexy body wasn't a good idea right then, so she led her to the bar area, where the beat was fast and furious.

Ryan was apparently trying to save a few minutes later in the evening, since she chose to begin their foreplay on the dance floor. The music pounded away in a quick, pulsating rhythm, but Ryan chose to dance in half time, swaying her sexy hips as she stared at her partner with unconcealed lust. She reached out and Jamie slid into her embrace. They held each other by the hips, feeling each gentle, rolling movement of the other's body.

As the song continued, they drew closer and closer together until Jamie could feel Ryan's thigh press insistently between her legs. With wide eyes she pushed Ryan away, shaking her head fiercely.

Ryan looked into her eyes, seeing embarrassment, not rejection. She gently turned her around, pressing up against her back instead.

Ryan's left arm tucked around Jamie's waist, pulling her tight against her body as she let the music take them away. The weight of Ryan's breasts pushed against Jamie's back, hips grinding against her ass, quickly escalating her arousal higher than it had been all night. Without conscious thought, Jamie's hands slid behind her partner and grasped her firm cheeks, pulling her in even tighter.

A strangled moan issued from Ryan's throat as she felt her partner clutch at her, and she dropped her head and bit down gently on the smooth column of pale skin that glistened with the evidence of their exertion.

"Whoa!" Shaking her head roughly, Jamie grasped Ryan's hands and pulled them from her waist. Turning in her embrace she gasped, "We're practically humping each other! We've got to go home."

"That's what I've been saying for half an hour. They're gonna turn the fire hose on us in a second."

Thankfully, when they returned to the back room after

hurriedly straightening their clothes, Sara and Ally were back in their seats. They said their goodbyes quickly, Ryan's full attention focused only on her partner.

As arranged, the Range Rover pulled up in front of the club fifteen minutes after Ryan placed the call to Conor. As she opened the rear door, Ryan was puzzled to find Kieran driving.

"Conor was circling for a kill," he said. "After I drop you guys off, I'll swing by to see if he was successful."

"Did you guys have fun?" Ryan asked.

"Yeah, I guess. The clubs down here are kinda weird—too loud to talk, too crowded to dance. I prefer the neighborhood joints myself. Conor seems to like them though."

"Conor's taste are very eclectic," Ryan decided, thinking that her brother liked any place that was filled with women susceptible to his charms.

No one was home, including Duffy, who must have been overnighting at Maeve's, so Ryan was able to chase Jamie down the stairs, loudly calling out, "You're mine, Jamie Evans! All mine!"

As soon as she reached their room, Jamie leapt onto the bed and welcomed her partner. "You don't see me complaining, do you?"

"Not yet," Ryan agreed, "but the night is young."

Her eyes were glittering in the warm lamplight, and Jamie pulled her close to kiss her. Surprisingly, Ryan resisted, keeping her lips just out of reach of her lover's seeking mouth. Frustrated by the game, Jamie grasped Ryan's neck and tried to pull her down, but the powerful muscles tensed and held, giving Jamie no satisfaction.

"I told you earlier that I was a big, powerful top," Ryan purred. "What makes you think that's changed in the last hour?"

Jamie blinked up at her, a jolt of arousal hitting her hard.

"Sometimes I have this...drive," Ryan said softly, her eyes reflecting the gentleness of her voice. "A need to express myself.

I feel like that tonight. My whole body is thrumming with pent-up energy." She ran her hands over her partner's face, smoothing the fine blonde hair off her forehead. Placing gentle kisses all over Jamie's face, Ryan said, "Let me lead you."

Jamie nodded slowly, consenting to be taken wherever Ryan needed to go. The thought flashed through her mind that this was the Ryan that most of her previous lovers had known—decisive, determined, strong, powerful and completely in charge. But whatever face it wore, love and tenderness shone through.

Ryan rolled off and got to her feet, then tugged Jamie up into a standing position. Sitting back on the edge of the bed, Ryan began to slowly undress her, pausing to run her warm hands over skin that was unhurriedly revealed. "Mmm…nice," she growled, unable to contain the deep satisfaction she seemed to feel from touching Jamie's body so intimately.

Jamie was shivering, slightly embarrassed to be exposed so slowly and determinedly. Ryan's eyes darkened with desire as her gaze lingered on the curves being slowly revealed.

"Touch yourself for me," Ryan said softly, her eyes never leaving Jamie's. "Run your hands all over your body. Show me how it feels to have your own fingers touching your skin. Come on," she said, her voice powerful and low. "Show me."

Swallowing against her discomfort, Jamie closed her eyes and obeyed Ryan's directions. Standing naked in front of her, she placed her shaking hands on her stomach and began to move them. One hand traveled up her abdomen, pausing to trace her muscles, while the other slid over her hip and skimmed up and down her thigh. Her skin felt silky smooth, except for the goosebumps that followed the trail of her fingertips, popping up as soon as her hand passed.

Jamie's eyes were closed, and though Ryan said not a word, her breathing was audible and slowly growing more rapid. When Jamie heard a swallow, she began to lose her nervousness and get into the game. Even though she was following Ryan's instructions, the power had shifted decisively; she realized that, for the moment, she was in charge.

Fingers skittering up her body, Jamie cupped and squeezed her breasts firmly, her low moan echoed with a matching one from her partner. Bringing her index finger to her lips, she licked the digit seductively, then circled the moist tip around each of her stiffening nipples, concurrently sending her hips into a slow grind.

Suddenly, her world was spinning, and she was thrown onto the bed, Ryan's ravenously hungry body plastered against her. Ryan was everywhere—kissing, touching, squeezing, and suckling on her tender flesh, that voracious mouth feeling like it was in three places at once.

Jamie grasped her partner's ass with both of her hands and pulled her in tightly against her need, shoving her hips roughly against Ryan's jean-clad thigh with a moan.

Ryan let her thrust for a few moments, then pulled her back from the edge, showing an impressive display of determination as she wrenched her body from Jamie's grasp and knelt astride her spread thighs, using her powerful legs to gently, but firmly draw them together. She grasped her partner's wrists and pinned them above and to the left of Jamie's head. Eyes wild with desire, Ryan leaned over until they were nose-to-nose and growled, "You're mine!"

The blonde head nodded slowly, dutifully impressed with the speed and power that Ryan summoned to cause her to submit. Even though she was totally under Ryan's control, she felt not a flicker of fear. She'd tried to push her partner, purposely trying to wrest control from her, and Ryan was only reminding her that they had a deal, and she was sticking to it.

Ryan got up and stripped quickly, leaving her clothing in a rumpled heap at the end of the bed. Staring at Jamie for just a second, she went to her closet and extracted the gym bag that housed her assortment of sex toys. After putting the bag on the edge of the bed, Ryan climbed on top of her again, her moist warmth leaving a trail across Jamie's belly as she slid down.

Leaning over until she hovered just above Jamie's face, Ryan said hotly, "I'm going to love you…a lot."

Jamie nodded, her gaze following Ryan carefully. Satisfied with the compliance, Ryan rolled off and started to love her again, pinning her wrists with one powerful hand, just to make sure there was no further insurrection. When Ryan's wanderings required both of her hands she tucked Jamie's hands under her butt, effectively letting her own body weight hold them in place.

It didn't take long to ratchet Jamie's desire even higher, and soon she was squirming continuously, fighting the overwhelming need to grasp Ryan's dark head and put it right where she needed it. Just when the need was beyond her ability to resist, Ryan kissed down her belly and began to lap at her throbbing, pulsing flesh. Jamie cried out in pleasure, the extraordinary discipline it took to keep her hands pinned making the thrill sharper.

The warm glow started at her toes and crawled up her body. Jamie's entire being was suffused with the beginning thrums of satisfaction, but just as shc was about to cry out, Ryan lifted her head and pushed down on Jamie's hips, forcing her hands to remain pinned.

"No!" Jamie cried in frustration as she tried to slither out of the hold, needing release immediately and not above providing it for herself.

The powerful body leaned over her, the determination not wavering a thread. "You're mine," Ryan reminded her fiercely.

Taking a few deep, cleansing breaths, Jamie finally nodded, feeling some of the pounding energy drain away.

Now Ryan flipped Jamie onto her stomach, placing her hands under her thighs to secure them. Starting at the back of her neck, Ryan supported most of her own weight on her elbows and knees, kissing and nibbling until Jamie's body began to move again. Dropping down to lie on top, Ryan began to move with her, their sweat-slickened bodies gliding smoothly against each other.

Ryan grasped her by the hips and pulled her into herself,

grinding her pelvis against Jamie's ass as she pumped against her. "Jesus, you feel so good!" she moaned as the sensations continued to build.

Surprisingly, Ryan released her grasp and rolled off again, lying on her back for a moment while she caught her breath. Jamie gazed at her in a silent plea, her lips slightly open, inviting her lover's touch. Ryan fulfilled her request, snuggling close to kiss her tenderly, letting the passion build again until they were hungrily sucking each other's tongues. She pulled away just as Jamie tried to extract her hand from beneath her thigh. Ryan didn't comment, but her sly smile and slowly shaking head let Jamie know that the game continued and her request had been denied.

Straddling her again, Ryan took up right where she'd left off, slowly working her way down her partner's back. She spent a long time kissing and licking the tiny indentations just above the swell of Jamie's cheeks, one of her favorite spots.

Jamie's heart beat faster as Ryan fed more insistently, licking and sucking with abandon as they rocked against one another in a frenzy.

"Please...please let me come," Jamie begged, her hips thrusting roughly.

"Soon," Ryan murmured, the word vibrating against flushed flesh. Her teeth raked across the skin, leaving faint marks that disappeared instantly as the blood returned. Jamie's hands were no longer pinned by her thighs; they were grasping handfuls of sheet to control herself as best she could. Her ass twitched and pushed against Ryan's hungry mouth as Ryan sucked loudly and grasped bucking hips to pull her close.

Dipping her head a bit, Ryan fixed her attention on the ultra-tender skin right at the base of the buttocks, one of Jamie's most ticklish spots. Today she was sensitized beyond ticklish. She moaned and growled as Ryan sucked and bit at the skin, her tongue sliding over the flesh again and again. Mewing in frustration, Ryan flopped onto her back, clearly trying to rein in her impulses.

Jamie forced her eyes open to see the vaguely unfocused blue eyes gazing in her general direction. From the set of Ryan's body and the longing in her eyes, Jamie could see she wanted more. Struggling with her feelings for just a moment, she had to admit she wasn't willing to go further. She was uncomfortable having that part of her body explored—for now at least. Seeing how Ryan honored those boundaries, even when she was wound up like a top, made her heart swell with love.

Jamie reached out and tenderly touched Ryan's cheek, the pink flesh warm to her touch. Ryan grasped her hand and kissed the palm, placing soft, moist kisses all over it. "I'm yours," Jamie said, sharing an emotion-filled smile with her.

"Forever," Ryan vowed as she began to kiss her again. Their tongues twined and touched gently, sliding into each other's mouths repeatedly. Jamie was still on her stomach and Ryan straddled her again, running her hands all over her back.

Jamie felt her partner's weight shift and heard some small noises, but she was almost oblivious by this point, nearly past the point of desire. Her body had been frustrated so many times it had given up hope of satisfaction, seemingly content to allow Ryan to play it like a stringed instrument.

Ryan grasped Jamie by the hips and lifted her to her knees, gently pushing on her shoulders until she dropped down onto her elbows. Once again Ryan shifted down and started to kiss and nip at Jamie's cheeks. It wasn't long before Ryan was moaning softly as she nuzzled against the firm softness, eventually pulling away with a loud smack.

Then Ryan's body draped over Jamie's back, holding onto her hips firmly as she ground against her again. Jamie felt something cool and smooth bump against her and she froze for just a second, unsure of what Ryan was planning.

Ryan ran her hands down her moist back, soothing her as she whispered, "Just relax and let me in."

Jamie felt a slick firmness at her entrance. She gasped when she felt the dildo poised to enter, but she took in a deep breath and tried to relax her muscles.

Her voice was thick, words almost slurred when Ryan murmured, "That's it, you're doing great. Open up for me. Just relax and open up."

As the smooth, firm cylinder slipped inside, Jamie grunted softly, calmed by the slow stroking of Ryan's hand rubbing her gently from shoulder to waist.

Ryan didn't move once she was inside, and after a few seconds, Jamie had stretched enough to comfortably accommodate her. The low moan that slipped from her lips this time was a sign of pleasure, and Ryan took her cue, starting to move, slowly drawing in and out, pulling out just a little and then slowly slipping back in, letting her get used to the sensation.

"Good. Feels good," Jamie murmured, her voice muffled by the mattress. Her right hand reached back and grasped Ryan's hip, pulling her in a little harder.

Responding to the overt signal, Ryan thrust deeper and more rhythmically, moving her hips in a smooth circle. Jamie's eyes rolled back in her head as the delightful intruder touched every sensitive spot deep inside her body. She had no idea how Ryan knew where every spot was, but she somehow had an intimate knowledge of every nerve, and knew just how long, how hard, and how often to stimulate each one of them.

Jamie was riding along on a cloud of sensation, barely aware of her body or her position. Her whole world had narrowed down to a few sensitive inches of flesh, every nerve in her body feeling like it was centered between her legs.

She scarcely heard Ryan's breathing pick up again, was not aware of her own matching the rhythm. She did, however, feel the golden glow that started in her extremities and traveled slowly but relentlessly through her body, finally centering and growing as it settled deep within her. The pulsing began to thrum and beat inside her, quickly becoming so insistent that it overtook all of her senses simultaneously, blurring her vision and filling her ears with a strange white noise. Jamie wasn't sure how long the sensation filled her, but she slowly became aware of her entire body again, and realized that Ryan was collapsed partially on top of her, still wedged deep inside.

With a puzzled frown, Jamie realized that both of her hands were between her legs and she twitched to extract them. Try as she might, they wouldn't budge. Even though Ryan wasn't fully on top, she was so heavy Jamie couldn't move.

Ryan must have sensed her struggle, and she slowly withdrew, slipping out so effortlessly Jamie barely felt the loss. Then the sweat-drenched body shifted and Ryan tumbled heavily onto her back, dropping the toy onto the floor.

Jamie did her best to roll over, so weak she almost needed to ask for assistance. She looked at her slick fingers in puzzlement, finally asking, "Did you give me permission to touch myself?"

"I'd like to see the person who could have stopped you." Ryan chuckled, the sound low and raspy. Turning her head, she made eye contact. "Have fun?"

Rolling her eyes dramatically, Jamie giggled. "You are the mistress of understatement." She patted Ryan's belly. "How about you? Did you...?"

"Have you gone deaf?" Ryan laughed languidly. "Thank God Conor's not home. He'd surely break the door down to save me from being strangled."

"Really?" Jamie asked, her nose wrinkling up in amusement. "I didn't hear a thing. I think I really was deaf there for a minute."

"That's possible, you know. It's happened to me a time or two."

"So, since I was unaware of anything but my own pleasure, would you say you enjoyed that anywhere near as much as I did?"

"I'd say so. I was in another world there at the end. I thought it was entirely possible that the top of my head would blow off."

"Still there," Jamie informed her, tapping her skull lightly. She struggled to sit up and see the floor. "What in the heck did you use?"

"Have you ever heard the expression 'two heads are better than one?' It's the gospel truth." Her laugh echoed through the room, and Jamie let the warm sound wash over her, feeling perfectly and fully loved.

After Jamie had thoroughly exhausted Ryan's spirit of generosity, as well as her tongue, she lay flat on the bed, totally naked, not even a sheet covering her. "If there were more women like you in the world, we'd cut our heating expenses by millions of barrels of oil. I know it's chilly tonight, but my temperature's so high I feel like the sheets might ignite."

Ryan chuckled at the joke, resting a hand on Jamie's belly for a few seconds then picking it up and shaking it, as though it'd been burned. "I guess a dozen orgasms can crank up your furnace." She rolled over on her stomach and placed her chin in her hands, then smiled peacefully at Jamie. "Happy?"

"Blissfully," she said dramatically. "That's the second time we've used that diabolical toy of yours. Is it a favorite?"

"Not really. But it does the trick when I'm too turned on to give you my full attention."

Jamie curled her index finger, beckoning Ryan to lie by her. When Ryan scooted up to share the same pillow, Jamie put an arm around her and cuddled her close for a moment. "I like it when you use your toy," she whispered into her ear. "You get all dominant. I go into another gear when you do that."

Ryan pulled back a few inches and wiggled her eyebrows. "Nice to know." She let her head flop back down as she lazily ran her fingers across Jamie's body. "How's it different from having sex with a man?"

"Sex in general?"

"No. Sex with a toy. Is it like having intercourse?"

Laughing softly, Jamie said, "I sometimes forget I have knowledge you'll never acquire."

"Never want to acquire it; just want to hear your

perspective."

Patting Ryan, Jamie said, "I figured that." She took a breath, then let out a long hiss. "It's hard to describe, but it's very different."

"I'd think it'd be about the same. Usually I think I have a real advantage over a guy, since I'm all about you, but when we use a toy I'm as focused on my own body as I am on yours."

Laughing again, Jamie said, "You'll always have an advantage. You're ridiculously talented in the sack, sweetie. I'll admit my history is limited, but it's night and day."

"But different," Ryan said, lifting her head to rest on her hand. "Tell me about the difference."

"Well, to be honest, I wasn't crazy about missionary position intercourse." She snuck a quick look at Ryan. "Do you really want details?"

"Yeah. I'm interested. I think of this as data acquisition, not something prurient."

"Interesting. We're different that way. I'd never want to know what you did with someone if you'd only had one lover. Much too personal."

"Doesn't bother me. Jack's out of my life." Ryan jerked her arm up and stuck her thumb over her shoulder. "Now he's data."

"Okay. I guess I didn't care for it because I felt trapped."

"Trapped? That isn't what I expected."

"Yeah. That's the best word." Jamie looked thoughtful, as though she were trying hard to recall her feelings and the sensations. "Jack weighed seventy-five pounds more than me, and he was a lot stronger. When he was on top of me, a lot of his weight would be here..." She made a vague gesture across her pelvis. "He used to put his hands on my shoulders and..." she trailed off and shivered. "I didn't like it much at all. When he really got going, I couldn't have gotten him off me."

"He was actually on top of you?"

Jamie looked at her as if she was slow. "Yeah," she said, laughing a little. "Haven't you ever seen porn?"

"Just gay and lesbian stuff. I mean, I've seen pictures, but the people have been doing it doggy-style. That seems like it'd be most comfortable."

"We were mostly missionary." She shrugged, unable to explain why that had become their habit. "Being on my back was uncomfortable, but not because it was painful or anything; I just didn't like the sensation. When he was almost ready to come, he'd drop his head right next to mine and really pound away. His beard would be rough against my cheek and neck, and his body hair would feel like wire on my belly." She made a face of pure distaste. "I always thought of dogs doing it. It seemed so... I don't know, gross, I guess."

Ryan made a face too. "It sounds it!"

"I think I'm in the minority on that. Ask Mia about having sex with a guy, you'll get a whole different perspective."

"Why didn't you try other things? There had to be other ways you would have enjoyed."

Jamie gazed at her for a minute, her eyes scanning over Ryan's face. "I'm still not sure. I'm certainly not afraid to tell you when something's uncomfortable, but I just let Jack pound me."

Ryan lay back down and stared up at the ceiling. "How does it feel when I'm pounding you?"

"You don't do that. Even when you're moving fast, you're very considerate of me. You always come at me at an angle, a little bit on your side so I don't have your whole body on me. Not that I'd mind if you did. I like feeling trapped by you." She reached over and grabbed a bit of skin, tickling Ryan's waist.

"Really?"

"Yeah. It's sexy. Actually, I really like it."

"You're really gay," Ryan said, laughing. "Way, way gay."

"Ya think?" Jamie slapped at her thigh, making a loud noise.

"Did you ever like intercourse?"

"Yeah, a couple of times I enjoyed it. But only when I was on top."

"God, I'd hang myself if you told someone you'd only liked

sex with me a couple of times."

"You'd know," Jamie said dryly. "If you had any doubts, you'd ask, and keep after me until you were sure I was telling the truth. You're relentless."

"Sometimes I have to be to pry things out of you. You can be a tough nut to crack."

"A girl likes to have some secrets," Jamie tossed off blithely. One she was planning on keeping was her attempt to keep Ryan just a little hungry. That hunger had lit the fire, a fire that was still simmering as she let her gaze move all along Ryan's length, considering the next round.

Chapter Nineteen

The family confab to discuss Jennie was set for Sunday night, supplanting their usual family dinner. Since it promised to be a warm evening, Martin suggested they barbecue. They'd barbecued just the day before, and seemed to do it for nearly every group meal. But Martin really knew his way around a grill, and having him in charge of the entree took a load off Jamie's shoulders.

She and Ryan had been to her grandfather's church for services, and were walking home in the bright sun.

"You don't think anyone will mind that I invited Poppa, do you?"

"I don't think so. I'm sure he's been involved in a lot more of these kinds of discussions then we have. Of anyone, only your mom might mind."

Jamie looked at her quizzically. "My mom? Why would she mind?"

"I'm not sure she will. But she seems determined to get custody of Jen, and there's a part of me that thinks your grandfather won't be supportive."

Jamie tried to stop herself from getting annoyed, but wasn't successful. "You've got to give her a break. She's changed a lot since I was a kid."

Ryan held her hands up in surrender. "You're awfully touchy about this, but you don't need to be. I'm crazy about your mom, and if she wants to spend the next few years focused on Jennie, I'm all in favor of it."

"There's something you're not saying."

"I'm saying everything I'm thinking. If your mom wants to get custody of Jennie, I know she'd be great at it. But she's talking about buying an apartment in New York to have fairly frequent contact with Giacomo."

Anger started to well up inside Jamie's chest. "Your father was gone for forty-eight to seventy-two hours straight, every week, and you turned out just fine. I know you think I was raised by the help, but mother was only gone for a few weeks every year."

Ryan tucked her arm around Jamie's waist and pulled her close. "You're never going to get me to say that your mom did a bad job of raising you. I don't think that, so I won't say it. All I've said is that raising Jennie would be very different from raising you."

"I know she's up to it."

Ryan pulled out her most confident smile. "I do too."

At four o'clock that afternoon, Charles, Martin, Maeve, Catherine, Jamie, and Ryan were all in the backyard of the O'Flaherty house. Martin had chosen the usual summer menu, going with Italian sausage, bratwurst, and hamburgers. Jamie wasn't sure why she and Ryan had been designated as the official potato salad makers, but they were once again assigned the task. Maeve made a green salad and Catherine brought beer and wine, so the meal was all set. Just to be wild, Jamie made a lemon meringue pie, which stopped Martin in his tracks when he saw it.

"You know how to bake?"

Jamie nodded. "I've been baking pies since I was five."

In a very serious tone, Martin said to his wife, "Not many people can bake a good pie. It's both an art and a science, and I must say I've never been good at it."

"Nor have I, Marty." Maeve put her hands on Jamie's shoulders and pulled her close to kiss her cheek. "I hope you know that from now on, you'll never escape making two or three of these. My husband loves pie almost as much as he loves his children."

"That's an exaggeration by half," Martin said, looking at the pie as though he was barely restraining himself from digging in right then.

Jamie and Ryan set up the ragtag collection of outdoor furniture into some semblance of order, and the family was all seated around the table asking them questions about the trip to Colorado. When they were finished with the main course, Maeve volunteered to go inside and serve dessert.

Jamie leaned over and said to Ryan, "Why did you keep staring at my mother?"

"I've never seen her eat so much," Ryan said, laughing quietly. "Who knew that her secret craving was for a bratwurst?"

Jamie joined in the laughter. "It's probably the first time she's ever eaten one. I think walking as much as she has been has given her a normal appetite."

"Maybe that's it, but if she breaks open a beer and starts chugging it, I'll know I'm in an alternate universe."

After Martin had praised Jamie's baking skills until she was blushing, they finally got down to the business concerning Jennie. Ryan led off.

"Just so we're all on the same page, I'll give a summary. Jennie's parents are both alive, and either could have custody of her. Her father has remarried, but his new wife and Jennie don't get along at all. Her mother has cut off all contact. That means she's either going to have to remain in the group home, or go back into the foster care system. She's been there three times, and has run away three times. I'm sure she'll do it again if it came to that."

Catherine caught Ryan's attention and said, "The group home she lives in is as good as it can be, but she's not flourishing there. She doesn't have a close friend, and one of the girls has caused her a lot of trouble. Ryan and Jamie think they've solved that issue, but one never knows when a new girl will come in and upset the whole house." She looked around at the group, pausing to make brief eye contact with each of them. "I have the time, the money, and the desire to petition the court for custody." She swallowed and took in a shaky breath. "This is something I really want to do."

Charles took advantage of the quiet to say, "How does Jennie feel? Has anyone talked to her about leaving the group home?"

"No," Ryan said. "We didn't want to get her hopes up. But I guarantee she'd jump at the chance to get out of the foster care system."

"No question," Jamie added. "I think Ryan knows her well enough, and knows kids that age well enough, to be a good guardian. But, selfishly, I'm not ready to take on that kind of responsibility."

Ryan put an arm around her partner. "I'm not mature enough."

Martin patted the table with both hands. "I think we can all agree on that." He smiled warmly at his daughter, showing he was partially teasing. "Maeve and I know that Catherine is a wonderful mother, and that Jennie would be lucky to have her, but I'm worried the girl would be too much for you." He looked directly at Catherine, continuing despite the fact he'd obviously hurt her feelings. "I know she's a good child at heart, but she's also headstrong and has a tendency to be deceitful."

"She's had to be," Catherine said. "The poor girl has been on her own for years. I want to give her the chance to reclaim the last bits of her childhood."

"I think that's what we all want," Martin said. "And of all of us, I think Maeve and I would be able to give her the blend of discipline and consistency she needs." He fixed on Catherine again. "I don't doubt your parenting skills, but I'm worried you won't be able to be as firm with her as she needs."

Doggedly sticking up for her position, Catherine said, "I don't think she needs much discipline at all. I think she needs love and understanding. I know both you and Maeve are wonderful parents, but Jennie doesn't know you well. To her, at least at first, your taking her in would almost be like another foster home."

"I don't think that's true, Catherine," Ryan said. "She's gotten to know Aunt Maeve this summer, and she's been around Da at least a half dozen times."

"From talking to Jennie, I've come to think she's had more than enough discipline in her life," Catherine said. "What she hasn't had is connection, and that's something she and I have. She tells me things I'm sure she doesn't feel comfortable talking about with anyone else. I know I wasn't a very good mother when Jamie was growing up…" Tears sprang to Catherine's eyes and she used her napkin to blot at them angrily. In a shaky voice, she said, "I promised myself I wasn't going to cry."

Jamie jumped up and went over to stand next to her mother. Catherine lay her head against Jamie's hip and accepted a gentle hug. "I want another chance." Crying in earnest, she stood up and went into the house with Jamie.

Everyone was silent for a few moments. Martin said quietly, "I had no idea this means that much to her."

"It means a lot to Jamie, too," Ryan said. "I haven't been able to figure out why, but I think I'm getting the idea."

Quietly, Charles said, "Let's be frank. Martin and Maeve have the experience and the living situation that's probably most likely to give the girl a stable home. But Catherine has something the rest of us are lacking—desire." He looked Martin in the eye. "You're a good man, and it's very generous of you to offer to take Jennie in. But I think it's clear you're doing it because it's the right thing to do—not because you want to have a difficult teenager in your house."

Smiling, Martin admitted, "It's not how I pictured my retirement."

Maeve added, "I'm very fond of Jennie, but she and Catherine do have a real bond."

"Hillary Clinton says it takes a village to raise a child," Ryan said. "Why can't we raise her as a family? Catherine can try to get custody, and when she travels, Jennie could stay with Da and Aunt Maeve. Jamie and I could be backups."

"That could work," Charles said. "I think Catherine has a good point. If Jennie had one person who paid very close attention to her, she wouldn't have as many opportunities to get into trouble."

"I have my doubts there," Ryan said. "She's almost fearless, and she doesn't seem to learn from bad experiences. I think she needs a pretty firm hand."

Seeing Catherine and Jamie coming down the stairs to the yard, Martin caught Catherine's eye and said, "We're agreed. You'll petition the court for custody, and the four of us will be there whenever you need us."

As the tears flowed again, Charles got up and wrapped Catherine in a hug. "The five of us will be there whenever you need us."

The next morning Jamie woke to the sounds of someone mowing the backyard. She blew air out between her lips, making a noise.

"Has our gardener woken you?"

Jamie turned to see Ryan sitting up in bed, reading something. Fluffing the hair from her eyes, Jamie grumbled, "I didn't know we had a gardener in Noe."

"Obviously my father wasn't happy with the way the grass looked when he arrived for breakfast." Ryan looked up at the wide window above their heads. "Good thing we have curtains. It wouldn't do to have my father see all of your gorgeous flesh." She dove for Jamie's side, playfully nipping at her sensitive skin.

"Stop it!" Jamie tried to cover up, but it was no use. Ryan was relentless, teasing and tickling until she begged for mercy. "Ryan rules!" Jamie finally screamed.

Immediately, Ryan stopped. She placed a dozen soft, gentle kisses on the same parts she'd just terrorized. "Better?" she asked, still far down on the bed. The morning light made her eyes sparkle, rendering them an almost ethereal blue.

"Come up here and kiss me like you love me."

Ryan flipped around, sending her legs into the air as she made a u-turn.

"Someone's in a good mood today."

She kissed Jamie tenderly, letting her decide when to break the kiss.

"I'd proposition you, but I can't consider making love with your father right outside."

"He used to be right upstairs every day." Ryan pointed directly above their bed. "Didn't stop you then."

"This is different. I'm not sure why, but it's different." She reached out and smoothed Ryan's mussed hair. "Why are you so chipper?"

Ryan scooted up so she was able to use the wall for a backrest. Lifting her knees, she rested her hands on them and acted as if she was going to make an important announcement. "I've finally, after many weeks of agonizing over it, decided what to do with my windfall."

"Nice word," Jamie said, grinning at her.

"I got it from you. In many ways." Ryan stuck her tongue out and easily pulled it back before Jamie could grab it.

Jamie put a hand atop Ryan's and looked into her eyes. "Have you been obsessing about it?"

Nodding forcefully, Ryan said, "It's been on a slow burn—more like a simmer, actually—always bubbling in the background."

"Aw, honey, I never would have done this if I'd known it would make you crazy."

"It's all right, Jamers." Ryan extended an arm and Jamie cuddled up against her. "I have to get comfortable with money one way or the other. You just pushed me a little."

"So, what's the big plan? Go to the sporting goods store and buy 'em out?"

Looking thoughtful, Ryan said, "Great! Now I've got to start over." She grinned like a chimp, showing all of her teeth. "No, I'm going to be a little more prudent. First, I'm going to start sending my Aunt Moira money every month."

"Good idea. We should have been doing that all year."

"I know. She's not as proud as most of the rest of the Ryans. I think she'll take it. I want her to cover my grandparents' expenses as well as give them a few luxuries."

"But how will she get them to take the money?"

"Not sure," Ryan admitted. "I've considered phony lottery tickets, anonymous checks, a government payout to World War II veterans… It's all up here," she said, tapping her temple. "Whatever it takes to drag them out of poverty."

Jamie leaned over and kissed her cheek. "That's an excellent plan. You'll feel much better if they're more comfortable."

"Right. Then I'm going to pay for Aisling's school expenses."

"Oh, right. Sure. That's a good idea too."

"And I'll pay for the rest of my cousins' too. I think they'll all go to university, so that's a long term plan."

"You don't have that much money, babe. That could be eighty or ninety thousand each."

"They won't have to pay tuition, since their government realizes an educated populace benefits the entire country. I'll just cover their student contribution fee and any expenses."

"Got it."

"I considered giving Tommy and Annie money for a down-payment on a house, but with prices like they are, they'd be saddled with a huge mortgage." She shook her head. "That just doesn't make sense. I think they'll be happy living in the OFC apartment. It's gonna be plenty big and they'll be able to live rent free in exchange for managing it."

"I thought it was a good plan when we came up with it. I still do. It doesn't make sense to have the kind of debt they'd have if they bought a house now."

"Right." Ryan slapped her hands together. "I have to leave the house to implement the rest of my plan. Wanna go?"

"Sure." Jamie slipped out of bed, turning repeatedly on the

way to the bathroom to make sure Martin couldn't see inside.

Before they took off on Ryan's mission, they went to their favorite coffee shop for breakfast. After a couple of espressos and a pair of muffins, they went back to the house and got on Ryan's bike. It was a beautiful day, with a brisk wind blowing all of the fog away, making the sky a beautiful clear blue.

"I love riding behind you on your bike," Jamie said when Ryan brought it to life.

"Warm enough?"

"Yeah. With you in front, my light jacket's plenty." She ran her hands down Ryan's shoulders and arms, covered only by a snug white T-shirt. "You're gonna freeze."

"I like a cool wind when I'm riding. Makes me feel alive."

Ryan carefully maneuvered through the streets, heading all the way across town. Jamie didn't say a word, mostly because Ryan couldn't hear her with the din of noisy streets, but also because she liked to guess where they were going. When Ryan started to cross the Bay Bridge, Jamie would have ventured they were heading to the Berkeley house, but Ryan didn't take their usual Berkeley exit. Instead, they wound up in a different part of town, one they rarely frequented. After threading their way through the heavy traffic, Ryan pulled up in front of the bank where they'd first opened their joint account.

"Ahh," Jamie said, as she took off her helmet and shook her hair free. "Memories."

Ryan smiled. "Yeah. I'll always remember the day you forced me to have a checking account."

Jamie slapped her on the butt. "A twenty-four-year old woman who kept her money in her shoe."

"Not in my shoe," Ryan protested. "In my savings account. I wanted my ridiculously low interest rate."

Inside, Ryan spotted the man who'd waited on them the previous year. He was alone at his desk and she sauntered right up to him, looking at his name plate. "Hi, Mr. Merriman," she said, extending her hand.

He looked up at her and then at Jamie, and they could both see recognition dawn.

"Hello!" He jumped to his feet and enthusiastically shook each of their hands. "How can I help you today?"

"I don't think we need help," Ryan said. "I'm going to make a deposit and…" She pursed her lips. "Actually, you can help me. I want an account in my name. I don't want to write checks, but I'd like an ATM card."

"Certainly. Why don't you both sit down and I'll get right on that."

He started keying things into the computer and Ryan could see his eyes searching wildly. Finally he found their names. She figured he'd remembered Jamie's and then found hers linked to it. "Ms. O'Flaherty, I can open a savings account that has an ATM card for withdrawals. You can make four withdrawals a month without any fee."

"Fee?" she said, narrowing her eyes.

"Yes, that's the terms of this account."

"I don't want to pay a fee to have access to my own money." She didn't add anything, just looked at him with a clear expression of unhappiness.

He started making keystrokes. "I'll flag the account. If you make more withdrawals than the terms allow, I'll override the fee."

Ryan showed a big smile. "Excellent." She took out the checks Jamie had given her for her brokerage account. "I want to close this brokerage account and deposit most of it in our joint account." She handed him a check that made him sit up straighter. "Then I want…six thousand dollars in my personal account. The one without fees," she emphasized.

"No problem." He took the check and went to a teller window, instructing the young man as to how to divide the funds.

"Six thousand dollars? What's the deal with six thousand dollars?" Jamie asked.

Ryan smiled, looking very relaxed and confident. "That's what I want for personal expenses."

"For the month?"

Eyes wide, Ryan almost choked. "For the year!"

Now Jamie was stunned. "You plan on living on six thousand dollars a year?"

"Yeah. This will give me the illusion that I have to budget and plan my personal spending."

"What personal spending? I don't think you've spent a hundred dollars on yourself all year."

"Exactly! This will be mine, and I might buy myself a few things. I've been wanting new running shoes but I hate to spend our money, and I hate to ask you if you think it's a good idea…" She made a circle with her finger. "Crazy thoughts spinning around in my head."

"If you think having your own little pile of money will help you buy what you need—go for it."

"I think it will. I hope it will."

Mr. Merriman returned, statements in hand. "Here are your receipts. Now I'll need to see some identification and have you sign a few papers."

Ryan filled out the rest of the paperwork while Jamie refused all offers of CDs, Money-Market accounts, home improvement loans, and all of the rest of the services he touted. When they were finished, they walked out into the bright sunshine and Ryan said, "How about lunch?"

"Uhm, sure. It's a little early, but I can manage."

"Hop on."

They went through Berkeley, then got onto a road that took them into the Oakland hills. As they climbed, Jamie thought about the first time Ryan had been in her car. They'd come to this exact spot, and for reasons she didn't realize then, she didn't want the day to end. She'd never been with anyone who'd held her interest so completely, and she was thrilled to acknowledge that hadn't changed a bit.

They reached the top of a hill and Ryan pulled over and turned off the bike. It was such a clear day they could see for miles and they silently looked out at the Bay and the city in the distance. Jamie put her head against Ryan's back and they sat just like that for another few minutes. Then they started off again, heading back down to Oakland. When they were still quite a few blocks away from their destination, Jamie knew where they were going. She was smiling when Ryan pulled into a legalish spot and turned off the bike.

"Our first meal together," Jamie said, squeezing Ryan's waist.

"Yep. I love this place, and we haven't been here since that first time. I remember how amazed you were at how much I ate."

"I remember being fascinated by every single thing about you." Jamie hugged her again, almost too tightly.

Ryan slid off the bike, then helped Jamie off. They stood in front of the deli for just a moment, then Ryan said, "Two things are different. One—I'm buying." Jamie grinned at her with unconcealed affection. "Two—when we're done eating, we're going to Berkeley to check our mail. Then I'm going to take you upstairs and do what I wanted to do the very first time I saw you."

Jamie gazed up into her eyes and blinked innocently. "Work on a paper together?"

Ryan's grin was feral. She looked like she could easily dip her head and take a bite out of Jamie's exposed neck. "That paper was the furthest thing from my mind." She moved a little closer, letting Jamie feel the heat that radiated from her body. "I wanted to seduce you."

Something about the way she said it made Jamie squirm. She wanted to skip lunch and get right to the seduction.

But Ryan was clearly having fun playing the game. She bent over until her lips were right next to Jamie's ear. "I wanted to get you alone and take off every bit of your clothing. I think you had on a...blue sweater and jeans. Your breasts looked awesome in that sweater, by the way. It was just snug enough to show them off. I had this vivid image of how rockin' your body was, and I'm glad to say I was totally right." She stood up, grinning when she saw that Jamie's pupils were dilated.

"Isn't it a little early for lunch?" Jamie's voice was slow and sweet and sexy. "We could eat later. Much later."

"Nah, we're not in a rush. It's summer, and we're on vacation. The sun's out, the sky's clear, and we have nothing but time."

Jamie couldn't help herself. Even though they were on a busy street in front of a busy deli at high noon, she had to lace her hands behind Ryan's neck. She leaned back, taking in her lovely partner. Words were unnecessary. She was completely content to simply gaze at her.

"We'll eat, then spend the rest of the afternoon in bed." Ryan looked up at the sky and took in a deep breath. "We'll open the window and have a nice breeze blowing over us. It'll be fantastic."

"Being with you is fantastic. Sometimes I wish I'd known who I was and what I wanted that first day so we could have gotten to the good parts faster."

Ryan shrugged. "You weren't ready. I probably wasn't either." She bent and kissed Jamie, making her touch soft and sweet and tender. "Now we are."

Jamie's smile was so bright it was almost blinding. "We sure are. Together we're ready for anything."

The End

By Susan X Meagher

Novels

Arbor Vitae
All That Matters
Cherry Grove
Girl Meets Girl
The Lies That Bind
The Legacy
Doublecrossed
Smooth Sailing
How To Wrangle a Woman
Almost Heaven
The Crush
The Reunion
Inside Out
Out of Whack
Homeconing

Serial Novel

I Found My Heart In San Francisco
Awakenings: Book One
Beginnings: Book Two
Coalescence: Book Three
Disclosures: Book Four
Entwined: Book Five
Fidelity: Book Six
Getaway: Book Seven
Honesty: Book Eight
Intentions: Book Nine
Journeys: Book Ten
Karma: Book Eleven
Lifeline: Book Twelve
Monogamy: Book Thirteen
Nurture: Book Fourteen
Osmosis: Book Fifteen
Paradigm: Book Sixteen
Quandary: Book Seventeen
Renewal: Book Eighteen

Anthologies

Undercover Tales
Outsiders

Visit Susan's website at
www.susanxmeagher.com

Go to www.briskpress.com to purchase any of her books.

faccbook.com/susanxmeagher
twitter.com/susanx